THE LANCASTER CROSSING

Christopher Oxborrow

Published in 2012 by New Generation Publishing

First Published by
Citron Press, London
1998

Subsequently Published by
iUniverse, USA
2003

www.newgenerationpublishing.info

This book is dedicated to my wife Elaine
And our four daughters.

*Cover photograph of the Aqueduct carrying the
Lancaster Canal over the River Lune
Completed in 1797*

Photograph by Peter Thomas

Chapter 1

The noisy clatter of the cart increased as it crossed the bridge, the horse suddenly finding his task made easier on the smooth paving after the loose, broken stones on the Kendal Road. Far beneath the hammering hooves, the ebbing water of the Lune exposed sloping banks of glistening mud. Ahead, he saw the ships alongside Saint Georges Quay, settling down on the ooze, their masts leaning, topsail spars at sharp angles above the rooftops. John stood behind his father who sat on the box guiding the cart through the port traffic. As they reached the quayside the turmoil increased. Carts waited in lines, bringing produce down to the ships or taking away their imports. To young John Weaver the scene was chaotic; barrels, casks, sacks, and stands of timber competed for space between the carts. Slings of cargo swung in the air as they were hoisted to upper floors of the towering stone warehouses. And, throughout it all, the continuous urgency of men, if not lifting or carrying, then hurrying with papers between the ships, the open warehouse doors and the steps up to the pillared portico of the Custom House. When the horse had been halted in line, the exotic smell of sacks of spices being carried by crouching men into the security of the buildings lent the whole scene the final touch of excitement, a reminder of the distant worlds lying far beyond the grey stones of Lancaster.

For John Weaver these days with his father had become a regular occurrence, minding the horse while his father concluded business on the quay and in the town. His alert, young eyes noted all the activities around him, sweating men struggling with heavy loads, sailors working on the ships, apparently unconcerned by the sloping decks and swinging spars. The inns were a constant source of entertainment to the young observer; an inebriated customer being ejected, or attempting to return. A drunkard's occasional fall into the dock, whether into water or low-tide mud added further excitement. John knew that in this man's world of ships and cargoes, he only women around would be readily noted by the bright colours of their skirts and the noise of their laughter. From his innocent observatory beside the horse he quickly appreciated the importance of these colourful women in the activities of the quayside.

'Hold Tempest, lad. And no talking to anyone. Understand?'

John knew his father's orders well. His strict manner belied his gentle nature at home, but the risks on the quayside were obvious. Even the horse, affectionately named after the storm raging at his birth, was of value in this harsh world of commerce.

As he stood guard he became aware of a boy approaching him. He was dressed in dirty white canvas trousers and a coarse shirt, and wore a woollen cap, which once had been red. His feet were pushed into ill-fitting wooden clogs. He studied John and the horse with care.

'This your horse? Can I touch him?'

John's first reaction to such a greeting was to satisfy himself this was not simply a diversion while the boy's accomplice was busy stealing from the cart. His enquirer seemed to be alone.

'Yes, he belongs to my father. Are you a sailor?'

'Deck boy, that's what I am. Been round the World, I have. Antigua, Jamaicy, Calabar. Seen black men, tall as a mast, shiny black, like your horse. Can I feed him?'

The juvenile mariner bent down and picked up half an apple from the cobblestones. He offered it to the patient animal, heeding John's warning to keep his hand flat. After the soft mouth of the horse had scooped up the fruit the young sailor turned to John.

'Want a cheroot? Here, have this.'

In the palm of his filthy hand lay two small bundles of tobacco leaves, each crudely formed into a roll. John shook his head, eyeing the proffered gift with suspicion. He looked at the thin, hungry boy with a feeling of pity. He was two or three inches smaller than John, and his rough shirt hardly concealed his narrow chest and shoulders.

'How old are you?' John asked, as a mark of friendship.

'Thirteen, they say. I'm the youngest they'll take on big ships.' He inclined his head towards the nearest grimy brig, whose wooden hull was below the level of the stone quayside. 'I'm Jake. Mighty Jake the Mate calls me. You a sailor?'

'No, I help my father. He buys and sells cargo, I think. We work together on the docks. I might go on a ship in a year. I don't know. My mother and father make me go to school when there's no work.'

'Do you live here?'

John pointed to the distant roof of his house, just visible across the river.

John's father re-appeared, holding papers and beckoning his son to lead the horse and cart through the piled-up cargo. The young sailor walked alongside, his clogs echoing the sound of the horses hooves. They stopped alongside a stack of cotton bales, on the top of which sat a small man smoking a clay pipe and gazing towards the distant estuary. John's father waved the papers at the man, and together they started to lift the bales on to the cart. John and Jake helped, until eight bales filled the small wooden platform. John turned the cart round while his father tossed a coin to the watchman and the youngster,

6

before scrambling up onto the box. John followed him and turned to wave to Jake, but he was gone. Responding to the whip Tempest trotted back across the bridge and took the road home to Ryelands. Hidden tightly between the cotton bales the thin body of Mighty Jake shook with the rocking cart. He hadn't been so warm and comfortable for months.

*

'That damned boy's missing again,' announced the boatswain. 'Hand him over to the constable, they'll flog some sense into the little toad.'

Captain Kenyon eyed the boatswain suspiciously.

'You're a bully, Mr Gains. You think you can treat these boys like dogs. I'd be very careful of dark nights if I was you. You may get a nasty surprise.'

'There's ten ships in this poor-man's town who wants me as their bos'un, sir. I just happen to like the 'Rainbird'.'

'Mr Gains, you like the shares you get. Not many ships have done so well in Guinea, and that's why we're all here. One hundred and fifty negroes loaded, one hundred and thirty-two landed and paid for, plus five girls off the manifest. In Liverpool you'd need to carry twice that number and still split your share with half the city. If that boy returns, I'll decide what happens to him. And don't you go talking out of turn to any constable. I find sailors and shore-folk somehow don't get along together.'

'Well, Sir, we'll be sailing a few light by my reckoning, and that's dangerous on the Guinea Trade.'

'That's my worry, Mr Gains. Now, get back to your work, and forget the boy.'

Captain Thomas Kenyon dismissed the bo'sun and turned to more pressing problems. The cargoes for Africa were being stowed at this moment, but he knew his own prosperity depended heavily upon such additional commissions he could carry out 'off the page'. But the enthusiasm of the Customs House and the Port Commissioners since the end of the war had made such enterprises more hazardous.

However, one advantage of the peace with France and Spain was the quantity of arms which could be bought in the right quarters. Muskets, pistols and blades found a ready market on the Guinea coast. Only a fool asked who would use the weapons. The new American states had a growing demand for healthy slaves, and he knew the sources on The Coast, and the violence that was necessary to procure the strongest tribesmen, able to survive the 'Middle Voyage' across the ocean and able to work hard on arrival.

Two days earlier he had loaded bales of sheepskin, each bale concealing muskets and short swords, and three apparently new sails delivered today were similarly concealing the means of undeclared profit, twenty-four new pistols in canvas pouches, powder horns and shot. The last thing he wanted was the constable looking for a missing deck boy. Anything which delayed him sailing on tonight's ebb tide was increasing the risk. The towering bulk of the castle looking down on the quayside only served to remind him of the fate awaiting him if his enterprise was discovered.

He left the confines of his cabin, scarcely high enough to stand in, and went on deck. Two men were loading what appeared to be a street-full of furniture from wagons on the quayside. One of the men approached Captain Kenyon and doffed a tricorne hat which looked as if it might have seen action in most of the colonies.

'Cap'n Kenyon, Sir? Compliments of Mister Gillow, Sir. He would like to see the furniture is correctly secured, and he will pay for extra dunnage if necessary. He will be here after noon to see what you may require.'

'Tell Mr Gillow he's welcome as soon as he likes, but the 'Rainbird' leaves this quayside at sunset, with our without his cupboards and tallboys. G'day to you sir!'

*

The cart creaked and groaned into the yard at the side of Joshua Weaver's house. His young son jumped down and released the horse from the shafts. He led it towards a tree and looped the reins round the trunk.

'The carter's coming up from Milnthorpe tomorrow, he'll take the wagon up the road,' said Joshua. He closed the yard gate and tied a rope round the stone post before turning to the load on the cart.

'Hullo, what have we got here?' He pulled on a small foot that was visible between the cotton bales.

With more effort, the thin figure of the deck boy, Mighty Jake was withdrawn from the load, who finally jumped down on the stones of the yard. He brushed evidence of the cotton from his tattered clothes with the petulant air of a dandy emerging from a chaise.

'Mother, we've got guests for supper tonight!' shouted Joshua, as he took the skinny shoulder in his firm grasp. The small boy looked at the man in a cheerful, almost truculent manner, and carelessly patted the horse.

'Thanks for the ride, Tempest. We'll all sleep well tonight, eh?'

The door of the house opened and a woman, dressed in a heavy, grey dress, with a dark red wrap round her shoulders, strode across the yard to look at the arrivals. She examined the young boy, holding his chin in her grasp.

'When did this poor thing last eat? Easter Day?'

'I don't know,' replied her husband. 'He jumped on at the quay. Thought I hadn't noticed.'

He turned to the boy. 'You off the 'Rainbird', lad?' he asked kindly. For the first time the boy looked frightened, and shied away from the woman's grasp.

'Don't send me back, mister. Just let me walk away. Don't send me back.'

The woman ignored the outburst and looked at her husband and the boys. She inclined her head towards the house.

'Hurry up, all you men. Supper's already on the table and growing cold. So bring some wood with you.'

She pushed Jake towards the open door, and smiled at her son as he gathered up an armful of logs from the far side of the yard.

Indoors, the most noticeable thing to the arriving travellers was the large, black fireplace containing blazing logs which was the only source of light in the room, and that was further restricted by clothes hanging on lines, casting shadows on the walls. In the evening twilight the room was becoming very dark.

'Boy! Wash your hands in the tub, there, afore you sit at the table, like everyone else.' She spoke easily to the young stranger, as if he was a regular visitor to the house.

When the three men were seated she placed a big iron bowl on the table and ladled out a thick stew, rich with the smell of herbs.

'Do you eat mutton, boy? Mother's mutton stew with mushrooms as big as plates,' enquired Joshua Weaver. The newcomer nodded silently.

Young John Weaver opened a wooden box on the dresser and pulled out a flat oatcake, which he broke into pieces and handed round to the diners. Already, the stranger was eagerly spooning up the steaming hot stew, scarcely noticing his hosts. He took the bread and tapped it hard on the table-top.

'Why do you do that?' asked John.

'Weevils. Shakes 'em out, if you don't like 'em in your stew. Mr Gains says they do you good. I think they keeps on eating when they're inside of you.'

He lapsed into silence, as if the last vital piece of information had exhausted his conversation. The others chatted easily, talking about the day's business, each casting an occasional eye on the stranger. When, at last, the large helpings of mutton had been eaten, Joshua reached over and picked a pipe off the dresser and slowly filled it with coarse, black tobacco from a stone jar. He reached forward and lit it with a red-hot ember from the fire. To his surprise he found Mighty Jake was holding out one of the crudely made cheroots between his thin lips, and Joshua offered him the ember. The room started to fill with clouds of smoke from the two smokers, and a curious smell.

'That smells good, Jake. What is it?'

'The best. Virginy baccy and Jamaicy rum.'

Mother looked at the young stranger.

'Now, Jake. Who are you? Where are you from?'

'Don't properly know that,' he replied briefly. 'My uncle put me on the ships.' He turned to Joshua. 'Ever heard of Rotherhithe, Mister? Terrible place, full of thieves. They put me on the ships to get some learning. The only learning they gave me was at the end of a rope.'

'Well, you can stay down here by the fire tonight and Mr Weaver will decide what happens in the morning. Isn't that so, Father?'

Joshua Weaver nodded, and made a signal to his wife.

'Jake, my lad, we'll give you a blanket and a sheepskin to sleep. Do you give Mother your clothes and she'll have them washed by tomorrow. And I'll dry your boots over the fire.'

'You mean, Mister, you'll make sure as I doesn't run away while you're asleep. That's right by me.' He looked at his hosts with unsmiling young eyes, reflecting the wisdom of a bitter childhood.

*

At midnight, as the tide started to ebb down the River Lune and the nightwatchman tested the warehouse doors, the brig 'Rainbird' shook out her topsails and glided almost silently down the river towards Sunderland Point and the open sea. On board, twenty-four men prepared for the long, lonely journey to Africa, but more than one of them looked back towards the grim outline of the castle against the starlit eastern sky, resolved to place a thousand miles between themselves and the fearful dungeons on the hill.

*

The following morning was bright and clear, the wind blowing cold from the northern hills. Joshua Weaver and his son had business in town, and they took care dressing for the occasion, clean shirts and cravats, and freshly brushed breeches. Joshua wore black boots with brown folded down tops. His coat was maroon red with worn gold frogging. He had recently bought a new, wide-brimmed hat, the only garment he owned which could possibly be considered in fashion. Likewise, his young son put on a black tricorn to compliment his grey coat. Sarah Weaver looked at her husband and her son approvingly, adjusting a cravat, brushing a coat, a final polish of a boot.

'Mister Weaver and Son, the city of Lancaster awaits you.' She laughed and curtseyed as she opened the heavy front door upon the spring morning.

'Keep our young visitor indoors until I can find out more about him. Any trouble, get Jed from the farm.'

'He'll be no trouble, poor child. Still sleeping, curled up like a kitten. Now, off to the Town Hall.'

Man and son walked briskly down the road into town, crossing the river by the ancient bridge.

'They're planning to build a new bridge higher up the river, but that will need some money. I suppose it's better than spending all our money on wars. You watch, son, there's many new things to be done in this land, new canals joining up all the towns, new and better mills, iron used to make bridges and even ships.'

The boy at his side laughed at his father's forecasts.

'Iron ships, Father? I don't think they'll do that, will they? I don't think I'd sail on one.'

'Then more fool you, boy. In Mr Brockbank's shipyard last week he had a small boat carefully made of iron sheets, rivetted together, the joints sealed with tar, so heavy it took two men to drag it to the water's edge. Yet, when the tide came in it floated just like a wooden boat. Mr Brockbank stood in the boat and opened a bottle of French brandy. Twenty of us stood on the bank and watched, each of us a sovereign the poorer. Never wager against the worth of iron, John.'

As they walked through the awakening town, John carefully watched his father and doffed his hat each time his father did so in greeting business acquaintances.

'Morning Mr Weaver'

'Good-morning, Mr Cleland. See you at the meeting?'

'Certainly, sir. Most interesting it will be, I'm sure. Bringing your banker with you?' He nodded in the direction of John and laughed.

'Master Weaver, Mr Cleland. I tell you this, Sir. If our Town Clerk could write a copy and keep an account as well as this young man, we might manage our affairs a little more expertly. I see last month we had even more gaps in the accounts, probably buying a new horse for a sailor or coals for a lodging with no chimney.'

'Joshua, you're an old grouse. I didn't hear a word of complaint from you at last months' meeting. Very good profits on your shares, eh?'

'Yes, Will, and justly earned.'

And so their progress through the bustling town proceeded. Joshua called at offices on their route, paying bills and collecting payments and documents. At each he was warmly greeted, until at one office they were ushered through the front office into a smoke-filled room where a dozen or more men sat around, noisily discussing the business of the port. Cups of coffee and chocolate were served by a girl from a counter at the back of the room. John had never seen so much activity, not only in the conversation between the men, but in the coming and going of youngsters his own age, clutching messages and documents. On one wall was a board which to John seemed to be the names of ships, names he had seen on his frequent visits to the quayside. He noticed the ship 'Rainbird' had the message 'Sayld to Guinee' scrawled under its name.

Yet more men entered the room, the smoke and general hubbub increased, until finally one man seated against the far wall stood up and banged his fist on the table to command attention. The room immediately fell silent.

'Gentlemen, we have news from Liverpool that more ships are handling the Guinea Trade, at our expense. Nevertheless, we've had a good winter, and I'm sure we all agree there's a good market in peacetime for all of us if we are sensible. But I have to tell you we have one ship ashore in Antigua, seven men lost and her cargo sold just as a clearance.' He consulted same papers on the table before him. 'Name, brig 'Cyclops' Captain William Clark, Mate James Prescott.'

One of his listeners cursed quietly under his breath. The speaker continued.

'There's a carriage leaving for Liverpool this afternoon, and we have a messenger on it, so anything to be taken must be with Mr Chatham at the desk by 2 o'clock.' He looked round the room. 'Any other business for the chairman?'

John Weaver got to his feet.

'Yes, Mister Chairman, I hear the new dock at Glasson is being finished. Now, I've nothing against that, but let's be sure that control of the port remains with us here in Lancaster. With Sunderland Point virtually dead, we need the opportunities of a bigger port at Glasson, but under our control. Is that agreed?'

A general murmur of assent ran round the room. Another man standing in the doorway of the crowded room knocked on the doorframe to draw attention to himself.

'Excuse me, gentlemen. Am I not correct in my understanding that we asked a Mr Whitworth to plan a canal for the city? Now, I know it's not our task in this room to do the job of the Council, but if I'm not mistaken, this is where the money will be found. My information is that the country is being channelled for canals as fast as the navigators can dig, which could leave us literally high and dry if we don't start digging pretty soon.'

Again, the room seemed to sympathise with the speaker.

Another man stood up. The room fell silent again.

'I don't know about digging, Mister Chairman. I'm told such a canal would need to be seventy or eighty feet in the air to cross the River Lune and the River Ribble at Preston.'

Amid the laughter which greeted this remark one of the audience stood up.

'I hear that a Mr Jeffries has crossed the English Channel by balloon! Perhaps we should send our cargo to Manchester and Rochdale by air!'

The room filled with laughter, and this seemed to be the signal that the formal business of the meeting was at an end.

As the audience returned again to informal discussions around the tables, Joshua sought out an acquaintance and drew him to a quieter part of the room.

'William, I see your 'Rainbird' sailed on the tide. Full ship, was it?' He made the enquiry sound casual.

'Aye, Joshua, full indeed. Grains, furniture, trinkets for The Coast. Why d'ye ask?'

'Good crew, Will?'

'Good enough. Captain Kenyon. Makes a bit on his own account, but no harm there. Runs a very tight ship, never any trouble.'

'Any difficulty getting a crew?'

William hesitated.

'We-ell, we took a couple from the magistrate to make the numbers up. Why? D'you want a job?' He laughed loudly at his joke.

'No Will, I mean were any missing at sailing time?'

'Oh, just a lad, probably run back home. London, I think. I expect he's in Manchester by now.' He looked Joshua straight in the eyes.

'Half-way to London, no point looking for him in Lancaster, Mister Weaver.'

'I quite agree, Mister Hunter. Right out of town by now.'

*

From the morning meeting Joshua and his son made their way to the Town Hall in the Market Square. Its pillared portico was crowded with small market stalls. Joshua made his way to a heavy oak door. Inside, the tiled hall had doors leading off and a staircase rising at the back. Clerks appeared and disappeared, doors opening and closing continuously, almost like a game, thought John.

They climbed the stairs and Joshua opened a polished door.

'John, this is a private meeting. You can sit here and read the Journal. See how well you can read the news of the day, because you can be sure I'll ask you about it on the way home.'

Joshua entered the committee room, and noticed the other members were already seated. At the head of the of the long table sat a man of obvious authority, his silk coat almost shining in the cool, spring sunlight, the pure white silk at his throat and cuffs in keeping with his smart pig-tail wig, neatly brushed back and tied with a ribbon. Joshua nodded respectfully towards the chairman and took the last vacant seat, in front of which a number of documents were carefully arranged.

The Chairman looked round the table. There was no need to call for attention, the ten men sat in silence and waited.

'Gentlemen, as I think you all understand, we have had a very successful period in the Guinea Trade, carrying hundreds of slaves with very few losses. But two occurrences must cause us disquiet. Firstly, Liverpool is making representations that our ships and their masters are becoming more corrupt and devious in their trading with the Africans, causing many riots and uprisings. Now, I readily perceive the Liverpool men want to cause us trouble, but the behaviour of two ships to my knowledge is a grave misdemeanour which could bring ships from this city under a cloud of suspicion. I intend, therefore, to place agents on some ships, well able to perform their duties as seamen, but with the secret commission to report in person to this committee on the conduct of our affairs on the Triangular Voyage. To make this a reality, these agents can be sentenced and put on the ships by the magistrates to assist in their deception. Any comments?'

The Chairman finished speaking and looked round his listeners with an air which almost defied response. A murmured approval was the only reply. He continued.

14

'Next. I am getting reports from Bristol and Liverpool that a Mr Clarkson is making overtures to Parliament to put an end to the slave trade. Now, my advice to shipowners is to pay close attention to new trades in case one morning we find Mr Pitt has suddenly taken the oil from our lanterns.'

This announcement brought an immediate response from many of the men round the table.

'He'll have the Duke of Clarence to deal with first!' exclaimed one of the men.

'And every stone-mason from London to Bristol. Five hundred negroes delivered to Virginia pays for some very pretty mansions in Bayswater!'

The members of the committee allowed themselves a brief laugh.

Joshua Weaver had heard enough.

'Mister chairman,' he began. 'I like to think we are all, in this room, men who have always looked forward to new opportunities, and see the coming of iron, and steam, and new ways and means. But I feel a wise man will always preserve that which has served him well until he is certain he has something better to take its place. In Africa we have the plums to put in the Virginian pies. The businessmen I have the honour to represent are proud to provide the ships to carry this trade as expertly as possible. I do assure you, a dead slave makes no profit for anyone.'

Joshua sat down amidst the combined tapping on the table as each man marked his approval.

'Well said, Joshua Weaver', said one of them. 'Find me a better cargo than two hundred healthy negroes, and I'll carry that as well!'

Laughter greeted this remark, and the meeting relaxed into the details of the port's business.

Outside the door, John Weaver sat silently by the window and tried to read the cramped, uneven print of the Journal. As he concentrated he was aware of someone watching him as he waited at one of the doors. John looked up and saw a tall man dressed in the best style of the city, white silk cuffs and bows, a blue silk coat and white waistcoat and breeches. He carried an elaborate hat with silver tassels and a small white feather at one side.

'Are you Joshua Weaver's boy?'

John stood up and took of his hat before replying.

'Yes, Sir. John Weaver.'

'I'm told you write a good hand. Is that so?'

'Yes, Sir. I have been taught by my mother and father and I can also keep books of account. I am learning tracing and copying maps and drawings.'

'And when you are older, what do you plan to do, Master Weaver?'

'I would like to learn navigation and perhaps own my own ship, Sir.'

'Do you indeed? Sounds as if I'm going to have competition in a year or two! My compliments to your father, Sir and to bring you up to Carnforth when he can spare the time. Tell him Squire Kerr would like to share an Oporto wine with him. I will expect you both at twelve o'clock on the day after tomorrow. I bid you g'day ,Sir.'

The squire bowed towards the astonished boy, who awkwardly returned the formality. When, once again he was alone John felt his knees shaking at the thought of the encounter.

Chapter 2

As they walked home together Joshua questioned his son about the news in the Journal, horrified to hear the list of the crimes of those on trial at Lancaster Assizes; young boys sentenced to death by hanging for stealing a horse, another for mysteriously re-appearing in the city when he had been sentenced two months before to transportation. Even hard-working men in his own employ had been branded by the magistrates on the palm of one hand with the letter M, the permanent stain of the malefactor.

'Well, lad, while you've been enjoying yourself I've been arguing to protect our living. Some of the whigs would like us to sell coals on the street corners instead of earning our livings across the oceans.'

As he spoke they turned into the yard at the side of his house. His wife opened the door and immediately Joshua sensed something was wrong. Her eyes were red and she seemed unable to look at her husband.

'Is that young villain still here?' He asked.

'Yes, he's here. He's sat by the fire, now, but he's been working all the afternoon. He can split wood as quick as a grown man, and he's put a new rope on the gate...' her words were lost in a sudden flood of tears. Her shoulders shook with deep sobbing and she turned from the warmth of the kitchen to go into the cold drawing room, only used when her husband had visitors from the city. He followed her and sat beside her on a settle by the window.

'Has that young villain upset you? What's he doing? I'll skin him alive.'

'Skin him alive, Joshua? He could slit your throat so that even the Lord wouldn't know you were dead. He could show you how to kill a man with a piece of string! And as far as he knows he was twelve years old in mid-winter. Twelve years old and a trained cut-throat! Did you know that? Because it was your trade who taught him his devilish tricks!'

'Not 'Rainbird'. Not one of ours.'

'Then that's all fine, I suppose. Not our responsibility, Mister Weaver? Just talk to that boy, just let his own childish lips tell you how to get the dead bodies out of the tween deck without unchaining the living ones. He could tell to you how to pick the clean girls for parlour maids in Jamaica. How they keep the best ones separate to keep them 'sweet' for their new masters. Joshua, he's the same age as our son, who we love and teach to write and keep a neat hand, who can make a ledger look like a scripture. I'm so ashamed what Jake has done to keep us well-dressed and fed..' She broke down again in terrible sobbing.

'John. Come here and sit with your Mother. Put that coat over her shoulders and keep her warm. Now, where's that young man Jake?'

He went into the parlour, where Jake was sat by the blazing fire, eating from a basket of oat girdle-cakes.

'Now, my boy, I want some truth from you. One single lie and you'll be in the Castle dungeon this very same hour. Understand?'

Jake looked directly at Joshua Weaver.

'I don't lie to you, Mister. I don't have to lie to no-one now.'

'Right boy, tell me all you know. First, when did you join the 'Rainbird'?

'In the summer. I was first on a three-master, Rotherhithe to Liverpool. Four lads from the orphan school, our uncle got us the job, but after many days we had almost no food and all the worst jobs aloft. Tom Thumb fell from the foretop and was broken across the windlass when we found him. Buried at sea off Skerries. The Mate told us to pray for his soul and to tell no-one except Jesus Christ. He was a very religious mate, always reading the gospels, he said.

'So when we gets to Liverpool we were next to 'Rainbird' and their bo'sun told me he needed a good man like me. And the masts were not so tall, and easy yards. So I joined just as they was leaving for the Africs. But it was a very hard ship, not enough crew, even before we got to the coast. It seemed to take for ever, and the sails were half rotten. In a good blow the main course would only last a day or two, and then down it came and we all sat round, drifting along under topsails while we stitched together rotten canvas. Two days later we'd be sewing the next seam to it.

'When we got to Sir Leon it was called, there were two ships from Bristol, the bo'sun said they had one thousand black men on board, and there were no others for picking so we sailed to Accra, where the London ships were already at anchor. The Captain said we would do better in Calabar, and when we dropped our anchor there we were the only ship.'

The boy looked pleased with himself at the way the foreign names came so readily to him. He took another piece of oatcake before continuing.

'The man they called 'The Agent' came on board with a black giant who had green and red feathers in his hair, and a rope round his waist with a man's bones hanging from it. When he walked along the deck the bones banged together like firewood.

18

'There was a big argument in the Captain's cabin, which we could all hear. The black giant walked back to where his small boat was waiting. He climbed over the rail to the ladder, and when he was holding on with both hands one of our sailors rushed towards him and put a piece of spunyarn round his neck and pulled it tight. His eyes bulged out, and the only way he could save himself was to climb back on board. When he did, all the sailors fell on him and they tied him to the foremast dead-eyes. He was screaming as soon as they took the yarn from his neck, cursing the ship and all of us. I think everyone was very frightened. I was terrified, even though no-one understood the foreign words.'

Young Jake stopped talking, looking very nervous. Joshua had some wine on the dresser, and poured out two cups of the crimson liquid. He gave one to the young boy, who drank it readily.

'Take your time, son, and remember, no lies or you'll be in a cold dark cell all by yourself for three months.'

The boy drained the cup and wiped his sleeve across his mouth before continuing.

'They shouted down to the boat, which had two black men with paddles in it. They told these men the chief was to be 'changed for one hundred and fifty slaves, and they must be brought out in the next ten days, or their chief would be killed. The Captain gave some of our sailors muskets and told them there must always be three men with muskets on deck, day and night. The next day boats and rafts started paddling towards the ship. The mate shouted to them to make sure only one boat was alongside us at a time. The black men climbed up the side and the bo'sun checked each one when he stepped on deck. After they had been seen by the bo'sun they had to pull up two big bundles from the boat, one was full of beans and food and the other was a skin for water. Then his hair and mouth were checked and then if he was wearing any cloth or anything, that was taken off and thrown away and the bo'sun looked at his prickle. If he was clean, a chain was put round his ankles and a leather round his neck to the next slave, but sometimes the man would kick out, and then he would be clubbed on to the deck. The seaman told me they never hit their heads, or they might not live out the voyage. They were led below five joined together, and I would go down to turn the keys, while the sailors kept guard with their muskets. It took many days, sending some back if they weren't good enough, or we had to wait for their food.

'Men went on the port side and forward on the starboard side. Women were also on the starboard side, and aft of that, what they called the chicken run they chained up the young girls. They were especially examined and had to show their parts to the Mate. The sailors laughed when the young girls came on board, and I knew what they was saying was lewd. If a girl was not clean between her legs she was pushed back down the ladder. One of the sailors told me some of the girls put sour milk in their openings to make them look unclean. I don't know anything about that.'

Joshua looked round. His wife was standing in the doorway, holding her shawl to her mouth in horror as the narrative continued.

'Now, boy, how many did you load at Calabar?'

'I'm no good with numbers, mister, but after many days the tween decks had two layers on both sides, except for the chicken run. When we had finished you couldn't have fitted a canary into the tween decks. That night, after we had handed back the chief, they gave him some bars of gold, some old muskets which didn't work, and two boxes of beads. As the ship was got ready for sea and we waited for the wind a canoe was paddled out to us with two men in it. They shouted up to us on our deck and told us for a rope to be lowered. The two men tied a big red bag on to the rope and paddled away. The bag was pulled up on deck and untied. Inside was a big mess of red and black, and I knew it was blood. My mate Tom says it's the head of a man, just the head of a white man, who the captain said was our agent. The Captain gave an order for the two stern-chasers to be fired towards the land, but by the time we had loaded black powder and balls both fell short and splashed in the sea. We weighed anchor and set sail, tacking away from the coast. That night the slaves started singing. I have never been so frightened. Twenty-four of us scared silent on deck, two hundred of them singing a long, low song, like Jesus knew what we were doing that was so wicked. They sang the next day, but never again after that.'

The fearsome story stopped as Mrs Weaver started weeping again, reaching forward to put an arm round the story-teller's narrow shoulders. Her husband turned to the lad.

'Right, boy. Blankets by the fire again tonight. I don't want to hear any more tonight, and we'll talk about this further in the morning.' He returned to the drawing-room, leaving his wife to comfort the trembling boy. Joshua sat by the empty fireplace and considered the account he had been given. The house of Joshua Weaver was silent throughout that forbidding night.

*

Joshua and his son, brushed and polished, took the Kendal coach as far as The Golden Ball at the Kellett Road crossing. When they descended they could look across the bay, where craft of all sizes seemed to be moving with a special urgency about their business to take advantage of the high tide. At the mouth of the River Keer two boats were in course of construction. The yard was overlooked by a large house with tall windows and, at one end a bell-tower, almost like a church.

They walked up the well-tended drive and could hear dogs barking as they approached the large, evenly-proportioned house which seemed to lie perfectly in the tree-clad meadowland which sloped gently down to the busy yard.

Joshua knocked on the oak door with a shiny black iron ring. It seemed to disturb the tranquillity of the house, and he felt uneasy at making so much noise.

The door was opened by a butler wearing a short black waistcoat and white breeches.

'Mr Weaver and Master Weaver to see Squire Kerr.'

'You are expected, gentlemen.'

He took their hats and Joshua's cane, then led them through the house and the tall french windows opening onto a terrace. He bowed and indicated where their host was standing at the end of the paving stones.

Squire Kerr welcomed his guests warmly and proceeded to point out the places of interest in the view before them. Sunshine and shadow gave way to distant showers of rain sweeping across the mountains and villages of Westmorland and Cumberland.

'Mr Weaver, I know from the reports you have made to your board that you are one of those always looking forward to new opportunities. As you know, Glasson Dock is nearing completion, and I am expectant that we could see a great rise in trade in consequence. Instead of having to share our cargoes with Liverpool we could grow our own trades here. When complete, more than a score of three-masters could moor in Glasson in nearly three fathoms of water.'

Joshua nodded in response to Squire Kerr's remarks and his son copied his father's action, excited by being included in the details under discussion.

'Mr Weaver, I want to build and own ships built in the bay, using local craftsmen and materials, and then setting them to trade for the benefit of the townsfolk of Lancaster and around. Let Liverpool provide the boats and, mark my words well, the profits will go with them, as will the guilds and crafts.'

'Aye, Squire, that is exactly my sentiment. The merchants I represent are all local men, but every day see the pressure from Bristol and Liverpool. But, Sir, we all forget what happens in times of war.

Then, the English Channel and the Approaches are full of French privateers flying any flag that's in the locker. That's when our northern ports come into full benefit. We can have our ships away in the North Channel while even a Liverpool brig is still pressing against the Mersey tide. But as soon as King Louis scribbles a treaty, the trade drifts to the south again.'

'By the Lord, Mr Weaver! You're a man of the same sail-cloth as me! And I'm sure your son here, Master Weaver, will inherit your good counsel.'

He turned to the youngster and once again showed all the formality due to a man twenty years older.

By now, they had walked, in deep discussion, into a large drawing room, lined with books, with a large desk facing one of the windows. John noticed the desk was covered with maps and charts, line drawings of ships' hulls and long bills of quantities. Beyond the desk was a detailed model of a merchantman, a three masted ship, with a protection of cannons on the open deck.

'My first step is to ensure we have the right ships for sustaining our ship-building, especially securing consistent supplies of timber and tar from the Baltic. Mr Brockbank's yard, like the others in the Lune find themselves short of masts and spars, and my yard is waiting for timber month after month. I am now altering a brigantine specially for this purpose. Do you know how?'

Joshua looked appropriately puzzled, although he considered he knew the answer. From many years experience of running committees he knew when to let an influential member be seen to originate an idea, even when the same invention could be found in the Minute Book of the previous year.

'I'll show you, gentlemen.'

He shuffled through the drawings on the desk and finally drew out a line drawing of a ship's hull, fully detailed to show every frame and knee, keel, stem and sternpost and the long, curving strakes, deck beams and planks. John had never seen so much fine detail in a drawing and tried to visualise the huge task of building such a intricate vessel. The squire pointed to the lines of the hull.

'See this, gentleman? It looks a little like a gun port, doesn't it? Like a hinged door in the side, four feet wide, but right up forward, nearly beside the stempost. When it's closed it is secured and strengthened by two elm-wood beams, nine inches square, as strong as any part of the ship. But see here. Swing the door open and we can load a single piece of timber nearly ninety feet long, slide it in like putting a sword in a scabbard. But this scabbard can carry as many swords as you like! Ha!

Look, slide the first one in, draw it to the side of the tween deck to make way for the next one, and so on. Shorter spars can be handled between the lower masts below deck. I've even designed the sheer of the hull to make it as flat as consonant with seaworthiness. Masts for men-o-war like matches in a box! My matchbox! Ha! How does that strike you Master John Weaver? One day you could sail my ship proudly through the Baltic to load Russian pines.'

John felt dizzy with the prospect which suddenly seemed like a reality. He gazed round the great room at the books, the ship models the drawings, and the infectious enthusiasm of Squire Kerr, which all seemed to focus his thoughts into one irrevocable direction. He knew must get away on a ship as soon as possible.

The two older men had wandered away to the end of the room and were speaking together in low tones. Shortly, the butler returned with a tray on which stood a dark bottle and some dazzling crystal goblets. Also, a large stone jug containing a cloudy liquid, which turned out to be a lemon cordial, its sharp bitter taste a completely new experience to the prospective young mariner.

Pipes were filled and lit, and legs eased as the three men sat before the terrace windows and watched the ships in the bay assembled into the remaining channels between the emerging sandbanks. The Squire raised his glass and turned to his guests.

'A health to His Majesty, and a good prosperous future to Master John Weaver. And good health to you, Sir and your Lady.'

*

On the coach journey home Joshua discussed their visit with his son, whose eyes still shone with the excitement of the Squire's comments.

'He would be prepared to take you as an apprentice, starting in his shipyard before serving aboard one of his ships. It is a fine opportunity for a bright young man which would give you experience to play a leading part in a trading house in later years. Let's have this out with your Mother.'

But once again, returning home gave them another surprise. The meal was ready to put on the table and Mighty Jake was clean and scrubbed. He had been dressed in a shirt, breeches and short jacket which her son had grown out of more than a year ago. John greeted him like a new brother as they gathered round the scrubbed table and watched the roast goose being carved into portions.

After a peaceful meal, Mrs Weaver suddenly made an announcement.

'Well, we have a little thief in our house.'

There was a long silence. Three pairs of eyes turned to the thin, smiling face of Mighty Jake. Then he realised what was happening.

'Not Jake, Missus. I've not thieved, not since Rotherhithe anyway. You could trust me with your purse all day long. Just try me out, Mister.'

'Huh! Don't you listen to him.' She felt in the deep pocket of her apron, and drew forth three gold coins which twinkled even in the dimly lit room. 'What's that, my little cutpurse?'

The small face looked at the coins in anger and reached out to take them.

'That's my shares, that's what that is, Missus. That's my right shares. I never stole nothing like that.'

He looked round the table with fear in his eyes, his young brain telling him a theft of such magnitude would cost him life at the next Assize. Stolen money earned more than an agonising brand.

Joshua looked at the boy, not knowing quite how to judge the pitiful figure across the table.

'Jake, boy, this is your last chance for the truth, or you'll be in the cells tonight. Where did that money come from? The real truth, now.'

'Mister, this is God's truth. When we gets back to Lancaster we are all paid up, wages less allowances, and then our shares.'

'How is that done, boy.'

'I don't know, Mister, they just call it share dividers or words like that...' he hesitated in his frightened confusion.

'Shared Dividend? Is that what they call it?'

'Yes, Mister. I think everything we buy and sell, if they're just black men and girls, bags of grain, tobacco or rum, and the Captain's Extras, we all get a divider.'

'Dividend,' repeated Joshua.

'Yes, it's the only reason I stayed on the ship. I could have lived in Virginny as a coachman.'

Mrs Weaver swept her husband aside.

'Then, my fine fellow, where was this gold when you came here two days ago? I washed you in that tub naked as your Lord made you. No gold to be seen then.'

Without another word the boy left the table and went to the side of the fireplace. Where the heavy black iron frame rested against the wall a crack was clearly visible. Joshua stood up and crossed to where the boy was pointing. He picked up one coin and tried it in the space. It nestled in, virtually hidden from view.

' 'Pon my life, Mrs Weaver, I think he might be right. Certainly it isn't our money, this looks like Spanish, if I'm not mistaken.' Once again he turned to the boy.

'Why did you hide it like that?'

'That's what we were taught, see. Never keep money on you more that you must. You could rob me all you like, cut my throat or just wait till I'm asleep. But hide it close at hand and you'll live forever, I say!' To everyone's amazement, the small philosopher made them all laugh.

'Mrs Weaver, I think this young man should become the manager of the Lancaster District Bank!'

Still Mrs Weaver seemed uncertain. She took the boy by the shoulders and stood him in front of her. Her mind was searching for the most effective words.

'Jake, do you remember your Mother?' He shook his head.

'Well then, do you know about Jesus Christ? Did you ever say a prayer to Our Lord Jesus?'

'Only when we was burying someone. We were taught to say 'Sweet Jesus, keep our brother's soul in Heaven'. None of them were my brother, but I called them that if I was told to.'

'Fine, Jake. Then can you say 'I promise to tell only the truth, or Jesus will strike you dead?'

'Yes, missus. I know that.'

*

Joshua Weaver stood up and took his pipe from the shelf, and puffed happily for a minute or two.

'Well, here's something for all of us. John and I have been with Squire Kerr today, and he wants to take our John as an apprentice, to start in his shipyard before serving his full time on board a ship. He will have him properly instructed and if he attends to his work he will sit for his certificates as a Master's Mate. Now, that's a fine prospect for a young man. What do you say to that, Mrs Weaver?'

She looked hard at her husband's smiling face.

'And will he have the honour of chaining up the negroes and their clean young girls, returning home to Ryelands with a pocket full of gold soaked in their blood? His 'Dividend' don't you call it?'

'No, Mother, not slaving. He'll be sailing round Denmark to the Baltic, to Memel and Saint Petersburg. That's the Squire's trade.'

'Until His Majesty goes to war with Spain. Then he'll have to go on the Guinea Trade.'

25

Joshua smiled. 'More likely to be hauled aboard one of Admiral Rodney's men-o-war. That's worse than slaving, and without a dividend.'

His wife shook her head with anger and turned away from the men's laughter. She gathered up the dishes and tried to ignore the conversation as it continued.

'Now, Jake, what are we going to do with you? What do you want to do? Be a farmer?'

'No, I want to fill my pockets with gold coins. I can't do that on a farm, so I'll have to get onto a good ship if I can. I don't mind the trade if the ship is good and the crew are properly run by the Captain and the Mate.'

'Then I tell you what I have in mind for you. A friend of mine has a special job to be done. You can live here until I find you a berth, you can eat properly, and if you are honest and truthful we will teach you to write and count. If you are lazy or untruthful you know exactly what will happen to you. Then, when the time comes I will see you are properly signed on a ship to Africa and The Indies. How's that?'

'Better than the Assizes, Mister.'

'Just about.'

Mrs Weaver wept bitterly as soon as she was away from the noisy men.

Chapter 3

In the long northern twilight the 'Kestrel' ran free before the westerly wind and a deep swell rolling in from the Atlantic, which bore the brig forward on its crests. To the south, flashes of summer lightning over the distant mainland illuminated the coastline.

Captain Tobias Cooper turned to the young apprentice at his side.

'Make hay, Master Weaver. In this light and with such a favourable wind it's safe to run through the islands like this, and shake the wrinkles out the canvas. But imagine what we will have to encounter returning home in two months time.'

He turned his gaze aloft, where the square-sails were full and straining, the spars and rigging creaking under the tension of captured wind. Occasionally the foresails rippled and crackled, their wind deflected in the lee of the squaresails.

'It's fine enough to run all night in these benign winds. Come November it will be pitch dark by the dog watch and a nor'east gale will see you skittling along under staysails, with ice clattering off the t'gallant yards!'

John Weaver heard the Captain's comments with some apprehension. His previous voyage as apprentice had been to Bristol and Dublin, an almost commonplace journey, scarcely out of sight of land. Yet Captain Cooper, taking his responsibilities very seriously, had his young apprentice constantly at work. No headland had been passed without its profile on approach and recession being minutely sketched in John's pilot book. Every channel sounding called out by the leadsman had been carefully recorded as sketch maps filled with detail, no church tower un-noted, every beacon and lighthouse marked and described. The Captain had warned John of the task which lay ahead, to accumulate a detailed knowledge of the appearance and dangers of every landfall and channel he ever had the opportunity to behold.

The 'Kestrel' was sailing from Lancaster with an assorted cargo of timber products, iron fittings and farm produce, bound for the Baltic. The most important purpose of the voyage would be loading much-needed timber, hemp and tar, all in demand by the shipbuilders and the other industries developing in the north of England. John Weaver was constantly aware of the greater difficulties, with a crew of fifteen, to hand the sails in the constantly changing and unpredictable weather around the coast of Scotland. Even leaving the River Lune had meant days of waiting for the westerly wind to veer to the nor'east, allowing them to join the urgent procession of ships using the ebbing tide and favourable wind to clear the hazards of the Bay. For hours the bay was flecked with sail, like a flock of birds disturbed from their nests and fanning out across the hazardous waters. Some, heading for Africa and the West Indies had set course to the south, joining the ships from Fleetwood rounding Rossall Point.

But the 'Kestrel', bound for the northern entrance into the North Sea had to work hard to take the North Channel. She was forced to tack into the ocean before Captain Cooper decided the wind was set fair to allow a safe passage through the Little Minch passage of the Western Islands.

In the ever-darkening night, Captain Cooper walked to the deckhouse and called to 'watch on deck', the four men who would trim the sails as the wind and course changed.

'Lee braces, there! Ease away, and tend your weather side. Helmsman, steer East'sou'east. And nothing to starboard.' This last command to the helmsman to keep 'Kestrel' clear of the final headland of Duncansby into the turbulence of the North Sea.

A scurry of men adjusted the sails, seeking the last benefits from the favourable weather.

As the ship settled on her new course and the watch took shelter in the deck house the Captain took his new apprentice on a tour of the deck, checking the set of every sail and the security of every line and halyard as he progressed. While doing so he questioned his young companion closely.

'I've known your father for many years, a man much respected by the traders of Lancaster. So I owe it to him to give you the best training I can. I will report exactly on your conduct to your father, and you will not know my report aforehand. So, heed to my instructions and you won't let your father down. But, if you think I can make life easy for you, then you'd better find another berth. Vous comprendez?'

John Weaver had already experienced the Captain's occasional flights into the French language, a mark, he assumed, to denote his extensive travels compared with the merchants he met in the city. John considered that the Captain's stocky frame and polished, red face would mark him out as a seafarer in any company. But for John, nearly fourteen years old, taller than the captain and probably half his weight, lean and muscular, the only hopeful mark of his trade was a short tight pigtail. With only a few months at sea his skin and complexion had not yet hardened and coloured in response to the harsh elements, unlike most other members of the small crew. The other exception was Mighty Jake, who had signed on under the name of Jake Tempest, a name of his own choosing. His pale, pointed face and small frame was in sharp contrast to his consistent good cheer and resourcefulness. Whilst the ship was waiting in Lancaster for a favourable wind and tide it was Jake who stepped ashore and returned within the hour with a wooden tray filled with some beef pies which had been overcooked in the bakehouse and couldn't be served at the dining tables in the Kings Hotel.

'Did you steal these, you scoundrel?' demanded the ship's carpenter.

'No, mister, I didn't steal nothing. I just made sure they was burnt. Friend of mine is pantry-boy. He can burn anything you want.'

The assembled sailors laughed at this new approach to a better life, and Mighty Jake's reputation was assured.

The Captain turned to John Weaver.

'Where did your father find Jake Tempest? Not a distant relative, surely?'

'No, sir. Just an orphan my father feels some responsibility for. I've promised to keep an eye on him while he learns his trade.'

'Well, I don't want any thieving, or I'll hand him over. Thieves on ships are worse than rats. So, Mr Weaver, instruct him in the rules of the game. Is that understood?

'Yes, sir.'

The Captain completed his round of the deck just as the mate appeared on the poop beside the helmsman.

'Hello, Mr Longman. A fair night, I think. Course East-Southeast, while this wind holds. If in doubt and it starts to blow, take in your fore-course but call me if necessary.'

The new officer of the watch acknowledged the Captain's instructions and checked the dimly lit compass card. He turned to the retiring Captain.

'We'll have to pump out again in the forenoon watch. We cleared a lot of water yesterday and I'd like to find out how serious it is.'

'Ah, Mr Longman, you Royal Navy seamen are all the same. Pump, pump, pump, two hundred matelots to keep busy. Believe me, the 'Kestrel' takes on water stuck in port, hogging and sagging herself on the mud at every low tide. Get her loaded and sailing well and her seams all settle down, tight and sweet. I'll wager tomorrow you won't draw more than twenty strokes on the pump.'

'Is that a real wager, Captain? A roll of my tobacco against a measure of your brandy?'

The Captain laughed. 'Done, Mr Longman. Have a quiet watch, and no filling the bilges while I'm asleep.'

*

At sunrise the following morning the wind had freshened and was blowing from the Nor'west. Sail had been shortened, all hands aloft, taking the main course in and shortening the topgallants. In the swell which was now at an angle to the ship's head, the masts swung in an arc across the cloudy sky, but John was confident of his skills in handling the canvas and the bunt-lines from the upper yards. He looked across to the other end of the same spar. The diminutive figure of Mighty Jake could be seen, working as fast as any man on the spar, getting the unwanted sail area reduced and under control. When all was secure, the small figure descended rapidly to the deck by the simple expedient of sliding down the fore-brace. He stood on the deck with an air of impatience as the rest of the foremast men scrambled down the shroud ratlines.

After crew breakfast, the pump handles were rigged and within a few strokes a jet of brown water ran across the deck. Captain Cooper looked down from the poop.

'I'm counting, Mr Longman.'

After ten strokes the jet of water stopped, and the pump plunger rattled in the dry bore of the pipe.

The Mate looked towards the Captain. 'Dry ship, Sir!'

'So I see.' He lowered his voice. 'His "Kestrel" is a very dry ship. I've carried cargo all round the North Sea, into the Baltic in mid-winter, down the Channel in a full gale, and never lost so much as a sack of black beans from water.' The Captain took the Mate's tobacco bag from his hands and filled a short, heavily stained pipe.

'Sail-Ho!'

The foremast look-out called down to the deck and pointed on the starboard bow. From the deck nothing could be seen, and the Captain handed his small telescope to John Weaver.

'Get aloft. Tell me what you can see.'

John scrambled half way up the main shrouds and tried to steady himself whilst focussing the glass. Images of the uneven horizon flashed across his field of vision. At last he could keep the distant vessel in sight long enough to study her outline. He could see billowing white canvas as the ship sailed fast across the bows of 'Kestrel'. In contrast to the clouds of dazzling sails her hull looked to John like a stone wall, clumsy and inelegant, compared to the shapely lines of his own ship. As they drew nearer he could see rows of gun-port doors, obviously tightly closed.

'Man'o'War, Sir! Three-decker, I think. No ensign flying.' He shouted down to the watchers on deck.

30

Presently, as he kept the approaching ship under scrutiny a large blue ensign burst open in the wind, still not easily visible, blowing down wind.

'Royal Navy, Sir! Blue Ensign hoisted. Escort ship astern of her. About a league astern. Ensign flying!'

The two distant ships were clearly adjusting their course to pass close to 'Kestrel'.

Both were now visible from the deck and as they drew closer John could see for the first time just how large the approaching man-o-war really was. The escort was faster and more manoeuvrable and passed ahead of Kestrel before backing her topsails to lose way and wait for 'Kestrel' to sail up to her starboard side.

Across the turbulent water between the escort and 'Kestrel' a voice was calling.

'What ship?'

The Mate took the megaphone off the hook on the mainmast.

'Brig 'Kestrel' Captain Cooper, Lancaster to Riga and Baltic ports.'

'Are you carrying any armaments or gunpowder in your cargo?' came the query across the water.

'No! Our cargo is iron fittings, some tobacco, finished timber, barrels of salt. What is the name of your ship and your command ship'

'Seventy-four gun 'Triumph' and escort 'Arrow'.'

As if taking offence at 'Kestrel's questioning the escort trimmed her sails to the wind, and like a fretful woman gathering up her skirts, swung contemptuously astern of the merchantman and took up station between the 'Kestrel' and the huge man'o'war. Within half an hour they were far out on the starboard beam.

The Captain looked quizzically at the Mate.

'Strange. Don't generally encounter His Majesty's ships this far north, and never in peace-time. He never has enough matelots for such cruising.' The Captain proudly exhibited his knowledge of all maritime activities in happy conjunction with his french language skills.

The Mate scratched his head.

'I understand, sir, some of the difficulties in America have persuaded our Admirals to get new ideas on tactics, and to exercise their ships and their crews in peacetime as well as in war.'

'Don't like all this questioning. If we have paid all our dues it's no business of theirs what we are carrying. I'll wager they don't stop the slavers in mid-Atlantic and ask questions.'

The mate smiled.

'No more wagers, if you please, sir.'

*

After four days of alternating weather, requiring many changes of course to stem the tides and make best use of the winds, the first hardening of the horizon gave warning of the low-lying land ahead. On the table in the Captain's cabin a much-used discoloured chart showed the land-masses guarding the entrance to the Baltic. Captain Cooper carefully showed John Weaver the task that lay ahead.

'That low land ahead is called Jutland, nothing very high to be seen there. The other side of the Skaggerak is bounded by Norway, high and rocky. Now we've made a landfall we'll sail north, following round the coastline, but we'll have the leadsman taking soundings as we go. So out with your pilot book and I'll name the headlands as we come to them.'

Back on deck John Weaver watched the passing land about two leagues abeam on the starboard side. There were more ships hugging the coast than he had seen since leaving Lancaster. Some passed close by and hailed the 'Kestrel', and one ship, flying the red and white flag of the Danish Navy sailed close alongside for over an hour without making any sign of recognition, except for the officers with telescopes to their eyes carefully examining the English brig. The naval ship suddenly went about and seemed to pay the same minute attention to a merchantman sailing south.

Throughout the night the 'Kestrel' groped ahead, reaching northwards to round the Skaw, a long, low-lying finger of land which was a crucial signpost to the Kattegat and the Sound which lay before Copenhagen. In the deceptive twilight, with misleading shadows creating imaginary land masses, the leadsman used the old seaman's trick of allowing the lead-line to hang 'up and down' at the mark five and wait for any evidence of the weight touching the sea bed.

As eyes strained to determine the sandy headland a moving shadow was seen moving parallel with the 'Kestrel', and Captain Cooper suddenly realised the danger. A small ship was hugging the coastline to round the Skaw in the opposite direction, with the possibility that he was unable to see the 'Kestrel' in the misleading darkness.

'Quick! Get some tar burning. Bo'sun! Hands on deck, prepare to go about. Chippy! I want some tar in a barrel, some canvas scraps, get it alight and Weaver here will haul it aloft.'

At the same time a big lantern was being trimmed and lit to hang below the main to illuminate the white canvas.

'Mr Mate, I don't want to be forced to go about if I can avoid it. We'll hold our course till the last moment and see if we can make him alter course instead.'

'Well, sir, he'll consider we've got the easier wind.'

'I know, but if we get forced up to the north now it could take us until morning to find our way back to the eastern side of the Skaw. The currents here can push you to the west without you knowing it.

'By the mark Five!' called the leadsman.

'Come up a point, helmsman. Steer north-east.'

'North East it is sir.'

The hands were trimming the braces, trying to keep headway on while the ship edged closer to the wind.

'By God, Mr Mate, that ship's got the current with her. Look at her fly, yet not much canvas set.' He passed the telescope to the mate, who watched the ship across the sandy spit of land.

'He'll pass ahead of us if he doesn't go about towards us too soon. Pray to God that he's seen us, that is!'

The two ships seemed to be converging, chasing relentlessly down each side of the spit.

'By the deep Four'

'We'll be ashore soon. We're drawing twelve feet at present.'

'Steady as you go, helmsman. Nothing to starboard!'

The helmsman repeated the Captain's order, aware that his helmsmanship could be critical in avoiding a disaster.

The Captain kept his gaze on the fast-approaching sails.

'They're getting ahead of us, they'll pass ahead. Keep your course.'

The spit of land finished and nothing separated the two sailing ships except a patch of turbulent water where the fast flowing current from the eastern side clashed with the deep-water current on the west.

'By the mark Three!' screamed the leadsman.

'Hold your course.'

The two ships were separated by no more than a few yards, 'Kestrel' slightly astern of the dark, fleeting shadows of the other sails. At one moment it seemed as if the bowsprit would actually foul the backstay of the other vessel.

The current round the headland carried them both to the west, mercifully less for the 'Kestrel' than the other ship. As its stern passed a few feet ahead of the brig, her name was just visible in the darkness. The cyrillic letters had a translation below. 'Prince Ivan'. From the deck of the 'Kestrel ' it appeared only two men were on the deck of the Russian ship. Within a few moments the grey canvas and dark hull were sliding into the darkness of the night, no light, no sound to give evidence of her fleeting presence.

'By the mark Five!'

'Bear away, helmsman. Steer East nor'east. Ease your braces.'

The Captain stood beside the mate as the ship settled on her course.

'Quite close, Mr Mate.'

'I think they took our suppers off the mess-room dishes!'

John Weaver stood in the waist of the ship, watching the fast disappearing sails and the low silhouette of the Skaw.

'Weaver! I hope you've got a clear picture of that in your pilot book! Make a note in your margin not to hazard your ship like you've just witnessed.'

The Captain gave no indication which ship he meant.

Chapter 4

In the strange stillness of the evening, the 'Kestrel' lay uneasily becalmed, her sails occasionally flapping idly, and sometimes, as a zephyr of wind stirred a cat's-paw on the glassy surface of the sea, the sails would fill and head the ship aimlessly before gaining steerage way. After twenty or thirty seconds, the breeze would drop and once again anxious eyes would try to judge whether any real headway had been being made against the current which flowed out of the Baltic for most of the year.

To the west, the city of Copenhagen lay in the shadows of the setting sun, a last flicker of golden sunlight reflected off distant roofs. The city skyline was pierced by tall, narrow spires, and a hundred gossamer columns of smoke. Closer to the waters of the Sound lay the harbour which, to John Weaver, appeared like a forest, crowded with the masts and yards of warships. He had never seen so many ships in one harbour, and they appeared to have spilled into the surrounding waters. The entrance to this busy channel was guarded by two low, angular forts rising out of the water, like the hulks of huge ships, which, in the sunset readily merged into the long, evening shadows.

The mate stood beside the apprentice and pointed out the features of the city.

'Built like a castle. Completely protected by the sea on one side and then by canals between the ramparts, all the way round the city. See those?' He pointed to the mysterious forts.

'They call them the Trekroner, the 'Three Crowns Forts'. But that's only part of it. On the shoreline is another fort called the Citadel. I expect they can put cannons on the ramparts if they feel threatened. You mark my words, youngster, don't ever try to sail into this place without an invitation.'

John started drawing the dark outlines in his pilotage book, trying as near as possible to indicate the tallest spires.

All round them, becalmed ships drifted, their sails hanging limply, slowly but relentlessly carried northward by the current. On the poop the Captain and Mate were in deep discussion, looking shoreward from time to time, the Captain using his telescope and a small hand-held compass to examine the distant forts. In the stillness, the crew sat around, waiting for orders to get the brig moving again, but none came. Mighty Jake silently shuffled up to John. He cast his eyes towards the un-moving canvas and shook his young head with great gravity.

'Need some wind up there, Mister, that's our trouble. Not like this in the Atlantic. More wind than you need most of the time. And hot! So hot you had to sleep under the sky. Even the black men who like it hot were crying with the heat. The mate used to chuck buckets of sea-water down the gratings. He called it 'Noah's Flood'. He laughed at the memory.

'Well, Jake, you're not on a slaver now, and you won't get too hot here.'

'Will it get hotter when we can sail away from here?'

'No Jake, forget the heat, this part of the World isn't like Africa, you know.'

'Well, then, I don't like it. That's all I can say on it.'

John took the lad by the elbow.

'Look here, my fine fellow, you're signed on the 'Kestrel' until the day that Captain Cooper signs you off. I hope you don't have any mad ideas about jumping ship. Do you understand?'

'I know that, mister. I want to get into the hot weather, nothing more than that. Honest, John.'

'That's fair with me, Jake, but no tricks on this voyage. My father has given his word, to get you some training as a seaman, so don't you forget it. And I'll give you all the help I can, if you want it.'

*

All hands were called on deck at 4 o'clock in the morning as the wind suddenly freshened, and sails on the scattered ships filled and bent to the first gusts. On every ship anxious eyes judged the effect of the wind and the position of other ships nearby to plot a clear passage. In addition to the constant movement of vessels to and from the Baltic, an equally busy trade existed between the opposing coasts of Denmark and Sweden, across a channel as little as four miles wide at Kronborg Castle.

Within a few minutes it became clear that many of the ships were being gathered up like autumn leaves and blown towards the city's waterfront before the freshening easterly wind.

The topsails were being furled whilst three sailors were hastily setting the fore-and-aft spanker sail and stay-sails to take best use of the wind to claw their way off the unwelcome shoreline.

'Bo'sun! Get the lead going. Were in dangerous waters here.'

In a few moments the calls were coming from the leadsman, skilfully heaving the seven-pound lead weight to splash into the water ahead of the ship, and being brought up to measure the depth accurately as the ship advanced in the ever-freshening wind.

'By the mark Three!' he called.

The 'Kestrel' altered course to avoid ships which had been caught unawares and were crabbing awkwardly across the narrow channel between the invisible shoals. Yet now a greater peril loomed out of the early dawn light. No matter how skilfully the mariner performed his task no sailing ship could head directly into the wind, and the angle the 'Kestrel' had to follow, even with her most favourable use of stay-sails and spanker was now going to bring the ship perilously close to the sheer, unforgiving stone walls of the Trekroner Fort. If there were no other ships in the fairway the 'Kestrel' could have tacked towards the north-east, but the crowded Sound presented even greater danger. The Captain and the Mate watched the impending danger, constantly assessing the variable elements around them.

'Mr Mate, we'll take another gamble. We'll have to stay on this tack now. If we are going too close we'll head up into the wind at the last moment, to take the way off her, and trust the northerly current will carry us clear of the forts. If there is a counter-current swirling round those massive walls, have the port anchor cleared away, ready to let go. Now, all hands to stations, and keep the lead going.'

The bo'sun and two sailors stood by the spanker-sheet, the most critical sail in this difficult manoeuvre, whilst the carpenter and one sailor prepared the port anchor, now swinging on its cable, its flukes dipping into the short, steep waves.

On the fort the watching guards calculated the danger and lanterns were lowered from the parapets, presumably in a landsman's attempt to reduce the risk. The tall, plumed hats of the soldiers could be seen clearly against the dawn sky, as they watched anxiously over the massive ramparts.

With the sense of speed greatly exaggerated by the closeness of the stone walls, the bare spars of the 'Kestrel' seemed about to strike them as the swirling current threw the ship round like a piece of flotsam, mercifully providing additional pressure to push the ship out of danger.

'Dear Lord God!' exclaimed the Mate.' That, sir, was a very close run.'

The captain stared over the ship's stern at the receding ramparts and raised a hand in salutation to the watching guards. Then all efforts were directed to steering the brig southward through The Kings Channel to break into the spacious waters of the Baltic sea and the five hundred miles to Riga.

*

In the vastness of the Baltic the 'Kestrel' rarely encountered another sail, and when sighted, they tended to keep their distance. To Captain Cooper this corner of God's globe had mixed memories. The conflicts of recent years, generally fomented by France recruiting new allies to contain Britain's mastery of the seas, produced treaties and alliances which were not easily understood by the itinerant mariner. Particularly difficult had been the Treaties of Armed Neutrality, the Convoys Acts and the privateers attacking merchant ships in wartime. In the bottom of the flag locker could be found a number of ensigns of countries having little connection with the Port of Lancaster, which had sometimes been more use than a broadside of cannon. Regardless of the view of the politicians, the merchantmen generally found a warm welcome from the shippers and merchants in every port of call. Cargo standing in warehouses, timber unfelled or stacked on quaysides earned nothing for anyone. Even in England, the sixty different rates of customs duties financed the politicians' grand schemes in peace, and armaments in war. Now, in the year of our Lord 1789, with Europe apparently at peace, trade was expanding, not only to make good the losses of war but in commerce with the new, expanding countries, like the United States of America. The Captain reflected upon the fearsome slave trade which had brought wealth to many of his fellow mariners, but which he had always avoided. Yet he knew he could well return home after four months in these northern waters with precious little profit for him or the ship. Whether true or not, the tales he heard in the Lancaster and Liverpool coffee houses seemed that 'The Guinea Trade' was the way to an easy fortune. He had heard it said that if one ship in three was lost with all hands and her cargo, the owners would still make a handsome overall profit from the other two.

He looked around at the 'Kestrel' with considerable pride, her decks scrubbed, her full sails drawing and creaking with a satisfactory tension, the mark of a well-run ship under full power. In the cloudy skies he could only estimate their progress, the chip log recording a speed of over seven knots on both timings in the forenoon and afternoon. Presently, he became aware of voices behind him.

The bo'sun was making rounds and checking the trim of every sail. He had with him the small figure of Jake Tempest. Not much more than a child, he nevertheless literally pulled his weight and more, always the first aloft and likewise the first back on deck. When he could see the bo'sun had finished his rounds Captain Cooper beckoned the boy over.

The thin figure scampered across the deck and stood straight as a marine, the sheepskin coat he wore reaching to his knees.

'Well, boy, how are you getting on? What do you think of my ship, eh?' Captain Cooper made his best attempt to sound stern, but all the time he knew the small figure before him could have been his own son, born while he was sailing from Leghorn, dead and buried in a Milnthorpe churchyard before Gibraltar was astern. He looked into the pinched face.

'Cold sir. I've been cold for weeks, sir.'

'Ha. Is that so? Well, just you tell the cook you're to get double helpings. Tell him I said so. Get some pudding on these bones. Are you always this cold? You don't feel ill, do you?'

'No, sir. My last voyage was so hot the pitch was melting, leaving black footprints on the deck planking. Bo'sun Gains said he'd kill anyone stepping in the pitch.'

'You were with Mr Gains? Were you slaving?'

'Aye, sir. 'Rainbird' of Lancaster, that was us.'

'Bo'sun!' The captain called to the man on the other side of the deck. He came over to the Captain.

'Yes, sir?'

'Bo'sun, we've got a steelyard in the stores, haven't we?'

'Yes, sir. We keep in for weighing damaged sacks and things like that.'

'Right, I want this young imp weighed every day, and you can tell the apprentice to write it in the log book. Every day, understand?'

*

The city of Riga required an element of good fortune to find from the open seas of the Baltic. It lay in one corner of the Gulf of Livonia, which was shaped like a boot with the city near the toes. The 'ankle' of the gulf was protected by islands so that the entrance was no more than twenty miles wide. Captain Cooper used the customary method by making the first sighting of land well to the south, sighting 'The Seven Hills' and then feeling the way northward up the coast until the gulf opened up ahead, 'like a blind beggar finding the door.' If the landfall was made too far north the hapless ship could sail half way to Petersburg three hundred miles away before giving up the search.

The heart of the city was a few miles up the River Dvina which flowed for over a thousand miles across the great Russian plain. The spires of Europe were replaced by the onion-shaped domes of an Eastern world. However, most ships were loaded and unloaded in the mouth of the river, where great cumbersome rafts of tree trunks floated or were secured to posts driven into the estuary. Trunks were joined end to end to form enclosures called 'ponds' for smaller timbers to be secured for different shippers. Each post and pond had a symbol or a number, by which the ownership of each consignment could be identified. Ships of many different rigs were idly swinging at anchor, great three-masted ships with cross-yards towering over the low shoreline, small coastal boats with triangular lateen sails, and even single-masted boats whose poles could lie flat to permit passage up stream under the timber bridges which were the only dry link between thousands of square miles of rich farmland and gigantic forests. Some of the largest ships showed signs of their age; dull, blackened woodwork, upper masts and spars missing, and bulwark rails cut away to allow great loads of timber to be carried on deck. As they swung at anchor, square openings could be seen in their transoms to allow great timbers to be loaded lengthwise. Such ships, nearing the end of their trading lives, would be rendered unseaworthy for extensive ocean voyages.

As the 'Kestrel' turned into the wind and dropped her anchor, everyone on board became aware of the clean, sweet smell of pinewood. The air was heavy, yet refreshing to the incoming crew, and held a promise of the luxury of dry land after the weeks at sea. But even as the sailors observed the activities of the busy port, they were being watched by inquisitive eyes. Two longboats were rowing towards them, the leading one clearly filled with soldiers or some uniformed militia, with muskets slung diagonally across their backs. Four oars were clumsily attempting to row the over-laden boat alongside, much to the amusement of the 'Kestrel's' crew, who cheered on their efforts.

'Bo'sun! Get those idle fools away from the rail! If you want to laugh at the Russian army, I'll tell you, they'll let you laugh for twenty years, through prison bars.'

He turned to the Mate.

'I don't know what the fuss is about, but I want strict behaviour, no talking from anyone until I know what is going on. Tell our jackasses to stand in a straight line and, if necessary, help our visitors on board.'

A ladder had been lowered over the starboard side, and presently the soldiers started the awkward ascent, their muskets and bandoliers making their task twice as difficult. The first man to stand on deck was a giant, towering over all of the sailors. His daunting stature was increased by a black fur hat, adding fully fifteen inches to his height. He silently stood on the deck, lifted his musket off his back and held it across his chest. Seven more men, not quite so impressive, but notably robust, stepped onto the deck and formed a straight line facing the hushed and surprised mariners.

With a clatter of sword and scabbard, an officer in a dark blue uniform coat, white breeches and black boots struggled over the ship's rail with as much dignity as he could muster. He was wearing a helmet, complete with plume and with a golden chin-strap, which had failed to prevent the helmet being knocked askew in his climb.

Captain Cooper, from long experience, knew when to attend to the correct courtesies. He swept off his own, well-worn tricorne hat and nodded to the impressive officer.

'I am Captain Cooper, master of the brig 'Kestrel' from the city of Lancaster. I have twenty three other sailors on this ship..'

As he spoke he realised the officer could not understand a word. He tried again.

'Bonjour, mon colonel, je suis Capitaine Cooper de cette bateau 'Kestrel'...

He could feel his French running out of words as he spoke. Further embarrassment was avoided when another figure climbed nimbly over the side. He was also clad in a fur hat, but not quite as smart as the stationary soldiers. He wore a sheepskin coat tied with a broad leather belt, from which swung a short dagger in a decorated leather sheath. He was, like all the visitors this morning, tall and very powerfully built. His face was the most remarkable feature noticed by the Captain. He had a thick black moustache which had been carefully groomed to extend more than the full width of his face. His weather-beaten face had high cheek-bones below black, piercing eyes. The fur of his hat seemed to be a natural extension of his face, like a predatory animal. He stood contemptuously in front of the officer and addressed the Captain in a heavily accented voice.

'Captain, sir. Ve haf been expectin' your ship many days now. I velcome you to ze city de Riga, monsieur. Ve must speak vis you in private now, if it please. Private, now.'

The Captain extended his hand towards the small companionway which led down to his cabin. The officer and the civilian removed their headgear and clambered down the stairway as formally as possible.

In the small, ill-lit cabin the Captain turned to the civilian.

'A little brandy, perhaps?'

Dark eyes lit up, coats were undone and the three sat round the table secured to the dark wooden panelling of the captain's cabin. When three glasses were filled Captain Cooper looked to his guests for some response. To his surprise, the officer was the first to speak.

'Messieurs, le King George of England.' He looked at the others with obvious pride.

'The King George of England,' they both responded.

'The Empress Catherine, Czarina of the Russias.' responded Captain Cooper, giving the widest possible scope to her dominions under the circumstances.

Toasts were drunk, health proposed, pipes filled and in the comfortable, seclusion of the cabin the formalities of rank were quickly disposed of as the brandy bottle was passed round.

The civilian, who introduced himself eventually with the rather unlikely name of Chef Popov, produced papers to demonstrate his authority as an accredited merchant in the Port of Riga. He had a letter of authority from two merchants' houses in Lancaster, although the dates seemed confusing to the Captain.

The officer leaned forward and looked straight into the Captain's eyes.

'Vous avez les informations de Paris, Capitaine?'

The Captain looked at Chef Popov for assistance.

Popov turned to the officer and with much gesticulation and head shaking, made a long speech in what Captain Cooper assumed was Russian. After a few more questions from the officer to which Popov appeared to give satisfactory replies, the officer stood up and drained his glass.

'Merci, mon Capitaine!' he exclaimed loudly, although in the cramped cabin he was no more than an arm's length from the captain. He turned and left the cabin, followed by the captain. On deck he saluted the remaining English sailors before descending the ladder into the boat, followed by his military escort. Captain Cooper looked over the ship's side and waved to the departing boat, once again deeply laden but now with the officer laughing and shouting, obviously under the influence of French brandy. The crew of the 'Kestrel' joined in the farewell, waving to the unstable boat.

The captain returned to his cabin and poured himself another drink and turned to offer the bottle to Chef Popov.

'No thank-you, dear sir. I've got to keep a clear head. I changed my glass twice with that numskull to keep him awash.'

The Captain looked in astonishment.

'I thought you only spoke a little English. What are you about?'

'Ah, Captain, it doesn't do to let these musket-mules know too much. I let them think I am a peasant who does what he's told and they let me make a few crowns on the side. In fact, I speak quite good English. I have been in your country and my father also worked in your country, learning to be a shipwright.'

'You astonish me, sir! I had no idea. Where did you visit in England?'

'Your great naval harbour at Portsmouth. Have you ever heard of a great warship called the 'Vanguard'?'

The Captain looked slightly embarrassed. His knowledge of the Royal Navy was strictly limited to the ships he had encountered on the high seas.

'Er, Mr Popov, I don't think I know that one. A sloop, I fancy.'

'Sloop, Captain? Nearly eighty cannon on that ship. It could blow St Petersburg out of this World if it was minded to! Well, we were commanded to Portsmouth to measure the masts. We travelled by land all the way to Hamburg to board a ferry to the River Thames, and started measuring and checking the drawings in your shipyards at a place named Sheerness then at Portsmouth. We were responsible for masts and some spars. When we returned to Memel we had to search for the best timber. I tell you, we earned our money.'

The much-travelled Mr Popov leaned forward and tapped the side of his nose with his finger.

'Captain, today we must be very careful. Two days ago a courier arrived on the way to the Palace at St Petersburg. He had a message from our Minister in Paris. The citizens are rising up against the government in Paris. They are not against the King, you understand, but the harshness of the government. A great prison called Le Bastille has been attacked and some of the prisoners released. That is why our city militias have been prepared to meet any unrest when the news spreads, and why our friend with the fine hat came on board. I had to give my word that you were not carrying arms or explosives.'

The captain nodded.

'You can rest assured about that. He may examine the cargo manifest if you so wish.'

'No, no, no, Captain. Your word as an English Captain is good enough for me. For this voyage, anyhow.'

'Pardon, sir? I don't quite understand. Will my word not be good for you every voyage?'

'Captain, I have certain information which leads me to the conclusion that soon some explosives may be the most valuable commodity you could put into your most attractive ship. Just between the two of us, some barrels of black powder could be a very pleasant treasure to find at the bottom of your hold. Don't you agree?'

The Captain looked at the wild face of Chef Popov. He noticed the flicker of a smile.

'Ha! You're joking. I thought so. I couldn't sail into here with a cargo of gunpowder under any circumstances, without paying duties in England and again when we land it here.'

Popov leaned back in his chair and laughed, before lowering his voice to a whisper.

'Then, if that is the case we won't land it here. I will arrange everything so that you can quietly land your treasure a little way down the coast. No need to disturb the good citizens of Riga, especially if it might blow them to their Maker in the middle of the night! Ha!'

He laughed loudly at his splendid joke.

The captain shook his head vigorously, and looked angrily at the strange man opposite him.

'You know what you suggest could put both of us in prison, probably to be hanged after they had got all the details from us. It is totally out of the question, and I think you know that when you ask.'

The cabin fell silent, the air tense with the Captain's anger. Popov eventually broke the silence.

'Captain, you don't quite realise. I represent the handful of men who control the finest timber forests in this area. When your Admiralty sent for me and my father it was because we could supply them with everything they wanted. If you don't play my game you can load your ship with all the firewood and kindling you like, and sell it in the street at, where is it, Lancaster? A halfpenny a bundle? Good-day, Captain. Tomorrow we will start unloading your cargo and settling the trading accounts. Good day, and my thanks for your kind hospitality.'

Chapter 5

In the home of Joshua Weaver at Ryelands the fires had been lit in the cool of the September evening. The dining room was prepared for his guests and his wife had hired two girls from the village to help serve at the table. In the kitchen a side of lamb had been roasting over the blazing fire, whilst fish, fresh-caught in the Bay was cooking on skewers each side of the sizzling, spitting carcase. The evening air was heavy with the smell of food in preparation and as each man arrived jokes were exchanged about the delicious smell.

Round the dining table five men enjoyed the food which the young girls carried to the guests. At the head of the table, as host, sat Joshua Weaver, wearing his best dark blue frock coat and white breeches. Like most of the others, he wore a short wig with side curls. Only Councillor Matthew Redfearn wore the more elaborate Codogan wig, his whole manner being that of one who expects to be in the chair at most assemblies. His pale blue silk coat was decorated with gold piping, his silk cravat was more embroidered than anyone else's, and buttons more numerous. He sat at the opposite end of the dining table, facing Joshua. His air was one of ill-disguised impatience, finding the meal an intrusion upon his customary duties of Chairman.

Captain Cooper, only recently back in Lancaster from the Baltic, was dressed as formally as possible, wearing his blue high-buttoned jacket which confirmed his distinctly naval air.

Of the two other men, one, William Provender, was very tall, with a long, grim face, dark brows joining above deep, piercing eyes. He had the appearance of one accustomed to bad news, and his dress was dark and sombre, in complete contrast to the last arrival at the table. When he entered the room he had introduced himself to the three men he hadn't previously met.

'Giles Wainwright's the name. An a-hem, an associate of Mr Wakefield, who sends his compliments.' He bowed formally to each of the others, with a broad smile upon his cheerful, round face. He was short in stature and stout, his bright red coat barely fitted round his ample waist, and every garment seemed to strain to cover his rotund body and limbs. His hands were similarly plump and pink. The overall effect was to add a slightly comical air to what otherwise seemed a very serious and possibly ill-tempered supper.

The pitchers of red wine were passed round the diners and goblets were filled time and again. Fresh helpings of meat were brought from the kitchen and Mistress Weaver carved at the sideboard. Gradually the conversation became more relaxed, Captain Cooper related some of excitement of the last voyage. William Provender listed the rising duties which were being levied by Mr Pitt's government, and morosely considered the future.

As the meal drew to a close the women gathered the plates and dishes together and carried them to the kitchen. Councillor Redfearn tapped the table with his spoon.

'My compliments, Mistress Weaver, for your hospitality and your well-prepared table. Gentlemen?'

He looked round the table. Glasses were raised towards John Weaver's wife, and heads nodded. She curtseyed briefly and withdrew.

Immediately the door had closed Councillor Redfearn tapped the table again, but this time his summons was much less good-natured.

'Gentlemen, Joshua has brought us to his table for a very specific reason. Much as I enjoy good food we have more pressing matters to resolve tonight and time is not with us. Without further ado I ask Captain Cooper to make his report. Tobias?'

'Thank-you, Councillor. As you know the 'Kestrel' has just returned with an excellent cargo of timber and flax, and just a small quantity of tar. There's plenty of trade there and much bigger ships looking for it. 'Seekers' from every European country waiting for cargo. Now, we have a new agent there who calls himself Chef Popov. Knows English and has been to England in the past. Everything we took from him looks the best. Operates from Riga, St Petersburg and Memel. Everybody at ease with the arrangements?'

The men gathered round the table nodded and raised their glasses briefly to the Captain. His last question was, in reality, seeking approval for the dividends each would have received in the past few days. They had no wish to speak in more detail in the presence of the rubicund Mr Wainwright. Councillor Redfearn responded.

'Fine. Gentlemen, we may now speak freely with Mr Wainwright on matters of mutual interest. Chef Popov has made a particularly difficult demand upon us. He wants gunpowder.'

A murmur ran round the table. With the exception of the cheerful face of Mr Wainwright the men seemed exasperated by the news. The lugubrious face of William Provender seemed to grow even longer.

'He'll have us all hanging from the Lancaster gibbet, that's what this means.'

Captain Cooper nodded in agreement.

'At least you'll hang at home. I'll hang at Cronstadt, a thousand miles from the River Lune.'

The chairman cleared his throat and the table fell silent.

'Mr Wainwright, perhaps you would explain to my colleagues assembled here what the attraction for gunpowder is at this particular time.'

The jolly, rubicund man took a long drink from his glass and wiped his face on the napkin.

'As I think you know, my Principal, Mr John Wakefield has been manufacturing black powder at Sedgwick for nearly twenty-five years, both for quarry-blasting and for the military. I know many of your ships have carried our products around the World. Ever since the government stopped using private manufacturers for their military requirement, meeting much of their need from their own mills, we have had to look for new markets at home and abroad.'

He took another drink from the glass which Joshua had kept filled.

'Now, gentlemen, just two years ago we made a big advance. A professor of science, the Reverend Richard Watson, who lives nearby at Heversham but teaches at one of our great Universities, invented a new way of making charcoal, by heating the coppiced wood in an iron drum. The method is a secret, but all you need to know is that 'cylinder powder' as it is called is much more powerful. The word is abroad that this new powder is available, so naturally the buyers are in the market. We can make a much better price at the present time, while others are still looking.'

Captain Weaver looked even more apprehensive.

'Twice as powerful, they'll hang us twice as high.'

Councillor Redfearn shrugged his shoulders.

'Don't get caught, that's the answer.' He laughed with a dry, mirthless chuckle.

Mr Wainwright enjoyed the joke.

'I think we can help. As you know, you must have no iron close to gunpowder for fear of striking sparks. As you may find, we take unusual protection in this regard. For this reason we make all our own barrels at Sedgwick. We can now fashion a barrel which is divided in half. The top half can be filled with anything you like. I know one boat left with a cargo of split peas in the top half of the barrels. We could make some big barrels for carrying cattle hides if you like, with just one third part for black powder.'

His audience appeared less than enthusiastic with what they were hearing. They expressed their concern in various comments.

'Why don't we just carry the constituent substances for making the gunpowder, even in different ships? Then we wouldn't have the same crippling duties and the prohibitions on who we can sell to.'

Councillor Redfearn looked angrily at the questioner.

'Money, man! One hundred pounds value of chemicals is worth one thousand guineas when Mr Wakefield has used his skill in making it into gunpowder, perhaps two thousand if it is the new powder. But wait too long and His Majesty's gunpowder mills in Waltham and Faversham will reduce the price to pennies again.'

Still the dissent continued. William Provender drew his black jacket closer round his gaunt frame.

'If the Revenue catch Captain Cooper sailing across the Bay on Tuesday we'll all be before the Assize by Friday. Why don't we take it by wagon to Liverpool and let them run the risk?'

Councillor Redfearn nearly exploded.

'Liverpool? Liverpool, Mister Provender? Are you mad? We build our own ships, we run the port, we have agents in Russia, and Mister Provender wants to send a horse and cart to Liverpool.' He pronounced the name of his victim with carefully enunciated disdain. 'If you think this is too risky for you, now's the time to get back to your farm.'

'I'm not a farmer, Councillor. I happen to own a bank. My reputation is a vital asset in my profession.'

'Yes, and so are the thousands of pounds which I and others pass through your bank. Unhappily for you, that money does not come from picking cherries off the trees in the summer sunshine. It comes from trade, Mister Provender. Trade in timber for our men-o-war, slaves for our plantations, iron cannons for our allies, and now the finest English gunpowder for the Empress of Russia. That's what pays for all of us round this table, for our sons at Public Schools and Oxford University. Really, I grow tired of explaining this to you bankers every week.'

The victim of the chairman's rage looked round the table for signs of support for his hesitation. Joshua Weaver sensed the need for a mediator.

'I think we are all agreed that this opportunity needs careful consideration. First of all, Captain Cooper is a trusted partner in this company. If each of us is running a risk, surely the Captain is bearing more than his share. If anything goes wrong, he will be the first to receive blame and the most difficult to acquit. I would like to hear his view.'

'The risk is very great, but to my mind the risk is reduced by reducing the number of voyages. Thus, one voyage carrying twenty tons is less risky than five voyages each carrying four tons. If we are searched and this is found, that will be the end. If we have an accident and catch fire, one ton is as lethal as one hundred. Additionally, I agree with the chairman. We make as much money by delivering the new powder as early as possible.'

Councillor Redfearn looked at the other four.

'Well?'

Giles Wainwright, the cheerful gunpowder merchant, cleared his throat.

'If you own the ship, why don't you build false bulkheads inside the hold to conceal the barrels. We could still make them divided into two halves and overload them with other cargo.'

'That had been my idea, Mr Wainwright,' said the captain. 'Also, if we filled the holds tightly with cargo, full to the deckheads, then no one could gain access to the suspect barrels. But what I need is the right cargo.'

The chairman's manner suddenly changed to one of genuine interest.

'Tell me what you want.'

'Right, Councillor. This is what I suggest. Firstly, as soon as the 'Kestrel' has finished unloading in Lancaster we make sail to Milnthorpe and load the black powder, creating as little attention as possible. Next, still in Milnthorpe, to avoid unnecessarily entering and leaving port, we load a cargo on top for which Chef Popov will find us a market in Dantzig. Coffee, cocoa, wagon wheels and iron fittings will all be readily negotiable, if you could find us the cargo coming in on your West Indies ships, Mr Weaver.'

'No difficulty,' he replied.

Once again, the lugubrious banker interrupted.

'And payment? I suppose your Chef Popov has the money ready when we have unloaded everything into his estate, and then he finds he has forgotten his purse?'

'May I, councillor?' interrupted Captain Cooper. 'The price has already been agreed, which will be highly advantageous to us. That is the justification for of our visit to the port of Dantzig. Half the payment will be made at Dantzig, which gives Popov a chance to make his own assessment of the cargo. It also lets him know we are in the locality so that he can prepare to meet us further up the coast north of Memel. We unload the black powder into his coastal boats and receive the balance of the money. Then we sail on to Memel and load a full cargo of timber. That is how I see this being accomplished. Now, anything any of you can do to ease our task, so much the better.'

The chairman glowered at the men sat round the dining table and waited for a response.

'I can speak on behalf of Mr Wakefield. We will build the special barrels at no cost to yourselves. Furthermore, in view of the risks you are running, we will offer you credit on one half of the purchase price until you have been paid for the first part, or within two months of departure from Lancaster. I expect the volume of powder available will be not more than fifteen tons, which, in false barrels containing seventy-five pounds of powder and twenty-five pounds of other cargo, say glass goods packed in straw, china-ware in wood shavings and so on, would require over four hundred barrels. That's a lot of work for all of us.'

The chairman nodded.

'That is most obliging of Mr Wakefield. I will provide warehousing at Milnthorpe to assemble the filled barrels, so that we can accumulate the full cargo for the 'Kestrel'.'

Mr Wainwright cleared his throat.

'Excuse me, Sir. To warehouse black powder in a town would be a most dangerous and unwise practice, and if any accident, however small, should arise, the effect would be quite devastating. We can create a stock ready to convey down the road in what we call the Expense Magazine. We could move out of the Sedgwick mill each night, you fill the upper half of the barrel at your warehouse and load directly into Captain Cooper's ship in the morning. I would rather not move such quantities in daylight out of the mill yard. The ship would bear the burden that no fires or sparks could cause a detonation until the barrels are loaded, secured and covered.'

'Is that agreed by everyone? Mr Provender?'

He nodded, silent for a moment's reflection.

'I can send two carters to the mill. But I would like to make a suggestion. We must give this material a name, so that everyone can make their invoices or whatever, without being party to the whole enterprise. I suggest we use the description 'Brewer's Grains.' If anyone makes an enquiry, the substance is used in the manufacture of ale.'

Councillor Redfearn had been making notes in a small notebook. He looked round the table at the four other men. He tapped the table with his silver pencil.

'Do I have your approval for the plan as devised tonight? All commissions will be notified by Mr Provender when known. The usual dividend on shareholding, although I would like to suggest an additional share to Captain Cooper for the added risk. I am prepared to contribute one half share if the remainder of the committee can find an equal amount.'

Once again, approval was given round the table. Glasses were filled and the chairman proposed good fortune to the venture, which was warmly acknowledged.

One by one the men left, but the chairman remained until he could speak to Joshua Weaver on his own.

When they had the room to themselves, the chairman took off his wig, for comfort, and revealed a pink, bald head.

'That man Provender is a most dour citizen. A first-class banker, who has certainly used our deposits to good effect. At times I think he is frightened of his own shadow. I have to sharpen him up from time to time, which is why I was not too polite in our discussion. I'm sorry if my rebuke offended my host.'

'Not at all, Sir. I fully understand the difficulty. It would certainly be most unfortunate to have to find a new bank at this time.'

'Joshua, I understood you to say you had a young man who could keep an eye on my Guinea Traders. I get so many tales about ill-usage of the slaves that I want to get at the truth. Who have you got to help me?

'Well, at first sight you may be surprised at my recommendation. But I have given your request most careful thought. I have in my care a young orphan boy who has worked in Mr Brockbank's shipyard and had sailed with Captain Cooper and given a good account of himself. At first I would not have trusted the boy, but I have put him on his mettle on a number of occasions. Trustworthy but up to every trick in the book. He was well regarded on the 'Kestrel' for pulling his weight, day or night, and never short of a new twist. I feel the sailors would trust him without further thought.'

'Can he read and write?'

'Not what you mean, no he can't. But he keeps a strange log of his life in a very original way. Look at this.'

Joshua spread out on the dining table a single sheet of coarse paper which was covered on both sides in narrow columns or rows of marks covering every inch of available space.

'See this? It's completely his own invention. These long columns of marks are actually days. Let me explain. Day one, regardless of date, which he doesn't understand anyhow, is this first 'box' at the top right-hand corner. If anything has to be noted, like leaving harbour, he draws a tiny picture which means that. I happen to know a triangle is a sail. Other signs mean other things, so he can make each day's entry long enough for all the signs he needs. If nothing happens he just draws a line to keep the number of days correct, and goes on until he wants to record another event. This simply serves to prompt his memory, no more than that. He can remember the smallest detail of events, so there is no risk of him being found writing reports. Look, if you like the cut of his cloth, ask him to tell you every event on this page. You'll be surprised, I promise you.'

The councillor looked unimpressed.

'Sorry, Mr Weaver, I don't like the sound of your young man. I expected someone older, say twenty-five years old, trustworthy and able to stand witness at the Assizes if necessary.'

'In which case I think you might have a funeral to attend to. I don't think any seaman would bear witness against his shipmates, no matter how great the crime. Dear Lord, we've had murders without any witnesses, when we all knew ten men were on deck at the time. If I'm not mistaken you had evidence of barratry on one of your own ships, but I don't remember any witness coming forward.'

'So what purpose will your boy serve?'

'He will at least tell you what is happening, nothing in writing and no risk of being before the magistrate. That's going to be the best you can expect. Furthermore, he has experience of the slave trade and wants to sail in the tropic sun again. He found the Baltic too cold for his taste. And he likes the dividends!'

'Tell me, Mr Weaver, do you not have a son of your own? Doesn't he seek a sailor's life?'

'Yes indeed, Councillor, but he is learning his trade in the Baltic under Captain Cooper. I don't want to interrupt his studies.'

'You're sure it's not the Guinea Trade he wants to avoid? Upset by the 'black ivory', is that it?'

Joshua knew his son would be revolted by the slave trade, but didn't want to admit as much to the head of the company. Councillor Redfearn enjoyed Joshua's obvious discomfort.

'Rather have your boy sailing with ten tons of black powder than a couple of hundred black boys, eh? Well, please yourself, Weaver. But I know where I would feel safer. Let me examine your young orphan boy, then.'

Joshua went to the door and called.

'Mother? Send Mighty Jake in here. Hurry, now.'

Mighty Jake walked into the room, dressed in clean white breeches and red and white striped smock. He carried a broad-rimmed hat which he proudly held at his side. He stood straight and still in front of Mr Weaver.

'Jake, this is Councillor Redfearn. He would like to talk to you. Answer his questions. Politely now.'

Jake turned to the frowning face of the seated man.

'Evening, Sir.' He touched his forehead with his fingertips.

'Boy, do you tell the truth?'

'Yes, if you want it.'

'What in God's name does that sort of answer mean?' exclaimed the councillor.

'If you want me to tell a lie, I'll do it. Like Captain Cooper. He told me to tell the soldiers in Russia we were forbidden allowed to have ale on the ship. They wanted ale for theirselves and started to turn the ship inside out looking for it. So I lied, the best I knew how.'

The councillor allowed a brief smile to flicker across his face.

'Suppose I wanted you to tell me everything that happened on a voyage, ale for the soldiers, perhaps mischief with the slaves, hurting them, any bad thing at all, would you tell me?'

'Yes.' The boy's answer was brief and uncomplicated.

'Suppose a shipmate of yours, a special friend, killed a slave, would you tell me?'

'Yes.'

'Suppose your friend went to prison because you told me what he had done, how would you feel?'

'Very sad, Sir.'

'Aha! So you might not tell me?'

'If you tells me, Mister, when you signs me on with the Captain that I must tell you the truth when we get home and pay off, I'll do it.'

'How old are you, boy?'

Jake looked towards Joshua for guidance.

'We think he's about fifteen, Councillor. He's been in my care for two years. I've no complaints.'

'How can I be sure you won't tell me lies.'

The small, standing figure looked to Joshua again.

'Can the Mistress come in here, Mister?'

Presently, Mistress Weaver appeared at the door, casting off her apron. Jake took her plump, work-worn hand in his and laid both clumsily across his skinny chest to lie approximately on his heart.

'If you tell me what you want, Mister, I'll tell you all the truth.'

The councillor nodded.

'Thank-you, Mistress Weaver. He's told us all I need to know.'

She left the room, with a brief, backwards glance at the small figure.

'Joshua, I think you and I and...'

'Jake Tempest, Sir'

'...and Jake Tempest have got an agreement between us. I bid you a good night and thank you for a most successful meeting.'

Chapter 6

The lane wound its way through tall, straight trees. On the right hand side flickering moonlight was reflected from a fast-running river, its tumbling water the only sound in the still night. Four horse-drawn carts stood under the trees and figures with dark cloaks moved silently through the shadows. Ahead, a number of stone buildings blended with the midnight shadows, as if they had been there since the beginning of time. Strange roof-high hillocks of earth, like monstrous molehills, separated each squat building from its neighbour, adding to the sinister, unreal atmosphere.

Joshua Weaver cautiously walked into the darkness, feeling for the rutted track beneath his feet as the only guide forward. Suddenly, the growl of a dog and the sound of the beast pulling on a chain caused Joshua to halt in his stride. A voice whispered out of the shadows.

'Who goes there?'

'I am the weaver seeking the loom.' He held his breath.

'The shuttle will fly tonight.' A lantern flashed briefly to show the presence of the speaker.

'Gideon Musprat at your service. Have you wagons?'

'Four wagons, Mr Musprat. Eight men for loading the 'Brewer's Grains.'

'Right, my friendly weaver, bring the wagons this way. There are only three of us here tonight. We'll go to the magazine. I'll provide the only light. Tell your men they must not smoke any pipes or light lanterns because of the grain dust. Make sure they understand that. No man passes this gate until he has been searched for any hazards'

The wagons rumbled forward, guided only by Mr Musprat's strange lantern. They wound through the trees, and the noise of rushing water grew louder. Then, without any warning, another fearsome sound filled the shadows, which struck terror into the visitors, a long, low groan, like a mammoth animal dying in pain. The very buildings seemed to shudder with the sound. Joshua Weaver felt his blood freeze as the horses whinnied with animal fear. Musprat appeared to ignore the sound.

'What in the name of God was that?'

Mr Musprat laughed in the darkness.

'It's just the watermill, turning against the brake. Quite harmless, but it keeps the thieves away. Some people in the village swear we have Russian bears chained to the trees!' The word was passed down the line of frightened men, and nervous laughter trembled in the gloom.

The storehouse to which the wagons had been led was surrounded on three sides by huge mounds of earth, and even the fourth side allowed only one wagon at a time to draw up beside the door because of another wall of earth a few feet away from the wall. The rough track was replaced by heavy baulks of timber laid cross-wise, with gaps between them. The horses hooves fell almost silently on the timber.

'That's to stop horse-shoes striking sparks,' explained Musprat. 'Your men must put these clogs on while they are working in the magazine.' The heavy wooden shoes, only crudely shaped to cover feet of all sizes, were kept in a sack. The overwhelming gloom of the occasion was briefly dispersed by the laughter of the men trying different clogs, seeking the best fit.

'Here we are. Now, you men, take these casks, but load them upright. Always stand them on their ends, is that clear?'

In the darkness, their eyes now becoming accustomed to the shadows, the dozen men started the long task of lifting the casks on to the wagons. Fortunately, the storeroom floor was built up to nearly the same height, so they could be dragged across more easily. Nevertheless, it took three hours for the wagons to be filled and the heavy rope nets spread across the loads and tightened down. Some pitchers of sharp-flavoured ale mysteriously appeared and were drained by the sweating men. The clogs were gratefully returned to the sack and the procession of heavily laden wagons set off down the road, the teams of horses now straining and panting. Joshua Weaver signed for the cargo at the gatehouse. He reached inside his heavy surtout and from one of the voluminous pockets produced a bottle of brandy.

'Our compliments, Mr Musprat.'

'Well, sir, that's generous indeed. I wish you a peaceful journey, wherever that may take you. Good night, sir.'

The journey back to the small port of Milnthorpe should take over an hour, and throughout the dark hours the threat of encountering a footpad, or revenue men was ever present. Stories had been devised and rehearsed, that these were casks of animal hides, whereas only a few casks had their contents covered with sheepskins and cattle hides. The casks were various sizes, some no more than small barrels, others big, unwieldy shapes, big enough to hide a couple of men. Some wooden chests were also used, the secret cargo covered with timber, later to be overlaid with a cargo of glass panes. But on every container, in an inconspicuous place would be the mark of two rectangles joined together. The left rectangle was inscribed with the weight of powder in pounds, the second rectangle showed the letter for type of powder, M for musket, C for canon and P on the small number of barrels of black priming powder.

*

As the four horse-drawn wagons made their way along the dark track the still night air was suddenly shattered by a loud bang, even louder than a musket shot. The second wagon in line heeled over at a crazy angle. The two horses struggled against the loose ground, their hooves beating, as the accompanying men threw themselves flat on the ground, waiting in fear for the attack to be renewed. When none came, the men started to look about them, slowly getting to their feet and running at a crouch to take shelter behind the heeling wagon. At last the truth dawned. The noise had been the collapse of the back cart-wheel, and shattered, splintered spokes clearly showed the extend of the damage. The load of casks had been tipped into the shallow ditch and the thick bushes which bounded the track. Joshua, who had jumped down from the leading wagon clutching a brace of pistols, took charge of the disaster.

'One man, you drive that front wagon to the port, unload and come back here straightaway. All you others, get this cargo behind these bushes, and remember to stand every cask upright. Then, we'll drag this cart to the side and try and get the others past. We'll use all the horses to drag this out the way if necessary. Smartly, now! And no noise.'

The handful of men worked silently in the dark, calming the frightened horses and getting the serviceable wagons on their way down the road to Milnthorpe. Four men, including Joshua, stayed with the damaged wagon and its cargo, and started collecting stones and rocks from nearby to build a support to lift the rear axle and allow the smashed wheel to be removed. But no one had either the tools or skills of a wheelwright, and they could do no more than wait for the autumn dawn to dispel the night.

As the light increased a flock of sheep appeared on the road, bleating in protest as they were urged along by a young girl and a stooped old man whose grey beard matched his sheepskin cloak and ragged cap. They passed the damaged wagon and the casks pushed into the bushes. The old shepherd waved to the waiting men and walked over to make his own examination.

'Ah, wossit?' he muttered, his words and accent almost unintelligible. He surveyed the scene from beneath bushy grey eyebrows.

'From the mill, is it? Gunpowder, like as not, I'll wager. More powder on this road than in the King's magazines.'

His listeners looked at each other in horror as the old man continued his examination.

'Pity we didn't have this at Yorktown. Never enough powder when it's needed.'

He scratched his head with a grubby fist and waved before returning to his sheep trotting briskly up the road.

The old man's announcement made the waiting seem even more hazardous, and it was broad daylight before the first wagon returned, with six men sat on the back. The cargo was loaded and the wagon turned round. One of the men had some tools and managed to remove the damaged wheel which he put up with the casks. The horses were all harnessed up, enabling the laden wagon and all the workers to complete the journey at a smart trot.

The 'Kestrel' was lying alongside the shoreline downstream from the town of Milnthorpe, the quayside appropriately named Sandsides. Smaller craft, like 'Old John' and 'Tickler' could enter the River Bela, but the 'Kestrel', over 150 tons burden, lay in the tidal estuary of the River Kent. This was the same river which flowed through Kendal and the gunpowder mill at Sedgwick to drive the waterwheels. Earlier attempts to float the hazardous material down the river to waiting ships had not been successful and recently presentation had been made to the planners in Lancaster to ensure that any canal being considered should pass through Sedgwick.

Wagon and carts of mixed cargoes were arriving at the quayside, for the ships 'Kestrel', 'Hope' and 'John' which were all busy loading. The clandestine casks and barrels could be mixed with the more conventional cargo without drawing attention to itself, but the tally clerks and revenue inspectors had to be watched from the upper windows of the warehouse. Councillor Redfearn had provided bills of lading and documents to cover all the casks. The 'brewer's grains' aroused little interest compared with the import duties levied on cargoes from Europe and America.

As the last wagon swung over the bridge in Milnthorpe the door of the warehouse opened to receive the long-awaited cargo. The revenue officer happened to be away from the town, examining a small boat which was mysteriously aground further down the estuary. Inside the cabin all that remained of her cargo were three wooden casks marked 'Oporto' which, unfortunately, were empty. Steps had been taken to ensure there was no means by which the revenue officer could possibly know the boat belonged to Councillor Matthew Redfearn.

At the end of that long, hard day the bars of the Bull's Head Inn at the town end of the quayside were more than usually crowded. The sailors from the ships joined the men who loaded and unloaded the cargoes, the carters and draymen. Like all harbour inns, there was always a secret market in the ship's broached cargoes, and conversation was frequently behind the hand, low voices and nodded responses confirming a multitude of transactions. Bursts of laughter and the shouts of women at one end of the bar made an easy screen for trade. In the upper rooms, the merchants took their suppers and gave final instructions to their shippers and sailing masters. Joshua Weaver had collected some money earlier that day and now made his way down to the smoke-filled bar. He stood at the foot of the stairway for a while and then slowly returned to the dining room. At intervals a man would climb the stairs and knock at the dining room door. Joshua would pay him off, a brief nod of acknowledgement exchanged before his place was taken by the next labourer. The last man to ascend to the room was, like the others, strong and obviously used to hard work. He had a grizzled countenance, with unruly hair and beard. He wore a patch over one eye, frequently the mark of a discharged militiaman. He entered the room and introduced himself to Joshua Weaver.

'Sergeant Musprat, Sir. I think you may have met my brother in your trade today.'

Joshua was hardly prepared for such an introduction.

'I think you have the advantage of me, Sir.'

'Are you not the weaver seeking the loom?'

Joshua was immediately on his guard. The password was not to be used in such a manner.

'Sergeant Musprat, I fear you have made a mistake. I am seeking no loom. I must ask you to offer your services elsewhere.'

'No, Sir. I offer my services to you. Sadly, the constable is also seeking my presence and I would prefer to be aboard the 'Kestrel' for the next few days rather than the waterfront of the River Kent.'

Joshua looked at the powerful man with disdain.

'The 'Kestrel' has a full complement of seamen, all able-bodied and experienced. We have no berths for military men. Good-night to you.'

The man didn't move.

'Oh, you'll be one man short, I'll warrant that. When you sail on Friday's tide you'll be looking for an extra hand.'

'And you feel you would make a good sailor? Have you ever sailed to the Indies, Sergeant Musprat? Can you reef a t'gallant in a gale? Can you steer a course for ten hours without a break? I think not. Six months in the Indies would still not make you a sailor.'

The man's single eye looked hard at Joshua Weaver.

'Without me on board you may never get beyond the Bay. If I'm not on board the 'Kestrel' then the revenue men will be. Your choice.'

'Ah, that's your threat, is it? Then I think you'd be better off with the constable, not on a ship. Now, sir, get out of this room.'

The man put a hand on Joshua's shoulder.

'Friday, or you'll never sail in five fathoms. I promise that.'

'Then, Mr Musprat, keep a good look-out behind you, and don't go out in the dark.' Joshua drew out one of the pistols he carried from the previous night's activities. He showed the polished wooded butt to the one-eyed man, who suddenly seemed nervous.

'Two barrels, Musprat. I generally say, 'one for each eye'. In your case, one for your eye, the other in the mouth, which seems to be your undoing. Is that clear?'

The unwelcome visitor left hurriedly and Joshua followed him down the stairs. When the man was out of the door Joshua turned to the Landlord behind the bar.

'Mr Scaife. My compliments. Do you know my visitor, man with a patch on his left eye? Powerful man, I would judge.'

'Aye, sir, he is as you say. Bad trouble. I'm told he killed a man with his bare hands. Strangled him like a chicken, they say. But they don't say it to his face.' The landlord laughed at his own joke. Joshua was not laughing.

'He told me his name was Sergeant Musprat. Do you know where he lives?'

'His name's not Musprat. His real name is Fox, but they call him Black Fox. He sleeps anywhere he can, and takes what work he can. I know all the Musprat family. They all work at the mill, no trouble there.'

'Well, Mr Scaife, I'm surely foxed.' The joke was unintentional, but they both laughed. 'If you can find me a room for the night I will avoid the Lancaster Road until daylight.

*

Three days later, Captain Cooper ensured the last few items of cargo were tightly stowed, so that much of the hold was completely inaccessible. The crew contained several old faces from previous voyages in the Baltic, and once again Joshua Weaver's son signed on as apprentice.

'What's happened to your young friend, what was his name? Jack?'

'Jake, sir Jake Tempest.'

'Aye, that's the boy. Made him admiral, have they?'

'No, sir. Signed on for the 'Triangular Voyages.' He thought the Baltic was a bit too cold.'

'Well, Apprentice Weaver, if we don't get this ship to sea and bend some sail on her we'll spend the coldest winter you'll ever know locked in the ice of St Petersburg. Ask the Mate to come and see me in my cabin. And you tell every man jack on this ship to be aboard at 4 o'clock for the doctor to examine. Any man missing the examination will not sail and will get no pay. Now, here's the muster list. You check every man is told. Understood?'

And thus it was at 4 o'clock on Thursday the twenty-odd souls who would be the entire crew of the 'Eagle' in the voyage to the Baltic Sea, lined up for inspection by the doctor. Joshua Weaver, dressed in a black coat and carrying a black bag played the role of medical practitioner, liberally sprinkling each man's head with lice powder. The Captain's Mate, Mr Mutch, soon realised Joshua was not what he pretended and quickly whispered his doubts to the Captain.

'I know that, Mr Mate. But I want this ship away on tonight's tide, without giving any of these fine fellows the chance to miss the ship. The doctor's inspection is the sure way to get the crew on board. They think they have another night between the welcoming breasts of the Milnthorpe maidens. Instead, the next women they see will be twice their size and stink of sour cabbage under their twenty layers of animal skins.'

The Mate scratched his beard thoughtfully.

'I think we'll have trouble tonight if we do that.'

'Then, Mr Mate, you'd better prepare for it.'

Mr Weaver was now examining each man's teeth and then examined their eyes. One man had an eye missing, and Joshua called the Captain across.

'Do you know this man, Captain?'

'Yes, I do, Doctor. Name of John Blossom. Sailed with me for three voyages. Any problems?'

'How does he manage with an eye missing?'

'Better than most men with two, sir.'

'Then, Captain Weaver, send him aloft with his mates and let's get those topsails set. I have two men waiting to cast your lines off, so I bid you farewell. A good voyage to the 'Kestrel''

With that, Joshua vaulted over the ship's rail and jumped the narrow gap to the quayside.

Captain Cooper waved farewell to the departing figure and turned to the Mate and the Bo'sun.

60

'There's your orders, gentlemen. Let us get under way.'

'Cast off your fore line!'

The last movement of the flooding tide eased the shapely bows of the 'Kestrel' away from the quayside and pointed her towards the middle of the stream.

'Let go your aft line! Set topsails!'

Released from her moorings, the ship responded to the fresh breeze and over-rode the tide to sail slowly towards the Bay.

On the quay, Joshua Weaver waved briefly to his son on the receding deck and watched as the canvas tumbled from the gaskets and rippled in the filling breeze.

With a feeling of sadness at the departure of his son, but pleased he had got the ship away so easily he turned towards the 'Bull's Head' where his horse was quietly munching hay.

'Come on, boy. Let's get home.'

He was unaware of the single watchful eye that observed his departure from the privacy of the snug of the inn. As the sound of hooves disappeared, Black Fox drained his tankard and slipped quietly out of the inn. In the same stable-yard he examined the two remaining horses, feeling their legs with the experienced hands of a horse trader. He selected one horse which had nothing more than a single bridle. With surprising agility for such a powerfully built man he vaulted on to the bare back and urged the willing horse forward. Once again, the stone houses of Milnthorpe echoed to the sound of flying hooves as the evening sun settled over the peaks of Westmoreland.

*

As the twilight deepened Joshua Weaver dismounted and tied his horse up in the stable-yard. He walked into the inn and saw the landlord setting-up a new barrel behind the bar.

'Ah, Mr Scaife, a gill of your ale and a wet cloth if you please.'

'Back again, Mr Weaver? Been in the wars?' He noticed the cut across his customer's cheek.

'Nothing serious, landlord. A low branch across the roadway. I didn't see it until it had slashed across my face. But I didn't feel able to go on like this.'

'Very wise, Mr Weaver. I'll get a room ready for you.'

He pushed the small tankard across the wooden bar-top towards Joshua's hand. His experienced eye noticed how the white cotton cuffs showed the unmistakable scorch-marks of gunpowder.

Chapter 7

On a fine June morning the centre of the city was bursting with activity. The market place was lined, as usual, with stands and stalls, some with brightly-coloured tilts to protect them from the showers of summer rain. Carts and barrows were piled with fruit and vegetables at the beginning of the harvest season. In addition, many visitors were in town, not just to take advantage of the thriving market but to attend at the Town Hall which overlooked the noisy marketplace. Carriages and horses continued to unload visitors, and every lad could earn a copper or two holding horses or carrying bags to the nearby inns and hotels.

The Town Hall appeared like a bee-hive, hurrying workers coming and going with an urgency which was not generally reflected in the town's civic affairs. The heavy doors had been opened since eight o'clock and now, as the clock above struck ten the council chamber was crowded to capacity, with perhaps fifty gentlemen seated, their fine coats and silks reflecting the summer sunshine flooding through the tall windows. But crowding every space around them were businessmen and merchants, less colourfully dressed in brown or black coats, white cravats, and carrying dark hats. In addition, the doors to the chamber were all wide open so that the adjoining corridors were filled with visitors straining to get a view of the raised benches within.

Mayor Atkinson, accompanied by his clerk emerged from a nearby office doorway and struggled to get through the throng, accompanied by shouts of greeting or calls for space.

'Make way for the Mayor!' 'Good day, Mayor Atkinson, from the parish of Halton' 'Votes for tenant farmers!' The good-humoured protests brought a smile to the Mayor's serious countenance as he pushed his way through the throng. Inside the crowded chamber, the smoke added to the smell of the sweating bodies and the noise of a hundred diverse conversations.

The mayor eventually reached his large, carved chair, which the clerk respectfully pushed under him as he sat. The Clerk looked round at the crowded council chamber and banged the table with a wooden gavel, at first to no effect whatsoever, but after several attempts the cry of 'Silence!' rang out through the chamber and the corridors. When the noise died down the mayor looked round the audience gathered before him, nodding to acquaintances, or a giving a wave of the hand in greeting to a dignitary.

The Clerk called out 'Pray silence for Mayor Atkinson. Let those who have business before the Council of the City of Lancaster attend today, the eighth day of June in the year of our Lord one thousand, seven hundred and ninety-one, for this special meeting.' The clerk then read aloud a list of announcements from several documents laid out before him which quickly lost the attention of the large audience, who resumed their various conversations. When he had finished he set about bringing the meeting to attention again, and at last Mayor Atkinson considered he could commence his address with a reasonable chance of success. As soon as he started the crowded building fell into absolute silence, everyone straining to catch his words.

'My Lords, Councillors, Gentlemen. I have convened this meeting today to consider proposals which have been discussed daily in every office, market-place and inn throughout the city and county. I refer you to the consideration of constructing a continuous waterway, extending from Kendal in the county of Westmorland to Westhoughton in Lancashire, and serving the cities of Lancaster and Preston. In the first instance, I ask Thomas Rawlinson Esquire to address you.'

Mr Rawlinson was seated at a table in front of the mayor. He stood up, and in so doing, revealed his dark green coat, with a high collar and silk cravat, to his audience.

'Mr Mayor, my Lords, Gentlemen. As many of you may know, some of us have been looking at the possibility of building a canal to join our great market towns with the factory towns of Manchester and Liverpool. It is twenty years ago that work started to build a magnificent canal to join Liverpool to the Yorkshire city of Leeds, an undertaking which will be over one hundred miles long when complete, crossing the Pennine Range by the ingenious use of locks, cuttings and embankments. The canal we are proposing today, one of a number of diverse routes, which has been surveyed by the eminent engineer, Mr Robert Whitworth, would join this great enterprise at the town of Westhoughton. But what many of you in this famous council chamber may not realise is that our engineers and navigators have already completed such extensive canals and navigations that the four great rivers of the Trent, Mersey, Thames and Severn are now totally joined together for all time. By linking the thread of our canal into this great tapestry of waterways we bring to every farmer, quarryman, manufacturer and merchant in the County Palatine of Lancashire and the County of Westmorland the opportunity of selling his wares in every town and city in England. That is the substance of our proposals for which we seek general approval to proceed.'

He sat down to a chorus of questions and conversation between his eager audience.

'The chair recognises John Pedder, Esquire, of Preston.'

'Mr Mayor, my Lords, gentlemen. I agree and endorse Mr Rawlinson's proposal. There will be a need to seek an Act of Parliament, to form a joint stock company and thereafter to raise the necessary finance. In this manner we are fortunate, because we can learn from those who have already started or completed such a construction, to observe how the carriage charges and tolls can generate revenue to pay interest on the substantial funds which will be required. May I tell this meeting that last month, at a meeting to raise finance for the Manchester to Rochdale canal, £60,000 was subscribed in just one hour.'

This remark drew forth cries of admiration from the chamber until, once again, the crowded room was enveloped in the hubbub of conversations, and several hands were raised to attract the attention of the Chairman.

'The Chair recognises Councillor Redfearn.'

The councillor's reputation for skilful negotiation and merciless examination brought an expectant silence to the attentive audience. His name was whispered down the corridors.

'I would like to ask some of our adventurous engineers how they will manage their constructions to join the great rivers of this county. I think I am correct in stating that the Rivers Keer, Lune, Conder, Wyre and Ribble will all intersect with our man-made waterway. How do you stop all the canal water flowing into the Irish Sea?'

He sat down, having set his trap with care.

Thomas Rawlinson rose to take the invisible bait he had been offered.

'Oh! Councillor Redfearn is badly informed. Our canal, sir, will not join any of those waterways. It will soar across each great river thirty, forty, even fifty feet above them, canal traffic crossing unhindered on great aqueducts, free from the demands of tides and the curbs of storms. You perhaps doubt our ability to devise such a structure which could contain thousand gallons of water without it leaking on to the land below? I can assure you that the method we use called puddled clay can contain all that water indefinitely.'

Councillor Redfearn rose, clutching in his hands a large roll of paper. His trap was ready to be sprung.

'I have no doubt of your ability to build a canal a hundred feet above the rivers if necessary, given enough of our money!'

His audience laughed and then fell silent as they awaited the thrust of his attack with close attention. Councillor Redfearn cleared his throat before continuing.

'That is not my complaint. You told this meeting that a link had been forged between the Thames and the three other great rivers of England, presumably, Sir, at the same level as the existing waters. But if we take your advice, Lancastrians will ridiculed by their countryman that the beautiful wide rivers which God has given us, especially the Ribble and the Lune, are, literally, beneath us. Instead of learning from England, Scotland and Ireland, all of whom have canals in use today, which take advantage of the existing rivers, we are going to ignore them completely. Now, if I could ask the indulgence of this meeting I would like you to examine this map of the whole of England. As you will see, it shows a number of rivers and their associated canals, which radiate like the branches of a tree, extending ever further inland from the great coastal cities, bringing the benefits of our ports and harbours to towns who have never seen the tides nor heard the cry of the gull. But Mr Robert Whitworth,' the councillor's voice was heavy with contempt. 'Mr Robert Whitworth has surveyed for us a route which not only lies parallel with the coast, it is, in places no more than a thousand yards from the sea itself, but never reaches it! Yet Kendal, Lancaster, and Preston are all served by fine rivers, and we have just finished the construction of a new the dock at Glasson, where the River Conder flows into the estuary of the Lune. I ask this meeting to abandon all talk of Lune-atic canals in the clouds and use one tenth of the money to place weirs and pound locks across the rivers to give us deep river water further inland and my friends Mr Brockbank and Squire Kerr will build you ships which can sail without any horsepower to Liverpool and Manchester, even to Bristol and London.'

As Councillor Redfearn sat down, with the air of a man who has vanquished his foe, Squire Kerr, the ship designer and trader from Carnforth caught the eye of the Mayor and was called to his feet.

'Gentlemen, my highly-respected friend, Councillor Redfearn has put his opposition most effectively. However, I would urge him to consider the purpose of the canal more carefully. If we can bring coal from Wigan quickly and economically it will reflect to the credit of all our businesses. In return, our limestone can be sold throughout the cities to the south. Even within the immediate surroundings of the canal, the rapid movement of farm produce will benefit all of us...'

He was interrupted by an unidentified speaker wedged into one of the doorways.

'It will also encourage the Manchester merchants to invade our towns with their wares. We can make our own cups and plates, we don't need the potters from Staffordshire and Cheshire selling their unwanted stocks...'

'You talk nonsense, sir!' shouted another voice. 'Will you tell Mr Gillow he can't sell his furniture in Manchester because they want to make their own? If we all talked like that there would be no trade for any of us.'

The Clerk was on his feet.

'Order! We must speak in turn and study every argument with care.'

A speaker was called from the back of the chamber.

'My name is Tobias Gunn, and I am an engineer. I think canals are soon going to be out of date. My considered method is for a tramway, consisting of iron rails secured to wooden beams. Cheaply laid, they can provide reasonably economical transport of wooden trucks, using horses on level routes, and steam winches or water ballast to draw wagons up inclines. These are quite widely in use already and have demonstrated how they can be moved quickly as the traffic grows or declines. In terms of effectiveness I give you the following actual figures. One horse can draw no more than two tons on a good level pathway or road. On a canal or river, one horse can draw between fifty and a hundred tons, and on a level tramway about eight tons. With the terrain through which such a tramway would run, with plentiful supplies of river water, a very economical system could be devised and for which I would be honoured to offer my services.' This remark was greeted with some laughter from those standing at the back of the room.

Mr Rawlinson was on his feet, unbidden by the clerk.

'I demand to explain to this meeting our assessment of the actual costs of carriage by canal. To convey one tun of limestone a distance of twenty-five miles, that is, from Kendal to Lancaster, the charge would be three shillings, eleven and one half pence. Thus, the cost for the full length of the canal, the seventy miles to Wigan, would be the sum of eight shillings and ninepence.' His voice fell almost to a whisper, causing everyone to remain hushed to hear the final point of his argument. 'As many traders in this room can attest, the present charge for such a freight by road would be three pounds! Three pounds, nearly seven times the price!'

As the sun rose higher and the heat in the council chamber increased so the discussion became less intense. By noon, many of the audience had left to quench their thirst in the crowded inns and taverns around the town. The market traders added to the noisy, smoke-filled bar-rooms. Good-natured arguments flowed back and forth, many of the most important merchants apparently swayed by the desire to be seen to support the latest engineering marvels of the day, even though the cold reasoning of Councillor Redfearn carried a great persuasion.

'Perhaps,' observed Joshua Weaver, ensconced in the corner of his favourite bar, 'if you are investing your money, you would not favour a canal. If you have neither the means nor the intention of making an investment, the novelty of having 'your own canal' would seem obvious.'

He turned to his fellow merchant, Mr Cleland.

'We are about to enter a new century, in just over eight years time. Mr Redfearn's sailing ships look a trifle unadventurous to some people in the town. But the farmers and country folk will always favour the tried and tested ways of the past.'

As the ales flowed the conversation turned to other matters of more immediate concern to the merchants. Mr Cleland spoke first.

'Do you hear all this news from Paris? I'm told the monarchy will fall soon, and then you mark my words, Europe will burst into flames. Our ships will be targets, our best crews will be pressed to serve his Majesty and taxes will double overnight.'

'You paint a very sombre picture, Mr Cleland. I could have sworn it was one of your captains who brought home a couple of prize ships in the last war.'

'I assure you, Mr Weaver, without the Letters of Marque many of us owners would have been finished. Two of my ships gave service to the Crown as privateers, but it is a fool who looks for such opportunities to sustain a business.'

Joshua looked carefully at his friend, sensing other worries lay behind his remarks.

'How are your ships faring in these peaceful days? I see ever-growing imports from the West Indies, so you deep-water traders must be doing better than the Baltic men. Timber is all very well, but every ship-owner in Europe is prepared to seek the trade. St Petersburg has armadas of ships waiting through the winter to be the first to sail when the ice breaks up. Feeding a crew for three months without sailing a ship's length sounds bad business to me.'

Mr Cleland called the pot-boy over and paid for more drinks to be brought to the table at which they sat. After the first sip, he turned to Joshua.

'Believe me, Joshua, you at least can sleep easy in your bed at night. Yet I find myself haunted by shadows every day and night, and can do nothing about it. Have you ever heard of The Reverend Thomas Clarkson? A man of God, Joshua, with the bravery of a lion. He has been in Liverpool, collecting evidence concerning the slave trade. He has statements from ship's crews, captains, mates and sailors, their minds so troubled by the terrors of the trade that they have unburdened themselves. He was here, in Lancaster, two years ago, and is collecting evidence to spin into a rope which may yet hang us all.'

Joshua laid a hand on his friend's sleeve.

'I doubt that, good friend. Why, the Duke of Clarence heads the list of public figures who endorse the value of our legitimate trade. I believe my Lord of Hawkesbury was himself awarded the Freedom of the City of Liverpool particularly for his support of the trade. The reason I know this was that my own son was himself starting his apprenticeship...'

'Not in the Guinea Trade, surely?'

Joshua hesitated.

'No, I confess I sought a berth in the European trade, having reason to keep him away from the excesses of your ships.'

'Why, what had you heard? It is only in the past few months that I had any idea of the extent of the murderous activities on the fearsome coast. What stories have reached your ears before mine?'

'Tell me, Mr Cleland, did you lose one of your agents in Calabar about two years ago? Have you any idea what happened to him?'

Mr Cleland looked puzzled.

'Yes, my agent was a Frenchman called Louis Bertrand. Lived on the coast for many years, and as honest as the day is long. One of our ships returned to say Monsieur Bertrand had moved inland and thus we had no agent. From that day to this we have never heard from him, although we still owe him a commission. Why, have you knowledge of him?'

'Can you recall the last ship of yours who dealt with him?'

'Yes, I can surely say that it would have been the 'Rainbird' because we have stopped using Calabar since then. The Captain was unhappy about the difficulties of working without a reliable agent.'

Joshua nodded in agreement.

'Is the captain still in your employ?'

'Why, of course. Captain Kenyon has been with me since I acquired my first ship. No need to worry about him. Why do you ask?'

'The next occasion you speak to Captain Kenyon ask when he last saw your agent.'

'Well, it was over a year ago, but I was assured he saw him the day the 'Rainbird' sailed from Calabar. In fact, I'm certain Monsieur Bertrand was the last person he saw as he left the coast.'

'Mr Cleland, if my information and my memory are both correct, your Captain was indeed the last man to see your agent face to face.'

'I'm sorry, Joshua, I don't quite understand your concern. What are you saying?'

'I'm reasonably sure that the last sight your Captain had was of the severed head of your agent, who had been executed by the African tribal chief in return for the barbaric way he had been treated by your ship.'

Mr Cleland's usually florid complexion was now greyish in colour. His whole face was in motion, as if the muscles round his mouth and his eyes were out of his control. He looked at Mr Weaver with horror in his eyes.

'For God's sake, what are you telling me? Do you mean he knew the Frenchman was dead, yet said nothing? And you knew this and also said nothing? I would prefer to say I don't believe you, except for one small thing.'

'And what is that one small thing?'

'As you can imagine, as owners we get all sorts of letters, from disgruntled crews or men who think punishment has been too severe or unjust. They scribble messages without names and when back home they get some wretch to deliver them to the cargo office. It's their only way of trying to get even with a harsh captain or mate. As most of them can't read or write, messages take strange forms, drawings, pages torn from Bibles, even knives with a possible victim's name scrawled on the blade. Hard men leading a hard life, Joshua. Captain Kenyon was not excluded from these threats, and in my private office I think I could still find the evidence. But as you will understand, I can't arraign a captain, with all his certificates, and ask him to account for the ravings of every sea lawyer in his crew.'

'Well, Mr Cleland, if it is any assurance to you, I learned of these grim events almost by chance. But I am well aware that not only the Abolitionists are seeking out this evidence, but owners and shareholders are looking to satisfy themselves that their ships are well-conducted.'

Mr Cleland considered the manner in which the morning's discussions at the Town Hall would be materially affected by his present difficulties.

'I can't help feeling the finance for this wonderful canal will be much harder to find if the profits from the Guinea Trade are no longer available to prime the pump. How would we justify the costs of sailing to the West Indies for your rum and tobacco, and all the fine timbers for Mr Gillow's cabinet-makers without a prosperous 'Middle Passage'? I see from the Customs Records that last year, 1790, ninety ships from Liverpool transported twenty-seven thousand slaves with a value of one and a quarter million pounds. I know we are much smaller in the

Lancaster trade, but those ships make a quite exceptional difference to the prosperity of the city.'

'Well, I don't think Mr Rawlinson's schemes will meet with much approval, particularly as Councillor Redfearn has such firm criticisms and a well-measured alternative. Certainly, he has caused me to have second thoughts, and I was one of the keenest supporters a couple of years ago.'

The two men finished their drinks. The unhappy Mr Cleland leaned towards Mr Weaver and lowered his voice, even though the general hub-bub of conversation in the crowded bar would seem to make such precautions unnecessary.

'I trust, Mr Weaver, our discussion here may be considered completely private. Would you not agree?'

'Why, most certainly, sir. I would never consider otherwise, you may rest assured of that.'

'Then, sir, I wish you a good day.'

As Mr Cleland left and Joshua Weaver returned thoughtfully to the Town Hall, his mind conjured up the awful vision of the severed head of the innocent and hapless agent, before his own haunting image of the bloody face of Black Fox falling into the dark waters of the Bela River, an image which did not fade with the passage of time.

The continuation of the meeting in the Town Hall was, as expected, much less crowded in the afternoon, most of the morning audience having heard the arguments as far as they wished to consider them. Throughout the rest of the day plans were considered which resulted in a working committee being formed to determine a route and the landowners who would be affected. The committee would be responsible for raising a working fund for the initial surveying and establishment, before the final decisions were taken and preparations made for obtaining an Act of Parliament.

At the end of a long day Joshua Weaver was still not quite how the decision was made to proceed even as far as a planning committee. It seemed to him, as he rode home, that the vision of 'our own canal' had been skilfully manipulated by the city leaders without the critical consideration which would be accorded to making better roads or building a sewer to improve the health and comfort of every citizen.

Chapter 8

While the enterprising merchants of Lancaster were contemplating the cost of digging a level trench fifty miles long, fifty feet above the level of the rivers and filling it with water to a depth of seven feet, Captain Waterhouse and crew of the brig 'Antoine' were lying off the coast of West Africa. For two months they had struggled with Trade Winds and Doldrums, loaded with manufactures for the colonies and goods they hoped to exchange for slaves on the Guinea coast. Brightly coloured textiles manufactured in Lancashire mills especially for the trade, imitating Indian cotton fabrics, with strange names, niccannee, cushtae and romalls would be welcomed by the chiefs in exchange for nameless tribesmen.

For Jake Tempest, the departure from Lancaster at the end of a bitter winter had been longed-for relief from miserable, bone-chilling cold. During the past three weeks, since passing Santa Cruz in the Canarias Islands he had once again felt the warmth of the tropical winds upon his thin body. The whole nature of life on the two-masted ship seemed to change with the hours of sunshine. With every day that passed, the cold and damp evaporated from the ancient timbers of the ship. In a fresh breeze the ship surged over the rolling waves with an easy stride, like a cantering horse. For a few weeks the weather made the setting and trimming of sails less of a burden, and the small crew found life quite bearable.

Ahead of them, the mysteries of the coast of West Africa remained to be revealed. It was common knowledge that the ship would be unwelcome at Calabar, as they had no agent there and Lancaster ships were generally excluded. The Liverpool slavers had taken advantage of the poor reputation that had grown up on the coast, although the name 'Antoine' would be unknown to them. She had been taken as a prize years ago from the French, but had only recently been pressed into the slave trade to increase carrying capacity. In England, like the rest of Europe, the abolitionist movement was gaining momentum, and demand for slaves was, in consequence, increasing before the threats of closure of the trade.

For the past few days the coast had been faintly visible over the horizon on the port side, until at last Captain James Waterhouse sailed closer to the coast, each day searching for the familiar landmarks which would help him determine the ship's position. Even the muddy outflows of the great rivers gave a signal to the anxious navigators; the brown waters of the Niger announced the approach to the Bonny River and the islands which would provide a safe haven for the ship. His many voyages to the Guinea Coast had given him the mariner's sixth sense to know when to close with the shore, risking the hazards of shoals in uncharted waters. Even knowing the birds in the sky gave him another piece in the puzzle of placing the small brig in the great expanse of the ocean.

With just topsails and spanker set, the ship cautiously headed towards the low coast-line, searching for openings between the islands. When they were within a league of the coast, a small boat with triangular sail approached the 'Antoine' and two men could be seen waving vigorously towards the ship.

'Put a ladder over, chief, but have two men with muskets standing by.'

The Mate looked over the side and was surprised at the ease with which the huge black man stepped from the flimsy craft to the rope ladder. He climbed easily up on to the deck, and the Mate helped him over the rail. The black man called down to the boat and immediately a line was thrown up to the deck. The newcomer hauled on the line and drew up a cloth bag and a long, elaborately decorated staff.

He untied the line and opened the cloth bundle, which contained a dark red tricorne hat, heavily braided with gold. He settled the hat on his thick black hair, straightened his brightly-coloured robes and, taking the bag and his ceremonial staff in his left hand, banged it twice on the deck and turned to the Captain's Mate.

'Take me to your Captain, Sir!'

Captain Waterhouse was watching from the afterdeck, standing beside the helmsman. The visitor raised his hand in greeting, looking at the captain with a grave face. His black beard was flecked with grey, and almost completely covered his face, except for wide, staring eyes, giving him a ferocious appearance. His robes reached nearly to his feet, and appeared to consist of many layers of varied colours.

'My name, Captain, is Prince Henry, and I can see you safely into a good anchorage and bring you the very best trade, sir. Here are my letters and licences.' He took out a handful of documents from the bag, which the Captain shared out with the Mate. They indicated their visitor should take a seat on the flag locker while they examined the documents.

'Any Lancaster ships, chief, let me know. See if you recognise any names.'

The documents consisted of references from ship's captains who had been satisfied with the bearer's services.

"Rainbird' here, sir. Good reference. Another here from Captain O'Fie. I know him. Sails out of Liverpool now.'

'Good. Hello, one here from Captain Kellett of the ship 'Betty'. Let me see, looks very good. I think we'll be alright, don't you, chief?'

'I agree sir.'

The captain returned to the seated visitor.

'Prince Henry? What are the manner and price of your services?'

'I can steer you into a safe anchorage, no more that an easy row from a safe landing. I am factor for many masters and can obtain the best black boys and girls of good health. There are other ships in the harbour, but they will be gone soon. I also have ivory and teeth in large quantities. Provisions and water are all available by me. I offer you a good and honest service.'

'And if I want three hundred and fifty healthy black boys, how long will that take?'

'Just a few days, Captain. No difficulty.'

'How long have the other ships been in the harbour?'

'Some weeks, Captain. One is loading six hundred and fifty slaves, the other about five hundred. We are now going many miles up country to find our boys. I have one hundred already on the road, they will be here in two days time. We will send messages for more villages to be visited.'

As he spoke he was watching the coastline and indicating with his huge hands the direction he wanted the ship to take. The mate and the bo'sun were giving orders to keep the ship under way, trimming the sails to follow the direction ordered by Prince Henry.

'Aren't you worried that there may not be enough slaves to keep all of us happy?'

'Captain, these good boys are breeding with our beautiful girls, so that for the years ahead we will have many more good and willing workers for you. Without your help, what would all these strong black boys do all day? And, Captain, we can make black boys quicker than you can sell them.'

He laughed loudly at the simple logic of his trading principals.

The brig slipped silently between the islands into the harbour of the River Bonny, the wind no more than an occasional puff, the water smooth. Several small ships were anchored in the harbour, and one large, three-masted ship towered over all the others. She seemed to be completely surrounded by small craft of every description, from which it appeared a continuous stream of people and produce was being hauled up the sides of the great wooden hull. As 'Antoine' drifted closer, the noise from the other ships became more insistent. A strange mixture of shouting, crying and, unexpectedly, singing floated across the water. To Jake the sound of the mournful singing struck a memory, a recollection of the frightening sound welling up from the hold of the 'Rainbird' five years ago. He felt a shiver down his back before dismissing the event when ordered aloft to take in the topsail. The orders were shouted round the ship as a space in the anchorage was found.

'Let go starboard anchor! Hand all sails!'

'Welcome to Bonny River, Captain! I will take care of all you require while the 'Antoine' is at anchor.'

As he spoke, boats were already making their way alongside, and once again the captain ordered two men with muskets to remain on guard. Prince Henry shouted down to the water, dismissing most of the small boats, beckoning one or two of them to come alongside.

'These are my brothers, Captain. They will guard the ship and keep all these black-faced villains off your valuable ship.'

Three men tumbled on deck, all tall, shiny black giants with colourful skirts and elaborate head-dresses made from animal skins, the tails of the slaughtered beasts trailing almost to the ground. They smiled broadly, exhibiting white teeth in startling contrast to the intense blackness of their faces. Without any prompting they walked around the deck, shouting to any boat which looked as if it might venture alongside to keep away from 'their' ship. When they were satisfied they had secured their domain they stood like guards at the top of the ship's ladder.

The Captain was introduced to them individually, with the clear invitation that they would be responsible for all contacts with the shore.

'For you, Captain, a special guard, to look after your needs.'

He leaned over the rail and shouted down to one of the boats. Presently, over the ship's rail another black figure appeared and stood silently on the deck. It was a tall, graceful black girl, perhaps twenty years old, dressed only in a knee-length skirt wrapped around her slender waist. It was made from an animal skin, sand yellow with regular black markings, which showed off the taut muscular curves and the blackness of her body. Her breasts were completely naked, with strings of many-coloured beads resting enticingly in the deep, dark valley between the firm, pointed flesh. Her hair had been braided in such a way that it clung tightly to her head. Two blood-red flowers had been thrust into her hair. Her flawless black skin shone like polished gun-metal, except across the full curves of her cheeks deep lines had been incised and stained dark red, giving her face the image of a beautiful but dangerous animal. She stood quite calmly, without any hint of embarrassment as the black men guarded her. The English sailors stopped their tasks around the deck, as if hypnotised by the untamed beauty that had stepped into their midst. Prince Henry stepped up to her and lifted the beads away from her breasts. With the other hand he lifted the firm flesh as if judging its weight.

'Look at her, Captain. Have you beauties like this in Lancaster? Does even my good friend King George have a queen as lovely as this? She is the daughter of a princess, a jewel I have plucked from the wild tribes fifty days march from here. As clean as the day she was born. Her name to you is Elli, and she will look after all your needs, cook your food and fetch you fresh fruit from the shore. She will guard you from trouble with the black boys. Watch.'

So saying, he made some comment to the woman. She reached into the overlapping folds of her skirt, as if to reveal even more of her most intimate charms. Every man on deck froze in silent anticipation. Instead, her hand swiftly re-appeared clasping a small steel dagger which glistened in the brilliant sunshine. The narrow blade was straight and tapering and she held it pointing forward at the level of her navel, her feet parted and knees slightly bent in a perfectly balanced stance, like an attacking animal. The threat to any possible attacker was obvious. The Prince clapped his hands and the three guards and the woman hurried to their duties. From the waiting boat a stone pitcher was carefully hauled up, and a metal cup was produced, which the Prince filled with a white liquid. He drank from the cup before passing it to the captain. To the Englishman the fermented liquid was quite unlike anything he had ever tasted, sweet, aromatic and evidently intoxicating. It seemed easy to drink, and the cup was passed round the men several times, but never to the woman, who stood in silent, savage dignity, the knife once again concealed.

The prince suggested the captain should decide exactly what slaves would be taken aboard, so the two men moved to his cabin. The chief mate set everyone to work, securing the ship for a long stay in port. Yards were lowered to the mast-caps, sails were tightly furled or stowed in the deck lockers. But the image of the beautiful princess and the intoxicating smell of the land, after many weeks at sea, filled every head with thoughts far removed from the unyielding canvas and salt-encrusted rope.

After an hour or more Prince Henry emerged from the captain's cabin and left the ship in one of the waiting boats. The captain called for the mates to join him in his cabin, while the 'princess' stood silently outside the door. The pitcher stood on the floor, still partly full of the mysterious white liquid. The captain found some more beakers for his officers and poured them a drink.

'Well, gentlemen, it's just as I thought. This is going to be a long job. These other ships have taken just about every black man and woman from the coast. Prince Henry has promised me he has plenty more slaves from the hills. Now, you all know what that means. We will have to wait while the weary processions of chained men and women make their way down through the hills. But what I dislike is having to put, maybe, one hundred negroes below and then wait for two weeks for the next procession to arrive. It might be tempting to load what we can and sail for Lagos or Sekondi, but the Liverpool and Bristol ships are thick on the coast like wasps round the apple trees. So I have told the prince we will pay well for every good body taken on board before the middle of July. After that, the heat lying at anchor will kill us all, so we will set sail and decide where else to look for blacks. In the meantime, the crew can take the long-boat, no more than twelve men ashore at any time, and if every man jack is fair and honest he can stay ashore for a day or more. I will issue some things for bartering for food in the villages, but when that's all gone, they must understand there will be no more. And instruct them not to bring black girls on the ship. I forbid it because I know what happens. You either have one woman for each jack or fights start over women. Understood?'

The three mariners nodded, well aware of the risks that already lay ahead. Sailors on ships were generally constrained by the need to keep the ship seaworthy. But on dry land in foreign countries they stole food, drink and other men's women. In a country where twenty thousand of their kith and kin had been taken into slavery every year, the hospitality of the local population was not guaranteed, by any means.

The captain continued with his plans.

'We will build a deck shelter while we are waiting. Chief, tell the carpenter to get ashore with four men and find the timber he needs to build a shelter between the masts. We can thatch it with those palms that grow at the water's edge. Nothing too elaborate, but we'll need every opportunity to get the blacks out of the hold with the hottest weather in prospect. If we can only get two hundred slaves I don't intend losing any by our own carelessness. I've heard that there is cholera further along the coast, so I want the holds kept clean and dry. Tell the carpenter I want eye-bolts every ten feet on the top deck so we can shackle 'em in the open air for a few hours each day. We'll set up the stoves, one on the top deck, forward, the other in the tween deck, but only for bad weather.'

The planning for the loading of slaves and for the 'middle voyage' to Port Royal, Jamaica, occupied the remainder of the day. At sunset, the ship rested in the cooling evening. Seamen brought their bedding on to the deck to sleep under the stars. When loaded to the fullest capacity with black slaves, shackled together below decks, there would be no pleasure in sleeping so close to the poisonous stench from the hold. The old gun-ports in the hull would be opened whenever possible to ventilate the lower decks where the hundreds of sweating bodies would be chained.

In the darkness of the tropical night the silence was occasionally broken by distant thunder as storms flickered across distant hills. As the night wore on, the beat of a distant drum would not be heard by any but the most attentive ear, listening for this herald of the approaching column of manacled slaves.

*

The following morning two men on horseback appeared at the landing stage. They were dressed in the flowing robes and head-dresses which identified them as arabs, some of the most feared of slave-masters and traders They summoned boats and were quickly paddled out to the 'Antoine' where they nimbly climbed the ladder. Each of them had a flint-lock pushed into a belt, and swords hung from their waists. The captain had been called by the watch and stood on deck, surrounded by some of the crew, three of whom had muskets.

'Captain? Are you dealing with that fool Prince Henry? We've got all his slaves to deliver to you. We've got two hundred tusks, if you can afford them.'

'I only deal with the Prince, so you will have to negotiate with him. I therefore order you to leave my ship.'

The captain turned on his heel, his back towards the two arabs. He heard the unmistakable sound of a blade being drawn from its scabbard. The captain looked to his left and nodded his head. He heard two sailors drawing back the flints on their muskets. Captain Waterhouse waited a few seconds before turning. The sword was being slowly returned to its scabbard, then the two arabs turned to the ship's side and descended the ladder with as much dignity as they could manage. As the canoe pulled away they drew their swords again and defiantly waved them above their heads.

'Take a pot shot, Luke. You can't kill them at this range, but you can put a hole in his burnoose. See how good a shot you are.'

77

The effect of the shot was remarkable. One of the arabs must have been hit because he doubled up in pain and promptly fell over the side of the small craft. The cheer from the deck of the 'Antoine' did nothing to restore the dignity of the arab as he climbed back into the canoe.

'Have we got anyone ashore at present, chief?'

'Yes, sir. The carpenter and one man went ashore by canoe to select timber. One of the prince's men was with them.'

'Well, I hope they don't run into our friends. I can't help feeling we've got some trouble with those two. No more allowed ashore for a few days.'

The captain looked towards the landing stage and saw the canoe disgorging its two angry passengers.

'Boy, get my telescope, and hurry!'

Jake disappeared below deck to return a few seconds later with the large brass telescope. The captain steadied his hands against the mainmast shrouds and focused on the figures on the shore. He watched as they mounted their horses and galloped off in the direction of the New Town. As they did so he could see the two white faces of his own sailors accompanied by the tall figure of the prince's brother. One of the arabs reined back his horse and was obviously speaking to the two sailors. Suddenly, one of the horses reared up and knocked one of the men to the ground. The guard appeared to be slashing out with a club, driving off the horse and rider. He could be seen gathering up the crumpled form on the ground and hurrying towards the landing stage.

'Six men in the long-boat! Four muskets! Get those men back immediately. If anyone tries to stop you, shoot 'em! Bo'sun, clear away the two stern chasers.'

By the time the long-boat was ashore the imposing figure of Prince Henry appeared with several black men. A small convoy of boats set out for the 'Antoine' and presently the deck was crowded with sailors and black men in excited conversation.

'You've made a difficult enemy there, Captain. They call him El Hindi. To fire a gun at an arab in an open boat is a very serious loss of dignity.'

'Well, Prince Henry, you get my 'Black Ivory' on board and we'll not trouble you for a day longer than necessary. How many have you got for me?'

'Seventy-odd by tonight. Another fifty on the road from Eket, well-guarded. There's some women and children up in the hills which the Liverpool ships don't fancy. Good healthy creatures, make good breeders when they get to the colonies. Breed like locusts if you wants.'

The prince spoke contemptuously of the black slaves as if they came from a different planet in the sky, instead of being his own race from the opposite side of a river, a gorge or a line drawn in the desert sand.

The captain looked closely at the prince.

'Don't generally take females or children. Cause too much trouble with the crew. Our lusty lads will spread them open like the parson's prayer-book and leave their book-mark in the Magnificat.'

'Take my advice, Captain. Keep your sailors away from the black girls. If the negroes see their women ridden by white men they will call up the black evil. Ten thousand chains won't hold them when the evil is afoot. That's why you have Elli, she's not of their tribes, so you can take her to your bed as you will. But, when you leave for the great crossing she must be returned to me. This is her home, I hope that is understood.'

Captain Waterhouse nodded, not used to be addressed in such uncompromising terms. The thought of such a companion on the middle voyage and the price which she would command from the colonial households in Jamaica presented a double temptation to the captain.

Whilst they had been talking the boat pulled alongside with the carpenter and one sailor, who had been kicked by the horse, and screamed in pain as he was helped up the ladder on to the deck. The ship's surgeon, named Doctor Bale, looked at the figure lying on the deck in agony, an open wound on the left side of his chest, surrounded by a dark red bruise. The surgeon placed a wet cloth over the wound and covered it with a bandage.

'Looks like a broken rib. May have entered his lung.'

The surgeon was a reticent man. His years of dealing with gunshots, cannon ball injuries and shattered bodies which had fallen from aloft had bred in him a professional indifference which enabled him to withstand the rigours of his task without resort to the brandy bottle, the general assistant for doctor and patient on the high seas.

'Put him on a cot and carry him below. Positively no movement for four days. And one sailor to keep him clean, please Captain.'

The captain looked at the calm face of the surgeon.

'Bad start for the 'middle voyage', Doctor Bale.'

'And I suppose the hundreds of black bodies you intend fitting into that dreadful hold will all be happy, laughing souls, with no fluxes, fevers or cholera. That, Captain, would be a fine start, even if we killed half of them on the way to the Indies.'

The surgeon, a man probably twenty years older than the Captain, turned to leave, but the captain seized him by the arm.

'You have a lot to say, Doctor, which I didn't quite hear when we paid out the dividend in Lancaster.'

'Nor will you, sir, while the welfare of the Children's Home depends on my donation, nor from others who benefit from this loathsome trade, but prefer to breathe the sweet air of Lancaster. When I cross the new town bridge I know every stone has been paid for by the torment of these savages.'

'I'll make damn sure your earn your dividend this voyage, sir! I'm buying three hundred slaves tomorrow, men, women and children, and we're out of here before this sun scorches our skins. So you'll earn your keep this time, I promise.'

Chapter 9

'The game is going to be a race between the black boys and this Devil's Oven. Whoever gave this furnace the name Bonny has never been here, that much I'll swear.'

Captain Waterhouse had been remarkably accurate in his view of the immediate future. As the searing sun rose higher in the sky, standing in the zenith at midday, tempers ran high, and the procession of slaves, culled from distant villages far beyond the shimmering grey hills, became more erratic. What had been promised as a group of two hundred revealed fifty-five men, women and children, some still being suckled by their weeping mothers. Examinations on the waterfront before being paddled to the waiting ship eliminated many of the captives. Mothers with small children were left behind whilst the infant's father was chained and roped to his unknown neighbour. The mothers were torn between relief from the hell-ship and despair at losing their menfolk. No farewells were allowed on the grim jetty, just the cries across the oily-smooth water in the lonely night that followed.

Great quantities of stores were being loaded; food and water for the crew in addition to the needs of the slaves. Many years of experience had allowed the captains of the trade to determine the minimum provisions necessary to deliver the 'black ivory' in a condition to command a high price, with the least deaths from poor feeding and disease. In the worst condition, gross ill-treatment had caused slaves to throw themselves into the sea in mid-ocean as the only relief from the hell below decks. Eight years earlier the owners of a slave ship named 'Zong' had been tried for attempting to defraud the underwriters in Liverpool by claiming that all the slaves had died in storms, whereas in reality sixty had died of sickness and one hundred and thirty-two were ill and unsaleable and were thrown overboard.

As a result of Captain Waterhouse's attention to the quality of his 'boarders' the ship was lying at anchor with only half its capacity filled, earning no money and having to bear the cost of feeding them whilst waiting for the sound of chains and the songs of lament which would announce the approach of more weary, beaten negroes. As each boat load was accepted on board, Captain Waterhouse supervised the exchange of materials in payment. Rolls of brightly coloured fabrics joined piles of metal pots, pans, cups and basins. These were tied together in bundles and carefully counted by the prince's brothers. Barrels of brandy, wooden-bound casks of gunpowder and four muskets joined the collection of assorted coats, hats, factory clogs and sacks of glass beads and maniloes for decorating wrists and ankles, which paid for the human cargo being shackled below decks. Accurate book-keeping was essential to ensure the profitability of the whole voyage and to satisfy the audit of the joint owners when the ship finally returned home.

Towards the end of July the captain was forced to make a decision which could influence the rest of the voyage. His records showed one hundred and seventy-four fully grown men, thirty-six women and twelve young boys and girls safely loaded on board. All appeared clean and healthy to the brief examination of the surgeon and the first mate. In addition, hundreds of sacks of ivory, weighing nearly one and a half tons had been stowed in the most secure part of the tween deck. In a separate ledger which the captain kept specially for the purpose were recorded the private transactions which produced earnings for all on the ship. Those of the crew who were experienced in the slave trade brought with them from England their own barter-goods. Knives, axe-heads, saws and spades, old coats and hats all had their value, and with care could be exchanged for African head-dresses, decorated shields and small quantities of ivory, generally of second quality. A willing woman in the village would satisfy a sailor's needs in exchange for a pair of scissors. But a good captain, intent on maintaining a quiet ship would buy slaves, the profits of which would be distributed in proportion amongst every man on board, wisely only paid on the safe arrival at home port.

'I want seven of your strongest black boys, good workers, and these will not be on the manifest. Understood? I will also take first quality ivory to the value of fifty-five guineas.'

Prince Henry returned the following day with the boys, as demanded. He also brought with him a small bag apparently made from an animal skin. In the privacy of the captain's cabin he opened the bag and shook out into the palm of his huge hand a small quantity of brilliant yellow, sparkling powder.

'Gold, Captain. Gold from the Caves of the Emperor. We have a jar half full of dust. It could make you rich.'

Whilst Captain Waterhouse was contemplating the possibility of such well-deserved wealth, Mighty Jake Tempest, with the cunning accumulated over years of planning his survival in the unforgiving school of the crew's quarters, was contemplating a barter which had the chance of great wealth, but also a considerable risk of total loss. He had been singled out for this opportunity as a result of his sound judgement in Lancaster market. He had seen on a stall, metal objects such as cow-bells, shining brasses in the shape of the apostles, bells and buckles.

The greatest treasure to his eyes had been a metal horn, of the kind used by coachmen. He had finally made the decision to buy as many of these items as one gold coin could secure. This had demanded careful negotiation as the value of the foreign coin was not readily fixed, and the stall-holder had demanded a cash value from a goldsmith before filling Jake's kerchief with curios and handing him the brass horn.

Now, under the tropical sun, one of the prince's brothers had his eye firmly fixed on the shining instrument. Jake had demonstrated the splendid sound it could produce, and had attempted to get the black man's heavy lips to achieve the same result. The noise had brought his brothers and their friends to examine the instrument, and Jake found himself in the happy position of awaiting the best bid for the horn while the unsuccessful bidders argued and agreed to purchase the other curios. The best offer was a leather bag which contained rough pieces of crystal, some blue or green, others colourless, probably looted from a distant village in the quest for slaves. They were of no obvious interest, except that Jake had seen similar crystals tipped out on the white table-linen in the Kings Head Hotel in Lancaster while three men argued about their value. The crystals now offered to Jake were much larger than any he had seen before. The largest blue one was the size of a man's thumb, the others somewhat smaller. Each one had at least one facet which was fairly smooth, like a single window in an old building, allowing the scorching sun to shine into the heart of each crystal. The leather bag contained fourteen pieces and the exchange was discreetly made. The other purchasers paid for their goods with broken pieces of ivory, and one piece of ivory, the size of a hand, which had been delicately carved into the figure of a black man with a majestic, erect penis. The vendor had explained to Jake, 'This good man, boss, he bring you good woman, good feelings all your life.'

Jake had already found the hiding places he required for the remainder of the voyage. The age of the ship and the arduous life it had survived meant that some of the timber frames and knees were split along the grain. He had found one such split where, with the careful use of a knife a piece of elm could actually be levered off. He had laboriously carved some of the wood off the back of the piece, so that the void could contain most of his prizes before the piece was wedged back in position. But he wisely ensured that not all his wealth was contained in one cache, and hid his crystals in two other crevices. The ivory carving hung round his waist every hour of the day.

The following night, the sultry heat gave way to a tremendous storm, the rain slashing down on the decks, filling the scuppers and drenching the captives below the deck gratings. The unexpected wind was cold and penetrating. Great streaks of lightning flashed across the black sky, momentarily showing the rain bouncing high in the air from the decks, and from every surface battered by the deluge. Every spar, yard and bowsprit, every locker and bulwark rail was decorated with a crest of bouncing water. The thunder which followed the flashes terrified the invisible tribes below the gratings, and at the height of the storm a great tongue of flame leapt down the foremast and snaked instantly across the deck, seeking the Earth's core to disgorge its fearsome energy. On deck, the bo'sun had two seamen checking round, anchor cable, ropes, braces and hatches. The captain emerged from the companionway and studied the ferocity of the storm with an experienced eye. He silently noted the tongues of St Elmo's Fire from the ends of the yards. No one else seemed to notice the ill-omen.

At sunrise, he called the Mate into the cabin.

'No men ashore today, Chief. Have everything ready to clear away, and be prepared to sail at sunset if the wind is still strong and off-shore. The prevailing wind is blowing on-shore, but I've noticed after these terrific storms the wind veers briefly round to the Nor'west, the only chance we have of sailing out of this hole. Otherwise it's fifty men on oars and paddles. All our debts are paid, and I notice the Prince's people go ashore at sunset. So today, we'll break out the brandy and let the Prince and his boys join us. Are you following me, Mister Mate?' demanded the captain impatiently.

'You mean we sail tonight with just the slaves we've got? We could load another hundred, at least.'

'And where are those boys now? A thousand miles away in the jungle. We'll wait no longer. Mister Mate, there is no-one on this godforsaken coast will know we are leaving. Do you follow me? You tell no one we are leaving. When it is dark, bend on topsails and we'll slip away at midnight. But, more important, the Prince and his court will be sailing on a sea of brandy.'

Late the following morning, as the scorching sun dried out the saturated ship, Prince Henry appeared on board with ten more slaves, six men and four young women, for which the captain exchanged additional materials.

'Prince Henry, time is getting on. I think we will wait for four more days only. Every healthy man you can get me in three days we will pay for. After that we will leave on the first good wind.'

The Prince nodded in regretful agreement.

'I would like to find you another hundred Ashantees. I prefer dealing with you Lancaster men. I have left the Liverpool ships to the arabs.'

The captain accepted the compliment as an excuse to drive the tap into a barrel of brandy, offering a mug of the golden liquid to his guest. As the day wore on, the prince was invited to return to the barrel, and two of his brothers, who had mysteriously got the message from afar, came aboard and joined in the celebrations. In the stillness of the afternoon heat the prince went into the slave deck and returned with three black girls, naked and sullen. With much shouting, stamping and clapping the three girls were forced to dance, a shuffling, stamping ritual. Adding their own shouts of encouragement the crew gathered round and watched the proceedings with amusement. Pieces of wood, belaying pins and iron shackles were joining in the rhythmic tapping to enhance the movements of the girls. A fiddle was produced which in the past had been badly played by the sail-maker. In the present circumstances even his inadequate fumbling added to the rising excitement. The prince and his brothers danced with the girls, and as the gyrations became more exuberant, their hands grabbed at the writhing bodies before them. In the airless heat the captain passed mugs of brandy to the dancing men, who forced the fierce liquid down the throats of their unwilling partners. The captain nodded across the dancers towards the Chief Mate. Unseen by any of the crew the captain's black girl Elli watched the hideous performance with no sign of emotion on her black, decorated face.

By sunset, the three black men were slumped on the afterdeck, leaning back against the deck sail-locker. The brandy barrel was much depleted, its fiery contents having made the three men incapable of consummating their final degradation of the dancing slave girls, who were once again loosely shackled to the bolts in the tween deck.

'Bo'sun! Help our guests into one of the canoes. Carefully now.'

With much laughter and shouting, the three men were hoisted up on a tackle on the gaff and lowered into one of the fragile-looking boats. Three men with paddles who had been sleeping in the boats started arguing about the difficulty of reaching the shore with such a difficult load. The captain sent down a jug of brandy, and the complaints ceased.

In the brief tropical twilight the captain waited until the canoe was half way towards the shore. He had been watching the wind gathering speed as it veered to the west.

'Chief! All hands aloft! Ready to set topsails and mainsail. Be ready to set spanker. Shorten anchor cable but don't break out.'

This would mean the ship would swing head to wind, just held by the anchor until the wind was strong enough to make the ship respond to her sails and her rudder.

Anxiously, in the growing darkness, Captain Waterhouse gauged the wind speed and direction. After the ruse of the dance party it was essential to get clear of the harbour and preferably over the horizon before sunrise. The very worst condition would be to run aground passing between the islands. Some monies might still be owing to the prince, not directly for slaves, but for stores and provisions. Furthermore, it was clearly understood on the coast that good service from a factor or agent would be recognised by an effusive letter of commendation, which would be the basis of his future employment. More serious than any breach of these codes, Captain James Waterhouse had found the animal passion of Elli a drug he could not surrender. He prayed that she was sleeping off the effects of a tincture of laudanum, more usually employed by the surgeon to ease the pain of smashed bone and flesh.

As the night-time breeze freshened and veered towards the nor'west, the 'Antoine' swung to point towards the dark shadows of the land. By setting the spanker and bracing the topsails aback the ship could be forced to swing on her anchor a couple of points off the wind.

'Heave aweigh!'

As the four seamen strained at the capstan bars, the anchor broke free from weeks embedded in the mud five fathoms beneath the ship, and once again, the 'Antoine' was free, in her natural elements of wind and water, responding to the careful calculations of the Captain and his Mates, harnessing the variable power of the wind against the river currents.

While the sinister shadows of the protective islands briefly delineated them in the dark night the captain attempted to gauge their distance, although the chart of the harbour was considered so inaccurate that little comfort could be derived from such estimates. Every groan of the weary hull, every sound from the filling canvas, seemed like the first signal of running aground to the tense mariners. No beacon had been lit for the unannounced departure, and by now every member of the crew realised the significance of the day's activity. Some cursed that they had not bartered all their private transactions, others that the women ashore would still offer their bodies for a remaining bag of glass beads.

The greatest regret of all was the realisation by the two hundred and thirty-nine frightened, hungry black men, women and children manacled ankle to ankle, wrist to wrist, that any chance of salvation, any hope of rescue, even a change of heart by the cruel black slave-masters who had sold them into this hideous bondage was now gone forever. This truth manifest itself in the only manner remaining. At first a single, weary voice, then a small group and finally a numberless choir, in the terrifying darkness joined in an awful, perfect harmony. Different tribes and tongues mysteriously joined in the slow, sonorous lament, chilling the sailors and drifting across to the unseen hills. No soul on God's Earth could ignore the haunting sound of such an epilogue. In the secrecy of his seaman's cot, Mighty Jake Tempest continued the strange, cryptic record of events on the slave brig 'Antoine'.

*

While the ship was clawing her way across the ocean, searching for trade winds to displace the calm of the Doldrums, the city of Lancaster was enjoying a pleasant summer. Commerce was booming, the new harbour at Glasson Dock was filled with ocean-going ships, and enthusiasm for the canal was growing daily. Money was readily forthcoming for the initial survey and costing of the project. Mr Samuel Gregson had been appointed as Clerk to the Committee, and had rented offices near the Castle. Shipbuilding was thriving on the River Lune below the new bridge at Skerton, where Mr Brockbank's shipyard and timber store filled the Green Ayre. This meant that ships still had to be slipped from their yards and floated down river below the old bridge to have their masts stepped. The timber for these ships was frequently brought from abroad. The new American colonies were proving a good source of long pines for masts and spars, as an alternative to the Baltic suppliers.

Lancaster quayside was crowded, its warehouses full of cargoes, and the lumbering wagons and carts made the highways almost impassable, a sea of mud in the wet weather, a desert of dust when dry. The busy market town of Kendal could see itself isolated by the poor quality of the roads at the very time its industry was set to increase.

Under these circumstances, the need for a canal was obvious. The only criticism seemed to be that it should have been so long delayed in starting.

Chapter 10

In January 1792 the icy grip of winter brought the river and the port at Lancaster to a standstill. The new harbour at Glasson proved its value, allowing even the largest ships to enter two hours either side of high water from the broad waters of the estuary. Blazing piles of scrap timber on the quaysides warmed the men struggling with ships' ropes and handling cargo. But ashore, the rutted roads had frozen into solid peaks and valleys of ice-hard mud, twisting the wheels from wagons, halving loads and trebling costs.

The 'Antoine' was home from her ill-starred voyage, having sailed for four months under the command of Mr James Blackman, Captain's Mate, who had taken charge on the death of Captain Waterhouse in mid-Atlantic. The cargo of slaves had produced a highly acceptable profit at the sales in Port Royal. The negroes had been delivered in good condition, only two having died on the Middle Passage. Two seaman had died, one from sickness after a chest wound, the other from a fall. James Blackman had shown considerable skill in navigating the ship to Jamaica, and then in securing a high-value homeward cargo of sugar, rum and several tons of a valuable wood called lignum vitae. The baulks of timber were so hard and dense they barely floated in water, and when shaped and smoothed the wood would shine with its own natural polish.

But the voyage had been overshadowed by the death of the captain, reportedly from one of the choleras thought to blow across the Guinea Coast. The surgeon had signed the certificate 'tropic fever' as the cause of death.

As soon as Jake had signed off his berth on the 'Antoine' and drawn his wages and dividend he sought out Mr Weaver on the Lancaster quays and had found him taking lunch in his usual inn.

'By God, Jake, these deep-sea ships agree with you! There's muscle on those bones! Look at you, lad, strong as a tree, I'll be bound.'

Joshua Weaver proudly introduced the young man to his friends. Jake was no more than average height, but stood straight, his fair hair tied back in a pig-tail, his skin bronzed and hardened. He was dressed in a sheepskin coat, moleskin trousers and black clogs. He carried a black, broad-rimmed hat, and bowed correctly to the men sat round the meal table, before taking a seat, his seabag at his feet.

'Are you coming home with me tonight, then?' enquired Joshua.

'If that's agreeable with Mistress Weaver.'

'Agreeable, Jake? She'd lock me out with the horse if I told her you were sleeping in Glasson tonight. You'll come home and tell us all your tales. Sadly, your friend John is waiting in the River Tyne for the ice to break up in the Baltic. Some foolish captain thought he could make a profit on a last dash before winter. Damned lucky not to be frozen in Petersburg for three months.'

'Profit! That's all you merchants think about now,' said one of the diners. 'You were all a lot more careful when the Frenchies were watching every move you made.' The speaker slapped his thigh to emphasise the wisdom of his remark, before turning to Jake.

'What trade have you come back from, lad? Been to the Indies by the style of your topsides.'

The speaker, using this almost unintelligible tongue, caused his neighbour to lean across to Jake.

'Never been on a ship, has Thomas here. Likes to talk like Admiral Hood, even if his longest voyage was across the river after the bridge fell down!'

The merriment at the table grew as the meal continued and drinks were passed down the length of the scrubbed boards.

'Were you on the 'Antoine'?' asked one of the men.

'Aye, sir. Deck boy, promoted able seaman.'

'Tell me, able seaman, these slaves. I hear you can do anything you want with their women. I heard some jacks were taking them two and three at a time. Primitive savages, I'm told, but willing bodies like no white girls will ever be. Is that right?'

'I'd treat them with care, mister. Their witchcraft can kill a man a hundred feet up a mast.'

'That sounds like a tall story!' This produced a fresh gale of laughter.

'It's true, as God made me, and no man who has seen it would deny it. I've see a black girl on deck shout the curse at a sailor up the foremast, make him think he was a bird and try to fly. They bring berries with them, black, bitter berries, which can turn a sailor into an eagle. That's what finished for Jed.'

'That I can't believe, even from a friend of Joshua Weaver.'

Jake swung round to face the speaker and lowered his voice.

'You'd believe it soon enough, mister, if you had never seen a breath of wind for twenty days, the sea as flat as the church floor, no sound, no clouds, no birds. Three hundred living souls and not a single whisper. You could believe anything on the twenty-first day, but mostly you'd believe that God had forgotten you were ever born.'

At this sudden change in manner, the diners round the table were silent. The young man's low voice and words carried a chill into the tavern which the crackling logs in the fire could not dispel. Joshua Weaver was conscious of the tension, and rose from the table.

'Come on, my young friend, you're frightening some of the richest men in Lancaster!'

Nervous laughter greeted this remark, allowing Joshua to take Jake out of the inn.

'You can jump up behind me on the horse, if you like. After all, you took his name!'

Together they trotted home to the house in Ryelands. The horse made light work of the terrible road, and they caught up with a carriage which was stuck in the great ridges of frozen mud. The single horse was struggling between the shafts, the coachman on foot leading it to the easier part of the track, tugging at the bridle, until slowly he got the carriage moving again.

'I recognize that carriage. I think it's Councillor Redfearn. He's probably looking for you, young man.'

As they drew level the passenger looked out of the window.

'Hello, Weaver, I'm on my way to your house. Is that Jake Tempest you've got there?'

'Aye, it is, sir. The road gets better further on. We'll see you at the house.'

The trotted ahead, to prepare the house for the councillor's arrival.

Jake swung down from the horse and ran towards the kitchen door of the house. He pushed it open and put his arms round Mistress Weaver as she worked at the kitchen table.

She turned in mock surprise.

'Jake, you great lout. Let's have a look at you. Dear Lord, you've grown, not fatter, but look how strong you are.'

They hugged and he smoothed her hair, as if he was stroking a favourite animal. She had tears in her eyes, which she pretended was caused by the cooking on the blazing fire.

Her husband came in and closed the door.

'Quick, you two. Redfearn's on his way. We'll sit in the drawing room, because he's bound to want to talk.'

Before he took his surcoat off he carefully took a shovelful of burning logs out of the kitchen fire.

'Jake, open the doors, and stamp on any embers I drop.'

He carried the logs into the drawing-room fireplace, and soon a reasonably bright fire was cheering up the drawing room, while the two men took off their coats and cleaned themselves up in the kitchen.

The coach entered the yard and pulled up at the front door. The councillor clambered out, muttering under his breath at the cold weather and uneven ground. Joshua took his ulster and showed him into the drawing room. He told the coach driver to go into the kitchen for a warm, and a bowl of soup.

'Now, Weaver, where's that young man Tempest? Get him in here and let's have a word with him.'

'Yes sir, he's only just this moment got home. He won't be a moment. A brandy, Councillor?'

'Well, that's kind of you, sir. It might keep body and soul together in this dreadful winter. It's uncommon cold in this city.'

'There's many manufacturers had to stop work completely. Can't get materials up the road, can't move timber or anything.'

Jake knocked on the door and stepped into the drawing room.

The councillor looked up.

'Well, Master Tempest, this sailor's life seems to agree with you. I've heard a good report of your service aboard the 'Antoine' since Captain Waterhouse died. That's when I judge my men, when things start going wrong. Weak men fail, strong men succeed.'

'Thank-you sir.'

Joshua poured out the brandy and the three men sat for a while as the logs blazed into life.

'Now, Jake, I want to hear your report. Our usual rules will be observed. The full truth, and no magistrates. But we have lost a sound captain and now I learn our very best factor will no longer trade for us. Something tells me these events are related. Am I right?'

'I say so, sir. No troubles on the voyage to the Africs. All going well, negroes safely below decks, but one day everyone knew some mischief was about. We could see the captain was going to make Prince Henry too drunk to know what was happening. The whole ship seemed mad, dancing and drinking, black girls pulled out the tween deck. Everyone went crazy. Sure enough, we sailed out of Bonny, slipped out in the middle of the night. No beacons, no pilot. Everyone knew we was leaving troubles and bad debts behind us. The sailors, we all knew the score.'

The councillor turned to Joshua, his face dark with anger.

'Good God, Weaver. When will these captains learn the foolishness of their tricks. We expect these factors to sell us their own kind and then we deal in bad faith. The factors can always get the better of us. Sell us bad water, rotten fruit or poison the blacks. I think somehow they poisoned the captain.'

'They didn't touch him, sir. No one had the chance, nor the want to. He was a good and fair man to us.'

'Then how did he die? Fever, was it? The only sick man on a ship of nearly four hundred souls, and he dies of fever?'

'No sir, He was murdered. He was cut open in his belly, sir.'

'Boy, you'd better be certain that every word you utter is the truth.'

'It's the truth, sir, there's twenty men or more could declare that. The captain had taken a woman, sir. She killed him.'

'How? Why was that?' The councillor was almost screaming, barely controlling his anger.

'She was Prince Henry's special woman. The sailors called her 'The Queen' and was the most wanted woman on that ship. There was not a man-jack who would not have given every day's pay for half an hour spread across her shining black body.'

Jake looked up as he heard Joshua's intake of breath.

'Sorry, Mister Weaver. I mean no rudeness, but she made everyone dream of her body. But Captain Waterhouse kept her in his cabin, so that we sailed holding her captive, instead of giving her back to the Prince.'

'The fool! The brainless fool! I know the deals, slave women for sale, by the hour, by the day or for the rest of their lives if you want, yet an experienced captain steals the one woman on the whole coast of Guinea who is not for sale. Go on with this mad tale, lad.'

Jake sipped the warming brandy before continuing.

'For the first few days she walked round the deck, like a black cat, silent and staring at the distant shore. When she was not on deck we knew the captain was using her. At nights some of the sailors told the others what they thought the captain was doing to the black Queen. Two men even hung over the transom on ropes to try and watch through the stern ports. I don't think they saw anything, but you wouldn't know so from the accounts they gave.'

Jake fell silent. Joshua offered him another beaker of brandy.

'Can I get my log?'

He went out of the room and when he returned he was carrying the curious pages of paper which represented his diary. He laboriously counted the days that had elapsed before the next event.

'Three days out of the Bonny, some of the sailors again released a few of the women slaves and tried to use them, you know, use their bodies. Somehow, the other slaves, even when they were left in the hold all day, knew what we were doing to the women and the noise the men made was terrifying. The captain made us put the women back in the hold. The crew were very angry because they knew what the captain was doing to the Queen.'

He took a gulp of the brandy.

'To quieten down the blacks, the captain ordered them to be allowed on deck, fifty slaves in the forenoon, shackled to the eye-bolts, changed for another fifty in the afternoon. They could get buckets of sea-water for washing and cleaning, and the last fresh fruit was given out. Then, one morning, the wind suddenly changed, to the sou'west I think. The mate went to get the captain, but he returned on deck, holding the black girl by her wrist. She was covered in blood. She had no clothes on, but I could see no place where so much blood had come from.

"She's killed him! She's killed him! She's slit him open!'

The Mate seemed to be out of his senses, shouting and screaming. He had blood on his breeches and his hands. I remember the girl left dark red footprints on the afterdeck. I've never seen so much blood since my friend in Rotherhithe fell from the foremast. Blood splashed everywhere like painting the topsides.

'The Mate got hold of me and said 'Jake, get the surgeon, get him to the captain.'

'I ran down to the lazarette and found the surgeon. We went to the captain's cabin. The captain was lying half in and half out of his cot. His belly had been cut wide open, just like you clean a rabbit for the pot. Wide open, he was. And blood...'

Joshua held up his hand.

'I don't think we need anymore, do we, Councillor?'

The councillor hesitated.

'No, I think not. What happened to the woman, Jake?'

'I think she jumped into the sea. Maybe the Mate threw her in, I don't know. I wasn't there.'

Suddenly the stern face of Councillor looked kindly towards the young sailor.

'Tell me, boy, is there any more I must know? Or can we leave the rest of your story for another time?'

'No sir, there were many things that happened on that voyage, but no crimes the magistrate could handle, unless he can deal in witchcraft. Have you heard of the voodoo as they name it in the Africs?'

'Jake, these are things for another day, I've heard all I need.'

Councillor Matthew Redfearn stood up and drained his brandy.

'Gentlemen, I don't think there is any need for this bitter story to go any further. The captain's widow and family would be in no happier position by hearing these details. Those who have taken life have also surrendered their own, so God has his justice done. We know nothing more than that.'

'Except for the surgeon, sir.'

The councillor looked at Jake.

'You mean he has a complaint? I thought he had signed the certificate?'

'I know nothing about that. He just said to wait while Parliament acts. That's what he said to me one night.' Jake shrugged his shoulders.

For a moment the stern features of the councillor seemed to soften. He touched Jake's sleeve.

'To Hell with Parliament and all their fancy ways. We don't see our Lancaster streets crowded with their carriages. Too far from Regent's Park, I expect.'

*

'We'll need to send a delegation to London,' said Mr Rawlinson, addressing the crowded room in the Town Hall. 'We are now in a position to press for an Act of Parliament, having today received subscriptions amounting to one hundred and seventy thousand pounds.'

A gasp of surprise greeted this remark, and the proceedings were halted while excited discussions drowned the speaker's address. Eventually he was able to proceed.

'The subscription list shows a remarkably broad spread of interest. Blackburn, Bolton, even Settle, in The West Ridings, have demonstrated their real interest, in addition to the cities along the route, obvious beneficiaries of our plans. With this ready response, we should, indeed, proceed with confidence.'

Once again, it was Councillor Redfearn who struck a note of caution.

'May I enquire what Champion we have in Parliament to press our claim for this 'heavenly' waterway?'

His ironic description of the elevated canal and its expensive aqueducts raised a weary cheer from the room. It was the Mayor who replied.

'Why, none other than The Duke of Bridgewater, a peer who knows more about waterways than anyone in the Kingdom, and whose name seems singularly appropriate to meet Councillor Redfearn's misgivings!'

Having dismissed the voice of opposition, the meeting began discussing the details of the undertaking. Without doubt, the bitter winter had made every trader, large or small, eager for an alternative to the frozen, rutted tracks which had been adequate for pack horses but not for wheeled wagons, carts and carriages. Thus, the most adventurous route surveyed by John Rennie was accepted by the working committee. He had drawn a line over seventy miles long, from

Kendal in the north to Westhoughton in the south where it could link up with the rest of the canal system. It would require two huge aqueducts and three smaller ones. Of equal difficulty would be a tunnel nearly a quarter of a mile long, and the construction of more than forty locks. All the engineering works would demand large quantities of stone, timber and skilled labour, which would mean most of the money would be retained in the neighbourhood of the construction, a very healthy inducement, if any were needed, to bring cheer to local businessmen.

'I assume, of course, Mr Rennie's line will connect directly with our magnificent new harbour at Glasson dock. This may at least prevent the canal being something more than an engineer's plaything.' The councillor's voice droned on.

The committee shuffled through their papers, before regretfully announcing that the existing line did not go near Glasson at all.

*

At Ryelands, Jake was distributing gifts to his guardians. For Mistress Weaver he had a polished wooden box, made of the mysterious lignum vitae, naturally coloured a lustrous olive green. The top of the box had been carved delicately to show a two-masted ship, all sails set, with a radiant sun in the sky. Jake proudly announced he had carved the top himself. For Joshua he had a bag of tobacco which had been cured in rum, its sweet, tropical aroma filling the room. He also gave him one of the blue crystals, the smallest in his collection.

'What's this Jake? This looks like a gemstone. Where did you get it?'

'I bought it on the Bonny. Looked good to me.'

'And to me, Jake. I'll take it to a friend of mine in the city next week. He'll tell me the real value.'

Jake had also, with great consideration, made a gift for his namesake, the horse, Tempest. He had made a rope bridle, decorated from end to end with elaborate knots and splices, treble crowns and walls, turks heads, and back-splices.

Sarah Weaver looked at the pleasure in the young man's face.

'Jake, you're a good lad. No more of your terrible stories this voyage, I hope.'

'No, ma'am. No more frightening stories. Just sailing round the World tying fancy knots in bits of rope. It's a good life for a young man.'

Chapter 11

By the month of June King George III had more things on his mind than simply signing the Lancaster Canal Act. His messengers from France were bringing ever more startling reports of the difficulties of King Louis XVI, although, surprisingly, the British Ambassador in Paris reported that 'the greatest revolution that we know has been effected with the loss of very few lives. We may consider France a free country.'

The city fathers of Lancaster, however, proudly returned with their Act of Parliament and the good wishes of the Monarch to the citizens of the Duchy of Lancaster. The news spread to the towns and villages along the route, landowners drank their port wine, stonemasons took their ale, and the 'navigators' their porter, to celebrate the start of the greatest enterprise many of them would ever see, with the opportunity of earnings for all.

The formation of a committee, responsible for seeing the canal through to completion, was the first priority and this in turn accelerated the sale of shares. The appointment of Thomas Worswick as Treasurer and John Rennie as Principal Engineer meant that the two essential tasks could start immediately. Tenders and contracts were studied, and resident engineers appointed. With over £400,000 committed to the new canal company, negotiations were starting with the landowners, not only to agree the price which would be paid, but to overcome some of their protests. Fears were expressed that rivers would be diverted from water-powered mills and factories dependant on supplies of clean water, although they had expressly been given Priority of Use in the Act.

The local townsfolk watched with some concern as the engineers brought into town the army of canal builders, known as the 'navigators', who would be the muscle-power to dig the rock and soil. Most of them had gained experience in other parts of the country and had heard of the new 'cut' being made in Lancashire and found their way to the limestone county. If possible, they looked for lodgings in the towns or villages, but otherwise might have to manage with a corner in a barn or out-house. But wherever they settled, the fear of theft and drunkenness, or worse, kept the newcomers apart from the local dwellers. Bolts were fitted on the doors. Wives and daughters were warned by their men of the terrible things that might befall them. The brewers who had built their breweries beside the clean rivers, wisely made plans for increased sales.

Within days of these events in Lancashire, the French king was overthrown, and at 10 o'clock on 21 January 1793 he was executed on a guillotine erected in the Place de la Revolution. Britain and half a dozen other European States, who had formed themselves into a Coalition, found themselves at war with the Republic of France. Once of the first actions of King George III was to issue Letters of Marque and Reprisals, the authority granted by the monarch for trading ships owned by his subjects to wage war on the ships of his enemies. Within a few months sixty-seven ships in Liverpool and several more in Lancaster accepted the conditions of the Letter of Marque and armed themselves to attack French ships on the high seas.

'Do you realise what this means to the 'cut'? Every stand of timber, every piece of stone or iron brought by sea, will be at risk from the French.' Councillor Redfearn, never the canal's greatest champion, viewed the war with his traditional pessimism. He glowered at his fellow traders.

'Have you seen some of these plans of Mister Rennie? We'll be importing brick and stone from every port in this country, and then scouring the quarries and forests in Europe and I'll lay money that the government will enforce a Convoy Act. A river crowded with merchant ships waiting for Portsmouth to send us a frigate for protection. Preposterous! Next thing the King's Navy will haul into the River Lune and put a press gang ashore.'

His listeners in the council room listened to his gloomy assessment with their customary ill-grace.

'If I was a French captain I would hesitate before I set a course to Lancaster to attack my enemy,' said one, 'when the English Channel will have plenty of ships for the gunners to practice on.'

'Then, sir, you know little of naval warfare. Have you considered how we will trade in the Baltic Sea? How much timber does Mr Rennie require for his great bridges?'

His audience laughed.

'I don't think wooden bridges will hold all the water he intends to use,' said one.

Another joined in the merriment. 'Councillor, wood floats in water, not the other way round!'

The councillor cast a withering look at the other men in the meeting room, who enjoyed the few moments of humour in the intense discussions surrounding the canal under conditions of war. Councillor Redfearn continued.

'Don't you realise that every bridge across the waterway, and especially the huge arches of the aqueducts, can only be constructed with massive wooden scaffolding formed to the shape of each arch, to carry the whole weight of the stone while the arch is being built. Tons of good quality timber will be required, good in length, not any scrap lumber. I would also like to acquaint you gentlemen with one other problem. This great cut extends across the countryside, miles from the towns. Does it not occur to you that this valuable timber, waiting to be used, may mysteriously disappear into the night, so that by the time we reach Kendal there won't be a sagging roof or broken gate in the county! I'll wager that for every foot of timber used for Mr Rennie's folly we'll ship in a yard.'

In fact, negotiations were well advanced with Mr Brockbank, the shipbuilder, who was also one of the largest importers of foreign timber. The design of the aqueduct had been approved by the committee, although it did not conform to John Rennie's original design. The engineer's original brick construction of the five great arches had been altered to use stone, which the committee considered much more in keeping with the style of the city of Lancaster. The great difference in cost sounded a wise provision to the committee. Consideration of the crossing of the River Ribble was 'referred back', to be discussed at a later date.

One of the earliest requirements would be for massive timber piles. The design called for the stone piers of each of five arches to be constructed on wooden platforms supported on timber piles. These platforms would actually be below the natural level of the river bed. Each site for these supports had to be surrounded by a coffer dam, like a robust timber palisade, within which the water had to be pumped out, day and night, and the soft river bed excavated. Manual pile-driving rigs were constructed which did no more than repeatedly drop a great stone weight on the head of the pile, for many hours, until the timber shaft extended up to thirty feet into the bed-rock. Thirty or more piles for each of six piers required a minimum of two hundred piles plus great quantities of well-cut timber to form the coffer dams. Poor timber would be impossible to make watertight, although a huge steam pump, delivered in pieces from Birmingham, was set up on the river bank to try and drain the leaking water.

*

John Weaver, nearly nineteen, waited to be examined on his skills as a navigator. The ships chartered to carry timber from the Baltic to England, for shipbuilding and for the canal, provided the experience he needed. Suitable timber had been located at the port of Memel, in

Prussia, and Chef Popov had secured the size and quality of timber demanded by the Lancaster masters. The 'Nancy' and 'Kestrel', relatively small and fast, had sailed without escort until arriving off Kronbourg Castle, where a British frigate was waiting to escort British ships into the Baltic. Close to the Danish shoreline a sailing cutter was streaking through the choppy water, spray thrown high over the sharp bows. It drew closer to the 'Kestrel' and as it approached, broke out two red and white flags.

Captain Cooper turned the ship head into wind and waited as the cutter came alongside. A rope ladder was thrown over from the 'Kestrel' and presently a Danish Naval Officer appeared over the bulwark rail. John Weaver took the visitor to the after-deck, where the captain stood beside the helmsman.

'Ship's papers, please. Payment for 'Sound Toll' to be collected.' He spoke in careful, stilted English.

Captain Cooper took the naval officer below to check the calculation of tolls on the weight of cargo being carried into the Baltic Sea. A Promissory Note was signed, the officer took a brief look round the deck and then descended to his cutter.

When the cutter was clear, the British frigate 'Zeus' sailed up the weather side, stealing the wind and effectively preventing the 'Kestrel' getting under way after the Danish visitor.

'What ship? Where bound?' came the traditional hail from the frigate.

"Kestrel', Captain Cooper, bound from Lancaster to Memel, cargo of manufactures and furniture.'

'Commander Williams, Royal Navy. I wish to board your vessel. Please allow my boat alongside.'

The captain turned to the First Mate.

'Dear God! What do they want?'

'Well, he'd be a magician if he could get into the hold right now. Jammed solid with cargo.'

'Well, keep thinking pious thoughts and hope he doesn't ask too much.'

The naval captain and a midshipman vaulted smartly over the rail and stood to attention. Captain Cooper saluted and held his hand out. 'How may we be of assistance?'

The naval officer smiled.

'Well, Captain, it's really for us to help you. We are indeed nervous at present. The Baltic States are united in their opposition to the French Republic, thanks mainly to our support putting them on the right tack, at least for the present time. The rumour has it King George is paying the brave, loyal Prussians fifty thousand sovereigns every month to stiffen their sinews. But you just watch them when the cannons start firing! Believe me, Captain, these kings and Tzars have got their peace treaties already written in French. So my instructions to you are that there are no circumstances under which you are to stop upon orders from any ship except mine. Any interference with your safe and unhindered passage will be dealt with by us.'

'That sounds pretty dangerous to me. We are in the Baltic six months of the year, so we're well known in these parts. We will anchor at the port of Dantzig to clear our papers, and then sail close up the coast to Memel. I think we're amongst friends.'

'So you may be, Captain, but there are some nervous fingers on the muskets these days. Make best possible speed and watch for signals from me. By night we will show a white light on our stern, which you are to follow. By daylight, make your own course. Good luck!' The Captain smiled and saluted. The midshipman, who looked about fourteen, did likewise and together followed Weaver back to the ladder. The Captain disappeared over the side. The midshipman turned to John Weaver with a frightened look in his eyes.

'Can you see my mother in London? I haven't heard of her for more than a year on this ship.'

Young Weaver looked kindly at the small figure in his smart uniform.

'Sorry, Admiral. We're a Lancaster ship. Never in London in my life.'

The boy's face seemed even more crestfallen as he climbed over the side. The two naval officers disappeared and the 'Kestrel' set course to clear the Sound.

Captain Cooper turned to the first mate.

'Just what we need. A Danish and a British warship to watch over us. The best protected gunpowder in Europe!'

'Well, sir, we've made this run three times before and never got caught. Let's pray our luck holds.'

'At least we're better prepared than our first run. Better casks, better papers. Apart from paying taxes we're almost within the law!'

The evening breeze freshened, and the 'Kestrel' heeled under the best possible press of canvas, easily keeping up with the frigate. With more than three hundred and fifty miles ahead, a good breeze should enable them to reach Dantzig harbour in three or four days. If the wind failed, or veered towards the East, a fortnight might be wasted waiting for a change.

To enable the Baltic ships to carry more timber of the best quality, some of them had been modified. The older sailing ships had frequently been cut open to allow more timber in the hold or on deck. The 'Kestrel' had been altered in Mr Brockbank's yard. In the stern a port had been cut, as if for a cannon, but four foot wide and nearly five foot high. A timber door could be put in position or taken out from within the tween deck. Called a 'sabord' in the timber ports of the Baltic, long timbers could be slid into the tween decks, although the task of heaving a single trunk, three feet in diameter and forty or fifty feet long and weighing six or more tons, was a long and arduous process. Crushed hands and feet, bruised legs and backs were the inevitable outcome. This was only the second voyage the 'Kestrel' had made using the sabord, and the captain viewed it with the same unease as the crew who would have to handle it.

When they approached Dantzig the frigate stood off at a respectful distance, while the 'Kestrel' carefully felt her way between other ships at anchor, to ensure that she could be seen from the dockside. She hoisted blue and white flags on both topsail yards, a recognition signal to those ashore. After about half an hour a boat rowed out to them and a pilot came up the ladder.

'I have an anchorage for you at the eastern end. Chef Popov sends his compliments and will visit you shortly.'

With great care the ship moved along the line of vessels swinging at anchor. At the end of the line, as the ship lost all movement, Captain Cooper ordered the anchor let go and awaited the arrival of the colourful Chef Popov. When the agent eventually appeared, his usual flamboyance was absent.

'Captain, we have troubles. Let us go to your cabin.'

Once below, with the bottle of brandy on the table, Chef Popov threw off his fur hat and unbuckled his fur cape.

'St Petersburg has got wind of our little subterfuge. Believe me, they are stocking up with gunpowder every day. The magazines must be full to the ceilings with powder, but not from England. Someone is making it for Prussia and the Russian Army. Now there is a prohibition on imports.' Chef Popov shrugged his shoulders and held his hands out with an air of helpless finality.

Captain Cooper looked at him in amazement.

'What do you expect us to do with nearly twenty tons of powder? Take it back home, or maybe sell it to the French?'

'No, I may be able to help, but it could be risky. You see, Captain, I have a friend, shall we say, who knows your powder is the best. He wants to demonstrate it to a buyer. Do you know what I mean by 'une epreuve', Captain? It is a test they make upon gunpowder to see how good it is. We must make this test. If we are better than the Russian powder, I can sell it, otherwise no chance.'

'And how do we make this test?'

Chef Popov scratched his head. It was obvious he knew a plan, but was hesitant to divulge it.

'How is the powder loaded this time? In casks and barrels?'

'Yes, but they would pass for wine barrels. They're exactly the same, and marked 'vin rouge' on the ends. The manifest is the same. although on loose pages, which the customs house has never seen.'

'Right, Captain. This is what we will do. Unload everything else in Memel, as normal, but keep the barrels on board. We'll tell the commissioners we have to go to Libau, which is about twenty-five miles up the coast. I have arranged some timber there to load for our friend Mr Brockbank. But first, we will be at anchor, and I hope we will be able to unload the powder in the night into my friend's boat. He will take us ashore away from the town and we will test the powder in his cannon.' He looked at the Captain with a nervous grin on his face.

'Is that your plan? How very convenient. And when your friend has happily got all powder on his boat and carried out his test, what happens if he decides he doesn't like it?'

'Then, I regret, it will have to be thrown into the sea.'

'Chef Popov, you disappoint me. I'll tell you what we will do. First of all, you will pay me half the price for the gunpowder, from which moment the cargo is yours, and we will carry it to any place you wish, and unload it into your friend's boat. If, however, he doesn't like it, it will be up to you to make a deal with him.'

'But Captain, how can I do that?'

'Because, monsieur, as security, we will have loaded the heavy timbers in Memel before we sail to Libau.'

'But, Captain, that is impossible. You can't load the timber until the holds are empty. No, it wouldn't work.'

The captain studied his guest.

'Chef Popov, you are forgetting the fine quality of my ship. We have the ports, what you call 'les sabords' which will allow us to load the biggest timbers in the tween decks, without any consideration of the cargo in the hold. If you refuse to load this timber, I will form the impression you do not wish to trade with us in future. The volume of quality timber is considerable, and many of your competitors would like to deal with us.'

Chef Popov had got up from his chair and glowered at the captain.

'You insult Popov. I have the quality of timber which Mr Brockbank requires. It would be very difficult to find this from another merchant at such short notice.'

'Well, Mr Popov, that is something you will have to judge for yourself. If you don't have the heavy timbers for us in Memel when we arrive, ready to load, we will assume our future trade is finished with you. We will apply to the Minister in Konigsburg for the name of a new supplier. He will ask why we are no longer content to deal with Chef Popov and we will explain what has happened.'

'But not about the gun-powder. That would put you behind bars for ever!'

'Not if we said you had cleared all the agreements with your government. After all, how could anyone unload so much contraband cargo without it being seen? We must think it was always legally correct.'

'No one would believe you! You must be mad!'

'Well, dear sir, these are all considerations you will have to balance. Remember, if you don't meet our request in Memel, my plan goes into action. Payment for half the value of the black powder, timber for Mr Brockbank, or we light the fuses!'

'A most unfortunate expression,' murmured Popov.

The voyage to Memel should have taken no more than a day, but a chill northerly wind forced the 'Kestrel' and her escorting frigate to reach deep into the Baltic before turning towards the land. With no recognisable landmarks visible, Captain Cooper decided to turn south and eventually found the distant spires of the town. Once again, the frigate signalled a farewell and the 'Kestrel' made her way into the crowded harbour. Ropes were run ashore and the ship was heaved into position against a long wooden jetty. The square stern of the 'Kestrel' was moored hard into the corner where two jetties joined. This would give easy access to the stern aperture for loading timber. The watching captain turned to his first mate.

'It looks as if our friend has agreed to load us, so let's hope he's got the notes for the powder.'

To John Weaver, his first view of the port of Memel was a strange sight. Great stacks of sawn and rough timber, straight tree trunks and twisted boughs seemed to fill every space around the port. The harbour had the usual rafts and 'ponds' of floating wood. Hand-cranked cranes, sheer-legs and rollers added to the clutter and confusion surrounding the haphazard collection of ships waiting to be loaded, their bare spars at crazy angles where they were pressed into service to handle cargo.

Horses and ponies appeared to be the principle source of power to assist the dockside labourers. Rising columns of steam and smoke in the distance showed the activities of steam-powered saw-mills at the edge of the bedlam in the harbour.

The following morning, a crowd of roughly-dressed labourers appeared on the jetty, standing in a group, as if waiting for the arrival of some dignitary. Shortly, a man appeared on horseback, dressed in a huge leather coat and a conical fur hat. He was trotting smartly down the quayside, the horse finding a clear way through the muddle. He pulled up beside the 'Kestrel' and tossed the reins to one of the waiting men. He jumped easily over the ship's rail and called for John Weaver to take him to the captain.

Captain Cooper came up on deck and approached the visitor. To the captain's western eyes the man before him looked as if he had come from the tribes on the other side of the World.

'I'm Captain Cooper. Who are you and what is your business?'

The visitor slapped the captain on the back as a greeting and laughed loudly as he introduced himself.

'I'm Boris Yanicz, the chief lieutenant of Chef Popov. At your service, Captain!' Another hearty slap on the back almost sent the captain sprawling.

'I have some valuable documents for you, and very special instructions, heh?' He amplified this last remark by placing a finger along his nose, and winking with an air of great secrecy which could have been seen half a mile away.

'Come below, er Mr Boris. Are we to start work today?'

'But of course! Why not? We have fifty men just waiting to empty your ship.'

Down in the cabin, with the brandy flowing, Boris was a little more restrained.

'The Chief told me to put this in your hands only. Please read it and sign the last part.

The document he was given was a promissory note, and Captain Cooper knew the necessary checks to be made. Payment in Liverpool was unconditional and was dated one month later that the day's date. Popov and two other signatories validated the document. A clever form of receipt consisted of signatures written across a vertical line. Captain Cooper signed across the line, and his guest signed underneath. When the ink was dry, Boris carefully folded the heavy paper and tore it down the line, so that he retained a slip of paper with part of each of the five signature, which would exactly match the rest of the document if ever confirmation was required. The captain's partners were now assured payment for the gunpowder.

Other documents from Boris referred to clearing the inward cargo and loading the timber for the voyage home.

'I have cleared everything, and we will completely empty your ship here in Memel, and you will load as much timber as possible for your Mr Brockbank. Chef Popov sends his regrets if there was any misunderstanding during your meeting in Dantzig, but that was caused by false information being given to us.'

The captain smiled. His bluff appeared to have been successful. His impression of the thousands of tons of timber requiring reliable shippers in Memel convinced him that Popov couldn't afford the risk of losing the custom of his British merchants. And still the rows of casks in the bottom of the hold, stowed deep underneath the other cargo, remained to be unloaded.

In the days that followed, the cargo was carried, lifted, hauled and dragged over the side and loaded on to carts and wagons of every description. At last the casks marked 'vin rouge' started to find their way across the deck and on to the shore. Some were swung over the side away from the jetty and stowed in a waiting boat, always surrounded with boxes and packages of general cargo. In the muddle on the quayside, Captain Cooper could readily understand that almost anything could be concealed from prying eyes.

Until, that is, a platoon of militia appeared unexpected and unannounced early one morning as work was about to commence. About fifteen men in blue coats with black breeches and boots, armed with long-barrelled muskets, stood in a ragged line facing the ship, as if to prevent an invasion. An officer on horseback shouted an order and the platoon turned about, with their backs to the 'Kestrel', facing the piles of cargo on the quay.

John Weaver was the first to observe this strange ritual and ran below to tell the captain and the mates. They scrambled up the companionway and watched in horror as the platoon appeared to guard the ship. The officer dismounted and strode along amongst the cargo. He drew a shining sword from its scabbard, and with its point indicated three casks on the jetty. He shouted some order to his platoon, and three men ran forward and with their bayonets set about prizing the ends off the casks.

On deck, the captain and two of the mates watched in horror.

On the quayside two of the casks were burst open.

The officer looked up at the ship and noticed the faces watching his activities. He laughed as he plunged his gauntletted hand into the first cask. In a profusion of straw, he at last drew forth a large, terra-cotta jug. This was followed by a bowl, painted blue, with a pattern on it. He moved to the second cask and reached inside. He lifted out a leather boot, then two more, then some shoes and clogs. As he dug deeper, so he threw his finds over the jetty in disgust. He stepped towards the third cask. The militiaman was still trying to get his bayonet under the lid. The officer roughly pushed him to one side and studied the cask. He said something to the man and pointed to the inscription on the lid. With careful examination the officer managed to read the words 'Vin rouge'. He shouted at the cowering militia man and then struck him across the face with his gauntlet, picked up one of the boots from the other barrel and again hit him round the face with the leather. Blood started from the man's wounded face as the officer mounted his horse, shouted some raucous orders to his troops and galloped away. His small army followed.

'Gentlemen, time for a brandy, I think.' Captain Cooper led the way to his cabin, his heart still pounding in his chest.

Chapter 12

Later in the morning, Chef Popov and his excitable lieutenant, Boris, appeared on the quayside. They hailed the captain before crossing the gangway to the deck. After the alarms of the visit from the militia, Captain Cooper was anxious to speak to the two men.

'Have you heard of our visitors?'

'What, the mad captain of militia? You mustn't worry about his sort. He'd be looking for silks or sateens for his woman! They're so stupid, if you gave him a barrel of gunpowder he'd probably cook it!'

The humour of his remark had his lieutenant in gales of laughter, so noisily that the sailors and workers from the shore turned and joined the raucous sound. The noise contrasted strangely with the real fear that Captain Cooper felt about the nearness of discovery of the clandestine cargo. Suddenly, Popov was serious again.

'Captain, my friend is demanding a test of the powder. I have told him we will oblige. I trust you will agree?'

'Well, it depends upon what is required.'

'He will be on the quay in about one hour, with a closed wagon. He will select two casks of powder and take them away. We can go with him for about two miles up the coast. The powder will be put into a cannon and tested. That's all I can say.'

The captain considered the full implication of this demand. The need for a test had never occurred before and the possible outcome seemed to place everything at risk. Even as he considered the threat this represented, he saw the strange, covered wagon coming along the quay. It was pulled by two horses, on one of which sat the driver. The wagon looked like a small hut on two large and two small wheels, with openings cut in the sides to act as windows. The openings were protected by vertical bars crudely bolted to the frames. Once upon a time it might have been a carriage, but many miles and many winters had reduced it to its present sad state. It drew up beside the 'Kestrel' and a short man climbed down from within. He wore a military-style tricorne hat and a long coat which almost reached the ground.

He climbed on board and with great correctness nodded to Captain Cooper and Chef Popov. He swept off his tricorne to reveal a shining bald head.

'Gentlemen. It is an honour to meet you today. Peter Fuhrmann ... votre service.' His voice was very quiet and calm, although he spoke with a pronounced accent, which required him to speak very slowly to maintain the correctness of his words.

'Let me assure the brave Captain Cooper that we have no criticism of the powder you have brought us in the past. But recently, powder has been delivered from other countries and they have tried to swindle us. So, dear sir, we have requested a proving test for all powder. The only reason we have to go so far away is to prevent 'certain persons' becoming alarmed at the sound of the discharge.'

Within thirty minutes the dilapidated wagon was loaded with two casks of powder, and Captain Cooper had selected John Weaver to accompany him to witness the tests, leaving the ship in charge of the first mate. The round figure of Fuhrmann squeezed in beside the two mariners and the driver whipped the horses up for the uncomfortable journey away from the harbour. Popov and his assistant waved to the departing vehicle.

The proving ground turned out to be a stone-built fortification beyond the sand dunes which lay behind the long, unbroken beach. The port of Memel was out of sight behind a low, grass-covered headland.

Inside the strange building were a number of cannon of different sizes, most of which looked worn out, their sinister, rusting muzzles pointing through the openings in the massive walls. However, at one wide opening stood what appeared, to the captain, to be a mortar, like a short, squat cannon, its muzzle pointing up at a sharp angle. The two casks of powder were brought into the yard, and with a wooden stave Fuhrmann eased off the end of one cask, revealing the black, gritty gunpowder. With a wooden scoop he filled a cotton bag with about two pounds of powder and weighed it on a balance hanging from one of the giant beams which supported the roof. On the other side of the balance was a similar cotton bag, presumably filled with powder.

'Monsieur le Captain. The bag contains our standard black powder, manufactured in mills outside Konigsberg. As you can see, we have an identical weight of your most excellent powder. Now, we will place our powder in 'l'epreuve' and propel a cannon ball. The ball weighs precisely three and one half times the weight of powder.'

As he spoke, he carefully fitted the first cotton bag into the mortar, which he rammed down the short barrel with a wooden club. Then he lifted the fist-sized cannon ball, which was contained in its own linen bag, and lowered it carefully into the mortar. The three men then withdrew to a small ante-room, with an opening in one wall permitting the touch-hole to be ignited by Peter Petrovsky with a taper on a long metal rod.

The detonation of the mortar shook the building and the air itself. The mortar had recoiled against its rope tackle, dust and smoke filled the air. Despite the impact on the ears of the three watchers, the terrifying sound of the spinning cannon ball as it arched through the silent, summer skies could be heard until it plunged with a spray of sand on the distant beach.

Anxiously, the two mariners ran towards the point of impact to see how far the ball had carried. Fuhrmann followed, carrying two wooded staves, one painted white, the other red.

About two hundred paces from the point of fire, the ball was half buried in the soft sand. Captain Cooper reached down, and found the iron was still warm. Fuhrmann arrived, panting, his face flushed and sweating. He marked the point of impact with the white stave.

John Weaver carried the cannon ball back to the fortification, and once again the mortar was prepared. The bore was cleaned and the captain was invited to examine the mortar to ensure that it was restored to the same position, pointing up at the same angle as before. The powder charge was lowered down the muzzle, and the captain invited to ram it home.

Upon ignition, the detonation seemed of similar ear-stinging intensity, but the scream of the spinning cannon-ball was much more pronounced. The captain looked towards the dunes, where the first stave was clearly visible. This time, the plume of sand was well beyond the marker. Instead of running, Captain Cooper tried to pace out the distance from the front of the gun emplacement, although the soft sand made this difficult. The first stave was reached after two hundred thirty-five paces, whilst a further one hundred and twenty paces brought them to the cannon ball, a sinister dull black shape in an otherwise tranquil coastal scene.

Peter Fuhrmann was jubilant at the proof of the British powder. He nodded with satisfaction to his two guests.

'We need no more tests. Your powder is, if anything, better than any we have had before. Let us return to your most excellent ship.'

He carefully lowered both barrels into a concealed magazine below the stone floor and took his guests back to the strange wagon.

'I'm surprised the horses weren't upset by the sound of the cannon,' observed the captain.

'Oh-ho! They're used to a few explosions. Old cavalry horses, they are, and this old wagon is generally used for taking prisoners to the firing squad. They've grown up with the sound of gunpowder!'

The return to the harbour was strangely silent as Captain Cooper and Apprentice John Weaver considered the previous possible passengers in the uncomfortable vehicle.

The first rumble of thunder rolled across the summer sky as they trundled along the rock strewn road towards the town.

'Strange,' mused the captain, 'doesn't look like a storm.'

A few minutes later, as they turned towards the harbour, a column of black smoke could be seen rising almost vertically in the harbour. A moment later, flames could be seen at the base of the smoke cloud.

'That was not thunder, that's a ship on fire!' exclaimed John.

Captain Cooper nodded. 'There's a ship on fire. Look! Her mast is falling! Dear God, look at those flames.'

Like throwing a log on a slow-burning grate, the falling mast threw the fire into a fresh outburst of flames, which leapt twice the height of the surrounding masts. The captain stared in horror.

'That's Kestrel! That's our ship, blazing there. Hurry, let's get out of this hellish cart!'

He forced open the door and jumped down on to the roadway.

'Come on, Weaver! Move yourself! Our lives depend on it.'

Breathlessly, they charged through the increasing number of people who had appeared on the busy road to watch the conflagration. Forgetting few people would understand his words, the captain was cursing anyone who got in his way. At last, after what seemed a lifetime fighting through the crowd, the two mariners reached the point where those around them were running away from the blaze, rather than towards it. Further on, hands were pulling at them, urging them to avoid the blazing hulk ahead of them. From time to time, low explosions shook the air, shooting fountains of sparks and flames into the air. The sky was now darkened by the diffusing clouds of grey-brown smoke.

Suddenly, the two Englishmen realised they were alone. Ahead, the hull of the 'Kestrel' lay at an angle to a blazing quayside, the timbers of which were, as they watched, falling into the wreckage-strewn water.

Crates and cases of precious cargo slid into the water, and from his vantage point Captain Cooper could actually watch the soaring flames destroy the last vestiges of his own cabin across the square stern of the fast-disappearing ship.

Then occurred the fearsome phenomenon of a ship afire, when the blazing wreckage is inevitably engulfed by the sea and the fire is suddenly extinguished with a hissing, spitting finality. As the flames on the quay died down, the stinking air was strangely silent. Captain Cooper looked round the wrecked area, looking for any signs of sheltering people, but the quay was deserted.

'Hurry, boy! See where any of the crew have got to. Get back to those people watching there, see if any of the crew are amongst them. Then meet me back here.'

In the wreckage hardly any structure was recognisable. Planks, frames and spars were no different than the flotsam of cargo. Pieces of sail canvas could only be recognised to his experienced eyes by the remains of bolt-ropes and cringles. Slowly, the fragments of his precious ship drifted away on the slow, Baltic current. As he watched the final tortured minutes of his dying ship, young John Weaver was hurrying back up the quay.

'Quick, Captain. Don't let them see you. Get down the far end of the jetty, where we can't be seen. Quick, Captain.'

'Not so fast, boy. This is the remains of my ship. I'm not leaving...'

'Yes, sir, you must. Those people will kill you if they find out who you are! They think I am a deck boy, but they know what you were smuggling, because the ship exploded and burned so fiercely. They've already worked out it must be gunpowder. We'll have to hide until we can slip away without being noticed.'

As they hurried towards the end of the quay, ensuring the stacks of timber hid them from the crowds who were now venturing back to look at the wreckage, the captain pulled John Weaver into a narrow passage between two stacks of sawn lumber.

'Boy, have you got a single coin on you? Have you got a piece of paper saying 'I am Mister John Weaver of Lancaster'? Have you even got a piece of pencil or a page of paper?'

John checked all his pockets, and produced a clasp knife, a short length of yarn and an apple.

'Well done, lad, that should get us back to the River Lune in grand style! Let's see what I've got.'

The captain produced a bundle of letters, some pages from the manifest, listing some sheepskins. He had two pencils, a small notebook, nearly filled with navigation workings, a couple of kerchiefs and some ribbon. John felt a chill fear.

'What do we do now, sir?'

'Stay together at all costs. Try and mingle with the crowd, look out for any of our boys, and look out for Popov. He's bound to be snooping around. Then, when it gets dark, let's see if we can find a British ship. The 'Nancy' has already left, I believe, but there are lots of British ships calling here.'

By nightfall they had found one of the seamen, who had been standing on the jetty when the 'Kestrel' exploded.

'Them's all dead, Cap'n. All gone in one great explosion. I've seen bodies flying through the air, like birds, they was, like birds wi' wings spread. But they was dead 'uns. There was two who was burning like tar barrels. Saw 'em with my own eyes. Jumped in the dock and never seen again.'

The captain listened and waited while the frightened man unburdened his soul of the terrifying sights he had witnessed. When he seemed more at ease the captain questioned him more closely.

'Did you see what caused the explosion?'

'No, Cap'n, I was on the shoreside buying some spirit. They were all shouting on the deck, some mad argument. I think a cask had split or was broke. The Fuzzies were off the ship like scared rabbits in a meadowful of dogs. Before the firing, two of our boys starts down the gangway, but they was thrown down by the terrible power of the flames. The old ship split open like rotten fruit. I watched the starboard side fall open like it was an old barn door, an' all tumbling out, boxes, cots, just like a cart turned over. Every piece broken, burst, burning...'

His voice trailed away as he recalled the horror of the moment.

'Well, sailor, what have you got on you? A thousand golden guineas and a map of The Baltic Sea?'

The sailor scratched his head at the question.

'No, Cap'n. I've got a knife, and these coins. Russian coins, I think.'

The captain looked at his two companions.

'Here's what we are going to do to save our skins. Now pay attention. From now on, I will be called the ship's surgeon. Understood? I am not to be called 'Captain' by you two. Next, we are going to spend the night checking every ship in the harbour. We need to find any British ship, or if not, any ship except Frenchmen. But as we go round every ship look in the water for anything from the 'Kestrel', things that float, like bodies, hammocks, duffel-sacks, and especially anything that looks like ship's papers. We will work downstream from the 'Kestrel' as our best chance.'

Yet even as they started their grim tasks, figures were looming out of the night and looking for prizes for themselves. In a strange, black silence, the occasional sound of lapping water marked the recovery of some Lancashire sailor's property by a local peasant. For a moment, John Weaver found his thoughts returning to the varied garments on sale in the Lancaster market, which tomorrow would be on Prussian backs.

As the early, summer dawn lightened the eastern horizon the three men wearily examined the few items they had managed to haul from the dark waters. They had found three bodies, only identifiable by their remnants of clothing. Unable to lift them from the water they could do no more than utter a brief prayer. But several sailor's bags had been retrieved, mostly just containing saturated clothing. Some of the clothing they bartered with the scavenging peasants in return for documents and books. The captain collected into one bag any papers, books or items which could have any practical value or interest. By a curious coincidence, John Weaver's duffel bag was fished out of the water close to the wreck, although the contents had be partly burned and soaked with water. His precious, hand-written pilotage book was burned across one corner, and saturated. However, it seemed worth placing in the meagre pile which represented their worldly goods.

Later in the morning, as the summer sunshine warmed the air and dried the clothes on their backs, they found a large, three-masted ship called 'Laguna'. There were no sailors visible from the quayside, and the towering masts and lofty yards carried no flags or ensigns. Further inspection revealed the poor state of the ship. Her old timbers were grey and cracked, and two gaping ports had been cut in her quarters, each side of what once had been a graceful square stern. In many places the bulwarks had been cut away, so that a clear opening to the upper deck would give no protection from the sea in heavy weather. Captain Cooper turned to his two companions.

'Keep out of sight while I find out what our chances are. I think this is a Liverpool ship, but it might have been sold by now. Keep out of the way, but keep a look-out for any of our old crew, who may yet be alive and looking for help.'

He crossed the gangway, and found himself on a deserted deck. To his professional eyes, the condition of the ship appeared even worse at this level. Standing rigging was clearly hopelessly lacking in proper care. Iron parts were rusted, shrouds were slack and ratlines, which formed the footholds for climbing aloft, were missing or hanging loose. The running rigging was not made fast or coiled up, but lay in tangled heaps. He could see where deck cargo had been carelessly loaded so that running rigging was trapped behind tons of timber. He walked up the chaotic deck to the companionway which led to the accommodation.

'Ahoy, below. Anyone aboard?'

He knew better than to descend uninvited, so he waited on the silent deck. After several minutes he heard a voice from below deck.

'Who's on deck? Show yourself, man.' The mysterious voice was certainly English, but not the least friendly in its tone. The captain stepped to the top of the narrow stairway. He called into the darkness below.

'I'm Jonathon Cooper, ship's doctor. I'm looking for an English ship. Can you help?'

'Wait there, Sawbones. I'm up in a minute.'

Presently, the sound of a person climbing up the companionway with much wheezing and coughing announced the arrival on deck of a startling figure. He was a large, heavily built man, who, at first glance, appeared red. His hair, his face and the huge beard which seemed to grow sideways and downwards in unkempt profusion were all bright ginger or red. In addition, his hands and bare arms were the colour of mahogany, but covered in red hair. His smock had once been blue but now was covered in stains, and there appeared to be more paint on his clothing than on the ship itself. His rheumy eyes looked suspiciously at the visitor.

'And where have you come from, ship's surgeon? I don't see any ships in this drain which merit the attention of a quack.'

'Well, sir, I was travelling on the brig 'Kestrel' which you may have seen, caught fire yesterday. I am anxious to return to England as soon as possible.'

'Ha! I bet you are! You bloody murderer! I know what you boys were up to. Gunpowder for King Wilhelm, eh? Making a few sovereigns on the side, and now you've blown up. Well, hard bloody fortune, Doctor!'

The captain listened calmly to the torrent of abuse.

'You misunderstand me, sir. I was travelling purely as a passenger, but I was paid one shilling to make me a member of the crew. I knew nothing of the ship nor her business. Forgive me, sir, am I addressing the Master of this ship?'

'You are, sir. Captain Emmanuel Hotblack, of the ship 'Laguna'.'

'Then, Captain, may I ask for your brotherhood to a fellow-traveller to give us the opportunity to work our passage back to England?'

'Us? Has our doctor suddenly multiplied into a hundred, a thousand? You have me frightened by your numbers.'

The mocking figure pretended to shrink from supposed superior forces.

'No sir, we are no threat, I do assure you. I have two able seaman, who, like me, are looking for a passage home. We think we are the only survivors of the disaster.'

'And how did you survive? Even from this distance I would have said every mother's son would perish in that inferno. I expect you were whoring in some tart's filthy bed while your captain was paying his just dues to the Almighty. What do you say to that?'

'No, Captain. My interest ashore was to study the flora of this coast. The plants, flowers and grasses, you understand.'

'Yes, yes, I know what flora is, Doctor. Sounds as if you had the good fortune to be picking the flowers at the right time. Well, I lost my ship once and was pleased to find a friendly berth from the Brazils to Liverpool, so I owe my Maker a debt. I will examine you and your companions and sign you on as deck men. But, you'll have to work, by God, you will. I've lost five crewmen, deserted ashore, the scum. I've got fifteen Merseymen to drive this dying hull home to Liverpool, so a few free hands will be welcome by everyone. Can you cook?'

'Cook? What, in a galley? Cook the crew's grub?'

'That's right. I'll sign you on as cook, and let's see what your shipmates are made of. Bring 'em on board. We're getting out of this place by the end of the week if there's as much as a breath of wind from the East. We will be overloaded by then. It's a fine thing when the timber in the cargo keeps the ship afloat!'

Jonathon Cooper looked around the dishevelled ship, at the tangled rigging and the piles of timber.

'I don't see your crew preparing for sea. Are they ashore?'

Captain Hotblack glowered at him.

'Ashore? Afloat? What's the difference? Drunken louts, probably sleeping with a gutful of Russian firewater or stinking of their accursed beetroot. They calls it 'borscht' or similar. Disgusting muck, but your scouse sailor likes it. I give 'em all the time they want in this hole, because, when this ship gets to sea, no one sleeps! Today they can strain their backs to pump their fat Russian tarts, because on Sunday, with a few prayers to the Almighty, they'll break their backs on 'Laguna's' pumps. Aye! Pumping for their very lives! Takes a sailor's mind off the women better than anything I know.'

His observation was accompanied by a bellow of a laugh, which rapidly turned into a choking cough. He tottered to the ship's side and spat into the water.

*

When the 'Laguna' sailed her crew went about their tasks with a quiet resignation. They viewed their three newcomers with complete lack of interest. When the time came to work aloft, setting sail from the neglected yards, it became clear that the ship did not carry a full suit of sails. The ship seemed to manage with topsails on all three masts, two topgallants, with a fore-and-aft spanker on the mizzen. A couple of triangular staysails completed the suit. The effect of this unusual spread of streaked, grey canvas was to make the ship hard to steer. With the timber piled as high as a man on the deck, lower sails would have been difficult to handle. But, as Captain Hotblack had predicted, the pumps were manned nearly every minute of the day and night. The sullen, uncommunicative crew seemed to have become accustomed to the continuous wheezing of the pumps and the wearying turns, hour and hour about on the pump handles at the foot of the mainmast.

As the grey outline of the ship sailed sluggishly towards Denmark and the hazards of the channel between Copenhagen and the shores of Sweden, they left astern the aftermath of the explosion.

In the town of Memel, throughout the following days, the militia were busy rounding up suspects, many of whom knew no more than the evidence of their own eyes, or caught with a few scraps of cargo salvaged from the wreck. Ironically, the wagon which had carried the two casks of gunpowder was once again pressed into service. A protesting crowd of foreigners, petty criminals and nameless peasants were rounded up and executed by an uncouth firing squad against the bare stone walls of the strange, desolate fortification set above the sand dunes. The last prisoner to die was named 'Michel Le Renard' and cried 'Co–te que co–te' as the fusillade of musket-ball shattered his breastbone.

Chapter 13

He swung himself off the big horse with surprising agility for a man of his bulk, and turned to help his companion dismount.

'I thought you mariners were well used to clambering aloft and alow. Here, put your foot on the wall, and then swing the other foot down on to the ground.'

Eventually, John Morgan stood upright and wiped his brow with a dark blue kerchief.

'Never did like horses, Mr Hindle. Unpredictable creatures, I'm told.'

As he spoke he reached across to untie the large brass telescope which had been strapped to the saddle. From where the two men stood at the side of the track, the city and coast were spread out below them, extending into the evening dusk. Far out to sea, the last golden light before sunset filled the narrow band between the mantle of cloud and the horizon, and was reflected from the flat calm waters of the sea and the river.

'I could imagine the Almighty had turned the cold grey waters of the Lune and the Bay into pure gold. A long way from the reality of the matter, Mr Hindle.'

The mariner rested the brass telescope across the convenient back of his horse and adjusted it to examine the distant estuary and sea. He examined small boats in the deeper waters at the middle of the estuary, and larger ships secured to the pier at Sunderland Point. Closer still, he could see the masts and yards of ships lying alongside at Saint George's. and the New Quay. Apart from spiralling columns of smoke from the homes crowded round the dominant castle, the autumn evening was crystal clear, the mountains across the bay seemingly within hailing distance.

'Well, Captain, what d'you see?'

'Very little, with the tide so low. The bay is more sand than water tonight. Not much moving out there.'

'And beyond?'

The Captain adjusted the telescope, and slowly scanned the sharp, dark line of the horizon from the low shadow of Walney, possibly twenty miles away, to the open sea southward. Nothing seemed to occupy the glittering sea. Then, precisely coinciding with the end of the land he saw the first sign of the mysterious ship. A glimpse of a vertical line, insignificant, almost invisible at the great distance, yet representing a possible threat to the commerce of the city.

'I've got him, Mr Hindle. Standing just off Walney, without a breath of wind, I should say. But he's there alright.'

He lowered the telescope from his eye and polished the lenses as he questioned his companion.

'Why are your Commissioners suspicious of him, Mr Hindle? Could be anything, even a Britisher frightened of the shoals, and wanting to enter the Bay.'

'Well, Captain, that's easily said. The message we got at the Commissioners was that the fishermen out from Furness had approached the ship. She was flying our ensign and one of the fishermen tried to sell his catch to them. But no one could speak English, and one of the sailors threw down a Dutch guilder in payment for a basket of fish.'

'So, how are we going to settle this? Wait for ever, and see our traders turn to Liverpool for their merchantmen? That one ship could lose us our trade for a month or a year.'

'I agree. We've now got three ships waiting to sail, twenty cannon between the lot of them, most never fired a shot in anger. Let me tell you my idea.'

As the Clerk to the Port Commissioners outlined his plan, the Captain continued his examination of the distant vessel through the telescope.

'We've got three ships in the river almost ready to sail, the smallest one hundred and thirty tons, all fully laden, wanting eight or nine feet of water at least. If we get them out of the river on the point of high water, with the wind anywhere except westerly they could show a clean pair of heels rounding Fleetwood and Rossal Point. But I want our visitor to sample our hospitality. If you took your 'Esperance' across to Walney, as if you were making for Whitehaven you could tempt our guest to come and take a close look at you.'

The Captain looked with deep suspicion at the portly Clerk.

'Let him blow 'Esperance' out the water? While the West Indies Traders earn their fortunes? Five hundred black boys and girls and fifty casks of tobacco homeward sounds a good deal to the Commissioners of the Port of Lancaster, in exchange for the destruction of the fastest brig on the whole coast!'

'There, Captain, you have missed the import of my plan, and hopefully, so has Johnny Frenchman. Stood out there, waiting for the wind, tempted by a fat brig, all sails set, flags flying. What a juicy morsel. And so, like a French lover he glides over to look at his English rose, a Lancastrian Rose. Better still. But you, Captain anxious to protect your precious virginity....'

The Captain interrupted Mr Hindle.

'By God, Mr Hindle, I think you can tell your Committee we've got a plan. But I'll need time to study the tides, and I need two or three more seamen, even just for half a dozen tides.'

'Soon arranged. And just one other thing, Captain. You'll need a good story. Put it about the harbour that you're sailing to Whitehaven.'

The Captain looked enquiringly at Mr Hindle.

'Does it matter? We'll be out and back in a couple of days, five or six tides at the most. Who cares why?'

'Because, Captain, there are plenty of strangers in town, listening to the talk amongst the sailors on the quayside.'

The mariner laughed.

'Have a difficult job getting the information out there' - he pointed to the ship on the horizon - 'before we are within hailing distance.'

'Is that what you think, Captain? And suppose I told you an unknown number of men stepped ashore at Heysham Head last night, stole five sheep, four bags of flour and a cask of ale, and at sunrise this morning all we could see were the signs of their boat having left the beach on the ebbing tide.'

'Probably just fishermen, Mr Hindle. Times are hard round the bay, as you know.'

'Except that they carelessly left an axe embedded in the door of the Crown Inn. 'Bolougne' stamped on the blade. And poorly made at that.'

Unimpressed, the Captain took a last look round the darkening horizon before struggling back into the saddle of the horse, the telescope rammed into his heavy pea-jacket. The two men rode back down the long hill into the darkening town, occasionally passed by more confident horsemen, all seeking the safety of the city streets before nightfall.

*

The 'Esperance' sailed with a handful of sailors gathered from the port with a cash advance of seven shillings and the prospect of being back in the river within a few tides. Mighty Jake relished the opportunity of some cash in his pockets after so long ashore. Working on the farms was not to his liking, and the shipyards on the Lune would only take on skilled shipwrights. A quick journey to Whitehaven to load coal for Lancaster seemed an easy way of keeping solvent.

His new ship seemed strange to Jake, the tall masts more than adequate for a relatively small hull. When clear of the estuary, Captain

John Morgan had his makeshift crew of fourteen setting sail as if he was sailing to the West Indies with a crew of forty.

The sailors watched the swelling canvas, thrusting the ship through the choppy water of the Bay at great speed. The Captain took the wheel from the seaman and finely adjusted the course, running before the North-Easterly wind, pointing closely to the distant headland of Walney.

Other sailing ships littered the Bay, but none seemed to carry such a cloud of sail as the 'Esperance'.

'Sail ahead!' called the lookout on the foredeck. The Captain had ordered that no man should remain aloft, so that urgent adjustments of sail could be made rapidly with the unpractised crew.

Nearer and nearer the speeding ship carried them to the mysterious vessel standing ahead with just topsails set. The Captain watched through his telescope and noted the row of black gun-ports. From her gaff fluttered a blue ensign, the union flag incorporated in the corner. He looked up at his own red ensign, hardly fluttering as the ship's speed so closely matched that of the wind. He put his telescope away as the two ships raced towards each other. He could see all he required with his practised eye.

Now it was clear he could pass astern of the visitor, with the land less than two miles away to starboard. As they drew within hailing distance the warship suddenly lowered her false colours and ran up a huge tricolour flag. At the same moment, the fore and mainsails tumbled from the yards and filled with wind. Gun ports were lifted and twenty cannon on the starboard side could be heard running out on their carriages. Captain Morgan had heard that thunder before and he knew what was to come. He knew the crouching gunlayers on the French ship would be at this moment sighting along the barrel of the aftermost cannon, waiting for the hull of the 'Esperance' to draw into view.

'Hard a-starboard! Man all braces!'

With a terrible thrashing of the canvas, yards swinging and sheet tackles whipping as the tension was thrust upon the opposite sides, the ship lost all way and seemed to spin before the wind. For a fearsome moment it seemed the ship would stand head into wind with her massive spread of canvas taken aback or flapping uselessly. But the ship's head kept swinging round until the sails could be trimmed as the ship settled on a south easterly course, the wind on her port beam.

The French ship, deprived of a good broadside, attempted the same manoeuvre but was already well astern of the fleeing British merchantman.

The chase across the bay was on.

'You, boy! 'yelled the Captain. 'Can you heave a lead?'

'Aye, sir!' shouted Mighty Jake, with pride.

'In the chains with you. Get sounding, and I want to hear it, loud as you can, or we're blown out of the water.'

The lead line was roughly coiled on a cleat on the foremast. Jake laid it on the deck before carefully re-coiling the line in his left hand. He climbed over the rail and wedged himself in the starboard shrouds and started to heave the lead, back and forth and then in a full circle swinging over his head, the lead weight just missing the tip of the foresail yard, then low over the skimming waves. At the critical moment he released his right-hand grip and the weight arced forward, plunging into the waves forty feet ahead of his position. He drew in the slack line as the ship sailed up to the point of impact. He read the marks off the vertical line.

The three tails of leather were barely clear of the water.

'By the mark Three!' he yelled with all the power of his narrow lungs.

The French ship was now in hot pursuit and Captain Morgan could see one of the officers in the bows eyeing the distance that separated them. Captain Morgan calculated the French captain would be anxious to avoid approaching the land too closely, but would expect to catch the English prize in the middle of the bay.

'By the deep and a half TWO!' screamed Jake.

Captain Morgan eased the ship slightly closer to the wind, but already the topsails were banging, occasionally backing against the mast.

'By the mark TWO!'

The 'Esperance' was now in intensely choppy water and seemed to be moving jerkily in the water. Captain Morgan bore away from the wind. Still the uneasy motion continued, the ship vibrating in the short, steep waves.

'By the mark TWO!' screamed Mighty Jake again, knowing the call represented just twelve feet of water for the ship to float in with safety.

A judder and a crack of canvas told every man on board the keel of the ship was now dragging across the sea bed, bringing the ship nearly to a halt. Every sail and rope was shaking, progress through the water was impossible to determine and the ship's head was swinging round towards the south, now pointing towards the distant shores of Fleetwood.

Then, like a hound slipped from the leash, the sea bed released its hold on the sliding keel and the ship leaped forward through the waves.

121

But fortune was not so kind to the pursuing Frenchman. The heavier ship was now completely stationary in the turbulent water and already the pressure of the wind was heeling the hull over. With the evidence his plan was succeeding Captain Morgan shouted over the stern towards the stranded ship

'Welcome to The Mort Bank, Frenchmen!' He rubbed his hands with satisfaction. 'See how you look after four more hours of ebbing tide! You'll be able to walk ashore from your starboard gun-ports!'

Already the boats would be setting out from every inlet round the Bay and the militia would be looking for boats to take them out to the rich prize.

Steering South before the wind, Captain Morgan set about reducing sail. As the canvas was furled the speed through the ebbing water decreased until, with a smart turn on the helm, 'Esperance' headed up into the wind, with the fore-topsail the last to be furled.

'Let go starboard anchor!'

As the ship gently settled back on her cable, the captain viewed the grounded Frenchman, already starting to list as she was driven harder onto the shoal and the wind pressed against her exposed hull. The French sailors could be seen aloft wrestling with the useless, thrashing canvas.

Captain Morgan shouted into the wind funnelling down through the Westmoreland hills. 'Bon soir, mes amis. Dormez bien!' He turned round and saw Mighty Jake securing the running rigging. 'Boy!' he called.

Jake ran down the deck, his bare feet almost silent on the timber.

'Were you the boy on the lead-line?'

'Aye, sir.'

'Well, boy, you did a good day's work today. You've earned a share of the prize, young man.'

*

Off Fleetwood, the 'Nancy' was also at anchor, unaware of the excitement a few miles to the north. She was waiting for wind and tide to carry her up the River Lune to Lancaster with the huge timber piles and the planks which were essential to construct the coffer dams. Timber was going to be critical in the construction of all the bridges and aqueducts along the route of the canal, and most of it would be imported. The hundreds of tons of stone were already being dragged out of the Westmoreland Quarries and stock-piled at convenient points.

John Rennie decided to start work on the aqueduct from the southern side of the river, being the most convenient to reach from the city. With his Agent, Alexander Stevens, detailed specifications for the structure of the five great arches were agreed. Each semi-circular span of seventy feet rested on great stone boat-shaped piers, nearly seventy feet long and sixteen feet wide. As the citizens came to watch the preparations for this great construction, it seemed highly unlikely that it would ever be practical to carry the canal so high above the river, especially as the land on the city side of the river was low-lying for a hundred yards or more, and would presumably require an embankment of massive proportions to match the height and majesty of the aqueduct.

Councillor Redfearn seemed to gather more critical allies to his cause as the work made its first impact on the natural countryside and the fast-flowing rivers. The unhappy coincidence of the French declaration of war and the start of the canal was not lost on even the most reasonable of critics, nor on the committee.

Samuel Gregson, Clerk to the Committee reported to them.

'I am concerned that the rising cost of materials being imported from abroad is further aggravated by the reluctance of some shareholders to pay their due calls for cash. Some people seem to be getting cold feet, yet we are busy recruiting labourers, all of whom need paying.'

Another member of the committee turned anxiously to Samuel Gregson.

'I'm told that elsewhere in the country work has stopped on building because of rising costs.'

'Well, gentlemen, if you have any thoughts in that direction you had better voice them now because tomorrow will be too late. On the aqueduct alone over two hundred men are labouring round the clock to take advantage of low tides to work on the river bed and high tides to bring materials upstream from the quays. The tides are not controlled by the committee.'

Uneasily, they agreed that work should proceed as planned and with the utmost urgency.

From Liverpool, news arrived that the first prize, a French merchantman named 'L'Agreable' had been taken by a Liverpool privateer, with a prize value of about £10,000, and Captain Morgan's exploit in grounding the French frigate had made everyone feel the war was easily managed by brave men. This also gave the committee confidence in calling for essential merchant ships to sail alone. The alternative was to wait for convoys to be assembled, invariably at the behest of Liverpool owners. Even from Leghorn, special materials were at this moment on ships sailing through the Mediterranean, unescorted, to meet the demands of the Lancashire bridge-builders.

To make the best use of available materials and labour, the first successful contractors set their labourers to work on a number of short stretches of the cut, so that each of perhaps a dozen sections were working outwards from twenty-four faces. The initial trench was twenty feet wide and seven feet deep, unless at that depth the ground was still found to be unstable. The towpath was levelled, on the western side of the cut, except in the crowded confines of the city, where the path had to be levelled on the landward side. When possible, a finished section would be filled with water by redirecting a convenient stream, so that materials could then be moved either by barge or wagon towards the working faces. Much of the rock hacked out of the 'cut' was set on one side, to be dressed and cut by the stonemasons for building bridges and canal banks. Samuel Gregson had ordered a fleet of timber barges from Mr Brockbank's yard, each sixty-eight feet long and fourteen feet nine inches beam. The agreed cost for each was two hundred and forty-six pounds and fifteen shillings.

The Committee had been somewhat less than generous in the pay for labourers engaged on such a great enterprise. Councillor Redfearn had doubted whether sufficient men would be found to work for half a crown a day, nor a stonemason for three shillings. Yet, to his chagrin, the work proceeded with surprising speed, and, at first, with adequate labour and quality of work. But as the canal progressed, and the contractors could see opportunities for saving money against their contracted price, so the craftsmanship suffered and even the line deviated from that surveyed. A saving on an embankment or a cutting beyond that determined by the surveyor, who had to consider the ownership of the land, produced legal difficulties which took time and money for the Committee to reconcile. Tempers flared between the contractors and the committee, the former generally trying to get a section puddled and filled with water before the latter could insist on re-alignment or inspection of the work done.

As the days shortened and the autumn skies darkened, the open workings of the canal became more difficult to manage. The soil turned to heavy mud and the tracks used for transport round the sites became more treacherous. In the city, the rain at least served to flush the streets before they, too, became difficult to use.

Joshua Weaver was making his weekly rounds, keeping up-to-date with the comings and goings in the port. By the middle of the day he was at his usual table in the coffee-house, comparing notes with shippers, brokers and one of the insurance underwriters who was daily looking for business in the congenial surroundings of the smoke-filled room.

One of the small boys who earned a living as a messenger, came through the door, and in a high pitched, childish voice, called,

'Message for Mister Weaver. Mister Weaver, please.'

'Here, boy. I'm Weaver.'

'Mister Weaver, sir. You are to go to Councillor Redfearn's rooms this instant, he says, sir. Them's his words, sir.'

'Good lad. Get yourself a hot cup of chocolate. Suzie! Chocolate for my messenger.'

As he got up to leave he flicked a coin towards the lad, who caught it deftly and immediately pushed it into his boot-top.

Weaver hurried through the rain to the office which overlooked the Market Square. At the top of the stairs an elderly clerk in a drab frock coat was bending over a high desk occupying one side of the dark room. He looked up at Joshua's approach.

'Mister Weaver, the councillor is waiting. Go straight in, please sir.'

He ushered Joshua through a door which led into an equally forbidding office, dark in the autumn gloom, three walls lined with rough wooden shelves which were filled with ledgers and deed boxes, each one bearing the name of a company or individual, many well-known to Joshua Weaver.

Before he could make any greeting, the councillor was pushing a large, heavy envelope towards him.

'Sit down, Weaver, and study that.'

Joshua felt a surge of anger at the brusque manner of his host. Nevertheless, he could sense unease in the air. He loosened his cloak and took the proffered chair. The envelope in his hands was more like a flat canvas bag, heavily stitched round the edges. Various labels had been glued to both sides of the bag, but at first glance they made little sense.

He opened the flap at one end of the bag and reached inside. The documents he pulled out were all written on heavy paper. He carefully spread them out on the desk. The first one had been sealed with red wax, which had been broken. Joshua carefully unfolded the heavy paper and suddenly felt the chill hand of doom on his shoulder as he slowly read the uneven, sloping writing.

To the Lancaster Owners Committee from yr servant & Agent Felix Popov, Gentlemen, Be you hereby informed yr brig named Kestrel of the City of Lancaster has this day been declared a total loss by cause of fire deemed an Act of God Almighty, being lost with all hands in a disaster in the port of Memel in the Kingdom of Prussia, this day being the twenty eighth day of July in the seventh year of the reign of King Freidrich Wilhelm the Second of Prussia, the year of Our Lord one thousand seven hundred & ninety-three. Do you take note that the mariners of this ship, believed to number twenty-four souls have no known resting place save that of the Sea, except for the mortal remains of four of their number who have been laid to rest in land decreed for this purpose without the walls of the city. Do you also take note that costs and duties levied by the Kingdom of Prussia and the City of Memel will become due within one month of this assessment being made and despatched to you.

Joshua Weaver looked up from the handful of documents he clutched in his shaking hands.

'Do you realise my son John was on that ship? My only son, killed in a foreign country and even now, decaying in the waters of the Baltic? Do you realise that, Councillor?'

He was shouting with anger and overwhelming grief. Councillor Redfearn came round the desk and awkwardly laid a hand on Joshua's shoulder, as if to comfort him.

'Keep calm, Weaver. There's another document in your hand, which at present I don't fully understand. Look.'

He took the papers out of Joshua's hand and sorted through them.

'Here, this is the one. From the Liverpool ship 'Laguna'.'

The message was brief and obviously designed to conceal the truth from prying eyes. Joshua read 'The barrel-maker and the cloth-maker and one more have lost their bird of prey and sailing by the Moon.'

'Now, Weaver, I don't want to create uncertain hopes, but I take that to mean Cooper, Weaver and a seaman have left the Kestrel and are returning to the River Lune. But I don't know why they should be so secretive. If they are being held against their will, or if they are being hunted because of the fire, this may be necessary.'

Joshua looked the councillor straight in the eyes.

'You know what 'destroyed by fire' means, don't you? That will have been the gunpowder. That's why any survivors are in hiding.'

'And why, if anyone mentioned that unpleasant fact, our insurance would be void. Our esteemed agent has been skilful in establishing the loss due to fire. But he may not know we have survivors. Perhaps they did not contact Popov after the loss.'

'More likely Popov was keeping out the way, if it really was the gunpowder. Perhaps the last person he wanted to see was Captain Cooper. Either of them could have been incriminated by the unfortunate truth.'

Joshua Weaver shook his head in sorrow.

Councillor Redfearn looked at him with sympathy.

'However we handle it, we're going to lose a lot of money out of this disaster. God knows what payments we've got for our export, plus the cost of the ship. By winter the widows will be knocking at my door asking for their dividend and compensation.'

'Then, councillor, that will finish me. I'll not mince my words. I'll be broken by this. But get my boy home, and I'll worry about these other matters afterwards.'

'Well said, Weaver. I'll try and get more information, and we'll call a private meeting of the Lancaster Owners at the end of next week. May we again use your house?'

'Yes, but I assume only you and I know of these facts. I will certainly not tell my wife until we know more. At least she has our young friend Jake to keep us busy.'

As Joshua returned to the docks he was surprised to see a commotion outside one of the inns. A small crowd had gathered, either to watch or to join in a struggle between two or three men on the wet roadway. As he drew closer one of the noisy crowd broke away and ran furiously past Joshua, and turned towards him to shout 'Hawks Abroad!' with his gasping breath.

Joshua heeded the warning and crossed to the other side of the road and slid into the welcome shadows. The dreaded Press Gangs were in town.

Chapter 14

Through the darkening autumn evening, the day's rain had turned the roads to muddy tracks, keeping wise people within doors. Joshua's hurried walk back to Ryelands was made even more depressing by the violence he had witnessed in the harbour. Until today Lancaster had mercifully escaped the worst depredations of the ruthless Press Gangs, but as the war progressed and the demand for young men grew, so the search widened. With ships of the Royal Navy in the Mersey and lying at anchor off Fleetwood, the Press Gangs knew where they could earn a good bonus with prompt payment.

In the past, warnings had generally been effected by ringing ships' bells, even on the partly built hulls waiting to be launched on the Green Ayre slipways. The alarm call 'Hawks Abroad' was not a common cry in Lancaster. But today's seizures had been a complete surprise. None of Joshua's contacts in the port had made any mention of the threat, yet by tomorrow some Masters would be finding their best seamen missing.

As he made his way home he considered the life which the Impressed men would find awaiting them. Apart from the relentless discipline and cruel punishment, he knew their wages could drop from the three pounds per month and twenty shillings paid to their families while they were abroad. This could be four or five times what they would be paid in the service of the King. It was widely understood naval pay had not been reviewed since being set in the time of King Charles II. Unlike the merchant ships, where the Masters and Owners both depended on getting reliable crews, where a thousand ships a month were sailing from the Mersey, all required skilled crews. The unpredictable hazards of wind and tide would be multiplied tenfold if experienced men were not available.

His thoughts had wandered from his immediate problems, but as he turned into the gateway of his house his troubles suddenly weighed heavily upon him. When Sarah Weaver opened the heavy door, she immediately sensed the tension which caused him to avert his gaze. He wearily drew off his mud-stained boots and his wet cloak, which his wife hung by the open kitchen fire.

'Sit down, Joshua. You look exhausted. Is the harbour so bad? Or have you heard nothing of our son? Is that the heavy black hand on your heart?'

Joshua looked straight at his calm, re-assuring wife, who had stood resolutely beside him all the years as he slowly built up his business and reputation. Now he felt he was about to reward her unquestioning loyalty with a single, destructive blow.

'We have confusing messages about the 'Kestrel'. And even more confusion about her crew. Let me tell you all I know, and you shall be the judge.'

He related the message about the ship being on fire, without making reference to the loss of the crew.

'We have also a message which seems to say that the Captain and our John are not with the ship, but perhaps making their own way home.'

'John? Are you saying our John is not with the ship?'

She seized her husband sleeves.

'How would you expect them to get home from... where are they, Russia? St Petersberg is it? How does an English boy get home from there? Walk across France?' Her voice was trembling with emotion.

'No, my dear. We think some of them may be on a British merchantman called the 'Laguna'. I have sent a message to Liverpool to speak to the owners of that ship. We can but wait. Where's Jake tonight?' he asked as casually as he could.

'Oh, he's working on the river. I think they're hauling the big timbers up to that great bridge. He has to work with the tides, I understand.'

His wife started serving the meal, in complete silence. When they sat down to eat, she turned to her husband and laid a hand on his sleeve.

'What really is the truth about the 'Kestrel'? How can it be that some may have survived, yet you don't know who? What about the ship and the cargo? That must present many different problems. Will you receive payment from the insurers?'

'We hope so. With the war and so many ships in difficulties, payment is not going to be either prompt or adequate. Of that we can be sure.'

The lamps burned low, the candles guttered in their sticks and the dark, rain-streaked night closed round the silent house. Joshua Weaver and his wife made no comment but each was waiting and praying for the safety of their son, and, more immediately, for the return of Mighty Jake, who had become like their own son. From his first visit, with the three gold coins, Jake had always brought surprises and excitement to the house. Now they awaited his return from the town with unspoken fear.

When the loud, persistent knocking broke the dark silence, Joshua inwardly knew what the urgency heralded. He drew back the two heavy black bolts and swung open the door. In the darkness he discerned the frightened face of Jed, his next door neighbour, who farmed the meadows between the houses and the river bank.

'Joshua, thank God you're awake. Young Jake has been taken by the Press Gang!'

Joshua pulled the excited farmer into the kitchen and closed the door behind him. Sarah Weaver joined the two men.

'What are you saying, Jed?' asked Joshua, as calmly as he could.

'Why, Joshua, I was travelling late. All day at Preston market, and slow riding home. When I got to Galgate, I couldn't believe my eyes! The Press Gang had stopped the stage coach, I suppose it was the Lancaster stage, and were pulling passengers off like pigs in the market. Shouting and screaming, calling for 'the King's loyal men to join the fleet', the women screaming, an old man raising his stick and they near clubbed him to death.'

Joshua was pouring out a mug of red wine which he handed to the exhausted man, who continued his account of terror.

'At the side of the road was a covered wagon, and your boy Jake shouted to me from the back 'Tell Sarah Weaver I'm here, and safe with the Navy.' As he said this he held his hands above his head, just long enough for me to see the ropes round his wrists. There were some marines in the back with muskets. That's all I could see.'

He drank deeply of the wine.

'Jake, I swear I rode here as fast as the mare would carry me. They had a crew of men and boys there, maybe a dozen or more. That's a bad deal, Joshua.'

He relapsed into silence while Sarah gave him a piece of chicken and a piece of bread. After a moment's consideration he turned to Sarah Weaver.

'Don't worry, Sarah. Your boy Jake can give a good account of himself wherever he lands. He'll be alright, just you believe me.'

'Dear Jed. Don't you worry yourself. You've been a good neighbour this night. Finish your wine and get home safely to Marie and give her our love.'

As they closed the door behind the heavily shrouded figure, Joshua reached out and embraced his wife. In the silence he sensed the softness of her body, wracked with deep sobbing. For many long, painful minutes he held her, each supporting the other. In a matter of a few hours they had suffered the cruel triple blows of nameless doubts; an impenetrable fog of the unknown enveloped the fate of their son, their adopted son and their own modest riches. Only tears and darkness filled their staring eyes that night.

*

In the morning, the city was alive with news of the Press Gangs. They had seized young seamen straight off ships alongside St George's Quay, and had waited in one of the dockside taverns for men who had been working away from their ships. Stories abounded concerning the tricks employed to trap the unsuspecting mariners into the Royal Navy. Offers of favours from big-breasted women had enticed more than one to an upstairs room. As the sailor eased down his breeches he found his arms pinned to his side and the King's shilling pressed into his hand. Any complaints, his jersey would be pulled over his head and he would be bundled out of the building 'drunk and disorderly'. But there had been many split heads and broken bones before the covered wagon was chased out of town. The comments round the coffee houses reflected this anger and despair.

'The Navy has two ships off Fleetwood, and we've sent the Mayor and the Chairman of the Port Commissioners by carriage to try and board one of the ships and demand the return of our seamen.'

'Ha! You'd do better to go to St Mary's Priory and ask for God's Deliverance.'

Joshua found it hard to give his mind and energy to his business, with concern for the young men never far from his thoughts. Only Matthew Redfearn knew about the loss of the 'Kestrel', but Joshua realised it would soon be common knowledge round the port, after which, questions would demand some very difficult answers.

Lying at anchor in the estuary was the captured French ship, 'Requin' which had been taken as a prize by the skilful seamanship of Captain Morgan in the 'Esperance'. When the French officers were questioned by magistrates it was discovered that the ship had been on station in the West Indies for two years and was returning to Antwerp. Having assumed the Channel would be crowded with British ships, the young captain decided to take the northern channel. An adverse wind tempted him to look for a prize-ship in the tranquillity of the Bay. He could reflect upon his misjudgement in the peace of Lancaster Castle while waiting to be exchanged for some British prisoners taken on Declaration of War from British merchantmen in Brest.

The ship itself was available for sale, but under the Navigation Act, a heavy additional duty had to be paid, to protect British shipbuilders. Consequently, the ship swung with the tide and the prize crew could do no more than pump the bilges.

The delegation sent to recover the Impressed seamen from the Royal Navy ships off Fleetwood had been humiliated by the Senior Captain of the Squadron. The Lancastrians were accused of failing to realise a war was being waged in Europe, and they were informed that in the South and East of England every able-bodied man and boy was liable to be pressed into service. The following day, the Town Hall rang with threats and promises that any press gang venturing into the city would be identified in good time, and warnings sent around the streets by ringing every bell in town, whether in church towers or the hands of street traders. It was also agreed that, like other ports in nearby Cumberland, a Rate per Ton would be levied as a Bounty, to be paid in lieu of men, to support the needs of a 'Triumphant Navy of England' if the call was made.

But, with the war nearly two years on, and the French attempt to close European ports to British ships, the Royal Navy was engaged in ensuring that the French ports, particularly Brest, were closed to prevent the French fleet putting to sea. Lancaster could still look to a continuing level of trade, her traditional markets keeping the traders and merchants busy. In addition, the opportunities offered by the Letters of Marque established the rights of privateers to operate under strict rules in prescribed areas of the High Seas. Joshua Weaver knew the local shipowners would be considering the advantages and costs of fitting out some of their ships to seize French merchantmen, with the chance of prize money far more bountiful than current freight rates. But he also knew the stories in the coffee houses of ships loaded with bullion and gold coins being captured by a daring privateer were hugely exaggerated. For some owners, the exemption from press gangs was the greatest advantage of being registered as a privateer.

But for Jake, jolted and shaken in the covered wagon, crowded in with a dozen cursing, frightened young men, his loyal service in trapping the French frigate was of no help to him now. After hours of darkness, the cold dawn broke as they were approaching the jetty at Fleetwood. On the hard stone quay stood a crowd of marines with their muskets held at the ready across their chests, marking a path towards an iron ladder which descended to the black water.

'In a line. Stand still and straight' shouted one of the marines.

The cold, shivering collection of men, dressed in an assortment of clothes, formed into some sort of straight line as the early morning wind whipped through their clothes. Two were barefoot.

'From the right, number!' The meaningless order produced a silence, except for one voice, which timidly called out 'Two'.

The marine became angry.

'Can't you Lancaster pigs even count?' He gave the order again, and, with mounting fear, the voice called 'Two', followed a moment later by a further voice, 'Three.' Jake called 'Four.'

Then silence.

The marine was red in the face. He stood barely a hand's breadth in front of the first boy, and punched him in the ribs once.

'One!' he bellowed across the bare quayside.

He took one pace to his right. Two punches. 'Two!'

And so down the line, punches, shout, punches, shout.

As he reached the end of the line, his assault was starting to make his young subjects fall under the rain of punches.

'To attention! Now we all know our numbers. Start again!'

Having successfully taught his class of fourteen the elements of numeracy and demonstrated the mindless stupidity of the lower deck, they were loaded in three waiting whalers and swiftly taken out to one of the two naval ships at anchor about half a mile off shore.

When they drew alongside the towering hull of the warship it appeared to Jake much bigger than any ship he had seen before. Up its black and white sloping side fixed wooden rungs gave access to the deck about fifteen feet above. He scrambled up and almost fell on to the deck. He was immediately surprised by how white everything seemed to be. The deck planks were scrubbed, smooth and white, the lower parts of the two masts were white, with red and black ironwork. In stark contrast, at intervals along each side, shiny black, squat cannons were secured, looking to Jake like sleeping monsters.

The deck seemed to be crowded with sailors, in a multitude of different uniforms. Orders were shouted all the time, men were heaving and straining, and to Jake's expert eye, the ship was being prepared for sea.

The fourteen pressed men once again were lined up, and numbers called. An officer, who looked the same age as Jake, about nineteen, was reading aloud from a leather-bound book, mostly unintelligible to his listeners, but references to loyally serving the Sovereign, his Lords, Officers and Appointees seemed to carry some import to Jake and one or two others. Then, in turn, they were handed a quill and told to write their signatures on the lower part of the open page. By the time Jake was handed the quill, the pages had crosses, a square enclosing a cross, and a circle struck through with a line. Jake dipped the quill in the ink-pot and wrote

      Mite Jake Temp.

          and handed the quill back to the officer.

'Are you a seaman?' he enquired.

'Aye, sir. Able seaman, sail-maker and leadsman.'

'Stand over there.'

When the ritual had been completed, four men had been added to Jake's group, and they were sent below for food, examination by the surgeon for lice, skin and genital diseases. Then they were each handed coarse white trousers, blouses and black pea-jackets. Everywhere they went seemed full, either of sailors, or stores. Barrels, casks, boxes and bundles seemed to be crammed into every space. Hammocks in nets, sails in long rolls, coils of new rope, and even spare lengths of timber were lashed down.

Each of the newcomers was allowed to either write a letter to his home or a friend ashore, or a junior officer would write it for him. As Jake waited he listened to two of his group who had been seized while they were herding some sheep. This meant that somewhere there was a meadow full of untended sheep, purchased just four hours before the men were taken, with their life's savings. One of the young men who had been dragged from the stage coach was on his way to Lancaster to buy a house in Heysham for his new wife. But no excuses were accepted, the only man sent ashore had a disease of his private parts which the surgeon said made him a hazard to the ship. Jake sent a message, which the officer wrote down, to Mistress Weaver, telling her he was safe and happy.

*

The frigate 'Hart' set her gleaming white topsails and headed gently northward into the Bay, and Jake, on the main topsail yard could see the Priory and the castle in Lancaster. The feel of a well-ordered ship was enough for Jake. Food, good companions and not too much cruelty would suit him.

In the approaches to the estuary the frigate anchored again, and all the crew, which seemed to number several hundred to Jake's untutored eye, were assembled on deck. An officer, who Jake assumed was the captain, was in earnest discussion with two other officers, and presently they started selecting men, almost like drawing teams for a game, thought Jake. Soon it became clear what the game really was. They were selecting a crew to take over the captured French frigate 'Requin', presumably to sail her into action as a ship of the Royal Navy. Jake was selected by the young officer he had spoken to before, and shortly three of the cutters were passing to and fro, taking the prize crew to their new charge. It seemed that the most that could be spared was one hundred men, including officers. Jake thought this sounded enough to sail round the World, but once the skeleton crew were assigned their tasks it suddenly seemed hopelessly inadequate.

On the deck of the 'Requin' everything appeared very strange. Having been sailing in the West Indies for many months there was evidence of damages, breakages and temporary repairs. The cannons on deck were streaked with rust, and this had also stained what had once been a smart wooden deck. The running rigging was grey and bleached by tropical sun and spray. Below decks the effects of running aground, causing the ship to heel, almost on to her starboard beam-ends, had been to throw loose items to one side. The handful of men who had been put on board to keep her pumped dry had given up their task, and water could be heard swilling from side to side in the orlop deck and lower hold.

As the essential work was allocated to the crew, the officers became more easily identified. Lieutenant Buckingham had been appointed in command, with one other lieutenant and a sub-lieutenant as his two watch-keeping officers. They were determined to get the ship ready for sea with the least delay, so that they could sail in company with the two British frigates. When the wind died down at sunset, the crew were sent aloft to set the sails, two at a time, so that the officers could see the condition and manner of the canvas. The crew could also learn the ropes. To take advantage of the calm weather, they worked until past midnight, first shaking out the sails from their yards and then taking them in and stowing them on top of the spars. Two sails were found in the sail locker and hoisted up to their yards, but found to be rotted, the seams ripping open immediately any strain came upon them.

At the same time, a continuous pump detail was kept employed, the dirty, sour water streaming across the deck and over the side, hour after hour.

By the time of high water the following day, which was just about sunset, the message came across that they must take advantage of conditions to weigh anchor and set sail to stand well off-shore. So, after hours of unrelenting work, the topsails were set and 'Requin' made a hesitant departure from the treacherous channels and shoals of the Bay. These had been the cause of her undoing, and now she carried in her weary crew the diminutive figure of Jake Tempest, whose skill with the lead-line had been one of the instruments of her capture.

Astern, in the city, fast disappearing into the darkness of the East, lost against the outline of the moors, melancholy families sat round flickering hearths, clutching terse notes of explanation, sorrowing over the dread absence of a breadwinner, a son, a lover, a reluctant loyalist to a distant King.

Chapter 15

Captain Emmanuel Hotblack looked aloft at the shabby collection of grey canvas which drove the weary, groaning hull of the 'Laguna' westward across the Baltic towards the Kattegat and the North Sea. Since leaving Memel he had accepted that the man posing as a ship's surgeon knew much more about ship management than he pretended. But Hotblack was beginning to enjoy the joke.

'Well, Doctor, which channel does the medical profession like to take out of the Baltic? The Sound and Kronborg, or The Great Belt?'

Captain Cooper played the same game.

'I would care not to see a ship of mine in the Great Belt. A wind change at the wrong moment could see you ashore in no time. And I believe the anchorages in the Sound are preferable in a blow.'

Hotblack laughed at the part Cooper was playing.

'Well done, Doctor. How about paying the Toll? I understand they pay less heed to English ships in the Great Belt. Could save your owners a purseful of money. Possibly beyond the ken of a doctor, eh?'

'Save a sovereign, lose a ship. Isn't that what they say in Liverpool?'

'Well, Doctor, this voyage, I think we'll try my route. What I like to do is make our decision when we reach Langeland. I know where we can anchor to wait for a favourable wind. A good, strong westerly can get us through the sixty miles in a day, mostly with sea room. Just pray for westerlies when you're mixing your potions.'

Since leaving port the crew had been reasonably well-behaved, and had got the ship into a semblance of good working condition. Additional sails had been repaired, giving a fair spread of canvas, but still without fore or main courses. John Weaver was surprised at the way such a run down ship and a motley crew each seemed to gradually improve once the ship was at sea. The bo'sun kept the men fully occupied, and at times the ship's progress was quite swift. Even the forbidding Captain Hotblack had become a calm, professional master. John could see the signs all round him that the 'Laguna' must once have been the pride of someone's fleet. His knowledge gained in the shipyards of Mr Brockbank and Mr Caleb Smith; oak and elm, capped with expensive mahoganies, single-piece lower masts, all bore witness to quality shipbuilding. Even below decks, elaborate panelling and decorative brass fittings, now dull and stained with verdigris, told the same story.

Now, in her present trade, in the hold and tween deck, huge timbers, particularly masts and spars, had been loaded through the holes cut in her stern, and the deck cargo included spars almost the length of the main deck, in places chocked up where the graceful curvature of the deck would not support the straight spars. Thus crossing from one side to the other could be an obstacle course.

John Weaver was readily accepted by the other members of the crew, and Albert Mutch, able seaman, kept them amused with his songs, which he claimed he had learned sailing with Captain Cook, and which no-one believed.

But the passage through the Great Belt, in a strong, rain-laden Westerly wind, made heavy demands upon the crew. The ship made a great deal of leeway, probably due to being very deeply loaded, and twice Captain Hotblack managed to claw successfully to the westward to clear the islands and shoals which littered the Sound. The ship had to be put about when sea room allowed for it, but poor progress was made, and at one point the 'Laguna' was heading South-South-West, directly away from the distant waters of the Kattegat.

On a later attempt, with the lee braces as tight and hard as iron bars, the ship squeezed tighter to the wind, putting water between herself and the lee shore, and making reasonable headway, but always towards the most difficult part of the channel, where islands and shoals limited the sea-room.

Then, without warning, the wind freshened and veered two points towards the North West. The rain slashed down upon the sails, suddenly taken aback and slapping uselessly against the masts. The great curtains of rain even flattened the wind-tossed waves for a moment. The willing crew clambered across the deck cargo to man the braces as the helmsman struggled to turn the ship 'through the wind' and hopefully draw ahead with the wind on her starboard side. Slowly, desperately slowly, the ship's head turned, the compass card swung through North, North-North-West and then stuck, almost head to wind, her modest spread of sail pushing her astern. The only salvation now could be found in the fore-and-aft sail on the mizzen, the 'spanker'. With every man who could get there to heave on the huge tackle, the sail was forced over to the port side, so that the pressure of wind would assist in turning the ship through the head-wind. But time was not on the side of the 'Laguna' in that bleak September dusk.

Even under the mounting wind the ship might have been saved had she not been driven astern with the result that the huge timber rudder was one of the first things to strike the sea bed. Within no more than a minute the ship was unsteerable, and now, with the stern held, like a hinge on a great door, the hull swung round.

'Let fly all sheets!' The captain screamed a desperate order, which would take all pressure of the sails. But it also meant the ship had no driving power whatsoever. The noise of thrashing canvas was like gunfire. The ship was spinning helplessly before the rising gale until arrested by the shallow shoreline. As the keel was pressed ever harder into the shoal the work-worn hull of the 'Laguna' began to settle at an angle on the windswept shore to the north of Halskov.

*

'Dear Lord Christ! I've had two ships perish under my feet in as many months!'

Captain Cooper was standing on the shore with the Captain and crew of the 'Laguna', watching the wind and waves driving the ship harder on to the pebbled beach. Every man had collected what he could of his own personal property before clambering over the sloping deck and swinging down to the waves breaking over the sand and stones. They had run a heavy rope ashore fore and aft, but could find nothing on the beach to which they could be secured. With every minute that passed, the chance of the ship floating off seemed ever more unlikely. As darkness fell it was decided by Captain Hotblack that Cooper should take three men and see what assistance or hospitality could be found in the nearby town, whose lights winked invitingly.

The small shore party found a rough track through the sand dunes, but after a few minutes met a party of men coming in the opposite direction, about ten of them, carrying lanterns, ropes and even a wooden ladder. Greetings were shouted but they understood no English. By signs they exchanged such information as they could, the Danish men explaining they could find shelter for the mariners. They all returned to the beach and took the Danes to examine the ship. They nodded and talked in low voices amongst themselves.

On returning to the town, the crew were taken to a farm, which had a huge stone barn, containing three horses, hundreds of bundles of hay and some sacks of grain. It was dry and free from draughts, and still carried the warm, inviting smell of summer. The only light was that which came through the open door. One of the Danes made it quite clear there must be no pipe-smoking or lanterns lit in the barn, explaining that it contained the entire stocks of winter feed for the farm. While the crew tried to find a place in the hay for the night, the local men promised to return with food and some blankets. Captain Hotblack, his red beard wet and bedraggled, took Captain Cooper to one side and stood outside the building, gazing into the stormy night.

'Do you know these folk at all?' he asked Cooper.

'Not really. I've docked on many occasions in Copenhagen and like the people there, but they're difficult to understand. A strange language.'

'Ah-ha! That's what you think. I can understand a word or two, and I can tell you, these boys are planning to unload as much cargo as they can as soon as the weather abates. And the truth of the matter is, I don't know what my rights are. I recall watching my countrymen salvaging the cargo off a wreck on Start Point, and I think there was nothing the owner could do to stop us.'

'Well, Captain, I don't like to be a bearer of bad news, but in my experience that hull will start splitting after a couple of tides. When that happens, we'll have the Devil's job keeping every scavenger in Denmark out of the cargo.'

'I agree. But those masts we loaded will be very difficult for anyone to handle. If you had seen the struggle, days and days of blocks and tackles, rollers and wedges, to get them loaded and secured, it makes me weep to think of them floating adrift for any Jack to take. The Admiralty shipyards pay mightily for those massive timbers.'

For once, the robust frame of Captain Hotblack seemed ready to fold under the strain of watching his ship settle on the beach. Cooper kept his silence. Presently, Hotblack seemed to draw renewed strength.

'D'you know, Mister Cooper, I've sailed half a lifetime on this ship, my first voyage as deck boy when my uncle owned her. Kowloon and London. Cape Horn, Good Hope, Bombay, everywhere there was a cargo to be loaded, 'Laguna' was there. Aye, a few hundred blacks have slept in those holds, over three hundred once, lost three, two jumped ship. Lord, there was some money in that.'

The Captain scratched his beard as he recalled the chequered history of the great dark hull which was settling fairly squarely on the windswept shore.

'A million miles left in her, if we had never seen this wretched Baltic Sea. Cold and bleak, warring Tzars and Emperors, I've had to suffer them all. But the ice is the most terrible, Cooper. You watch your ship, three months or more, within sight of St Petersberg, and then you hear the ice, squeezing every plank, every frame, until in the night, at its very coldest, you hear the timbers crack, oak as thick as your thigh, cracking like a ship's biscuit. That's what signs her death sentence...' His voice trailed off.

The two captains stood side by side in the night, sharing the vigil over the crippled ship, whilst the rest of the crew took advantage of the warm stabling on the edge of the town.

With sunrise, as the pigeons gently announced the tranquil dawn, the local folk turned out to see the strangers, some with loaves of nearly black bread, and one buxom woman with a stone jar of cow's milk, still warm from the first milking. The barn gradually became a centre of interest as the day began. Women teased the men in their coarse, sea-stained clothing, children laughed at the strangers' incomprehensible language, daring each other to ask questions in Danish just to hear the Mersey sailors' reply.

By noon, the last of the rain had given way to a gentle autumn day, the waves quietly lapping on the beach. The two master mariners returned on board and inspected the ship, and drew up plans to secure her while deciding what to do.

Their deliberations were interrupted by an English voice calling from the water's edge. The two men on the ship saw a man on horseback waving his broad-brimmed hat and calling to them. They descended by the rope ladder dangling over the side and waded ashore to meet the newcomer. He was tall, with fair hair, not wearing a wig. His clothes, whilst muddy from riding in the wind and rain, were obviously of good quality, his tall riding boots of polished leather. He was about thirty-five years of age, and spoke English with a quiet, confident manner. His pale blue eyes showed no surprise at the sight of the captain, red and unkempt.

'Am I addressing the ship's master?' His voice and language was nearly perfect English, but with unmistakable traces of a foreigner.

'Captain Hotblack, master of 'Laguna'. Doctor Cooper, my adviser.'

'A bad affair, gentlemen. I heard you were ashore, and felt I ought to offer my services. My name is Lars Nyborg, I have shares in several ships, but my interest is in trading. I have a desk here in Halskov and one in Copenhagen. Now, I presume you are carrying timber. Is that so?'

Hotblack was hesitant.

'Some timber, yes.'

'Well, I tell you what I propose to you.' His command of English was nearly perfect. 'As you know, tides here are not great, but in about ten days we should make a higher tide than today. If I can help you afloat I will buy your timber at a good price. Then you may look if you want to take your ship away...'

'You mean we could unload in harbour?'

'Why not, Mister Black? Perhaps we unload some timber here in Halskov to make the ship less heavy..er..lighter, do you say. We make her lighter, yes? Then do you think we carry your anchor by boat to well out to sea. Twenty men on the windlass, eh Captain?'

140

He could see that his proposals was having the effect of brightening Captain Hotblack's bristling countenance with every word he uttered. In his enthusiasm the Captain shook the Dane's hand vigorously.

'By God, Mister Lars, we can work together, can you and I. How about you, Doctor?' He winked broadly at his compatriot.

'I'll be pleased to join in the enterprise, if I may.'

Mister Lars Nyborg shyly nodded to the two Englishmen.

'Then, gentlemen, let us get to my bureau in Halskov and make our plans. And we can make a proper meal for all the fine English sailors before they fall in love with our girls.' The two captains looked at each other in astonishment and then burst into laughter.

'Sounds a fair exchange to us!'

*

Over the following days, whilst the captain anxiously watched tide and weather, one or two of the crew considered the possibility of making for Copenhagen overland, with the chance of joining a British-bound ship. Captain Cooper offered to stay with Emmanuel Hotblack to supervise the repairs to the 'Laguna'. It was possible the ship, less heavily laden, could complete the homeward journey to the Mersey after the necessary repairs, but to retain the present crew for such a contingency was too expensive to consider. By the Articles of Agreement their pay would have ceased one day after the ship ran ashore. Not unreasonably, this provoked a storm of protest from the men. Furthermore, one of their real fears was that landing in England far from Liverpool, perhaps on the East Coast, would leave them liable to the press gangs. Stories were already circulating that merchant ships entering the estuaries round Britain after maybe two years in the East Indies were having their best seamen seized and taken off in cutters, to serve in Royal Navy ships just about to depart to the West Indies or the American colonies.

Over the following days the crew divided into groups. Five seemed to like the friendly reception they had received from the people in the town, and decided to take a chance with the 'Laguna'. One even thought he would like to be a farmer in such a welcoming town. Most of the others decided to make a journey overland to Copenhagen, where they felt there was a good chance of getting aboard a ship, homeward or outward bound. John Weaver felt he was honour bound to stay with Captain Cooper. But Lars Nyborg had other ideas.

'I would like you to come with me to Copenhagen. There is much planning to be done there in my office, and a man with knowledge of taking ships to England is just what I require. With Mister Cooper's approval, you understand, I would like to offer you work in my office.'

When the Dane had left, Captain Cooper took John Weaver to one side.

'You're going to make a fine sailor, and if I can I will help you, either through your father's committee of owners, or when you have an offer like this. These people are very like the best of the English, and you could find yourself happily trading to England, so your family would still see you.'

John considered the offer. He thought of his mother, her only surviving child now permanently out of the home. He confided once again in Captain Cooper.

'Sir, I'm worried about my mother and father. I feel certain the loss of the 'Kestrel' will have a very serious effect on my family. I don't know what my father's share was, but I think he will have lost much of his money.'

'You've spoken a true word there, Weaver. Your father and I have lost heavily. And with the war, all expenses will rise. My suggestion is to let them know you are well and in good spirits, but in your place I would keep out of Lancashire until the loss of the 'Kestrel' has been forgotten.'

'How do I get a message home from here. It seems impossible.'

'This is what I have arranged with Mister Lars. A ferry boat sails regularly from Hamburg to Dover, and carries pouches for all the shippers and merchants. To make sure, we will all write our notes, each listing all the names who are safe. These notes will go on different ferries, to give the best chance of at least one getting to the Town Hall safely. So get to work with your letter, and mention that I am safe and seaman Mutch is safe and staying in Denmark to keep chickens with a Danish beauty. If he has a wife, that should make her flap her wings!' He laughed at the thought.

John Weaver climbed on to the outside of the coach, having seen how crowded the inside was. Lars had bought him a heavy, fur-lined coat and some breeches and shirts. They both sat amidst the luggage, out of earshot and away from the smell of the other passengers. In the autumn sun, despite the bumping and swaying of the coach, the ride was quite pleasant, and Lars pointed out the small villages and streams which were the only features of the almost flat countryside. Windmills were often the tallest feature of the gentle terrain. The road, whilst no better made than in England, seemed much easier for the horses to negotiate, with no difficult hills and valleys. Many of the streams had no adequate bridges, and then some of the passengers would get down, to cross on foot, whilst the horses struggled to pull the coach across and up the opposite bank.

Lars soon proved to be an amusing travelling companion, talking about his business and his family, and the plans he had for trading with England. He had spent a lot of time in England, learning banking and trading. He had realised the English language was going to be important, and checked his usage every few minutes with John. He addressed John as if he was already a business partner, and asked his opinion on the possibilities of trading with the western ports in England, like Bristol and Liverpool, 'The Gateway to America' as he called it. John described the activities at Lancaster, a new name to Lars. John explained that his father played a major part in the conduct of business in the port. Lars Nyborg rubbed his hands with pleasure.

'Excellent, excellent. Just what we need.'

The coach stayed overnight at a small town, where a very inadequate inn could only offer them a shared room with one other traveller. The room consisted of not much more than three benches against the walls, with a pile of blankets and sheepskins for warmth. A breakfast of cold meats and some dark brown bread with a mug of hot chocolate or a jug of ale was to see them through the day. When they had boarded, fresh horses drove the coach briskly through the sunlit morning.

The approach to Copenhagen was made along a coastal road through a town with its name, Koge, on the tall wooden signpost. John tried to pronounce the strange name. Lars laughingly explained it was called 'Ker' by the local people. Its small harbour was filled with ships, and the sea beyond, flecked by a fresh wind, was speckled with sails in all directions. From the remains of his pilot book, burned and stained, at the bottom of the bundle which contained all his possessions, John recollected the low-lying land at the northern end of the bay. And then, at last, the spires and domes of the city of Copenhagen could be seen rising above the low city ramparts. As the coach drew nearer, John's attention was drawn to a building on higher ground, well outside the city's defences. The road appeared to skirt the edge of a great wooded estate. He asked his travelling companion what they estate might be.

'That, my friend, is Fredericksberg Castle. One of the King's Residences. Be alert, now, we're nearly home!'

The carriage clattered over the cobblestones on the bridge across the canal which reinforced the massive ramparts around the city. At the end of the bridge a number of carts, wagons and carriages were waiting in line.

'This is the Western gate, called Vester Port. We all have to pay a toll to enter the city. Here we go, we're on our way. Welcome to my home town of Copenhagen. I hope you will enjoy it.'

To John's eyes the city seemed to be bursting with people, the streets crowded, men and women going about their business with apparent urgency. Some of the buildings looked like the stone houses at home in Lancaster, but many looked quite new, constructed with a mixture of red bricks and dark timber. Some of the street appeared to be built to a strict plan, straight and lined with identical houses. The carriage pulled up in a large square, surrounded by three-storey buildings with evenly-spaced gables. The weary travellers tumbled out of the carriage and waited while the two coachmen handed down the baggage and parcels from the roof. Most of the passengers seemed too tired to speak, but John couldn't contain his excitement.

'This is a very pretty town, Mr Nyborg. Many of the buildings look almost new.'

'Ah! My friend, many of these are what we used to call 'fire houses', built to a common design. When my father was a boy, much of the city was destroyed by fire, just like London in earlier times. So the king proposed a plan for the city. It didn't quite work in the way he would have liked, so once again we have many different designs, just sometimes they all seem to fit together.'

Lars led John across the square, and down one of the streets. He turned in at the third house, through an archway into a courtyard. Across the other side, a double door gave them access to an ornate entrance hall. Lars called out, and presently two women servants emerged, curtseyed briefly and took the luggage and the men's heavy coats. Then, from an upper floor, a woman's voice called down. John couldn't understand a word, nor the reply Lars gave, but followed him as he ran up the stairs, two at a time. John waited on the curving staircase whilst he heard hasty conversations and laughter. Lars turned.

'Please, Mr John, I am most rude. Welcome to my home. And may I introduce you to my sister, Eugenie. My dear, this is John Weaver, Captain's Mate, who has come to see our business and stay with us a few days.'

Eugenie held out her hand and nervously John raised her hand to his lips. Whilst not an action he had ever learned in his own home, he nevertheless felt the graceful woman would expect some particular formality.

'Lars, what a pleasant change to be introduced to an English gentleman.' She turned towards the nervous, blushing John.

'Mister Weaver, my brother spends so much time dealing with Prussians, and, oh! Dutchmen, who seem to think they own Copenhagen. They are so ill-mannered.' She turned and led the way into the drawing room. This gave John an opportunity to take a more careful look at his hostess. She had the same honey-coloured hair and blue eyes of her brother. She had delicate features, a small nose and softly pointed chin. Her hair had been tied back and elaborately dressed, which, to John's inexperienced eyes, looked as if it might have taken several days to arrange. He noticed her plain white dress, tightly fitted above the waist, then billowing out like a soft, silken sail. He had no way of assessing her age, and could only consider she was the most beautiful creature he had ever seen.

In the softly furnished drawing room John felt very out of place, his clothes coarse and ill-fitting, dirty and stained from the coach journey. He nervously sat on the brocade-covered chair which Eugenie indicated to him.

'Lars, you two have certainly been travelling, for days on end I expect. Look at you both! Like a pair of chimney sweeps. I'll tell Beth to get the tub filled.' She laughed at the obvious discomfort of her guest. Her brother was quite stern.

'You don't seem to understand, dear sister. Mister John has been shipwrecked and lost nearly everything he owns. We must buy him some clothes tomorrow. Tonight, I can lend him a robe.'

Eugenie laughed again and turned to John with an air of mischief, speaking in almost perfect English.

'Shipwreck? That sounds very frightening. You must be very brave. These great, tall sailing ships frighten me.'

Lars turned to John.

'Tomorrow we'll get you fitted up with new clothes, something suitable for the city. We can get your heavy weather clothes later on.'

Eugenie looked at the young man with a careful eye.

'You two ought to go to the Italian tailors near the port. I believe all the naval officers buy their uniforms there. Probably much better value than this side of town, where the prices are too high, for ladies dresses at least. Some of the dressmakers appear to think they are in Paris or even London.'

John turned to Lars with a helpless gesture of his hands. Lars chided his sister for her enthusiasm, and John tried to explain that he had no money whatsoever.

'Money? I can advance you money to buy clothes, don't think about it again.'

For the astonished and embarrassed John Weaver, life seemed to have taken a strange, almost unreal turn in the few brief weeks which had passed since his old world disappeared in the blazing wreckage of the 'Kestrel'.

Chapter 16

The following morning, in the soft autumn sunshine, Lars took John down to the harbour. The houses and business buildings in the city gave way to a long road, with tall, well-built warehouses on one side, moored ships crowding the quay the other. In some places the ships were moored two abreast, and in between, smaller boats were secured, sometimes just stern-on to the quay, sufficient to allow cargo to be man-handled up and down narrow gangways.

'Everybody looks very busy this morning,' observed John, assuming his most business-like air.

'John, my friend, we have never been so busy. Our trading with the rest of the World is at its best. The normally gloomy merchants refer to the past few years as 'The Halcyon Days.' I am sorry to say, John, that while your country has been fighting wars in France, in America and nearly everywhere else, Denmark has remained resolutely neutral. We carry everybody's goods in our ships and do not take sides. Some people think we are too small to fight wars and win, others think we will be dominated by the French or even the Russians one day. Meanwhile, our trading reputation and the skills of our merchant ships increases. So much of what you see is new, the buildings, the harbour and the ships. I think your ship 'Laguna' had seen better days.'

John, reluctantly, had to agree with the observations of his charming host.

Across the harbour, in the great naval dockyard, where the peaceful country kept its fleet of warships, John could see dozens of hulls, their purpose signified by the rows of black painted gun-ports in their sides. Most of the warships were a curious sight to a mariner, with their top-masts and all yards unshipped, so that the huge hulls just carried the bare poles of the main masts. At the far end of the distant harbour, an elaborate crane mounted on top of a stone tower, was at this moment cautiously lifting the mast out of a naval frigate.

The movement of cargo took preference over everything else on the quayside, and the endless procession of carts, hand-trucks and wagons, some drawn by four or more horses, their hooves scraping against the cobblestones, made even walking hazardous. A heavily-loaded wagon would never stop just to avoid a man on foot.

Lars led John through a wide, oaken door in one of the great warehouses. Early morning greetings were shouted across the bustling floor. Men with bills of lading and other documents hurried across to pass information to Lars. His position as manager of the trading operation was clear to see. John noted the way he was able to give prompt replies and positive responses to the many queries that were brought to him. They ascended one stairway to find an office which overlooked the quay and gave an unrestricted view of the ships in port. The walls of the office were covered in black-boards, and a clerk was continually making notes and amendments to the columns of names and figures. In one corner of the office there was an immense desk, constructed of elaborately carved wood, stained nearly black, most of its top covered with bundles of documents, some tied with coarse string, some with coloured tapes.

'Now, John, this is where my trade is secured. Like your father, I expect, I bring cargoes and ships together. I have a share in the ownership of several vessels, and also I know where to charter other ships if the cargo demands it. Otherwise I may place the cargo on another ship, simply because it is sailing to a convenient port. As you can see, we are bursting out of our breeches here, so I now have desks in other ports, all working on my behalf. Let me show you.'

He drew out of the desk drawer a map which showed all of Europe, including the British Isles and the Mediterranean Sea.

'Look at this. Copenhagen. Right, there are two ways of entering and leaving the Baltic, either by the channel between Copenhagen and the Swedish coast, or through the Danish islands, as your Captain Hotblack was attempting on the 'Laguna'. So I have a bureau in Halskov to look after ships in that area. I am now planning the same thing in the port of Esbjerg, which lies on the West coast of Denmark, the closest point to England and the Atlantic Ocean.'

John looked at the map as Lars carefully developed his ideas.

'Now, Mister Weaver, this is where you can help me. Look at the map. The closest reasonable place in England for shipping to Denmark and the Baltic Sea is here, on your River Humber. There are ports and harbours all along that coast. But, if the French or the Dutch start making war against England, those ports may be closed to us. So, my plan is to have a bureau for trading with your ports on the west coast, Liverpool and Bristol I understood were the biggest ports. Now you tell me about Lancaster. Show me where that is, if you please.'

John studied the map. Fortunately the name was marked, but in very small print.

'This is the port, up the River Lune. But we have just built a new harbour at the entrance to the river, called Glasson, which can take twenty or more of the largest. I understand from my father that we are going to build a canal which will mean that all these places you have mentioned will be joined together by rivers and canals. This will mean that goods can cross the country quickly and cheaply without ever using the roads and turnpikes. Just load them into a barge and they can be hauled for hundreds of miles by horses, without ever having to lift the cargo from one barge into another.'

Lars looked at the enthusiastic young mariner.

'John, my good friend. This is exactly what I was wanting to know. One of my worries is that the Navigation Acts, which demand that British goods must be carried in British ships, could damage our trade. I would like to find some British ship owners who would like to form an association with us, using each other's ships to steer an acceptable course around the hazards created by our princes and politicians. I'm sure you and your father's associates will understand what I mean.'

As he spoke he searched through the drawer of the desk. Eventually he found a thick black crayon and drew a broad line across the map.

'Look at that! Memel in Prussia, Copenhagen, Halskov, Esbjerg and now Hull and Lancaster. They make a straight line across the map of Europe! What a plan!'

He turned to John and shook him warmly by the hand.

'How would you, Mister John Weaver like to be my agent, my eyes and ears in England? You can sail between all our ports and tell me whether our ships are well run. I need people with ideas to find new ways of making good business. Excuse me, my English is letting me down. Now, my young friend, lets buy you some clothes. Then we can talk about your money, and get you on a ship home.'

As the two men walked round the harbour area, John realised that Lars was skilfully learning more about his guest without asking direct questions. Lars passed documents across for him to read, noting how quickly John could absorb the written information. When they stepped aboard one of the busy ships, Lars asked his opinion of the vessel and the way in which the cargo was being handled. In return, John was trying to form an opinion of the position Lars occupied in the affairs of the port. Certainly, most people they met on their tour of inspection greeted him with a degree of respect and deference which John likened to his meetings with Squire Kerr.

As they made essential purchases of clothes, the small tailors' shops agreed to have the garments delivered to the house when the necessary alterations had been made. Unlike buying clothes in Lancaster, no money changed hands, and in one shop the owner insisted in serving a spiced drink whilst measurements were taken and materials selected.

When, at the end of a long day, the two men returned to the gracious home in the centre of the city, John found himself secretly longing to see Eugenie again. He felt himself blushing when they found her awaiting their return. John carefully watched her when it wasn't too obvious and decided she was possibly younger than Lars by a few years, but this was not a subject upon which the young man could claim much experience. Beautiful, graceful women had not filled his days, nor even his nights. Now he became aware of the perfume which seemed to surround Eugenie with the freshness of flowers. He had on many occasions smelled the perfumes of some of the women who worked in the inns and taverns around every dock. But those had been sickly sweet essences, mostly used to overwhelm less agreeable smells of the wearers. What John was breathing now was as if every rose in England was bending in a summer's breeze. He wondered whether she was just a little more carefully perfumed and coiffed than their first meeting.

When the supper was served by one of the maids, Eugenie questioned John closely about his day, and then, as the meal progressed, enquired about his home in Lancaster and his working life. After he had told her some of the events which led to the loss of the 'Kestrel' and his voyage on the 'Laguna', she listened attentively as he explained how his mother would still not know anything about his fate.

'But that is tragic!' exclaimed Eugenie. 'My brother must send a messenger immediately. What do you do, Lars? Send a rider to Hamburg?'

'Please, dear sister, we did that three days ago. Now, if you two will excuse me, I must write my own letters.'

Eugenie turned to her young guest.

'You men have all excitement, not like us ladies. You can fight for your life on a ship in a storm, sail round the World, meet all these strangers. Yet all I can do is visit the dressmaker and imagine it is London. Do you call it Pall Mall? Tell me, what's it like?'

John didn't care to admit that he had never been within three days' ride of the capital, that he bought his clothes in Lancaster market and even his father had only been to London a few times, to his best knowledge. He hazarded a guess about Pall Mall.

'Oh, they are very smart in London. What with the King and the Dukes, you know, people like the Duke of Bridgewater. Very important...' His knowledge of London life was exhausted before he had begun. He tried again.

'Acts of Parliament, that's our worry. Acts to get the canal built. My father is very much concerned with Parliament and the Duke of Bridgewater.' He realised his conversation was now locked into a circle, from which he could see no escape except silence.

Eugenie smiled inwardly at the young man's embarrassment, and feigned not to notice.

'Oh, Pall Mall must be wonderful! You are so lucky.'

Across the table, in an enigmatic silence John gazed spellbound by the enchanting woman who seemed to relish every word of his halting conversation. He noticed her bare neck, surrounded by a necklace of twinkling jewels.

'Do you like my diamonds? My brother bought them for me last year in Amsterdam.'

Suddenly, John emerged from his silence and found himself saying, 'Are you married?'

'Alas, John, I am a widow. My husband was killed in Sweden. Some years ago, it seems now.'

'I'm sorry, Miss Eugenie. I was very rude to ask.'

She smiled and laughed quietly.

'He was a most unusual man. He fought in the Swedish Army, for no reason except excitement. He found it very dull to own farmland in Jutland, so joined up with the Swedish King. Suddenly I found I had inherited hundreds of farms. I didn't know one thing about keeping a farm, so Lars looked after them. When a new ship is being built, we sell a farm, I think, to pay for it. I'm not quite sure how it is done. I expect you understand, you've done all these things.'

'Oh, yes. I have worked in Mister Brockbank's shipyard. I have built ships. Do you know, in Lancaster we are considered so important for our ship-building that we even take down the town's bridge to get them down the river to the sea?' He looked at his attentive listener. Her eyes watched his face as he spoke. No one had ever paid quite so much attention to his words before.

'My goodness, John, you have done so much in your life, and I'm sure you have learned so much more.'

John nodded, realising how little he knew about many things, particularly fair ladies with pale blue eyes, who listened to his stories.

That night, anxiously waiting for sleep to overtake him, after a day of discoveries, his mind turned to the delicate beauty of his hostess. But he also recalled the secret, lurid tales which Jake had recounted as they sat together on the sea wall at Sunderland Point, tales of the shiny black girls submitting to the seamen of the 'Rainbird,' whose demands had sounded so much greater and more brutal than his own courting of the young women of the town.

Two days later John was being introduced to Captain Berg of the three-masted ship 'Stellar' which was to convey John to Liverpool. Thanks to the practical generosity of Lars Nyborg, his kit was now quite substantial, consisting both of town clothes and his seafaring gear. The few items which he had salvaged from the 'Kestrel' included his pilot book. Captain Berg studied the sketches of headlands, harbour entrances and views of coasts round the Baltic and the North Sea.

'Mister Weaver, zis is a most waluable book. I haf not seen such care wif mine young mariners. Keep it well, keep it, how do you call it, up to the date?'

The Captain's English had a style of its own, possible because he seemed to have an impediment in his speech, even in Danish.

'Mister John, zur English and Danish are like brothers. We haf good ships and good sailors, we work well in the partnerships.' He winked at John. 'Ve also hate zur same people, French and the Ruskies, of zur Prussia ve are not sure. Heh?' He laughed at his simple summary of World affairs, and John shared in the easy manner of the ship's master. Captain Berg was possibly not more than thirty-five years of age, fair - haired and sun-tanned, like most of his countrymen. He wondered what he would have made of the bearded, florid countenance of Captain Hotblack and his exhausted ship.

The 'Stellar' lay alongside in the harbour, close to the warehouse, fully laden and waiting for a favourable wind. For days it seemed fixed from the Nor-West, and it became apparent to an experienced eye that as each day passed, more ships had completed loading and were also waiting for a favourable wind. But for those heading into the Baltic, departure could be made, rounding the Trekroner forts before running free before the wind. As the days passed, ships were towed out by boats with a dozen oarsmen and anchored in the channel, to make room for arriving ships, and also, to keep impatient crews confined on board.

In the days of waiting Captain Berg introduced John to his First and Second Mates, and John found himself treated as an experienced navigator in addition to being a business associate of Lars Nyborg. John quickly realised it would be considered bad manners to question the Captain about Lars, so had to content himself with picking up minor comments, not easy when most conversation was in Danish. However, it quickly became obvious that Lars was considered a rich and successful trader who had the ability to see an opportunity before others. Captain Berg interrogated John on a point of ship design.

'It is my opinion, Mister John, that we should change the rig of our big ships. Ve haf small boats rigged as schooners, vich ve sail ver' close to zur vind. See?' He had a sheet of paper on the desk-top and sketched out his idea of the benefits of a fore-and-aft rig in the relatively confined waters of the Baltic and the North Sea, compared with the great ocean passages, where the huge spread of canvas could drive the ship before the wind for weeks on end. He pointed across the harbour at small two-masted schooners which were able to leave the port and make their way into the Kattegat.

When finally, the wind backed to the South-West the exodus of ships made an armada of billowing sails, crowding the channels between the city and the shadowy shores of Sweden to the Eastward. Every ship was fighting to make headway and John noticed the skill with which the 'Stellar' was handled to make the best possible speed and to minimise the distance on each tack to gain advantage over the rest of the fleet. The beautiful lines of the ship and her spread of canvas appeared to drive faster than John had ever sailed before.

Because messages had been arriving in Copenhagen that the English Channel was full of warring British and French ships, Captain Berg decided to take the Northern route round Cape Wrath, and as the chill autumn winds gave way to the first gales of approaching winter, the 'Stellar' fought her way to the West. As the days shortened, John Weaver's thoughts turned to his return to Lancaster and the parents who, even now, might believe he was dead.

*

Far to the south, in the English Channel, the frigate 'Requin' was being brought up to Admiralty standards by her crew. Having been repaired and re-fitted in Spithead, the vessel was training her crew in the ways of the King's Navy. The two most important functions were gunnery and changing sail, which required every seaman to learn to set and hand every sail, by day or by night, to recognise every halyard and every brace in total darkness. As few of the sailors could read, the only means of recognition was by sight or by touch. A mistake could lose the driving power of a sail, or could injure or kill a shipmate. For this reason, the sail-master and bo'sun used the rope's end with complete freedom, to instil total understanding in the crew.

Naval gunnery was a science of its own. The obvious dangers of gunpowder, the weight and behaviour of cannons and the need to follow an iron discipline in bringing these two dangerous elements together required constant practice. Errors were almost always fatal, whether from a limb crushed under the recoiling carriage of a cannon, or a smashed face, caused by a new charge of powder being ignited by burning material remaining in the gun barrel from the previous charge. The other feature of the relentless training programme was to accustom the landlubbers in the crew to the horrific noise of the gun-deck. Even the smaller cannon of the frigate, firing a nine-pound ball, created a noise which left the ears painful. Less fortunate, untrained sailors, who met their baptism of fire in the lower gun-decks of first-raters, firing a single broadside of fifty cannon, could be stone deaf for the remainder of their lives, or lie in their hammocks after the action, waiting for the blood to clot in their ruptured ears.

For Mighty Jake Tempest, the outcome of gunnery drill was a sense of great achievement, only heightened by the unbelievable noise and commotion. The race to quench and re-load a cannon before any other crew on the gun-deck was a matter of supreme pride. No matter how painful the bo'sun's slashing rope across sweating backs, every six-man gun-crew strained to fire more shot at the floating target than any other gun. Record times were carefully chalked up on the bulkheads, the dazed and deafened sailors urged on to greater efforts.

The 'Requin' was training to cruise off the French Channel ports, to seize their merchant ships or to give warning of the emergence of their battle fleets. One of the reasons for this selection was due to the French ensigns, signal flags and even code books which had been captured with the ship in Morecambe Bay. It was not beyond the imagination of the Admiralty for the frigate to change her identity in the night. Furthermore, the Royal Navy knew the best way to defeat a foreign navy was to prevent it leaving port. Warships and their conscripted crews needed constant training; ships unable to leave port became ineffective fighting machines.

The stories spread rapidly round the lower deck that capturing a valuable French merchantman would mean prize money for every man on the 'Requin', whether Captain or powder-monkey. Jake's account of the capture of the 'Requin' on the shoals of Morecambe Bay was not believed by any in the lower deck, and he was ridiculed by his shipmates. However, word of his exploits reached the officers mess deck, and the sailing master noted the enthusiasm of the bean-pole sailor. In the rapid manoeuvres of the nimble ship, a practised sail hand was worth his weight in gold, and could set a good example to his younger, inexperienced shipmates, to whom the swinging yards and unmanageable canvas were a real terror. To consider handling them in the heat of battle was beyond imagination for many of the young men.

Mighty Jake, as usual, viewed his present position with equanimity. A well-ordered ship and regular food seemed a good basis for the excitement of bringing the frigate up to fighting standard, and the prospect of adding to his modest savings seemed thoroughly worthwhile. Although mostly concealed in the stable at Ryelands, Jake had taken the precaution of always carrying one of his gemstones with him. He hoped to return to Deptford one day. He had been told that in

London there were many traders in gems who would give him an honest offer for his treasure. Just like selling slaves, he knew that best prices were only offered when there were a number of potential purchasers. In such a market, the 'Rainbird' had made a substantial profit, both for the slaves recorded on the ship's manifest, and the additional unrecorded slaves which had been sold for the benefit of the ship's officers and crew. The untimely murder of the captain at the hands of the black girl only served to increase the share-out to those remaining.

Jake was eagerly learning the essential rules of commerce in the School of Experience.

Chapter 17

In the bitterly cold days of February the first of the giant timber piles which the sailing ship 'Nancy' had successfully brought back from Memel was lifted over the timber walls of the first cofferdam. The labourers inside the dam, thigh deep in the icy waters of the River Lune, struggled to position one end of the pile in the river bed. The surveyors on each bank squinted along their sights, signalling for the pile to be moved, first two feet this way, a foot that way, a hand's breadth forward, until frozen limbs could take no more and the timber was left suspended from the crude sheer legs. The much-heralded steam pump on the bank was beginning to lower the level of water in the first coffer dam, but more importantly, its hissing, trembling boiler was a welcome source of heat to the labourers. To them, the coal, scrap lumber and dead trees which were daily consumed in great quantities was the most important part of the whole dubious undertaking. From the wet, muddy pit of one of the dams, the vision of five elegant stone arches rising into the sky to carry barges laden with merchandise from far-away cities seemed an equally distant dream.

When finally accurately positioned, driving the pile into the rock beneath the river bed began. A rectangular stone, weighing about two hundred pounds was suspended by a rope over a pulley. On the free end of the rope, three or four men raised the weight and then allowed it to drop on to the head of the pile. Sometimes an iron collar was secured round the striking point of the pile to prevent the timber splitting. Frequently, the strata through which it was being driven would deflect the line of the pile, and one of the surveyors would decide whether its position was acceptable, or whether a new one would have to be driven beside it. Thus it was that amidst acrimonious arguments and violent refusals, nearly two hundred men were to toil for a year simply to construct the secure timber foundations in the river bed, which would never be seen again. By day and by night, the back-breaking rock was hauled up and dropped, time without number, in pitch darkness, in moonlight, rain and shine. Desertion, drunkenness and frequent breakages slowed the work down, changes of contractors were made to try and speed the work up. As winter made way for spring, anxious members of the committee were joined on the river banks by young women, all happy to see these labouring giants bending to their tasks.

John Weaver had anticipated his return home with some misgivings. He knew the loss of the 'Kestrel' not only endangered his own life but would have cost his father dearly. Reputations were also at risk. The clandestine cargo of gunpowder, if revealed, would be considered a criminal act, although in times of war such transactions with the Country's allies might be more generously considered. These thoughts filled his mind as he attempted to find some comfort in the stage coach heading north from Liverpool. The smell of his fellow passengers and their assorted habits made seafaring seem a pleasant pastime by comparison. Whenever the labouring horses failed to keep the carriage moving, one or more of his travelling companions would jump down, either to urinate at the roadside, or to find the nearest tavern for fresh supplies to fill his bladder. Two women passengers at first expressed amusement at the frequent calls of nature demanded by the men, but as tempers became more jaded, arguments followed. John sought refuge on the 'outside' of the swaying carriage, and eventually sat beside the driver, wet and cold, but breathing nothing more unpleasant than the smell of the horses. At Preston some of the passengers were set down and fresh horses were harnessed between the shafts. Large bowls of hot broth were available at the Royal Hotel before the journey resumed. As John climbed back to his seat high above the road he noticed the name on the mud-spattered side of the crowded coach. 'Lightning'.

In darkness the coach hurried across the last few miles to Lancaster, joining other wagons and carriages all seeking the comparative safety of the city, rather than the open country.

The coachman turned to John and pointed towards the western side of the road.

'See that, son? Them's navigators. 'Navvies' the locals call 'em. The biggest bunch of bully-boys you've ever seen. Black-hearted Irishmen, digging and burrowing through the night. Steal a sheep, skin it and eat it before it's stopped bleating, they say. I'm told they're building a canal to London.'

John peered into the gloom and could just make out the figures moving against the dim light of lantern and flares. In some places, big fires were blazing, and shouts could be heard above the sound of the coach's wheels. The coachman pointed towards the distant flames.

'Keep your women indoors when they're at large, boy.'

As he spoke he quickly showed John the butt-end of a pistol inside his heavy cape. They passed through the village of Galgate and a crowd of men could be seen at the side of the road. The driver whipped up the horses and charged between the houses without giving way to anything. The noise bounced back from the buildings, which seemed to encourage the horses to even greater efforts. The shadowy figures at the roadside hesitated long enough for the coach to leave them behind.

In Lancaster the road ran down hill towards the end of Market Street where the coach swung through the arch into the courtyard of the Kings Arms. Horses jostled with passengers, grooms, stableboys and baggage as other coaches prepared to depart. Two or three passengers jumped down as did Jake, shouting their farewells to each other as they left the lights of the Inn and set off into the gloom. John had decided to make for the coffee house in the hope of meeting his father there, rather than at home. As he pushed through the door he was recognised by one or two of the merchants.

'Bless my soul! Joshua Weaver's boy! How are you, son?'

Another trader, who he knew as Simon, hurried across with his hand out.

'John Weaver! Home safe and sound. That's some good news anyhow.' He pulled out a chair at one of the tables in front of the crackling fire.

'Why, Simon, what's wrong?' John looked at his worried face.

'Oh, John, things change so much. Some of our best young men have been taken by the press gangs. Some of our ships can't sail for want of a crew. Did you hear of your young friend, er, what was he called..?'

'Jake? Mighty Jake? What's wrong with him?' John felt his heart sinking.

'Press gang. Took twelve good young seamen one night. I'm told he's alright. I was with your father today, he said you were on the way home.'

'Are you sure, Simon? Are you truly sure my father has got my letters? I dare not go home until I know Mother and Father are expecting me.'

'Lad, if you don't mind the ride, I'll take you home on my dog-cart. Not too comfortable, but get you safely to Ryelands. Let's set sail, eh?'

He called a few messages across the room and led John by the arm to the rear of the building. The small cart with just two seats back-to-back meant he was facing backwards with his seabag on his lap as the horse trotted across the bridge at Skerton. When they approached the house at Ryelands John jumped down and opened the gate. Simon carefully led the dog-cart into the yard while John ran across to the kitchen door and rattled the handle. He could hear movement behind the heavy door, and then his father's voice calling, 'Who's there. Give your name.'

'John Weaver, Captain's Mate, and a friend.'

Above the sound of the heavy iron bolts he could hear his father's voice calling to his wife. 'Sarah, it's John. Quick, John's back home.'

The flood of warm yellow lamplight illuminated the two travellers. In the doorway Mistress Weaver was straightening her hair, and then extending her arms in welcome to her laughing son. As they embraced in silence, Joshua stepped forward and greeted Simon.

'Well, you are the bearer of good tidings, Simon. Come in and take a glass of wine with us. What a happy day!'

In the large kitchen, the everyday objects seemed to offer their own welcome to the young man. The firelight and the candles on the table flickered and twinkled off the polished pans and shining crockery on the hooks and shelves. The tang of burning logs mixed with the welcoming smell of baking loaves and John noted the basket of cobs beside the oil lamp on the dresser.

The trials and terrors of the Baltic, the opportunities and discoveries in Denmark seemed to have occupied another world. He was home at last.

*

Once again, as the lamps flickered, the events of the past months were recalled and discussed. The effect of the war not only meant Jake had been pressed into the King's service, but in the big cities food was becoming scarce. The cost of everything was rising, and some of the port's trade was affected. Taxes and duties were levied on every transaction in the port to pay for the war.

John's mother pressed him for more details about the loss of the 'Kestrel' but John knew better than to talk about the loss of the ship without his father's prior approval. Instead, he regaled his parents with outrageous stories about Captain Hotblack and the strange ship 'Laguna'. In turn, the tale of the capture of the French frigate, which had taken on a certain heroic quality was related by Joshua, including Jake's presence on the 'Esperance'. But no one knew their young ward was at that moment climbing into his hammock on the gun deck of the captured French ship.

Joshua was particularly interested to find out who Lars Nyborg was, who seemed to have rescued his son from disaster, and taken such care to ensure John's letters were sent by the most secure messengers from Denmark.

'Tomorrow, Father, we must talk more seriously about Lars. Tonight I can't think of business. I hear your canal is growing across the county every day. We saw the workers from the coach.'

His father looked cautiously at Sarah before replying.

'Don't take any chances with that lot, John. Councillor Redfearn warned the committee before it all started. There's some wild men abroad these winter nights. Keep your doors bolted, and put the animals in the barn before sunset. It's that bad, they tell me. But the worst is down on the River. A mile upstream from the city it's like the Bedlam. Water, fire and steam; hundreds of men working day and night; the only sign of profit at present is with the brewers. I'm told that we pay a labourer twelve shillings a week for working every day except the Sabbath. We give them free beer, and free hay to sleep on in the barns and byres. Who can blame them for stealing a sheep, or taking the poor-box off the chapel wall?'

'Listen to me, Father. In Denmark the merchants and traders are expanding every day, while we are fighting the French. That's where we should be making our fortunes, not worrying about the navvies, as you call them.'

His father nodded and gazed dreamily at the glowing embers in the grate.

'John, you may well be on the right path. But perhaps you don't get the news from France as readily as we do in the Town Hall. Not content with executing hundreds of their own people, they are determined to conquer their neighbours in Europe. So King George tries to form an alliance with Prussia, and Spain; even Russia and Austria joined the agreement. But it seems to many of us it was left to England and Holland to pay the bills.'

John listened attentively to his father's words.

'I've heard this before, Father. Yet the ports in the Baltic are crowded with ships. Timber, hemp and tar I'm told, are much in demand. Anyone can see there are fortunes being made by someone out there.'

'Aye, son. It was ever thus.'

He prodded the logs with the black iron poker. He gazed steadily at the last embers.

'Sleep well tonight, my son. Tomorrow, you stay at home with your Mother and help her in the house. On Friday I meet with Matthew Redfearn, and perhaps he would like to hear from you about the events in the Baltic Sea.'

*

In the morning, Joshua Weaver left his house early, before the winter sun was above the horizon. He had many transactions to deal with that day, to leave himself free for working with his son on Friday. He knew

Redfearn would be interested in first-hand trading news, particularly as America was becoming more reluctant to trade with the warring states in Europe. American voices were already talking about a Neutrality Act. Joshua fell to thinking about 'finding who your friends are when the bugles blow.' His footsteps led him naturally to the bridge while his mind contemplated the deeper meaning of War.

His train of thought was brought to an abrupt halt by the figure of a man in a huge dark cloak which made him seem like a giant, stepping clumsily from the shadows to block the pathway. Joshua instinctively grasped the thick handle of his stick more firmly. He kept walking at his normal pace until he was within two paces of the figure. Joshua stepped smartly to one side to avoid him, but to no avail, as the figure stepped again to block his way.

'Step aside, sir,' called Joshua.

'Step aside yourself, Joshua Weaver.'

Joshua felt he could give a good account of himself, even if he had to run for his life. He looked straight at the cloaked man. He noticed he was wearing a hat which might once have been a tricorne, but the brim at the front fell forward, casting a deep shadow over the wearer's face. Joshua could see nothing by which to identify the man.

'Name yourself, sir, and then be pleased to let me pass,' demanded Joshua, his voice firm and clear. At this hour he knew many people would be heading into the town, so he expected some form of assistance, or at least an observer before too long. The figure spoke in a low, coarse wheezing voice.

'I've been waiting for you, Joshua Weaver. You and the other owners of the wretched ship 'Kestrel'. I've some news for you and your friends. Do you want me to tell you my news here, or shall we find a friendly tavern for our meeting?'

Joshua thought quickly. Time was critical and one false step now could destroy the last hopes of recovery from the loss.

'You have the advantage of me, but I'm interested in anything I can learn concerning the loss of one of my ships. I suggest we meet in the private room at the 'Shovel' Inn. I will tell the landlord I have a private visitor at ten o'clock this morning. What name shall I tell him?'

The figure reached up to briefly raise the brim of his hat. A single, bloodshot staring eye gazed unblinking at Joshua.

'Tell him Black Fox has urgent business with you. And no constables, neither.'

*

When, later in the morning, Joshua made his way to the shabby inn near the brewery he was surprised to see how busy the bar was. The noise from the low-beamed crowded room would cover any private conversation elsewhere, and the appearances of many of the eager customers were not too far removed from the fearful countenance of Joshua's guest. He allowed the landlord to conduct him into the private bar, and served him with a tankard of ale. His guest was stepping through the door as the Town Hall clock struck the hour. Joshua ordered another tankard of 'your strongest ale' and took it from the landlord's hands, closing the door of the private room behind him.

'Now, Mister Fox, I understand you have some news for me. Let us get to business.'

'Not so fast, Weaver. I've got a throat as dry as a hayloft. Better tell your landlord to bring one of these every strike of the quarters.' He nearly emptied the pewter pot with his first drink, before he even loosened his cloak. He cast it over the back of a stool and then carelessly drew off his concealing hat. In the full light of day his face was terrifying. Joshua felt his legs tremble when he recalled that the last time he had seen that grim countenance had been several years ago on the Milnthorpe Road, drenched in blood.

'Aye, Weaver. Take a good look. And look at this while you still have two eyes.'

He roughly tore at the filthy neckerchief and shirt to reveal his right shoulder. The flesh was torn and twisted with badly healed scar tissue. Savage black and red marks extended across his shoulder and up his neck to his jawline.

'Aye, Weaver, your pistol did that. Thought I was dead, you and me did. But there's many tried to kill Black Fox and failed. They tried to hang me once, but I jus' walked away while they was stringing up a child of ten for taking a pudding. Now it's my turn to get some justice.'

He finished the ale in the tankard and brought the empty pot down on the bare table with a noise like a gunshot. Joshua felt in mortal danger. Yet he found himself forced to gaze at the damaged face before him.

'Now, Weaver, there's two men in this town whose lives are protected by God in heaven. You and me is nearly as safe as the bishop in his palace. Why? 'Cause, Joshua Weaver, I can't let you die, you are my paymaster from today. And, by a stroke of good fortune, you can't let me die because the day the parson at Carnforth lowers my coffin into his churchyard he will hand to the magistrates the confession of this poor sinner. That document will account for some deeds of mine. But, it will tell the whole story of the 'Kestrel' and her evil owners, of

162

the tons of gunpowder smuggled out of Milnthorpe, of the money made and duties saved, and the poor souls who met their death in foreign waters jus' so Weaver and Redfearn and Banker Provender and their bagmen can live in comfort.'

Joshua looked at the twisted, snarling face, and noticed a faint smile on the thin lips of Black Fox. Joshua knew he had to make a response, or forever be in this man's clutches.

'You have a vivid imagination, Mister Fox. Apart from the last voyage, when most documents were lost with the ship, the Commissioners have every document and manifest for her voyages. You must be mistaken in your information.'

'Not quite so fast, Weaver. I've watched and waited for this day since you first started your midnight passages from Sedgwick mill. Every day and every barrel has been written down. But jus' you give me a good job, good money, and you gentlemen will be safe as the Priory.'

The landlord opened the door and handed the next pot of strong ale to Joshua.

'Thank-you landlord. Our meeting will finish in a few minutes, I'll thank you for the account and trouble you no further.'

Joshua turned to his guest.

'I'm grateful to you, Mister Fox, but I don't think we have any business together. We don't listen to dockside gossip any longer.'

'Ho, is that so? Then just look at this, just one corner of one page.' Fox reached inside his grimy coat and drew out a page of hand-written text, arranged in neat columns. He spread it out on the table, carefully smoothing out the folds. He kept one giant, grimy hand across the lower part of the page allowing Joshua to read the upper part. Immediately he recognised it by the names 'Kestrel' and 'Capt. Cooper' across the top. He assumed it was part of the manifest, but examination showed it was a list of stores, mostly provisions for an earlier voyage. Joshua was puzzled by the significance of such an innocent document. He feigned consternation.

'How many of these have you got, Mister Fox?'

'All of them! Pages and pages, all these lists of black powder, packed as leather boots, cotton shirts, curtains and carpets! I've got all I need to put you in the prison for years.'

Fox was suddenly beginning to relish his position of power. Presently, the landlord returned with the bill. Joshua tossed a couple of coins on the table.

'Landlord, a pen and paper if you please, and sealing wax if you can manage it.'

After a few minutes the pot-boy returned with the pen and paper. 'Gideon says I've to go to the bank for some wax. I'll be back here in a minute, mister.' The small boy left.

'Right, Mister Fox. What do you want?'

'Why, I want a letter to say I am a manager of yours and you will give me a good reference if I ever need it. Simply write that and sign it.'

Joshua took the quill and started to write:

The Lord is my shepherd, I shall not want. He maketh me to lie down in green pastures, He leadeth me beside the still waters, He restoreth my soul, He leadeth me in the paths of righteousness for His name's sake.

With shaking hands he turned the paper for Black Fox to read. The single staring eye slowly scanned back and forth across the paper. Joshua waited without daring to breathe. Finally, the eye turned to stare at Joshua.

'Right, now sign it.'

Chapter 18

The meeting in the afternoon was held in Councillor Redfearn's austere offices. Winter light had difficulty penetrating most of the room, so that the five men sat as close to the window as possible, crowding round one end of the long, bare central table. A small fire barely raised the temperature and occasionally a gust of wind would blow smoke into the room. Redfearn sat with his back to the window, with William Provender, the banker and a newcomer, Charles Fitton next to him. On the other side sat Joshua Weaver and his son. After a few pleasantries and what had now become commonplace in the city, complaints about the 'ruffians building the canal,' Redfearn called the meeting to order.

'Gentlemen, this meeting is called because we have with us Joshua Weaver's son John, who served under Captain Cooper on the 'Kestrel'. He will give us a full report on that loss and other matters. We also have Mr Charles Fitton, who represents the interests of Captain Cooper, and we will discuss that in due course. For our newcomers, may I stress that discussions in this meeting are not recorded in writing, they are totally confidential, and may not be spoken of to others outside this room. I will ask Mr Provender to tell us about the bank's position on the loss of the ship.

'Thank you, Mister Chairman. I have given each of you the financial statement of the ship's business, and you can see we have got good payments for nearly all our exported cargo. Every barrel of the powder was paid for and no longer on our manifest at the time of the fire. This is due in no small measure to the skill of Cooper in securing payment on the day of arrival. Of the ship, I'm afraid those who we represent must bear a large part of the loss. We have some of the cost underwritten in Liverpool and here in Lancaster, but they will be claiming war risks and reducing their liability, as they call it. By a stroke of good fortune, no one in Memel has posted any complaint that we were carrying gunpowder, probably because too many people had a finger in that particular pie. That's all I can say at this time, until any more news comes from the Baltic.'

'Then I would like to hear from John Weaver his account of the loss.'

Nervously, John licked his lips. He had mentally rehearsed what he wanted to say, and was aware that even his father was not cognisant of all that had happened.

'Well, sir, we all knew things were more difficult in Dantzig when they talked about the war. Later, in Denmark they said hundreds of people were killed every day in France by the new government. When we arrived finally at Memel, I understand the captain was told the gunpowder had to be tested and he required me to go with him and the strange man who conducted the tests. It took us about three hours, or maybe longer, to load up and go to this fort on the coast to fire the test cannon. We were told the tests were very good indeed, so we all headed back to the harbour and the captain was the first to realise that the smoke we saw was from our own ship, blazing in the harbour. When we got there, not much was left and as far as I know, only the captain, me and one seaman survived. We looked around as well as we could, but with hundreds of ships in port, twenty or more sailing or arriving every day, there was no way we could make a greater search. The first night we just looked in the water near the ship hoping for anything which might have survived, but we only found a few small things. We also found four of the bodies of the crew, and we did our best to identify them. I think the captain sent you their names. Captain Cooper said we must be careful in what we did and on no account let anyone know what we knew about the ship. He called himself Ship's Surgeon to avoid difficult questions. He found the three of us a safe berth on the 'Laguna' which got us out of Memel, but we ran aground in Denmark.'

The committee members questioned him on one or two points about the fire, particularly because a letter from Popov had revealed a French spy had been executed by firing squad for setting fire to several ships in port over the previous few weeks. There was a story, much improved in its frequent retailing, that the spy had been 'led' to the 'Kestrel' by the military, letting it be known smuggled black powder was in the cargo, so they could entrap him and catch him red-handed.

Charles Fitton asked further questions before referring to Captain Cooper.

'We have a number of messages from the captain. It would appear he intends staying in Denmark for a while to try and bring the 'Laguna' home with Captain Hotblack. As you gentlemen will be aware, his contract, as for every member of the crew of the 'Kestrel', terminated immediately upon the loss of the ship. But his partnership in the syndicate continues until his death, so I am here to protect his interests as a partner.'

The intonation in his voice warned the other members round the table that Mr Fitton was not one to be taken for granted. Redfearn made a discreet shake of the head, seen only by Joshua. The captain's rights as a ship's officer in the employ of the syndicate were certainly confused with his position as a shareholder, particularly where the distribution of profits or the allocation of losses was concerned.

The meeting continued, discussing the future in the Baltic, until Fitton asked to be excused from further discussion. His last remark identified his views clearly. 'I will come and see you when the accounts have been agreed, so that final distributions can be made. If you are considering a widow's fund to ease your consciences, make it out of your own dividends, not Captain Cooper's. I think you will agree he has done more to earn his share than any of us here.'

When he had gone, Redfearn reached into a cupboard and drew out bottles of wine and some glass beakers. Drinks were passed round, and the meeting became visibly more relaxed and good natured.

'I find Fitton a difficult man, Weaver. Once this matter is reconciled we must ensure he does not remain on the committee.'

'I agree, but until that time we must treat him with care.'

Joshua Weaver asked that his son should be allowed to speak about his experiences in Denmark with Lars Nyborg. John once again had rehearsed the important points of his remarks, and began by referring to the kindness he had received from the Danes he had met. He then swallowed hard and outlined Lars' plans for a co-operation with British shipowners.

'My benefactor, Lars Nyborg, has a very large shipping operation which joins many of the Baltic ports with the rest of Europe and America. I think he has worries that some countries only accept their own ships, not foreign owned ships, to carry their manufactures. He feels we could work together, using British and Danish ships, whichever is best suited to the particular trade and locality, especially in times of war. The fact that my father is so closely concerned in a similar trading business was a useful coincidence. He tells me he owns ships or has shares in others, he has men in his employ in Memel and in other parts of Denmark. He would like to discuss joining up with some Lancaster owners. Before I spoke, he considered Bristol and Liverpool were the only real west coast ports. I explained about Glasson and also the canal. He was very impressed by what I told him about our activities, although I said nothing about the slave trade. I don't know what Denmark thinks about that sort of business.'

'Ha! I'll tell you.' Councillor Redfearn's interruption was almost derisive. 'They'll be as sanctimonious as the rest, but still make a fortune 'over the horizon' shipping the Ashantees to the Caribbean. And quite legally, too. But I wouldn't allow anybody to share in the business we have built up in the Guinea Trade. What do you say, Weaver?'

Joshua nodded his head.

'We need to build up our strength where we are weakest. The American routes, all the Baltic trade, and our longer routes to India could well be strengthened for the very reasons my son has so clearly pronounced. Baltic timber, particularly mast timber is in great demand, and there's a fortune to be made for the ships who can get it home. With France threatening us all, strength must lie in co-operation with foreign owners who think and trade like us. But a word of caution. The Danes are like the English, they learn their seamanship with their mother's milk. And a properly run merchant fleet is their pride. I most surely wouldn't make a similar proposal about most other countries. Holland has stood shoulder to shoulder with us in this war, but I fear an alliance with them. The French army seem more than a match for them on land, although I understand the Dutch battle fleet is most effective. I'm glad to say these are matters to leave to the military, and you can be sure we are the people they will come to when they've run out of money or able-bodied men. Until then, we'll keep our own counsel.'

Redfearn exerted his position as chairman of the small meeting.

'Then, gentlemen, I suggest we should draw up a proposal of sharing ships and cargoes, and send a first draft to Mister Lars Nyborg. Then I ask Mister Provender to start finding out more about the man and his business. We have an embassy who will help there. And if John Weaver here continues to serve on our ships to Scandinavia and the Baltic he can be our eyes and ears. We will prepare a list of the questions for which we require answers. Do you think you can handle this for us?'

'Yes, sir. I would be pleased to do so. But I must add Mister Nyborg has made me an offer to act for him. If you accept that my interests are equal between here and Copenhagen, then I would expect to deal truthfully with both. I would therefore request that neither the committee nor my father should ask me to act in favour of one or the other.'

Councillor Redfearn looked to Joshua Weaver and laughed.

'By God, Joshua. Your boy is in the same mould, eh? I'm not sure your honesty will make you rich, but it might make you contented.'

Joshua Weaver patted his son's arm.

'You spoke well, John.'

The meeting then turned to discussions on the replacement for the loss of the 'Kestrel' and the new ships being built on the river. Once again it was John who made a major contribution to the debate.

'I think many of the captain's who are having to watch and wait in the narrow waters around this coast and Denmark, waiting for a favourable wind, day after day, are feeling we are using the wrong ships. We see the schooner as the ship of the future.'

The councillor scratched his head.

'Ships seem to have traded quite happily for centuries. What are you out to change?'

'Well, sir, trade won't always wait for a fresh wind. The latest designs of ships with large single sails fore and aft, instead of square-rigged ships, will be much more useful in all sorts of wind. I watched a schooner sail from Copenhagen harbour, out of a hundred ships waiting, she was the only one daring to sail to the north in a nor-west wind. I don't know what everyone else was thinking, but when I own a ship it will have two great gaff sails, which will also be handled completely from the deck. Fewer crew, more profits, less time in port.'

'By God, Joshua, truthful and a businessman! You've got competition there!' exclaimed the councillor with a hearty laugh.

Before any further comment could be made, the meeting was interrupted by an urgent banging upon the heavy door of the office. Joshua got up from the table to open it, but before he could do so it burst open and a tall man in a red and black cape doffed his hat and bowed to the men in the room. His face was flushed and perspiring, and he wiped his neck and eased his collar as he spoke.

'Constable Leadbetter. My excuses, sirs, but we have a serious problem which we are investigating. We have a suspicious death upon our hands.'

The speaker appeared to be alone, except for the office clerk, yet he continued to refer to himself as 'we'. He continued.

'I believe one of you gentlemen is conversant with a citizen who calls himself Black Fox. Is that so?'

Joshua nodded.

'Indeed, constable. I know Fox. He occasionally works for me. Has he caused some trouble?'

'Not caused trouble, sir. He has killed hisself, so to speak. What we call 'taken his life'.'

Joshua looked pale and shocked.

'This is unbelievable! I was with Mister Fox at one of our meetings earlier today. You may ask the landlord at the 'Shovel' inn.'

'I have already done as you suggest. The landlord, one Gideon Gorse' he read carefully from a note in his hand before repeating the name, 'Gideon Gorse has informed us you were with the dead man, alive of course, at the time, in a meeting in the said inn or alehouse. I must ask you, sir, what was his nature when he left your presence?'

'He seemed much as usual. He was asking for some money, as is his custom.'

The constable looked closely at Joshua's face.

'Was he drinking?'

169

'Only a tankard, the same as me. I paid for all drinks.'

'So the inn-keeper has notified me...'

Councillor Redfearn jumped to his feet.

'Yes, yes, yes. For the Lord's sake, get to your point, man. What has happened? Come in and sit down and tell us what this about.'

When the constable was settled at the committee table he seemed more at ease.

'Well, gentlemen, this is a most strange occurrence. I've never seen the like. We know Fox as a trouble-maker, and would like to hold him for a number of serious crimes in the city and the county likewise. But he's sly and tricky, and his step is always one ahead of ours. Then, at midday we was summoned by a person, of the public, you understand, to accost a man who was stood on the parapet of the new bridge.' Joshua smiled inwardly at this reference to a bridge built six years earlier. The constable continued.

'When I get to the Skerton Bridge, I sees this tall man in a great cloak, walking along the top of the parapet. I accosted him and demanded he should step down. Thinking he was a drunkard, I took out my stave. But he spoke without any drunkenness in his speech, and his walking along the very edge of the stonework was not the step of a drunkard. I thought I recognised him and asked if his name was Fox. He didn't reply properly and I argued with him for some minutes, gentlemen, but he kept saying, and this is his words, as I can best recall, he says 'I will never have to walk again'.'

The room was silent as the strange narrative stopped for a moment. The constable wiped his hand across his mouth and cast an eye towards the wine bottles on a side table.

'Here, man, have a drink.' Redfearn hastily poured out a beaker of red wine. The constable drank deeply and continued.

'After some minutes, he would not listen to my reason, one or two of us tried to take him by the ankles, but, in spite of his great size, he avoided our grasp, our grasps.... then, of a sudden he calls out 'I shall fly like a great bird.' He spreads his cloak, like the wings of a huge black eagle and, gents, he tries to fly off the bridge, just like a cormorant off Warton Crag. For one second even I thought he was going to fly, he made everyone who saw him think for that second he was a bird.'

The beaker was swiftly emptied of wine.

'But he fell, straight down, like a stone, straight and true into the river.'

'And he died from drowning?' enquired Joshua, as calmly as he knew how.

'Indeed, no, sir. The river was at high water at midday, plenty of water to break his fall, at least. But Mister Millar, in charge of the bridge for the canal up stream, had six horses hauling great timbers up the river on the high tide. As Fox fell the timbers just floated from under the arches, and his falling body was smashed upon the great wooden beams. He was as dead as the beam that killed him.'

The room fell silent and the Sign of the Cross was made by each person in the bleak room, William Provender muttered 'May God rest his soul.'

After a moment, the constable drew a document from his pocket.

'Life is a very strange teacher. Black Fox would be in my lists as a bad citizen, and no great loss to this town. Yet, when we examined his poor shattered body, do you know what we found?'

The room waited in silence, perhaps expecting to learn the secrets of the Creation.

'Look. On that poor soul's tortured body, he carried with him the words of the scripture.'

He passed the crumpled water-stained paper round the table to his audience. Joshua read aloud, 'The Lord is my shepherd....'

'This is a very sad event,' said Councillor Redfearn. 'Is there any way in which we may help you further?'

'No, gentlemen, unless something comes to you which may explain how he became like an angel just before he died. That's all.'

The constable finished his wine and bowed before leaving the room.

William Provender was the first to speak.

'Did he say 'Angel'? Black Fox was the biggest cut-purse and cheat in the county. I don't think there is any businessman in town who will not breathe easier at his departure.'

'God rest his soul.'

Joshua looked at the others round the table and spoke in a low voice.

'I had better warn you that Black Fox knew exactly what we had been doing in the 'Kestrel' for some time. I have reason to suppose that he had a contact in the mill at Sedgwick.'

'Well, that's news to me,' said William Provender. 'But I had crossed his path at the bank. He made many false claims for payment against Promissory Notes which were always found to be false. Of course he claimed he had accepted them for payment in good faith. I'm still very disturbed to think he knew anything about the 'Kestrel.' I presume there is no way his evil influence can reach us from the grave.' The banker laughed uneasily.

The councillor interjected.

'Don't let this get out of hand, William. What do you say, Joshua?'

'I say we'd better prepare our defences.'

*

As John and his father returned home the conversation naturally turned to the day's events.

'Well, that's been a remarkable day, and no mistake. I've never seen those two so excited as they were over your ideas. Generally they greet new ideas like an attack of the quinsies. Listen to them bleating about the canal, yet you had them listening to every word you said. That has been a good skirmish for you. I suggest you find a berth on one of the Baltic ships and get back to Denmark. You obviously like it there.'

Suddenly, the young man's mind was filled with the image of the elegant Eugenie, and for a moment he considered telling his father about the woman who had such an influence on him. But when he considered that she may be eight or more years older than himself, maybe nearly thirty, he didn't think his father was ready for conversations of this nature. He didn't dare think about his mother's reaction.

'Yes, Father, I'd like to get sailing again. But first I would like to go to the shipyards, perhaps I could try and meet Squire Kerr again at Carnforth. I'd like to know what he thinks about new designs of ships.'

'Well, I might be going to a funeral there, so we shall send a note to the Squire to see if he could spare us some of his precious time.'

John turned to his father.

'That was a very strange affair with the constable. How well did you know Black Fox.'

'Oh, you understand, just a casual labourer. But he could always find men for heavy work. That's all.'

John looked at his father. 'How strange. Otherwise I would have sworn that the words of the Scripture were written in your hand. But did you notice the signature on the bottom? The signature was King George himself.'

'How remarkable,' replied Joshua Weaver.

Chapter 19

'I observe the English Channel is once more filled with the English and French battle fleets. We must take advantage of our position, so far removed from the conflict, whilst our valiant sailors in the South take great pleasure in the victories of their superior aggression. A Victory to His Majesty, I say!'

His audience in the Town Hall produced a desultory cheer in response to the Chairman's loyal remarks.

'In the meantime, I'm pleased to note the progress made by our engineers and the stout hearts who are, at this very instant, hewing our superb canal out of the living rock of Lancashire and Westmoreland. Each day we observe the mighty works to create the great aqueduct. However, I am told that the crossing of the River Ribble has not yet started. Perhaps Mr Gregson would be so kind as to tell the committee the present state of progress?'

Mr Gregson, who had enjoyed the eloquence of the chairman's opening remarks, now found himself having to criticise the 'stout hearts' who, he knew, were neither adhering to the standards nor the line laid down by the contractors; that he had demanded some of the stretches of the canal, which had been partially filled with water for floating small boats and barges of material, would have to be drained for inspection.

'This is a regrettable occurrence which produces unwanted costs and delays, I will admit. But when our structures are examined two hundred years from now our kinsmen will acknowledge the quality of our craftsmanship. In addition, we are encountering a problem in the section south of Preston. We believe that in the past, mine shafts have been sunk and then the workings have been exhausted and abandoned. If we were to construct the canal basin across an unidentified shaft, with no more than a few feet of rock laid across timber beams, a collapse of such a closure could be disastrous. For this reason we are having to consult local records and indeed, seek directions from local people who may have been employed in these old mines.'

A murmur of disapproval rumbled round the room as his listeners contemplated the effect of their fifty-mile long waterway draining without warning into a disused mine-shaft. The chairman questioned Mr Gregson in his most magisterial manner.

'Could Mr Gregson tell us where he considers the waters would go under such a circumstance?'

The room burst into startled shouts of 'Yes! Yes! Answer!' which gave Gregson an opportunity to consider a suitable reply. He could save his breath. A wag in the audience, mercifully concealed from the troubled scrutiny of the chairman, called out, 'It will squirt two hundred feet into the air through the Duke of Devonshire's fountains, and cover Chatsworth in best hearth-coal!'

The meeting exploded with laughter, as if in relief from the grim thoughts of a moment earlier. The clerk pounded the oak table with his gavel. Eventually, order returned to the room and the deliberations continued. Gregson's manner was becoming more aggressive. He turned to the audience, his anger clear to see.

'These are not subjects for jest, even though some people seem to think so. When finished I calculate the cut will contain nearly half a million tons of water.'

A stunned silence fell upon the gathering as the considered the magnitude of the possible disaster. Eventually the chairman spoke.

'May the committee enquire progress is being made in the means of crossing the River Ribble at Preston? This must be crucial in our plans to join with the Leeds and Liverpool Canal Company.'

'Yes, Mr Chairman, that is quite correct. However, as many of the problems to be encountered will be the same, we should complete the Lune crossing, with all its difficulties, before starting at Preston. I must, however, once again remind the committee that upon your insistence that stone masonry be employed instead of the finest brick, this will cause much additional cost. We will be wiser when it is completed, Mister Chairman.'

'Much wiser, I fear. I sincerely trust our shareholders understand the reason and the wisdom of our decision.'

'To hell with the shareholders! What about our customers? There's no money for anyone without customers.' Councillor Matthew Redfearn had not lost any of his critical powers where the canal was concerned.

'While Mr Rennie engages himself upon the problem of his bridge across the Ribble, could he spare some attention to the means by which this great waterway will ascend to the town of Kendal, which I am confidently informed lies one hundred and fifty feet above the sea water level in the bay. And no less, how it will descend to sea level to serve the new harbour at Glasson. He may be encouraged in his endeavours when I tell him that today the dock contains twenty-one large merchant ships and a dozen smaller vessels.'

The chairman nodded moodily towards the councillor.

'We take note of Councillor Redfearn's encouragement and feel our engineers will not be found wanting. If I understand Mr Rennie's drawings correctly, a series of locks, already widely used in other parts of the country will enable the water-borne vessels to ascend and descend in stages, fully laden and with little delay.'

Throughout the morning the questioning continued. When the meeting finally broke up at midday, Redfearn met Joshua Weaver and his son at the Kings Arms to take a meal together before taking the 'North Briton' coach to Carnforth, on its way to Penrith.

*

As the wheels rumbled over the stony roadway, conversation was difficult, particularly as the two other passengers were unknown to them. The councillor referred obliquely to the unpleasant task ahead.

'Never have relished a funeral. If it's a poor man, there's too much grief and too many hungry faces. If it's a rich man, the churchyard fills with smiling faces and words of unreal sorrow. I don't think there will be a full muster today. He had few friends, I believe.'

Indeed, he was right. In the cold graveyard a handful of men and women, dressed in shabby black coats, capes and shawls stood round the dark cavity in the untended rain-soaked grass. The parson looked around at the small gathering, and noticed the councillor, John Weaver and his father standing to one side, uneasily separate from the mourners. He rapidly read the funeral words from the prayer book. Three of the mourners stepped forward to take the ropes which ran under the plain wooden box. By a slight movement of the head, one of the men invited Joshua Weaver to take one rope end. He stepped forward, and as the parson intoned the final words of interment, they clumsily lowered the coffin into the shadows.

As the mourners departed, the parson stood to one side and nodded his head to the small family group. When councillor Redfearn passed by, the parson gently touched his arm.

'Strangers to our parish, are you?' he enquired. He was a short, white-haired man with a countenance well-suited to the funereal task. He wore the appearance of eternal grief, with a deep, sonorous voice to suit. 'Business friends, perhaps.'

Joshua nodded. 'Yes, Mr Fox was an occasional worker in our endeavours.' Joshua strangely found himself adopting the same gloomy tones of the parson.

'Ah! Gentlemen, you must come and see our modest place of worship. Modest, but deeply revered by those who use it each week.'

His words seemed to make a careful separation between the regular congregation and his present visitors. He unlocked the church door with a large, black iron key. Inside the dark building, the winter air was cold and smelled of dampness. If the visitors had expected an inspiring interior they were to be disappointed. The parson led the three men up the nave and pointed out various small features of interest. Family tombs, old inscriptions and engravings on the uneven stone walls bore witness to the history of the church, and possibly to its present meagre congregations. The parson was speaking in his low tones, as if carefully rehearsed over many years. To the right hand side of the chancel a studded oak door, not much higher than a man's shoulder, responded to one of the parson's keys. He led the way, crouching through the door and lit a lamp inside and with an outstretched hand invited the three men in. He carefully closed the door before taking out a bottle of Jerez and some small glasses from a cupboard in the corner. For a moment a glimmer of light and warmth seemed to invade the room. Upright wooden chairs surrounded a table and the parson invited everyone to sit down whilst he poured out the drinks.

'It's not the communion wine, I do assure you!' His manner became much more relaxed as he made his remark. The four of them drank as he whispered 'Jason Henry Fox, may God rest his soul.'

The three men murmured some response. The parson appeared to be relieved of a great weight. Suddenly, his manner was that of meeting long-lost friends.

'A difficult man, was Mister Fox. Deeply troubled by his sins, which sadly, seemed to be sufficient for a whole parish, instead of just one man. Yet, only a few months before his untimely departure from this life he made his full confession. He and I sat in this very room. For a long, cold winter's evening he made me list all the sins, all his victims, and the pitiful sums he had swindled from his friends and enemies alike.'

The parson refilled the small glasses, and then reached into a drawer beneath the bare tabletop. He drew out a brown paper package, once secured with coarse string and clumsy red seals, but now open at one end.

'A strange epistle, indeed. But as I wrote I thought of Our Lord, and the pitiful sinner before me. And then he passed me documents, page after page, names and dates and quantities of goods; what he, in his own poor way, called his Crimes of Partnership. A strange term, which I never fully understood. I expect one of you gentlemen, being in the city every day, would quickly recognise and understand.'

The parson deftly removed one page from the contents of the package, revealing no more than the first few lines of hand-written text. Across the top in a firm hand ran the heading.

Record of unlisted goods and dates of loading Milnthorpe 1790.

Joshua Weaver and Others will be pleased to confirm.

As soon as he started to read, the parson leaned forward and took the page out of Joshua's sight.

'A written confession is a sacred document to a priest of the church, you understand. Particularly so when the fabric of our beloved church is in such need of repair. To preserve this fine building to the Glory of God and the resting place of Saint and Sinner alike, we mortals have to pay our tithe to Mother Church while we still have time to show our devotion to the memory of those who have gone before.'

He smiled at his guests with a benign sweetness which had been completely absent from his manner in the cold churchyard, where it would have been more appreciated.

Councillor Redfearn spoke in a quiet, firm voice.

'How much is the tithe?' he asked briefly.

'Twenty-five sovereigns, donated without any name, should meet the needs of this humble place of worship.'

'And would that sum enable us to study at our leisure the depth of contrition of our dear departed brother in God?'

The parson handed the package towards the councillor.

'But of course. Saint Paul's Epistle to the Corinthians was delivered in writing, that they might read and study his words. I look upon this writing in exactly the same light.'

Joshua Weaver touched his son's elbow and they both stood up, as did the councillor. With great reverence Joshua intoned 'We all say Amen to that.' They bowed their heads in silence for a few moments, while the parson muttered a prayer. He turned to Joshua, who handed him a small leather bag.

Not one word was exchanged as the parson drew open the heavy door and bowed his head in silent farewell.

*

At Squire Kerr's gracious residence they were expected, and after the cold church the brisk walk had dispelled the gloom and chill of the funeral. Possession of the documents in the package under Joshua's cloak gave a lightness to his tread and to his words.

'A most useful funeral, I think we could say. We have buried more than one heavy body this day.'

John Weaver, unused to funerals and mystified by the parson's strange behaviour, was much more interested to meet the ship designer and builder, and thus to put the affairs of the church out of his mind.

Squire Kerr greeted his visitors with his customary courtesy, taking them to his office facing towards the bay. Councillor Redfearn listened to the designer's latest ideas for building better ships. When John outlined his own ideas about building schooners for the Baltic trade he found an enthusiastic listener, who had apparently already given a great deal of thought to the subject. Squire Kerr eagerly drew out a sheet of plain paper and sketched out a profile for a three-masted schooner.

'My own designs to build schooners seem to place constraints on size. To achieve a spritsail comparable to a square rigged ship would call for very large sails and spars, to carry the same burden. But in narrow seas their advantages would outweigh any restraint on size.' He turned to the councillor.

'I have found, from experience, once a ship builder presents the shipowner with a vessel of the greatest practical burden, the owner always wants his next ship to be bigger! Is that not your experience, Councillor?'

'Ships, cotton-mills and coal mines, no matter what we have, we always want the next one to be bigger. Even canals! Once upon a time we used to widen the river and bring our ships ten miles further inland. Then we started crossing the country with narrow canals. Now Mister Rennie is contracting Mister Brockbank into building boats fourteen feet wide for our grand waterway. One day we will wake up and find Bradford has its own fishing fleet.'

'Well, councillor, I'm sure that's what you call progress, but some of us call foolhardiness. Look at this young man here. He wants a ship that he can handle, not a ship too big for the waters it trades in.'

John blushed at the complimentary remarks, and following so quickly after the sombre episode with the parson, Squire Kerr's entertaining conversation and good hospitality put his guests at ease. Conversation flowed easily about the rising fortunes of the shipping trade all round the bay. When he produced some fine French wine, with a golden clarity and delicate taste, the setting sun over the distant hills seemed to mark the end of winter and the beginning of a new spring.

Reluctantly, as darkness fell, the visitors had to depart. The squire placed his coach at their disposal, and soon the coachman had whipped up the two horses and they were bouncing down the road to Ryelands and home. No further reference was made to the strange parson at Carnforth. John's mind was full of plans to return to Copenhagen, hoping he would be given the authority to talk with Lars Nyborg about his ideas.

*

Within a few days a letter was delivered to John which had been carried to Liverpool on one of Lars' ships and then on the mail coach. It contained an invitation for John 'and any member of his Company' to join his ship 'Falkon' as his guests to visit Copenhagen. It was finally agreed by the committee that John should travel alone and carry a document which would list the ships either owned or available to the 'company' which regularly sailed out of Lancaster. Details were given in a voluminous document prepared by the Commissioners showing the capabilities of the River Lune and the New Dock at Glasson, giving the dimensions of the berths. The canal company were reluctant to place dates against their elaborate plans, which showed a continuous link from the town centre of Kendal winding its way southward to pass through the heart of Lancaster and Preston, before terminating in a junction with another canal which appeared to cross the country from coast to coast with ease.

The purpose of sending the young man unaccompanied was to allow the Lancaster merchants a means of exchanging information without being forced to reveal any more of their plans than necessary.

In the hurried preparations for his departure John gave little consideration to his own personal needs, until the merchants purchased a gift for Lars Nyborg. It consisted of a carved mahogany plaque showing the castle, the river and Skerton bridge, made by one of Mr Gillow's apprentices some years earlier, possibly to present to some dignitary when the bridge was first opened. John realised he should likewise take a personal gift both for Lars and Eugenie. He searched in the market and found a pair of leather riding gauntlets for Lars, and a ladies' silk kerchief for Eugenie. On returning home with his various purchases his mother noted the carefully-wrapped silk but made no comment.

For the last few days he was home John found himself entertained by merchants and shipowners, and, to his surprise, the Lune shipbuilders suddenly seemed to recognise the possibilities the co-operation with Denmark. Mr Brockbank gave him a detailed specification of a three-masted ship with a length of eighty-four feet and a burden of nearly four hundred tons which he considered he could build for about four thousand English pounds, supplied with masts and spars, but all sailcloth to be purchased separately.

'Bring me a few orders for those, John Weaver, and we will all reap the benefit.'

'I can understand that, but when you see the industrious ports and yards in Denmark I don't know whether we could take business from them.'

The master shipbuilder looked at the young man who would be his ambassador.

'Never forget, John, that there is more than price in deciding how to buy a ship. The design and the craftsmanship are vital, but also the way we collect our payment is important. If our banker is prepared to lend your friend in Copenhagen some of the purchase price on the understanding that the ship must be built in Lancaster, that could be beneficial.'

As John received his final instructions and the documents from the various companies and traders interested in his journeys, he began to realise the ever-widening possibilities, and when they gave him a purse containing thirty pounds wages in advance he knew he was starting a completely new chapter in his life.

However, the rigours of the coach seemed to dispel his elation after the first uncomfortable few miles. His mother had taken care to oversee his preparations for the journey, including a new fur hat and a heavy cape which had once belonged to his father, but, nevertheless, the journey was cold, wet and uncomfortable.

Returning to Liverpool in the swaying coach re-awakened all his feeling of excitement. Much bigger than any other port he had been to, it proudly displayed the value of its world-wide trade. John had never seen so many tall buildings, graceful squares and elegant statues. And casting their presence over everything, were the towering masts of hundreds of ships tied up along the quaysides and riding to anchor in the fast-flowing River Mersey. In the city, every street, every office seemed dedicated to the business in the harbour, and the population which crowded them appeared to have come from every quarter of the globe. Chinamen with pigtails half-way down their backs, black men in blue or crimson robes, bearded arabs with flowing head-dresses passed quickly along the cobbled pavements, incongruous in the cool Lancashire air, yet mixing easily with the city folk. On his previous visit to the city, the darkness had hidden its exciting variety. Today, in the spring sunshine, he could feel the industry and urgency of the hurrying figures as he headed towards the docks, clutching his two bags.

On the quaysides and in the wide-open warehouses, goods were piled in huge quantities, far greater than he had ever encountered in Lancaster or even Copenhagen. The familiar smells of bales of wool and cotton, freshly-sawn timber and sacks of grain now mixed with spices, oils and tobacco. For John, well versed in the ways of the seafarer, he nevertheless experienced a new thrill as he proudly became a part of the intricate machinery of commerce.

While he walked along the dock roadway, sometimes weaving between great wagons loaded high with bales or sacks, he read the boards on the walls listing the ships in that particular section or basin. Sometimes the name of a foreign port followed the ship's name; Kowloon, Pernambuco, Alexandria, Piraeus. The magic was tangible to the young mariner. From time to time, carters would climb down from their boxes and, holding their delivery notes, scan the lists of ships' names, or, more frequently, ask a passer-by the whereabouts of a vessel. He knew that most of the carters and drivers would not be able to read, and counted on their sixth sense to find their way across the country to deliver their loads safely.

As the day wore on, John was forced to seek help to find the Danish ship 'Falkon'. At last, moored against the sea wall, the smart, three-masted barque was pointed out to him. From the stone quayside a steep wooden ladder had been placed to allow access to the deck, twenty or more feet below. He looked over the edge of the dock and called to a seaman on the deck.

"Falkon!' May I come on board?'

The figure below looked up.

'Zis is no strangers to come on der Falkon. Go avay, der Falkon ist sailing.'

John tried again.

'I am to sail with the 'Falkon'. I am friend of Lars Nyborg.'

Immediately the figure stood up, and hurried across to steady the ladder. 'Pliss, come on zer 'Falkon.' You are to be treated special. Wait, here is rope for your bag.'

He threw the end of a heaving line up to John, who made it fast through the straps of his bags and lowered them to the deck, before descending the ladder. Once on board, the sailor carried the bags and took John quickly to the companionway at the break of the poop-deck.

'Zee capitain is on land still. Our first mate is Pieter Mann. Here he iss.'

The cabin to which the sailor had led him was small, and cramped, but he immediately noticed the wooden panelling was brightly polished, as was everything in the cabin. The timber seemed to give a golden light to the tiny space, even though the only light came through a circular brass porthole, not much bigger than would allow a man's head to pass. The cabin was empty, but John could hear the conversation outside. Presently, the First Mate introduced himself to John and, in clear English, welcomed him aboard the 'Falkon.'

'This is really the flagship of the Nyborg fleet. We carry several passengers, but you will have the best cabin, next to the Captain. Do I understand you are a navigator yourself?'

'Yes, I have not passed my exam yet, but I have sailed in the Baltic and round Britain, of course. I have also studied ship building.'

As he spoke he watched the tall man who almost folded himself up to sit in the cabin. He was probably ten years older than John, about thirty, with ginger hair and a wide, drooping moustache which gave his face a rather sad look. But when he spoke he had a friendly, cheerful manner. When he took John on deck to show him round the ship, he uncoiled to stand well over six feet. He noticed John smiling at his difficulty.

'If you design ships for us, will you please make them big enough for real men, not pygmies?'

Pieter explained that they had finished loading virtually everything that was offered by their agent, but in a few days time some casks of tobacco may be delivered. The captain, whose name was Per Eriksson, was expected back from the city any time, and he had already prepared the ship to sail if the wind and tide were favourable before the final casks of tobacco arrived.

When the Captain finally arrived on board, just as darkness was falling, he announced that the ships leaving the Mersey on the next suitable wind would be sailing in convoy. The Royal Navy had two frigates off the Great Orme, and the route would be through the English Channel, to suit the ships for the East Indies and the Mediterranean. As the 'Falkon' carried only the lightest of defences, two light cannon mounted at the stern, he had little choice. To take the northern passage without an escort under such circumstances would not be practical.

They waited for the tide, so the captain took John round the ship and explained the nature of their business. The 'Falkon' had a crew of thirty-two, including two captain's mates. Captain Eriksson, unlike most Danes who John had met previously was dark, with a black beard, neatly trimmed, which gave him a slightly sinister appearance. He had a habit of narrowing his eyes, which seemed to indicate his disbelief in what he was hearing, and John soon learned to keep his more critical ideas unspoken. But Captain Eriksson was not short of his own views, particularly where it affected his trading.

'Mister Weaver, you note carefully, with the Terror as they name it in France, spreading its evil everywhere, soon neighbour will fight neighbour, brothers will take up swords against each other, while politicians sit in their congresses and make treaties. When were you born, John?'

'First of July in seventeen seventy-five, sir.'

'Then you won't mind if I remind you that when you were five years old, Catherine, the Russian 'coche', lined up all the Scandinavian and Baltic states like toy soldiers and declared the great Treaty of Armed Neutrality, so that we demanded the right to carry the weapons and stores of Britain's enemies, whether America or France. We travelled, like today, in armed convoys, to prevent you searching our ships. Now we are all friends again. But did anybody ask me if I wanted to be England's friend or enemy? Did we ask the Russians if they would protect us if England attacked us?'

John was beginning to feel uneasy at the direction the captain's protests were taking, and pretended to be completely ignorant of the recent history.

'Mister Weaver, I just hope you never have the opportunity to see England at War with Denmark.'

The dark, glowering features of the captain's face seemed to be in contrast with all his earlier experience of the Danish people. John carefully considered the proposition. He thought of the growing friendship between his friends in Lancaster and Copenhagen. His thoughts turned to the beautiful Eugenie.

'So do I, sir.'

Chapter 20

The hidden terrors of Land's End and the Isles of Scilly, graveyard of ships from all nations, kept the Mersey convoy well to the westward. Great rolling waves and gusting westerly winds from the Atlantic tossed the ships and kept sails shortened. Naval frigates circled the fifteen merchantmen, flying coloured signal flags. Their task was to separate the ships who were sailing south across the Bay of Biscay to Cape Finisterre from those who were sailing up the Channel towards the North Sea.

The 'Falkon' joined four other ships gathered together by a fast frigate which took pleasure in sailing close under the stern of the merchant ships, like a sheepdog snapping at the flock to drive them across the hillside. On one such pass John could even read the name across her stern, 'Requin'. The name seemed familiar. With the wind astern, the small fleet ran free up the Channel, past The Lizard and then Prawle Point before the great sweep of Torbay opened to the North.

To the astonishment of Captain Eriksson and his crew, the relatively sheltered water of the bay seemed full of ships, great first-rate men-o-war, some with their towering canvas driving them hard across the bay, others at anchor. Lesser ships, smaller and more manoeuvrable, tacked round the lines of battle-ships. Occasional puffs of smoke and the delayed sound of explosions showed where gunnery practice was taking place. From the south, a large man-o-war was approaching close-hauled, the wind just aft of her beam. She was heeled in the wind and judged her course and speed accurately to sail across the stern of the last merchant ship. An observer on deck would have seen the hand-held flags dropping as each gun-crew simulated firing at the merchant ships.

The Danish captain watched nervously as the great ship passed without mishap.

'The English Navy at their cannon practice look so powerful and well-trained, except I know how many of their deafened, frightened gunners were milking cows before the press gang made them into sailors overnight.'

As night fell, yet more sails were visible on the darkening eastern horizon, causing the captain to send two men aloft to keep a sharp look-out. With the same fear, the other ships reduced sail and nervously edged along the coast, just matching the ebb tide as they lay off Portland.

'There's some fighting afoot,' commented the captain. 'I noticed admirals pennants among that fleet, probably getting ready to take the battle to the French. You English like to keep the cork in the French bottle. I suspect in Brest you could do that with a couple of good third-raters, but that fleet in Torbay was expecting much better fish to fry. Is that the correct words?'

John Weaver nodded and smiled at the captain's nearly perfect English. He had found him good company, but very critical of the ease with which the European states went to war so eagerly. His ship was run very smoothly, with little shouting. The crew appeared experienced and kept the ship tidy. Trimming or handing sails, even in heavy weather, was quickly done, and after any adjustment, all lines were cleared away and coiled on cleats. John enjoyed taking his share of the work, keeping watch with the First Mate, fixing the ship's position by identifying the headlands on the port side. He took the opportunity to keep his pilot book up to date in the new waters he was passing through, Captain Eriksson and his two Mates giving him assistance and comments on the passages round his own country. Since leaving the Mersey he found it strange for a Danish seaman to be teaching him, an Englishman, the sights and hazards of the rock-strewn coast of England and Wales. Once again, John sensed the strange fellowship of sailors, who were constantly reminded that the wrath of the sea was much more fearsome than any threat of Kings and Princes. He had heard stories of ships fighting, each attempting to destroy the other with ball and grape-shot, fire and bomb. Yet an enemy sailor, drowning in the sea would be rescued by boat, manned by his aggressors, his wounds bound by the same surgeon who tended the gun-crew who sank his ship. He had heard his father relate how French sailors, taken prisoner from the raider off Walney had been sent to France in exchange for English sailors, each providing men for their aggressors.

The following morning a shift in the wind made the small convoy take to the French side of the channel, so that they could sense French eyes watching their progress. Yet the only interest they aroused was from British warships blockading the harbours of Boulogne and Dieppe. The Danish flag flown by the 'Falkon' gave cause for close examination by one ship, who sailed astern of her for nearly two hours, two officers clearly scanning the deck through telescopes. Then, with a contemptuous alteration of course, it overtook the merchantman on the weather-side, 'stealing' her wind.

Captain Eriksson look across to where John was standing watching the hastening warship.

'I think your British sailor is tired of waiting for the guns to start firing, and has to show off his skill to someone.'

The English Channel eventually opened into the North Sea, where the oceanic seas funnelled up the channel were replaced by the short, steep seas and cold, easterly winds slatting down on the remaining ships. Now, the sea was populated with ships passing between England and the ports of Holland, in addition to the ships like the 'Falkon', on passage to and from the Channel, and the largest merchantmen making voyages of a year or more to India and the East Indies. Just as he had viewed the activities in the great port of Liverpool, so this busy, crowded seaway, which John had crossed on former voyages, gave striking evidence of the level of trade centred on England and the western shores of Europe. From time to time he was able to identify the coastline as it slid past on the starboard side, although more frequently it was far beyond the horizon.

When, at last, the 'Falkon' rounded the northern tip of Jutland he remembered his first voyage, and the excitement of competing with other ships to make fast passages into the Kattegat.

*

The wind and tide did not help their approach to Copenhagen. Several times, the current and unfavourable winds carried them to the north, and fighting back towards Kronborg, in the company of many other ships similarly frustrated in their attempts to enter the Baltic, put tempers on a short fuse.

And then, at last, the first view of the familiar spires and towers of the city could be seen in the cloudy weather to the south-west. But as the sun disappeared behind the city a mysterious glow, like twilight, spread across the shadows. At first it could only be seen as a golden sunset, then suddenly it became obvious that part of the city was in flames, that illuminated the darkening sky and the cloud of smoke which was settling across the city.

All eyes were turned towards the land, and as the captain's telescope scanned the scene he called out names of churches and tall buildings, presumably, thought John, to estimate the location of the fire. From the north-easterly approach it was clear the seat of the fire was on the far side of the city. From John's limited knowledge of the layout of the streets, this would seem to be in the general direction of the Nyborg house. Yet he didn't dare ask the question of his shipmates. With every yard the 'Falkon' progressed towards the harbour entrance his fears became greater. He willingly climbed aloft to help take in the topgallant sails to allow him a better view of the fire, which now seemed to be dying down. The other sailors aloft were shouting to those on deck, each nervously calculating the locality.

When he was back on deck, the captain spoke dismissively to John.

'Looks as if it's the Slots Plads has burned. It certainly isn't the harbour, thank God.'

John knew this was the palace he could see when walking from Lars home to the harbour district. His fear of tragedy, that the beautiful home in which he had first met Eugenie was now under threat, he dared not discuss with the captain, lest he betray his innermost feelings. Instead, he busied himself with the process of arriving in port, observing the captain skilfully calculating the effect of wind and tide to carry the ship as far as possible into the narrow approaches to the harbour.

As the last sail, the fore topsail, was handed and stowed, so the first mooring ropes were taken ashore by rowing boats and dropped over mooring posts. The ship was pulled down the crowded harbour by winching up the rope and then casting it off the posts and carrying it down to a further post, or at one point, actually rowing the ship forward by half a dozen men in the boats.

Finally, in almost total darkness, the 'Falkon' was secured alongside a wooded jetty, to await further laborious moving in daylight.

To John's surprise, the only person on the quayside to meet the incoming ship was an elderly watchman, who spoke no English. The crew were anxiously asking him about the fire, and it became clear it was at the end of town, near the palace, distant from the port where most of the crew had their homes. There was no sign of Lars, and John's heart sank.

As soon as possible, he made an excuse to get ashore to find out what had happened. Without wasting time to change from his deck-coat, he wiped his hands and face on a napkin and, grabbing a hat from his cabin, he walked purposely down the narrow gangway and hurried down the jetty. Once on the quayside he estimated the general direction he needed to go. His sea-legs, not yet attuned to the steadiness of hard streets, carried him uncertainly through the streets, dimly lit by the oil lamps. At one point he felt completely lost, then recognised a square, a statue, a church, before hurrying on his way. With each step, the smell of fire, the acrid smell of smouldering timber, stung his nostrils and choked his panting lungs.

Suddenly, on the far side of a narrow canal, he could see the last remains of the fire. He knew this area was where they had been building the Royal Palace. Now, it seemed to be steaming in the flickering light from three or four fires. Even as he hurried by, a falling roof sent flames and sparks high into the night sky. The sound of frightened horses pulling wagons laden with furniture gave brief warning as they surged through the darkened streets. Men were lifting buckets of water from the canal, and two hand-operated pumps, their clumsy leather hoses snaking into the water, were being wearily worked by half a dozen men on each handle.

At last, he turned a corner and recognised the well-ordered street where Lars lived. He easily found the archway and ran across the courtyard to the front door. His footsteps crunched on the litter of fallen ash. He had never needed to ring the bell before, and he searched in the darkness for a rope or bell-pull of some description. At last he found an iron ring high up on the wall, and without thinking further, he pulled down with all his strength. He could hear a bell ringing in a distant room, and he waited nervously. After possibly three minutes a light flickered through a ground floor window, and then a man's voice growled through the heavy timber of the door.

'Who ist dat?'

'I'm a special friend of Mister Nyborg. My name is John Weaver.'

He spoke as slowly as he could, trying to convey to the invisible guardian that he was an honest visitor. He had no precise idea of the time, but estimated it must be nearly midnight, a late hour for unannounced visiting. He could hear some discussion behind the door, and presently the bolts were being drawn and the door opened about six inches. In the blackness of the night he could make out very little of the face which was examining him.

'Hello, I am John Weaver, a friend of Lars Nyborg,' he carefully repeated.

Suddenly, he was aware of the sounds he yearned to hear, the unmistakable voice of Eugenie. Even in the present crisis he could imagine her calling down from the landing to the old servant. Presently, the door opened a foot more and he was beckoned in. The old man was saying something about the smell of the smoke, and hastily shut the door behind him. John had the sense to enquire whether Mr Nyborg was at home.

'No, he is in another town, sir. He is not in the house. Please wait here. Do not move yet.'

The old man started to climb the staircase. Then John looked up. At the top of the stairs stood Eugenie. From the light of the lamp she carried he could see she was wearing a heavy cream-coloured cape with a hood. It seemed to cover her completely from head to foot, with just her face illuminated in the lamplight.

'Is that John Weaver I can see down there? Come on up. Klaus, bring some brandy and see if there is any food in the pantry. There should be some salmon. Bring it up and then you can go back to bed.'

John waited for the old man to descend the stairs before running eagerly up to the first floor. As he reached the door of the drawing room Eugenie was standing with her arms outstretched. He took her hands in his, as if to kiss them. Instead, she pulled him towards her into the drawing room and slid her arms round his neck to pull his face down towards hers. She kissed him urgently on the mouth, and he responded by enclosing her in his arms. As he held her closely he was aware she was trembling. He had no idea of the time, no idea of how long it was before the lovely creature finally relaxed in his arms and responded to his first expression of untutored love.

'I've been so frightened,' she whispered.

At last she gently pushed him away, just as the servant could be heard returning, bearing a tray, the glasses tinkling against a decanter of golden liquid. A blue-rimmed plate covered with slices of salmon was carefully laid out on a table which stood by the remains of a log fire. The servant lit two more lamps and then bowed to Eugenie and John before departing.

In the brighter lamplight John looked at Eugenie, and suddenly realised he had left a dark stain of soot across her cheek and on the material of her hood.

'You're safe, thank God. I have watched the flames above the city nearly all the day, but we only entered the harbour in the dark. Is Lars not here?'

'Dear John. Lars left two days ago to go to Holstein. I've been alone, hearing the commotion in the streets. I believe it's the Christianborg Palace. The fire started during the early morning, where the builders and carpenters are working on the palace. All day, there have been flaming pieces falling from the sky. You could see the ashes and glowing pieces after sunset. The noise and the smell, oh! I've been so frightened. The maids have been like nervous rabbits. Old Klaus has been very stern, making the maids bundle up baskets of food in case we had to leave the house.'

John looked at his host in surprise.

'Do you mean that? Was there really that sort of risk?'

Tears started in her eyes.

'We were all worried, because our parents always used to frighten us with stories of the great fire years ago. Then the city blazed for three days and nights. Suddenly, we all remembered those childish stories.'

Again, she started to tremble, and covered her eyes with a white kerchief.

John, who was sitting on the opposite side of the small table got up and stood by Eugenie's chair. He laid a hand on her shoulder, and felt her shapely body through the cape. Clumsily, he smoothed the soft material. She took his hand and kissed it, pressing it firmly against her lips. She held it against her cheek with one hand, whilst she slid her arm round his waist and drew him against the side of her face. In the flickering firelight they comforted each other solely by the closeness of their bodies.

John was still in his coat, and his hands and face were dirty from running through the smoking city streets. Eugenie pretended to suddenly notice how grimy he was.

'Look at you, like a chimney sweep. What am I thinking of? Come with me.'

She led him through two doors and along a passageway to a room which he knew was her private apartment. They entered a room with a wash-stand beside the window. She had obviously washed before retiring for the night, and the perfumed water remained in the huge decorated porcelain basin, still slightly warm.

'Here, take off your coat and you can wash in this water, it's still a little warm. Here, I'll help you.'

He looked nervously at Eugenie.

'I don't think I can, with you...'

She laughed, throwing her head back as she did so. The hood of her cape fell back, revealing her hair, loose and flowing. It reached down her back like a golden cascade. John had never seen her like this and was so confused he had started to remove his cravat before taking off his heavy coat. All the time he was protesting that he shouldn't...that he could manage on his own.

'John, don't you have a sister?'

'No, I don't. Why do you ask me that?'

'Well, you'll have to look upon me as a sister, just helping you after the terrible fright we have both suffered. Now, let me wash your face and neck.'

She took a large thick napkin which had been folded over the side of the basin and rinsed it in the cool water. She reached up and wiped his face carefully, the way a mother cares for her new-born infant. Round his neck, behind his ears, the fabric searched out every fold. The intoxicating smell of the perfumed water seemed to encourage John to ever greater longing for cleanliness and he threw off his coarse shirt, revealing his muscular chest. Eugenie rinsed and washed the taut muscular flesh before taking one of the rough towels off the wash-stand. She dried his body with the gentle, dabbing action known only to ladies who expect to pamper their bodies. John had no idea that bathing and drying could be so wonderful. In the black tub in front of the fire in Lancaster, the process was generally carried out with the greatest urgency to minimise the chilling discomfort. Tonight, bathing had become a luxury.

'Wait here, I'll get you a gown. Don't walk about the house without your shirt. Stay here.'

She left the room. John had the first opportunity to look around. A full-length cheval glass reflected his image. He had not seen his reflection for weeks of travelling, and he was surprised how tall and elegant he looked, wearing just his breeches and buckle shoes. He noticed that beside the glass was a row of wooden hooks. Hanging from one was a garment he didn't recognise, which he visualised would cover Eugenie from shoulder to ground, but even to his casual glance it was clear it did not fit closely round the neck. He stepped closer and placed his face close to the gossamer-like material. The smell of perfume, which was beginning to haunt his life, tingled through his nostrils.

'Do you like it?'

He turned, blushing. She ignored his discomfiture.

'That is a perfume from the Orient. I'm told it's one of the most precious perfumes in the World.'

She handed John a woollen garment like a shepherd's smock, with a silken rope round the waist.

'Put this on and then we can have some supper. Leave all your things here until you have had some food. Hurry up, because you've got to bring the fire back to life.'

She smiled at the young mariner as he laughed at the possible meaning in the innocent remark.

In the dining room, with a little encouragement, the logs flickered into flame, warming the two occupants, even if it left the far corners of the room cold in the darkness. The fresh fish and a tumbler of brandy with fresh spring water soon brought a mellow glow to John's face. As he ate he told Eugenie about the voyage through the fleet, his plans and the interest of his 'company' in Lancaster. He explained how he was representing almost the entire city. He just had one more glass of brandy and water. Eugenie's blue eyes never left his face as he spoke.

At last he could no longer hide his weariness, and she smiled as he tried to conceal a yawn.

'You can sleep in the front bedroom, if you don't mind the old woollen blankets. I can't disturb the maids after what they've had to put up with today.'

'I could sleep on a staircase, the way I feel.'

'Then make yourself comfortable in bed and I'll bring your drink in a minute.'

He walked into the large, panelled bedroom, which was cold and dark. A candle flickered on a table beside the bed. He took off his shoes and breeches and then he gratefully slid between the coarse covers before removing the strange borrowed garment. For a minute he lay coiled up, not daring to push his feet to the chilling extremities of the big bed. He started to unwind, slowly pushing his feet out, then suddenly froze. He was aware of the perfume before he felt the weight of Eugenie sitting on the side of the bed.

'My Sailor John. I'm sorry this bed is so cold and unwelcoming. I've brought your drink, and now I must make sure my beautiful guest is comfortable. Is that quite agreeable to the company's ambassador?'

His mouth was dry. He could neither speak nor swallow as he felt the weight of the smooth sleek body of Eugenie sliding against his when she eased into the large bed. Softly wrapped in the silk robe, the contrast with the rough material of the bedclothes was just the first of many new experiences of that night. He easily surrendered to her skilful touch as she spread the full weight of her body across his muscular torso, consuming and devouring him with moist, eager lips. In the flickering light of the candle and the distant fires the warm softness of her body glowed and created secret shadows. The reality of her passion was greater and more insistent than the dreams he had harboured since their first meeting, nor even his past, unskilful couplings on harvest nights on a moonlit fell. The delicate fragrance and soft touch of her firm flesh was quite unlike the cheerfully eager, sweating maids who had unlaced their had bodices in a chaff-laden hay field.

Eugenie whispered in the darkness of the night.

'I never dared think this night could be mine.'

'Dearest Eugenie, I have dreamed of nothing else,' he replied.

Her hungry, demanding body caressed him through the night, whilst in the city, shouts and cries and hurrying wagons echoed through the street and the leaping tongues of flame finally succumbed to the sputtering hoses.

Chapter 21

The Danish Captain had been correct.

The great fleet of warships which the crew of the 'Falkon' had seen assembling in Torbay was preparing to take the battle to the enemy observed secure in the port of Brest. In early May Admiral Howe, nearly seventy years old, known round the fleet as 'Black Dick', had withdrawn his blockade ships to lure the French out of port. He was getting reports which led him to suspect a vital French grain convoy was crossing the Atlantic from America. His target must be to intercept the convoy and to attack the escorting French warships.

However, the English convoy from the Mersey required him to detach eight of his fleet under Admiral Montagu to escort them and other merchant ships through the French privateers' hunting grounds across the Bay of Biscay to Finisterre and the Mediterranean.

On the frigate 'Requin', captured from the French in Morecambe Bay, Mighty Jake Tempest, now promoted fore-topman, was again excited by the sight of the fleet setting sail. The iron discipline and relentless training he had been subjected to gave him little sense of pride, until the well-ordered ships sailed in their carefully rehearsed formations, a demonstration of maritime power. The distant observer would know little of the cruel conditions on board the magnificent ships. Nervous of actually putting into port for fear of losing their crews by desertion, the anchorage in Torbay at least kept the crews on board, whilst essential stores and provisions all had to be brought out by small boats. As few of the crew would have been paid for many months, even being on dry land would not be the end of their misery. In the cramped conditions in the lower decks, finding what comfort they could between the cannons, discussion invariably turned to means of escape, even if few of them knew the geographical position of the ship. They couldn't even be certain whether the gentle hills and rocky headlands were their own homeland or just an ally's shore, and the ship's officers had no intention of telling them. Even the names of their own officers were not widely known.

The 'Requin' was detached to sail westward into the Atlantic to form part of a screen of ships searching for the French convoy. She was fast in a strong wind, and a carefully devised search pattern should give her the best chance of finding the enemy and being able to get back to the main fleet with the vital intelligence.

Yet they found nothing, and on the third day retraced their track to report back to the fleet. In a strange swirling mist the 'Requin' sighted a great line of warships to the south, ghostly shapes looming out of the dawn. Several ships passed before it became certain this was the French fleet, by which time any deception was too late. One of the French ships had altered course to pass close to the 'Requin' on the opposite side to the rest of the fleet. The frigate was effectively trapped between two ships, so the captain went about to pass astern and to present the minimum target to the approaching ships, with the forlorn hope that the mist would envelope her before more than the first shots could be fired.

The captain knew the conventional French tactic was to fire high with the first broadside, to damage masts and sails. The English frigate only had her upper deck gun-ports open, due to the heavy seas running, and the gun crews were loading and running out the port twenty-four pounders. The gunnery officer was demanding faster preparations, and shouting to the gun-layers, who would sight the gun barrels.

'Aim for her rudder! Aim for the rudder! Any good shot under her stern, a prize for a hit!'

As the two ships raced towards each other, the Frenchman fired as each cannon came into line with the frigate sailing directly towards her port beam.

The first shots from the Frenchman passed overhead with a ghostly whistling sound. But later shots passed through the fore course and then tore the canvas into long vertical ribbons. One ball hit the fore topsail yard and split the timber in two like a matchstick. The broken yard swung round, allowing the topsail to fold up in the wind. The noise of the splitting yard and the uncontrollable canvas was joined by the next shots from the French ship. The main-mast was hit a glancing blow, the ball crashing to the deck in a hail of splinters. Still the 'Requin' was pointing straight at the side of the Frenchman and unable to fire. She was now so close that the shouted orders of the French gunners could be clearly heard. The explosions of the next cannons to bear on the frigate were at a range of less than a ship's length. For many of the British crew this assault was the first time they had heard cannons fired in anger, let alone been the sitting target for such an onslaught, and the impact of the five or six guns that fired tore more of the canvas to useless shreds. The screaming, clattering chain-shot was the most effective way of damaging canvas.

The captain directed the quartermaster to steer right under the elaborately decorated stern of the towering French ship, until Jake, crouching low behind the bulwark, could look up and see the gilded carved balustrades almost over his head.

'Requin' fired her twelve cannon like the beats on a gigantic drum. As each cannon came into line, the mind-numbing explosion fired the ball as near as possible to the rudder head. Timber could be seen flying, but real damage would only be shown by the erratic steering of the French man-o-war, and 'Requin' did not intend staying for proof. With most of her sails showing signs of damage and two yards split, she turned away from the other ship and waited for the mist to cover her retreat and to lick her wounds. The French fleet would be anxious that the British ship should be prevented from relaying back the news of their existence. But the brief, violent exchange of fire had been loud enough to alert the British ships groping blindly through the mist. The limping frigate shortly found herself passing through the line of British men-o-war, and the yeoman on the 'Requin' shouted out the message being signalled from the British line.

'Enemy warning received by your valiant action.'

Two men had been injured, but superficial wounds could be bound and left for further treatment until a friendly port. However, Jake had calculated that this was one of the ways of getting ashore, not in haphazard flight, but in a carefully planned escape from the pain of the ship. The long, enduring horrors of the scorching slave ships could not be as bad as the cold, brutal misery of the overcrowded frigate, manned with more and more press-ganged sailors. The terrified, inexperienced newcomers merely placed more work and trouble on the experienced hands, so that the mastery of the ship was reduced, and the rope's end flayed bent backs and straining shoulders more often.

In the fresh westerly wind the damaged ship made good progress through the following sea, and eventually turned to port, making a slow, rolling passage northward towards the coast.

In darkness the 'Requin' dropped anchor between the protective headlands which Jake learned was the approach to the great sound at Plymouth.

Alert to the fact that the gunfire would have been the first taste of bombardment for many of the new crew, the captain placed marine guards on deck to halt the dreams of any deserters. Supply tenders tying up alongside were examined with particular care.

After several days waiting, new spars and canvas were brought out, and the back-breaking task of raising the spars aloft to replace the damaged ones could only be accomplished with the noise and fury which had become the normal way of work. With crushed hands, split fingers and bruised legs the spars were hoisted, the parrels secured to hold the yard across the mast, before the running rigging was secured. The works continued through day and night until completed, whilst on deck damaged sails were stitched, five stitches to every inch of seam. Hands more used to scything standing corn were turned to driving the needles through the unyielding canvas. The prowling figure of the sail-maker vented his wrath upon the laggardly sailors.

'I know every man jack working on this sail! One splitting seam when we're under sail and I'll know whose back to split. Five to the inch, you pig-men!'

As soon as the ship could boast a reasonable suit of canvas, hands were piped to stations for weighing anchor and the capstan bars were shipped into position for the task of raising the anchor. To the accompaniment of half-hearted shanties in the evening light, 'Requin' once more set her sails. Orders had been presented to the captain by the senior officers who had paid a brief visit of inspection before departure. They had also pinned to the hatchways leading to the lower deck a notice from Admiral Howe commending the brilliant action of the fleet in destroying eight of the French men-o-war, capturing six ships as prizes and securing over three thousand prisoners. The notice wisely made no reference to the one hundred and seventeen merchant ships fully laden with precious American corn which had entered Brest unharmed on that 'Glorious First of June.'

*

Lars returned to Copenhagen, burdened by the news from France which messengers were relaying round the cities of Europe. The execution of opponents of the Revolution, by the newly named Committee of Public Safety, scaled new levels of horror. It had been reported to Lars that in little more than twelve months as many as forty thousand men and women had been executed by one means or another.

'I'm told there is a terrible shortage of food, and there are riots in the towns and cities. Only the farm workers seem to have full bellies.'

John listened in horror to the stories of civil war and the attacks on the neighbours of the new French republic. In particular, that the French navy was suffering from the zeal of the revolutionaries, who insisted on officers being removed from command, ship-board decisions being made by committees of the crew. In consequence, many ships were hopelessly handled until a more rational system prevailed.

'Well, John, my friend, there's excellent chances for trade with France for those who have the courage to handle it. The value of the French franc is lowered with every day that passes. The only way we will trade will be by barter. I have already found cargoes of wine, earthenware and some short timber, which can be bartered for food. So we will look for grain and bean supplies. The nearest port we can ship to that I can see would be Antwerp on The Schelde.'

196

'I think you may be standing into danger if the Royal Navy find you.'

Lars laughed quietly.

'That depends on how we ship it and to whom we make our consignment. I have traders in Antwerp who can handle little difficulties like that.'

John looked at his mentor. Lars smiled.

'John, the whole purpose of securing our merchants into a great partnership is that we can certainly find a way of moving goods from the people who make them to the people who want them, without having to read every peace treaty, every declaration of war and pact between princes. That's why our new company will be trading successfully. And John, for your report to Lancaster, please note I am going to repair the 'Laguna' and use it in the Baltic for large timbers. I've offered Captain Hotblack and your friend Captain Cooper employment on the ship. Hotblack insists we have no right to ownership, but I have to disagree with him. He abandoned it, with all his crew. We are technically called 'the salvors' and can demand the full price of the ship and our costs, or keep it for our own use.'

John looked worried at this statement, although it was not a subject upon which he had any experience.

'I think the committee in Lancaster, if it was one of our ships, would expect to pay all your costs of salvage but still call the ship ours.'

'Understand, John, that my proposal is that otherwise I will covey them to Liverpool on my next vessel as free passengers. At present I do not enjoy their highest regard, which I regret. However, they do not have many choices.'

John reluctantly agreed with Lars' attitude, with a feeling of foreboding. This was not the first time he had observed the quiet resolve in Lars' attitude to the conduct of business. No dramatic speeches or gestures accompanied his determination to take every advantage of circumstances.

Fortunately, Lars had made an arrangement with John that he would be paid every day he was on one of Lars ships or ashore anywhere in Denmark. Thus, it was possible for John to find lodgings in Copenhagen and lead a life of comparative comfort. Many evenings were spent with Lars and Eugenie, and his sojourn in the city was a completely new experience for the young man. Eugenie had made no reference to sharing his bed on the frightening night of the Palace fire. Her manner had been correct at all times, always charming and friendly, with never more than a kiss on each cheek by way of greeting. But when she introduced him to her friends he was aware of knowing glances and giggles, as the exchanges in Danish were greeted by gales of laughter and admiring looks.

Lars and Eugenie were active people in the social life in the city. Parties, dinners, dances, even balls at one of the royal residences seemed to fill their evenings. John was able to buy sufficient clothes to see him through one or two events, and Eugenie even borrowed from Lars' ample wardrobe to find a change of attire for him.

On one such evening he found himself seated beside an elegant Englishwoman, dressed in pale blue silks, with her hair piled high and decorated with pearls discreetly tucked into the tightly-pinned curls. Like the other ladies at the ball, her gown was cut to reveal the expanse of her bare shoulders and the shapely, shadowy curves of her breasts, which became more obvious when she leaned forward to speak. John was surprised to observe that her skin appeared to be covered with a white powder which failed to conceal pale marks and fine creases. He considered she might be twenty years his senior, but seemed very interested in his presence and insisted on questioning him closely about his reason for being in the city. Suddenly she turned to him and exclaimed 'But you must be Captain John? I've heard so much about you. How exciting! I'm told you've been shipwrecked, blown up by those dreadful Prussians, and now you represent half the ship owners in England. How much you have done, and yet so young and energetic, like a colt.'

'Madam, I really fear you exaggerate...'

'Captain, never deny a favourable exaggeration. Take my advice, in this town they're just a bunch of farmers in silk coats. Good people, but slow to serenade, if you understand my meaning.'

'Forgive me, madam, I'm afraid we have not been introduced. My name is John Weaver of Lancaster. May I enquire your name?'

'Certainly, John Weaver of Lancaster. My name is Elizabeth. To be correct Lady Elizabeth, wife of Sir Richard Bowen, First Secretary to His Majesty's Ambassador to the Royal Court of Denmark.' She watched her young listener as she slowly pronounced her title. John felt the blush creeping up his neck and cheeks.

'Madam, I apologise. I had no idea...'

'Don't apologise, young Captain John.'

Presently, the Secretary to the Ambassador walked across the space cleared for dancing to address his wife.

'Elizabeth, my dear lady...'

'Richard. This is the famous Captain John Weaver. You know, dear Eugenie's friend.'

The Secretary, a portly man whose face was almost completely concealed behind snowy white whiskers, muttered under his breath. He shook hands before taking his wife to one side for a whispered conversation. He then turned back to John.

'I understand you're one of Nyborg's fellow merchants. It sounds a very powerful company you traders are creating. Keep in touch with the embassy, if you would be so kind. I often require a good messenger. If you are travelling between England and Copenhagen there could always be a bag to be carried. Just between you and me, Captain, you will have a Letter of Free Passage when working for the Embassy, so it does have some advantages.'

'I'm very honoured, sir.'

'Well, I'd heard your name from Lars and his charming sister. With all these villains in Europe we need good people like you travelling between our countries. And if you think I can be any help, visit me at the embassy. I bid you good-night. If you like to keep Lady Elizabeth dancing you have my thanks. G'night, Captain.'

When he left, Eugenie came hurrying across the room, and eagerly drew Lady Elizabeth and John to her side.

'There! I knew you two would be up to some mischief as soon as my back was turned! Has Sir Richard departed, dear?'

John was still reeling from the pace at which things were happening. In this small group of people it appeared that friendships were very quickly established, and everyone seemed to have a reason for knowing the others in the group. Nothing in his life had prepared him for this unusual social life. The memories of Lancaster seemed far away.

Eugenie took John by the arm.

'John, you must learn to dance. Here, let me show you. None of the Danes like our dances, except my brother. They prefer to talk business. The Englishmen like dancing, but we never have enough to make up pairs.'

For the rest of the evening, as wine flowed into the goblets, Eugenie and Lady Elizabeth tutored John in the gavotte, the two-step, and a strange formation which took him into the arms of six or more unknown ladies who crowded the dance floor. Eugenie remained elegant and graceful throughout but Lady Elizabeth was flushed with excitement and John noticed the tell-tale streaks on her white powdered skin. From time to time he caught sight of Lars swirling round with one of the ladies, and smiling broadly at John.

In the middle of the night, when John had lost any sense of time, the carriages were called. Lars mysteriously disappeared in the company of a young woman with long, dark hair in curls and ringlets round her face and over her bare shoulders. Eugenie and John were invited to share Lady Elizabeth's coach. When they climbed into its red-lined interior, John sat facing backwards whilst the two women sat side by side looking towards him. Although the coach was quite narrow, made more crowded by the ladies' cloaks, the two women pulled John towards them and insisted he squeezed on to the cushions between them. Amid much laughter he had to place an arm round their shoulders in the restricted space, and they could only rest their hands on the white linen of his breeches, steadying themselves in the jolting coach by clutching his knees. The ladies' conversation during the journey back into town unashamedly compared the merits of the gentlemen with whom they had danced or the style of the other ladies, even to the extent of estimating who was sharing whose bed-chamber.

As the coach drew up at the steps of the embassy residence, Lady Elizabeth leaned forward and kissed John with great passion, full on the lips, whilst Eugenie pretended to scold her. Mysteriously, he was aware of a gloved hand caressing each thigh, one in white silk, the other in palest blue. Eugenie tapped her companion's wandering hands.

'I'm greatly surprised, Lady Elizabeth, that you should take to your bosom this innocent young mariner. I don't know what spell these Englishmen cast upon their women, but I would be grateful if you would restrict your caresses to the gavotte.'

'Or perhaps the horn-pipe!' Lady Elizabeth laughed at her own wit. With much chuckling and a final pressure on his thigh Lady Elizabeth released the startled young man and opened the door of the carriage. John jumped out and helped her down the steps to the ground. The door of the residence had been opened by a servant, and John simply had to take her to the door.

'Good night, ma'am. It has been a pleasure to meet you tonight.'

'Good night, Captain John. I will expect to see much more of you next week.'

John climbed back into the carriage, and the coachman took his two passengers back to Eugenie's house.

'You must stay here now, there's no other carriage tonight. Thank-you, coachman. You may go.'

She gave John a large key from her cloak pocket.

'Open the door, John, and don't wake the servants. And put the bolts on before you come upstairs.'

'What about Lars? Won't he be home?'

'My dear John, unless I am much mistaken, my brother is taking to the bed of the cousin of the French Ambassador. None of them dare return to Paris, and Lars sees an opportunity for enlarging the circle of his friends.'

John smiled at the possible meaning of the words. But Eugenie was taking him by the hand, leading him once again through the doors.

'Tonight, our rooms for guests are not good enough for you. You shall have the best bed in the house. With the whole of the city admiring my young hero, he shall have the rest he deserves.'

With growing confidence and excitement caused by the lovely woman who was already releasing her elaborate coiffure from the jewelled pins and slides, John threw his cloak over the foot of the bed.

'I assure you, madam, I shall enjoy the rest.'

*

In the morning Lars was in a jubilant mood. He had arrived at the warehouse office at the same time as John. No reference was made to the events of the night before. John had soon recognised this was a characteristic of his new employer and readily adopted the same manner.

'John, I have had the most exceptional good fortune. I have a friend in the French Embassy who is not in full accord with the new government in Paris. What is important is that this person can put us in touch with many trading people who can move goods easily round the country. Payment in gold or by barter can be arranged.'

John carefully considered the events of the previous evening.

'Then, Lars, I may be of further help. I have been invited to be an occasional courier for the British Embassy. I don't understand what this may demand, but I am told I would have a Letter of Free Passage, which surely must be useful to us.'

'So, my friend, I think it is up to us to explore these highly desirable avenues of trade.' He winked at John. 'In my report to your committee in Lancaster I will mention these vital associations. We must impress them with the determination we are bringing to our activities.'

Chapter 22

The winter which followed the creation of the Northern Trading Company was considered to be the worst of the century. The seas and rivers froze, even 'the milk in the milkmaids' pails froze like marble' as reported in the London Gazette. The Dutch Texel fleet of fourteen ships-of-the-line were captured, while they lay imprisoned in the ice. The seizure was made, improbably, by a French lieutenant-colonel with a squadron of hussars and a company of infantrymen. The movement all of ships was severely restricted. In the Baltic most of the harbours were closed, at a time when demands for timber, particularly mast poles, were urgently made by all the European navies. Lars Nyborg took a philosophical view of the harsh weather. He explained the problem to John during his next visit to Copenhagen.

'The very best mast poles are felled in forests hundred of miles away from the Baltic ports. In my experience, the longest are available for shipment after a severe winter, when the plains are frozen solid and heavy timber can be dragged across the ice. I've seen mild winters, when the ground has been soft, and nothing much longer than sixty feet has been brought down on the rivers. Timber of that size does not earn the best rates. You watch the Admiralty Stores in Deptford. They'll pay anything for a presentable pole over ninety feet.'

The old sailing ship 'Laguna' had been patched up and was ready to sail to Riga and St Petersberg as soon as the ice started to break up. Captain Hotblack as Master and Captain Cooper as his First Mate were willing employees of the new company. In addition, Lars had an agreement with two Russian ships lying alongside in St.Petersberg, who would be amongst the first ships to sail with a full cargo of timber. Everything depended upon the great thaw and a favourable wind.

In Lancaster, the same changes in the elements were awaited by traders and canal-builders alike. With no work available on the frozen farmlands, labourers applied for work on the canal. The arches of the aqueduct started to rise from the foundations on each side of the river and the four stone piers which were now just visible above the high-tide level in the icy water. The short hours of winter daylight restricted the handling of the great pieces of dressed stone, each weighing several tons. The timber framework, or centering, which would form the temporary support for the huge arches, was being constructed on the south side of the river. For reasons of economy, just two such frames would serve for all the arches, being dismantled and moved along to the next span as required.

The bitter winter was the final blow to two of the contractors on the canal. Poor workmanship, shortage of good quality stone and timber were all exacerbated by the numbing cold and blocked tracks. The ground was even too hard to steal root crops.

By the end of winter the committee of the canal company authorised the two contractors to be 'measured up' and paid off. At this time, Mr Millar who, for a year, had been resident engineer, adopted a new method to try to improve the quality and speed of the work.

He decided to award small contracts to thirty or more contractors, each responsible for perhaps quarter of a mile of canal, or building just one bridge. If work was slow or unsatisfactory, the aggressive Archibald Millar would simply dismiss the offending contractor and pass his contact to a proven performer from another part of the canal.

The continental war was continuing to force up the price of food, although the farms which surrounded the city of Lancaster protected it from the worst effects felt in the great cities of the south. In the cotton mills around Manchester rioters attacked the factories, demanding cheaper food. Thefts from warehouses led to commotion in the streets, although when the militia were called upon to control the angry crowds, they frequently refused to do more than contain the disturbances into one area. A grim report was circulating in the Lancaster coffee houses that the Reverend Dr. Drake in Rochdale had ordered the Volunteers to shoot upon the rioters. Two were killed, and thereafter his church remained empty. Charity was a scarce commodity in the towns.

In March, the French, despite a multitude of difficulties at home, were quickly increasing the grip on their neighbours' lands. The Treaty of Basel effectively removed Prussia from the Grand Coalition, and Holland's defeat drove the British army back to Hamburg where they waited for the British fleet to rescue them.

'Now, John, you can see where the strength of our new trading company produces its best harvest. Danish flags carrying Danish goods will sail unhindered into the Prussian ports of Memel and Dantzig, where your Union flag would not be quite so welcome. As a consequence the British admiralty will be happy to pay even more for their mast poles, and overlook the Danish flag.'

John was now a frequent traveller between Lancaster, Liverpool and Copenhagen, harmonising the activities of the fledgling company. He could see how the ships were managed, and exchange the wisdom and ideas of each part of the operation. In addition, the shipments into the Royal Navy yards along the Thames gave an opportunity for the City of London to add its contribution to the widening interests of the company. Lars had tried to encourage the reluctant Lancastrians to look to London as the financial centre of their company.

'With Holland seized by the French, I can see the business heart of Amsterdam looking for a new home. Copenhagen will never assume that role, so I am depending on London becoming the real centre of banking for us traders.'

For the first time in his life, John Weaver was apprehensive. The great city, which, in spite of better roads, still took at least two days arduous travel by the expensive stage coach from Lancaster, seemed remote and unwelcoming. He had heard reports from his father of the crowded streets, riotous inns and licentious women. And the Press Gangs, particularly keen to sniff out strangers and visitors. But Lars already had an agent who looked after any of his ships in the long, straggling dockland of London, finding outward cargo and warehousing the incoming freight. His name was Albert Gurney and he lived in a terraced house in Southwark. He crossed London Bridge for his visits to the City, but most of his work with ships' cargo kept him on the south side of the river, at Rotherhithe, Deptford and Greenwich, particularly for supplying timber to the Admiralty. The great naval shipyards which extended down the Thames estuary as far as Chatham and the River Medway were the principal users of Baltic timber, hemp, flax and tar brought in on Nyborg's ships.

John Weaver's first sight of the great city was from the poop deck of the three-masted barquentine 'Diamant' arriving from Halskov, her last port of call after three months in the Baltic. Like many ships attempting to navigate up the estuary, the strong ebb tides would carry the ship downstream, in spite of a favourable wind. As a result, the incoming ships frequently were forced to lie at anchor on the ebb tide and resume their hesitant progress up the narrowing waterway on the next flood tide. Groundings and even collisions with other ships, although not dangerous, made the progress very slow and frustrating to John. When at last they reached Rotherhithe a weary crew tied up on a riverside berth. This meant that twice a day the ship 'took the mud,' settling at an angle on the sloping river bed. The flow of water from the great city up the river carried the detritus of nearly a million souls, fouling the air even on a cool day.

Mr Gurney was waiting to step aboard as the ship tied up. After greeting the Captain he introduced himself to John.

'Albert Gurney, shipping agent, at your service, sir.'

His short, stocky frame seemed to be enclosed in many layers of tweed materials, partially secured with rows of buttons, so that it was not immediately obvious whether he was a fat man or not. His cheerful, florid face, with white side whiskers which were lovingly brushed to double the width of his face, seemed in a permanent state of laughter. He wore a black top hat, which added a few extra vital inches to his height. He explained to John how much of the timber was destined for the naval dockyards. This would be loaded on to flat rafts and old boat's hulls where some of the deck planking had been removed to give easier access for loading. These strange craft would tie up on the off-shore side of the 'Diamant', under the control of a naval coxwain or boatswain with a handful of seamen who used the tides to navigate the river, supplementing the efforts of the seamen on long rowing sweeps. Sometimes, two such hulls would be lashed together to take long spars or keel timbers. Thus, a number of these craft were continuously coming and going as the longshoremen struggled with the great timbers. Compared with casks of tobacco, sacks of spices or even building stones, timber was not welcome cargo to those unloading it. In his strange, clipped accent, Mr Gurney looked momentarily gloomy as he surveyed the great baulks of oak and pine in the hold of the ship.

'There's some split 'eads an' broke backs getting that lot ashore, Mister John. That's as 'ow we earn our money, eh?' He finished this observation, like most, with a laugh and a pat on his ample girth.

Sure enough, on the third day, one of the great poles rolled across the sloping lower deck as the ship lay heeled on the mud at low tide. The tortured screams from the man trapped against the ship's side by the spar told its own story.

'Cracked rib, like as not,' opined Mr Gurney. 'Get 'im a cart, take 'im to 'ospital. Look sharp, now!' He urged the longshoremen to carry their comrade ashore. He put a couple of coins in the drayman's dirty hand. 'Roverhive. Tell 'em friend of Mister Gurney.'

Day by day, the unloading continued. As new hulls drew alongside John was surprised to hear the bos'un in charge shouting at one of the sailors.

'Tempest, you lazy cur! Heave this barge for'ard. Sharp, now!'

John looked across at the ugly boat, and in an instant recognised the thin figure of his boyhood friend. Even as he watched, the bos'un screamed yet louder.

'You're all lazy scum! Quick, get a line ashore! Jump with it, you goat! Jump! Go on, jump!'

The thin figure eyed the distance between the old hulk and the black paintwork of the 'Diamant' and then leaped from one to the other, across a space of several feet. Miraculously, he landed on the deck of the 'Diamant', clutching the mooring line. He writhed in agony on the deck, holding his bare feet which had taken the whole impact of his landing. John ran to his aid.

'Jake? Is that you, Jake Tempest?'

The crumpled figure looked straight into John's face.

'My God, John. It's you, is it? John, you must not recognise me. Please, you don't know me.' His voice dropped to a whisper. 'If they find we have a friend at hand they keep us locked in the gun deck. Pretend you're helping me. Say I'm hurt. Go on, John, for God's sake!'

John looked across at the bos'un

'Your man's hurt. He landed hard on the deck. He can't stand yet. Just leave him be a few minutes.'

The bos'un was still raging.

'Hurt? That little bastard is always hurt! I'll hurt him when I get him back on board.'

John made a great labour apparently carrying the injured man to sit on the hatch-coaming, with his back to the other boat.

'Jake, what's up?' He looked at the haunted eyes of his friend.

'John, my friend, I'm on a ship of the devil. How long are you in port? Quick, before they come for me.'

'The ship will be two or three weeks at this rate, but I am trying to get back to Lancaster on the stage in two or three days.'

'Do you live aboard this ship?'

John nodded.

'John, I'll be here, in the middle of the night. Don't fail me.'

Before he could say more, the sailors from the hull jumped over the bulwark rail and, each taking a limb, carried him back to the hull.

The captain of the 'Diamant', hearing the shouting, had come on deck and watched the injured man being taken away. He turned to John.

'You English may have the greatest navy, but you've got the cruellest system in the World for getting the best out of your seamen. Look at that swine now!'

He pointed across to the hull. The bos'un had a rope's end, with which he was belabouring the returning party of seamen.

'You lazy pigs! Get this filthy hulk made fast alongside and keep a look-out for thieves. Five men on deck, and one man injured. I'm ashore for an hour. Anything or anyone missing when I get back, then ten lashes to the others. And no talking to these foreigners.'

He jabbed his thumb towards John and the captain as he spoke.

The bos'un jumped on to the deck of the 'Diamant' and briefly saluted the captain as he made his way down the trembling gangway. John watched the receding figure as it made for the door of 'The King's

Mariner.' A gale of laughter and shouting escaped from the door of the tavern as he pushed his way in.

Nearly one hour after the sun had set, when all work had finished on the ships, the bos'un appeared at the foot of the gangway. The tide was in, and the climb to the deck was quite steep. The crew of the 'Diamant' watched with amusement. A woman from the inn appeared to be helping the sailor to climb aboard. He was obviously very drunk, and at each step he shouted 'Yes!' with great joy, as if each pace was an achievement.

At the top of the gangway, the woman disentangled herself from his draped arms and propped him up straight. She stepped back to admire her feat of balance and called 'Goodnight, my beauty,' before turning and trotting happily back to the bright lights of the tavern. The drunken man remained upright for many seconds and appeared to survey the deck in front of him. Suddenly, he crumpled like a broken puppet. He finally collapsed and pitched forward over the handrope of the gangway and plunged head-first into the dark chasm between the ship and the timber dock wall. A terrible thud signalled his headlong impact on to one of the dock timbers. For a second there was a chilling scream of pain, and then silence.

'Lanterns! Hurry, get a light over the side!'

One of the Danish sailors was putting a rope over the side while others were finding deck lanterns and a rope ladder. The sailor lowered himself down and shouted something in Danish to his mates on deck. John recognised the word for 'dead' and presently, with many ropes and much heaving, the wet body of the bos'un was hauled back on deck. The top of his head was smashed like an apple, and gushed blood to mix with the black stinking dock water that poured from his clothes and from his gaping mouth.

John had come from his cabin to see what was the commotion, and felt the vomit rising in his throat at the sight of the smashed skull. Soon the deck was crowded with sailors from the timber hulk, who laughed at John's nausea.

'That bastard's dead,' observed one of their number.

'How unhappy that makes me,' said another.

The six young sailors laughed. John looked around in the darkness.

'Is that you, Jake?'

'Yes, brother. Mighty Jake Tempest and this is the happiest day of my life.'

The thin young man looked round at his five shipmates.

'Funny thing, isn't it. Bos'un Cogwell falls over the side, drunk as a lord, and kills himself. Here's the body. Yet able-seaman Jake Tempest jumps over the side to save the beloved bos'un and dies between ship and jetty. Unfortunately, we never found his poor, crushed body. So sad.' He mockingly makes the sign of the cross and looks heavenwards. 'May God rest his soul.'

He looks round at the puzzled sailors.

'Any question, me mates? I'm drowned, dead n' gone, body lost on the ebb tide. Understood?'

At last, the young men nodded and laughed at the ruse.

The captain had joined the party and immediately took charge.

'You, go to the tavern and get that tart who was with the bos'un. Next, one of you sailors, get back to your dock and tell them two men have been killed. Tell them to bring a barrow or something for the body.'

He pointed to the retreating figure of Jake.

'Sailor! Come here!'

Jake returned and stood straight and tall in front of the Danish Captain.

'Name?'

'Mighty Jake Tempest, able seaman, sir.'

'English?'

'Born in Rotherhithe sir.'

'If you leave that hulk, what will you do? I can't give you a job. Is that clear?'

'Clear, sir.'

'Have you family in London?'

'No sir. My family is in a distant town. Lancaster.'

'Well, Jake, I know Lancaster. Hard people there. Have you heard of 'The Golden Ball' on the River Lune?'

'Aye, that I have. Home of the Press Gangs. I've sailed with lads from there.'

'And do you know what the navy do with deserters?'

'Yes sir. They hang 'em.'

'Then, lad, get your things, but remember, leave enough for evidence that you haven't deserted. But get off this ship immediately. And here's the cost of a meal or two.'

John had been watching the exchange between the captain and the seaman.

'Excuse me, Captain. I'm travelling to Lancaster when I can get a coach. Why shouldn't he travel with me? I can keep an eye on him.'

'Tempest. Do you hear that? But you'll have to find the money. Perhaps you can find a rich widow in Bishopsgate looking for a young sailor fresh ashore to serve her bedtime needs!' The captain laughed at his joke.

'Right, stay below, we'll find you some clothes. But keep out of sight. Understood?'

'Aye, sir. Understood.'

The following morning two marines, armed with muskets, and two unarmed sailors arrived at the dockside with a wooden barrow. They had also brought a tarpaulin sack with them. With much struggling, the corpse was put into the sack. With a chilling expertise they quickly flushed the deck clean with bucketfuls of river water before the two sailors carried the grim sack down the gangway. One of the marines requested to see the captain, who gave him a detailed account of the loss of two sailors and the difficult recovery of the one body which had got trapped between the ship and the jetty. The marine made some pretence at writing the story in a red log-book. The captain also suggested he should interview 'Miss Molly Lickwell' in the nearby tavern. The marine saluted, marched smartly down the gangway, his musket banging each stanchion as he passed. He sent the barrow party on its way, escorted by his colleague. Then, after straightening his tunic and breeches, went into the snug bar of 'The King's Mariner' to conduct his lengthy interview with Mistress Lickwell concerning the death of bos'un Cogwell, one of the most brutal bullies in the service.

Two days later, the timber hulk was found aground above the highwater mark near the village of Purfleet. Of the four sailors who were meant to steer it down river, there was no trace. If they had left anything on board it had probably been taken by the three local men who were busy sawing the planks and frames into convenient sized pieces when the navy found it.

*

When they left the ship together, Jake had been fairly kitted out with some reasonable clothes over which he wore a long black cloak, which, in conjunction with a braided tricorne, made him look tall and slightly sinister. John was wearing a heavy cape in anticipation of a cold journey on the outside of the coach. But he also wore his maroon jacket and breeches with a white neckerchief. They two young men hitched a ride as far as London Bridge with one of the carters. They had been told that coaches left regularly from Blackfriars for Oxford, which sounded like a good direction in which to travel. As they jolted their way into the centre of London, Jake asked how well John knew the roads of the City.

'Not at all. This is my first visit. I think St Paul's is the centre, and many of the roads lead outwards from the cathedral.'

'Have you ever heard of a place called Hatton Street?'

John confessed his ignorance of the City's byways.

'Then you will have to ask the way.'

John looked at his companion with a puzzled air.

'Who do you know in Hatton Street? A rich widow, I suppose.'

'As good as a rich widow, but without the falling hair and bad teeth. I heard this from a rum-pot captain who had gambled all his money and the purser's allowances for victualling, that he could sell his mistress's jewels in a shop in Hatton Street, near St Pauls in London.'

'And did he get the money?'

'I don't know. He was found with a musket-ball in his head. I'm told there was no sign of his pistol, but they think that might have been stolen by the woman who found him. It had a pretty pearl handle.'

'And, my dear friend Jake, don't say you are selling your mistress's jewels. Or has Lady Lickwell given you her diamond tiara for your the ride you gave her at Epsom?'

The two travellers sat back and rolled with laughter as they exchanged stories and jokes about their experiences. But Jake eventually had to ask the driver where Hatton Street was.

'Hatton Street, mister? Never 'eard of it. P'raps you mean Hatton Gardens. That's where the nobs see their physicians and their jewellers. Rocks and Rheumatics, yer might say.'

'That's the place then. Hatton Garden. How do we get to this garden?'

The carter directed them across the bridge and then to make their way past St Pauls to Lud Gate and then head up Shoe Lane.

'Better ask from there, admiral. Isn't too sure meself.'

The street in which the carter set them down led towards London Bridge. To the two strangers it appeared as if half of London was trying to cross the river. Carts, wagons, coaches, sedans occupied the centre of the roadway, while foot passengers struggled on the pavements. Everybody seemed to be carrying something, whether baskets of flowers for sale, a sweep's blackened brushes, a woman with a load of clean laundry on her head, even gentlemen with small valises, with leather straps securing the case to their waist, which John presumed was to prevent snatchers or pickpockets. Such was the crowd on the bridge and the city streets which led towards the cathedral that it became clear most well-dressed gentlemen either avoided the area or kept to the safety of a carriage. The roadway underfoot was thick with horse manure and rubbish which sweepers occasionally tried to clear away, particularly in front of the large buildings with ornate front doors and pillared porticoes.

*

When finally the two young men walked between the houses on Hatton Garden, Jake rehearsed John in the procedure.

'Open your coat to show off your silk, act as if you did this every day. I will stand close behind you and he will think I'm your bodyguard. Then you will ask him to value this stone.'

Jake reached down inside the front of his breeches, and drew out a small leather bag, from which he selected and withdrew a stone about the size of a cherry.

'If he asks, say you got it from the Africs. Otherwise he will think it is stolen. I'll stand behind you. If I push once against your back, that means yes, two times means we'll say our thanks but depart until another day. I think he will tell you this is a gold topass or something.'

The jewellers seemed to form a row of narrow shops, each with a door on one side and a window beside it. They chose the third shop along the row. The name on a brass plate beside the door read 'Ab. Schine' and the word 'Lapidiary'. Inside, a single counter was covered with a black cloth. Behind the counter, looking through two small windows, two faces watched them enter. One of the faces disappeared and presently re-appeared in the shop. A small, hunched man with a pale, bespectacled face surrounded by ringlets of black hair surprised both the young men by his appearance. A long black beard, streaked with grey reached down his chest. The man wore a decorated skull cap atop his unruly hair, and a silky black cloak which shimmered in the small amount of light which filtered through the outside window. As he approached he appeared to be washing his hands in invisible water.

'Now, young sirs, how may I be of service to you? A piece of silver to sell, maybe. Or are you looking to purchase some small gift?'

'Neither. I want your estimation of this stone. I may sell it if I consider it well-valued.'

John placed the stone on the black counter cloth.

The jeweller picked it up delicately between his thin finger and thumb. Like a magician, a small lens appeared in his hands, which he placed in one eye, having pushed his small spectacles into the security of his bushy hair.

For a while there was complete silence. The jeweller finally sniffed with a great snort.

'A pretty morsel, which, for the right lady would make a very welcome present. May I humbly ask whence you acquired this little piece?'

'I've just returned from a long voyage from Africa. All the coast, you understand, from the South to the North. Some of the finest gems are being found there, I'm told.'

'So I believe. I should like to weigh it, if you will excuse me.'

He turned to leave the shop, but Jake's hand shot out like a ramrod. He seized the jeweller by the wrist.

'Bring your scales in here. This jewel doesn't leave my master's sight, ever.'

The jeweller called for the balance to be brought into the shop, and then some small brass pots, like tiny narrow tankards.

The jeweller, having recovered his composure, sniffed thoroughly again, and then started weighing and measuring. The tiny shop was silent except for the sniffing of the small hunched man. At last he looked up from his studies.

'This is called a topaz, a golden topaz, with an uncut weight of nearly three hundred grains. A useful shape, it could cut quite prettily.'

'And tell me, sir, what would be your best estimation of value for this stone?'

'Well, sir, if I was paying in cash, Bank of England notes, I would venture a price of one hundred and fifteen pounds.'

'And this?'

Jake had placed on the black cloth a stone of smaller size, this one clear of colour, with one facet that caught the ray of the morning sun.

The jewellery took a quick glance through his lens before gently placing the stone on the balance pan, the metallic ring the only sound in the room.

'This is diamond of a good quality. With Amsterdam closed by the French, this stone is valuable. Tomorrow, next week, next month, if we can get stones from Amsterdam its value could be half of that today. This day I will pay one thousand pounds.'

Chapter 23

'What are you going to do with your money?' John enquired.

'Make it earn its keep, Johnny boy.'

John Weaver and Jake were riding on the back of the lumbering coach from Kenilworth, passing the hours relating their experiences in the wide World. John quickly recognised that Jake had managed to make money from a variety of enterprises, particularly his good fortune in bartering for the uncut gems from the slave traders. In addition he had earned sums of prize money and bounties and John detected a cunning instinct which appeared to guide his boyhood friend to make the most of his gains. The highly satisfactory outcome of their visit to the Hatton Garden, securing the best value, was occasioned by the French seizure of Holland. They had made visits to a number of jewellery merchants before selecting the first merchant, Abraham Schine, as their man. He required two hours to obtain the money, while the two young men decided how to protect their wealth. At the agreed hour, they presented themselves to the shop, the door was locked behind them, and the task of checking the stones and the money began, while their coach waited outside. When all was agreed to be correct and the money spread into different inside pockets and pouches, the jeweller opened the door of the shop and crossed the narrow pavement to open the coach door. The two men nodded to Mister Schine and hurried across the pavement. As the door closed the driver whipped up the two horses and the coach lurched forward. As soon as it was moving, Jake opened the opposite door and waited for the first corner to be turned. When he felt the lurch on the turn he signalled John to leap out, following himself, stumbling on to the dirty, crowded pavement. As the coach continued on its way Jake pointed. Sure enough, clinging to the luggage frame at the back was a grubby urchin, either hoping for a free ride, or worse, following the two customers from the jewellers. Now they were safely on their way home.

'John, my friend, I have always wanted to own my own ship. Maybe a small brig, but mine own. How much would one cost me?'

John looked in amazement.

'Jake, we are buying two masted brigs at three thousand pounds from the shipyard, and spending another thousand fitting out to our requirements. We have to go to the bank and raise the money on a loan, or the company issues shares to buy a new ship.'

'Right, John, then show me your brigs which are too old, too small, that you want to be rid of. I'll take one of those, and gladly. But I have heard of these privateers. If you are an able seaman you get a proportion of the prize money. But if you own a share in the ship you get ten times as much. Why don't you join me, John?'

'I'm sure it's harder than you think. The King grants a thing called a Letter of Marque, which I'm told allows you to attack the King's enemies. Several privateers work from Lancaster. I'm sure my father knows the people. He'll help you.'

'You're a good friend, John. Look, I've taught myself to read, most things I can manage, but I can't get the right books to read. I don't write well, yet. Have you not ever been caught by the gangs?'

John confessed that he had never even seen the gang at work.

'Friend, it's Hell on Earth. Slavery? I tell you, we treated those negroes in chains no worse than we treat our own shipmates, except we have to fight for His Majesty, with Frenchies pouring blazing tar barrels on you. Slaves? Three months on the Middle Passage and then a lifetime in America or Jamakee. That's the life. My shipmate on the gun deck had never been off that hell ship for two years, never felt the smooth skin of a woman, nor even stepped on dry land, lest he desert. John, I've seen grown men, their backs and their brains scarred a hundred times by the cat, jump into the sea and swim for land ten miles away.'

As the uneven road unrolled across the countryside, the tales continued. John related how he had become an important person in the operation of the Northern Trading Company, and how this had brought him into the city life of Copenhagen, something which he felt didn't exist in Lancaster. He started to explain how the trade was found in the Baltic, even in unfriendly countries, but Jake quickly interrupted him.

'You can do anything with money, John. If you've got the right money you can forget the King and Willy Pitt. On the 'Requin' we were sent to protect a convoy of three ships sailing from the port of Maldon. We had to escort them to the mouth of the River Shell they calls it in Holland. And do you know what we was escorting? Oats, John, hundreds of tons I should think, which should be feeding women and their babes in London. But the men in the River Shell paid more money for it than the London merchants.'

'But Jake, that's the whole meaning of trade. We are buying timber in the Baltic for our men o'war just because we know we will get more money for it now than last year or maybe next year. We will make a great profit from the King's Navy!'

'Then I hope the King keeps his promises, me bucko lad, 'cause no one else will.'

*

The journey required them to stay at inns for two nights on their journey. The first night at Banbury was uneventful, but in Manchester they arrived too late at night to find good rooms at the inn, and had to survive sleeping in the lounge of the King's Head inn at Salford, where they could catch the 'Umpire' coach for Lancaster. All night the noise of the drinkers continued, and the laughter of a handful of women in the bar seemed to rattle through the night. In the early dawn's light, though, a painful stillness had descended on the large room, broken only by the occasional snore of one of the many sleeping figures. Jake woke John and together they went in search of some food. They found a ham and some beef on a table, and Jake expertly cut half a dozen slices of meat which he placed in a slightly grubby napkin from the table. In the fruit bowl were some apples and pears.

'Fill your pockets with those, John, and we'll buy a couple of bottles of wine from our generous landlord.'

When they boarded the coach they got the best seats outside, where they would be protected by the driver's bulk from the worst of the weather. The four horses were quietly munching hay from the roadway, where the driver had tossed it from a loosely-tied bale at the side of the inn. Another bale was slung under the coach. When it was time to leave, the driver took blankets off the horses' backs and thoughtfully offered the warm coverings to the passengers on the 'outside'. He whipped up his team and the coach lurched into the city's morning traffic, joining the queues of slow-moving wagons, laden with bales of cotton and bundles of woven materials.

The city lived under a pall of grey cloud which produced a drizzle until the coach started to climb uphill, away from the grim factory surroundings. In the open country on the way to the Ribble Bridge at Preston, the sun broke through the clouds, as if welcoming the travellers back to their home county. The final twenty miles, with occasional glimpses of the sparkling sea to the west, and the rising columns of smoke to indicate the direction of Lancaster, brought all conversation to a stop, except to point out familiar landmarks to each other.

Down the hill towards White Cross, the great scar of the canal could be seen crossing the countryside. Freshly turned soil, honey-coloured stonework of the new bridges and cuttings gave way to the tall warehouses being built on the banks of the canal on the edge of the city. John felt a pride in his heart as he pointed out to Jake the exciting new construction of the town.

'Jake, just imagine, one day we will travel across the country in elegant canal boats, served wine and cold meats on real plates as we cross county after county, as smooth and level as your own parlour.'

The orphan boy from Rotherhithe, sold to a shipowner at the age of eleven, looked at his closest friend, and then swept off his own shabby hat in a mock gesture of salutation.

'John Weaver, one day the King will personally collect us from our own brigantine, maybe called the 'Sarah Weaver', in Deptford and take us to Lancaster Town Hall in his own carriage. But while I'm waiting for His Majesty to arrive I'll make a few pounds for myself. And truly, I tell you to do the same.'

*

They arrived on foot at Ryelands in the late afternoon, carrying their packs. Mistress Weaver had no knowledge they were even in the country, since it was nearly two years since Jake had been seized by the press gang. Then, his brief note had been the last message received at the house. Her husband knew the terrible truths about the gangs, that more than half of those taken died at sea, even a few from the action of an enemy.

The familiar kitchen with its blazing stove seemed to Jake to be just as he remembered it. But Sarah Weaver appeared more careworn and older than his firm memories of the generous, welcoming woman who had first given him love and protection ten years earlier.

With a mother's instinctive wisdom she knew precisely how to balance her love for her own son, her only surviving off-spring, and the needs of the young orphan who had entered their home so unexpectedly. She could afford no jealousy bred of favouritism, lest she lose either of them.

'Let me look at my two young men. Stand straight now.'

She pretended to squint across the tops of their heads.

'Jake, I do declare you are taller, but I suspect John is heavier.'

John picked up his mother in his arms and stood her on the red-tiled floor between them.

'Looks like you've got shorter, Mother. They won't even have you in the Volunteers at your height!'

The three laughed, and Jake stood Sarah on the wooden chair.

'There you are, missus. Tall enough for the Hussars, but, I'm afraid, not quite thick enough in the head.'

'Set me down, you bullies. Now, help me get some food. Mister Weaver will be along soon, and won't take kindly to you wanderers taking his supper.'

She looked into the iron stewpot which was sat on the blazing grate, her own tears making an unheard whisper on the sizzling metal.

'There's just a hare in the pot, and a handful of turnip. I'll drop in some more vegetables and then you can have some home-made cheese if you have any spaces to fill. Now, get your hands washed.'

'Missus, that's exactly what you said to me the very first day I came to your door. In the navy you don't wash your hands between one battle and the next. They say Nelson never washes both hands!'

When Joshua came home he welcomed the two young men with his arms round their shoulders, patting them like young horses. He went straight through into the drawing room and returned with a bottle of sack and some small, glasses. The heavy wine was carefully poured, and the glasses distributed.

'A welcome home to John and Jake, and our thanks to God in these troubled times for their safe return.'

The glasses were drained and refilled, although mistress Weaver surreptitiously tipped her wine into the rich stew, quietly steaming on the stove.

As the men talked into the night she watched from the shadows of the flickering firelight. She knew that every adventure, carelessly re-told and discussed, every tale of victor and vanquished represented a gamble for life and limb. When she at last withdrew to bed, she knew the men would open those chapters always excluded from the distaff.

It was Joshua who first ventured into this private ground.

'Jake, I know young John has his eye on some Scandinavian beauty. He doesn't say as much, but in my experience nothing keeps a man away from his hearth as readily as a soft face and a well-filled bodice.' He looked at his son out the corner of his eye. Jake was silently laughing. 'How about you, Jake?'

'Well, sir, lucky John. I had my chances in the colonies, and I took some. After that, women were beyond reach, the frigates and hulks unholy monasteries. There's a maid of Poulton who I was to meet the day I was snatched, maybe still cursing me for being a pig!'

'I hope she's not still sitting by the hayrick waiting for her able seaman.'

Amidst the general merriment John summoned up his courage.

'I would happily wed Miss Eugenie, but her brother may have other ideas.'

'And who is this all-powerful brother?' enquired Joshua.

'Your Danish associate, Lars Nyborg.'

'You mean you're getting into bed with your Master's sister?' asked Jake, with a look of incredulity. To him, such recklessness sounded like madness.

Joshua asked whether Lars was aware of the liaison, and if any understanding had been made. John had to admit he was nervous about asking Eugenie or her brother.

'Well, lad, take my advice. Don't miss the chance. But don't say anything to your mother until your plans are laid.'

*

In the early morning a horseman arrived at the door of the house.

'Message for Mister Weaver from the Mayor.' He handed a sealed envelope to John and then spurred his horse back down the road to Lancaster.

Joshua took the envelope and opened it with a table knife. He read the note more than once and then sat down with an air of despair.

'Well, I'm astonished. Councillor Matthew Redfearn died during the night from winter pneumonia, they call it. His physician had been treating him for months. But, listen to this.'

He carefully read from the letter.

'Please be advised in strictest privacy that M.W.'s personal affairs were in a very bad state. He had debts with banks in Lancaster, Manchester and Liverpool, which had been secured against deeds to properties to which he had no title. The Old Preston Bank has taken ownership of his shares in many undertakings in Lancashire, including the Northern Trading Company and the Lancaster Canal Company.'

Joshua stood up and made the Sign of the Cross. 'God rest his soul in Peace and forgive him his sins.'

He sat down and looked round the table at his family.

'Here's a fine kettle of fish, and no mistake. I wonder why he required to borrow so much money. Most of us are trading at a profit, with some prices so high our commissions are better than before.'

'Does it affect the trading company?' asked John.

'Only if Matthew was using the company to cover some secret trade. You see, John, if your customer knows you are trading 'off the page' he knows you can't easily recover a debt. I fear we might find he has been smuggling.'

'Well, Father, we've all been in that bed.'

'Yes, lad, within reason. And mercifully, no bad debts.'

'The next few days will tell,' observed John.

Two days later, in an unwelcome rainstorm that flooded the road and pavement, a heavily-cloaked figure dismounted from his horse outside the Preston Bank. He shook the rain from his cloak and his black-brimmed hat before pushing his way into the stone buildings of the bank.

'I wish to see your manager, or chief clerk. And jump to it.'

The young man behind the counter disappeared through a heavy door and presently returned with a black-suited man who bowed to the visitor, thus displaying a large bald patch in his white hair.

'Are you the manager?'

'No sir, my name is Burke. I am the chief clerk. May we be of assistance?'

'You may. I understand you have a quantity of shares in the Northern Trading Company. I am prepared to purchase those shares at face value plus fifteen percentum.'

'In what name is this purchase to be made?'

'John Sparrow. Please tell me the sum you require.'

The clerk disappeared for several minutes. When he re-appeared his face was smiling.

'The consideration will be three thousand four hundred and eighty-five pound and no pence.'

'Here is one thousand pounds on account. The balance will be paid in cash on collection of the certificates.' The cloaked figure reached inside his cloak and drew out four bundles of notes.

'Yes, Mister Sparrow, sir. I will just prepare your receipt and transaction note.'

*

The full import of Matthew Redfearn's financial dealings did not become apparent until several days after the elaborate funeral at St. John's chapel. The mayor led the city fathers in mourning the death of one of their sternest critics, ignorant of the creditors who were awaiting some reconciliation of their accounts. But it soon became apparent that an elaborate search would be needed to uncover the accounts in other names which harboured his true wealth. By carefully examining documents, banker William Provender established that Matthew Redfearn had purchased nearly all the low-lying land at the estuary, which he subsequently sold for the construction of the New Docks at Glasson. By the same reckoning, he probably bought much of the land required for the route of the canal from hard-pressed farmers unaware

219

of the earliest ideas of Abram Rawlinson. To Joshua Weaver's horror, each day seemed to reveal a new page of Redfearn's duplicity. There were several others in the county far more concerned that their associations with the former councillor might yet be revealed.

It was not only those suffering the hardships of the disastrous harvest who slept uneasily in their beds at night.

Chapter 24

John Weaver had summoned up his courage to seek Lars' approval of his desire to marry Eugenie. Neither man had pretended that his courtship had been anything less than intimate, yet his host always appeared to welcome John's presence in his household. Lars was his usual calm but stern self.

'You do understand that Eugenie is a widow, for whom I must accept some responsibility? Would I be correct in believing she told you her husband died fighting for the Swedish king?'

John nodded his assent.

'Then, my friend, I must tell you in confidence that such an account is not strictly true. He was, in fact, a brutal, licentious man, to whom my sister was hopelessly attracted. He had considerable wealth from his family, and he invested in my business. But every day he spent more than we could ever earn, and I could see both my sister and my business eventually being destroyed by this terrible man. If I stopped the flow of money from my business, Eugenie would suffer. You may be wondering how fighting for the King of Sweden should have caused his death. You will never know, and I expect the matter is never discussed again.'

'But, of course I wouldn't, it would presumably been most distressing to Eugenie.'

'You are very wise. Let me also explain that Eugenie is not a rich woman. She has some farmlands in the country and I make her an allowance, of course, and leave her to assume whatever she will. If you marry, I would expect to make you an active partner in my own business, whatever the Trading Company may wish to find for you. Now, what do you consider your own family will say to your plans?'

'My mother will be very sad, I fear. I am her only surviving child, so you may understand why. My father is, as you know, a very active trader in Lancaster, like you, with his own interests and those of the Trading Company. I imagine he would expect me to take over his interests in the years to come.'

'And where would you expect to set up your home if Eugenie accepts you?'

'I had considered I should live near Copenhagen, but not in the city. I would like to live beyond the lakes, if possible.'

'Then, John, I will give Eugenie her own house, not as any mark of distrust in you, but so that I know, in this turbulent age, she will always be safe, and so you will be while you are at her side. But let her down, just once, and you will lose your wife, your work and your house in the same day. Do I make myself clear?'

'You are most generous, Lars. I had considered that I could support her, but your kindness gives us great security.' He shook his hand warmly.

By some happy chance, Eugenie entered the sitting room at this moment, smiling innocently at the two men.

'Always talking business, you serious old men! Why don't you take a few hours away from the balance sheets and brigantines to invite some ladies out for supper?'

Lars looked at her and laughed. He went to a small bureau in the corner and penned a note. He rang the bell-pull and presently the elderly servant arrived.

'Klaus. Get this note to the Russian Legation, and ask the messenger to wait for a reply. Here's a crown for his trouble.'

Supper that evening was taken in one of the new, fashionable dining rooms in the newest parts of the city, rebuilt after yet another fire had destroyed more of the older buildings. Lars had arranged for a discreet table in one corner of the elaborately decorated room. Candelabra provided a soft, golden light, complimentary to the ladies' powdered complexions. Eugenie was dressed in a new silk gown, the shimmering material the colour of bronze. Her maid had dressed her hair with her usual care, piled high on her head, with a matching golden-coloured ribbon. The high waist of her gown presented the soft contours and subtle shadows of her breasts to their best advantage. As John leaned forward to kiss her on each cheek he was aware of the delicate yet sensuous essence of her favourite perfume.

Lars had directed the carriage to Bredgade to collect his guest for the evening. When she joined them in the carriage, Lars briefly introduced her to a startled Eugenie and John as the Countess Irena Kaminskaya of St Petersberg. She was wrapped in a snow-white hooded fur cape which covered her from her head to her ankles. But when they arrived at the dining room, servants took their cloaks and the countess was revealed in all her unusual grace. She was a stunningly beautiful woman, possibly slightly younger than Eugenie's thirty years, taller, and dressed in palest blue. Black, shining hair, with carefully-tended curls framed a face with high, pronounced cheekbones and dark, narrow eyes, whose outer corners appeared to be drawn upwards, adding a feline intensity to the soft triangle of her face. The movements of her eyes, her face, her whole self was slow and deliberate. When John spoke to her, her head and her eyes turned to look at him with such unhurried calmness that he felt as he was for one brief moment,

222

the most important person in her life. In the carriage she had spoken in French and in English. John was nervous that he would be unable to follow the conversations of the evening. Yet, as the servants drew back the chairs for the guests, the Countess turned to John and whispered behind a gloved hand.

'English gentleman, you must not let me make a mistake in this elegant room.'

Eugenie heard the request and smiled at the beautiful woman.

'He will protect you most carefully, I assure you!'

When they walked across the room there was silence at the other tables. Twenty or more diners watched in polite interest as the two men escorted the graceful ladies to the table. As the murmur of conversation returned, greetings from friends were called across the room and glasses raised in salutation. Servants busied themselves bearing salvers of food to the table whilst others charged the goblets with French wines.

Lars stood at the head of the table and once again, as the room noticed him, the talking ceased. He cleared his throat.

'Gourmets, feinschmeckers, I would invite you to take wine with me tonight to celebrate the betrothal of my only sister, Eugenie Madaleine to Captain John Weaver of the Duchy of Lancaster.'

As the servants circulated with fresh bottles of wine, the diners started clapping, until it reached a crescendo of noise, stamping of feet, tapping of wine-glasses and calls of approval across the room. Nervously, John reached across the table and took Eugenie's gloved hand in his. They both stood to nod their thanks to their well-wishers and once again, glasses were raised in happy salutation.

When they sat down, the Countess was the first to speak.

'Lars, you didn't tell me what a special occasion this was.' She slowly turned her dark eyes upon John. 'You are a singularly fortunate man to have the hand of such a lovely woman. I wish you both great happiness.' Her eyes then rested upon the blushing Eugenie.

'My new friend Eugenie. You shall be very happy, I am so certain, with this wonderful Englishman at your side. They are used to living on their little island and don't stray too far away. In Russia, the few beautiful men that there are can ride for a thousand leagues and still be in the Empire but far away from their wives and families.'

The meal was thus taken in an air of celebration. Other diners came to pay their respects at the table, sitting and chatting for a few minutes. Every man in the room took the opportunity to introduce himself to the countess, who had insisted to Lars that she should just be called Miss Irena. Every man felt the slow, penetrating look of her dark eyes, whilst every woman was aware of the flawless pale skin which swelled above the scooped neck-line of her bodice.

Between such interludes, the countess seemed to pay particular attention to John, questioning him on the way he travelled so frequently between England and Copenhagen. John had already received a secret signal from Lars, a finger placed on the lips, which both knew meant 'Discretion in Business.' John had recently learned, in the tangled politics of the Baltic that the less said on some occasions, the better. Whilst Lars claimed with some justification that the Company could outwit kings and princes, the death of Catherine of Russia possibly represented the eclipse of the last friendly havens in the Baltic.

The dining room had tall, curtained windows along both sides, and as the night wore on, the curtains were drawn back, on one side to see the last of the lights shining across the roofs of the city. On the other side of the room, the tall windows could be swung open to allow access to a balcony which ran across the full width of the back of the building. Although the view was simply of the street below, it at least gave the diners a private space for taking the air after the stuffiness of the crowded room. So, after the food had been cleared from the tables, couples moved freely around the room and the balcony, adding further to the conviviality of the occasion. Congratulations were repeated, and kisses exchanged with the betrothed couple. Then John felt a hand slip through his arm. He realised, without looking, that the countess was gently directing him towards one of the open doors. His heart was beating, having never quite understood the code of Copenhagen salon society. But he scarcely considered their relaxed view of flirtation extended to the occasion of one's betrothal announcement. Yet here was one of the most exciting women in the room unmistakably guiding him towards the darkness of the balcony. When they were clearly out of sight of the other diners she relaxed her hold on his arm and leaned gracefully over the balustrade, apparently unaware of the cold night air.

'Dear Captain John, do not misunderstand me. I have no designs upon the groom of dear Eugenie. My interest is much more important than that. Do I understand from the chit-chat round the table that you have access the government of King George of England?'

'Well, I carry state material at times and I am entitled to Freedom of Passage. May I help you, Countess?'

'You English! So correct, so gentlemanly, is that it? Then let me tell you. And I beseech you, never mention where you heard this. Every city in Europe is full of spies. In this room there are men who are wondering who I am.'

She noticed John's slow smile.

'Oh yes, some because they want me in their bed. I know that. But there are some, watching me, suspecting I come from Paris or Petersburg, whether I am a spy on their side or not. Shall I tell you, Captain John Weaver of the, what is it? The Duke of Lancashire?'

John smiled, and found himself captive to every word spoken in halting English by this remarkable woman.

'John, there's a woman in this room watching every move I make, who would happily put her husband into my bed, in fact she would happily put herself in my bed, if only she could find out what I know about Czar Paul and his communications with certain people in Paris. You understand, France is victorious in fighting her neighbours, but is in turmoil within its own borders. France will either dominate Europe or it will become a state fractured into pieces. And, my English John, if France found the right leader the outcome would be obvious.'

John was beginning to feel out of his depth. He considered his response should be to keep this conversation flowing for as long as he could. He ventured a few harmless observations.

'Of course, as Baltic ship owners and traders we all were concerned by the death of the Czarina. I'm sure her son will follow in her footsteps...'

'Never!' Her response was like a muffled pistol shot. Then her voice dropped to a low husky whisper, which, in other circumstances, might have been singularly alluring. Now, it carried its own menace.

'Never, I tell you. Cousin Paul is un cerveau brul,, a mad hat I think you say. Now, dear John, you must tell your King that our Czar Paul has a secret hatred of the British. I know, I have lived in the same house as him. He is deeply set in his animosity of the British and sees in France a chance to destroy you. He sees France placing all the warring countries into a Continental Alliance, he calls it, to destroy the English. The English, you understand, because France has already attacked Ireland in the hope that the Irish would rise up against your King.'

John felt reality sliding away as the conversation progressed.

'You know the Czar?' he enquired, scarcely able to suppress his surprise.

'I am a cousin of some distance. In our house he was always called 'Poor Paul' because he was possibly going to follow his mother, and so was taught by generals and politicians, while we were playing with the boys and learning the balalaika. When he grew up he studied wars, from Caesar, Alexander the Great, Ghenghis Khan, all the expert murderers. Now his heroes all carry muskets. You, John, must warn your King, and be alert. I cannot yet tell you if Cousin Paul supports the

Republic or the Monarchists in France. And I believe that is the question I must answer for you.'

'But you could easily meet friends of mine at the embassy and...'

'That I could never do. I am shadowed everywhere while I am in Denmark. Even more so in Petersberg. But if I can communicate with your shipping company no one will need to know. And if, like tonight, I am with you, it is just a little coquetterie, non?'

As she spoke she moved close to his side and one gloved arm wound round his neck and pulled his face down to hers. He found himself kissing her on the lips. Her perfume was rich and heavy, unlike Eugenie's, and he knew it would linger on the shoulder of his coat.

In the distant shadows a figure stood watching. Out of the corner of his eye John saw the flowing silk moved silently back into the anonymity of the crowded dining room.

*

The following day he reflected upon the confidence which had been entrusted to him. Lars had often told him the Baltic was dominated by madmen. Even in Denmark, King Christian VII had handed the reins of power to his son, the Crown Prince Frederick, due to his own malaise. In Sweden, the seventeen-year-old king, who inherited his murdered father's crown, had a insane hatred of France, which was equally liable to be directed in many other ways. He had insisted Sweden and Denmark should declare a Treaty of Armed Neutrality, enabling both countries' ships to carry provisions for belligerent states without harassment from British warships. The new Czar Paul reputedly had a grudging admiration for the French Commander in Chief appointed earlier that year, one General Buonaparte, who, at the age of twenty-seven years seemed to have an unerring instinct for successful land battles.

Yet throughout these uncertainties, Lars had been able to use his merchant ships with discretion to carry cargoes between the hostile nations around the Baltic, and particularly into England and France. The new designs of ships, schooner-rigged, built to designs of the English and the Danes were proving more economical in the difficult waters around Northern Europe, although the older, square-rigged ships carried the greatest loads of timber. Lars found the Lancashire merchants, whether sailing from Liverpool or Lancaster, had the same sound object to maintain high levels of trade, taking advantage of the demand for materials of war. For the first time in more than ten years he now had a good reason to visit England, both personal and professional.

Whilst Lars and John discussed their day-to-day plans for securing vital materials for the shipbuilders in England, and finding freight in return, a messenger arrived at the office on the Copenhagen harbourside. The messenger had ridden hard from Hamburg to Stralsund, the strange Swedish province embedded in the north coast of Prussia. From there he had taken a ship to Copenhagen. The documents in his satchel seemed to give no reason for his urgency. When he was sure the busy office was empty, except for Lars and John, the cloaked rider reached inside his tunic and drew out a heavily sealed package and handed it to Lars. 'Your own hands only, sir,' said the messenger.

Lars carefully broke the seals and drew out a handful of letters, which he started to read.

'Dear God. John, I must warn you, there's bad news afoot. The French army have landed in the west of England, at a place called Ilfracombe. They have been repulsed by your Yeomanry and the' ..he hesitated over the words.. 'Cardigan Militia, at a place called Fishguard. Now you hear this. Secret plans have been captured, showing they were intended to attack the sea-port of Bristol, to set the city afire. I don't understand this.' He hurriedly ran through the other documents.

'What's this? This is a note warning that the value of the British notes is falling fast. To accept payment from England in silver only. This is terrible. If Napoleon has plans to invade England now, we are in trouble. Remember, he landed a small army in Ireland only a few months ago. John, this is very serious.'

'I would like to make steps to return to England, if that is agreeable, Lars. But first I think I should call at the British embassy, to see what they say.'

'Certainly, get there straight away. I should go on foot. But I'll wager we have as recent news as they have. My messenger-post is very fast.'

When John arrived at the embassy, he asked for Sir Richard Bowen and was promptly ushered into a small sitting room in the large building. In the centre of the room stood an ornate inlaid table, with matching chairs each side. Presently, Lord Bowen entered, accompanied by a young man, who acted as a secretary.

'Ah! Captain John Weaver. I understand your visit is urgent. Not too urgent, I hope.'

He smiled behind his whiskers at the gentle joke.

'I have heard about the French invasion in Wales and Cornwall, sir and I...'

'The what? Invasion? What damned invasion is this?'

'Well, sir, we have just received a message from England that the French have landed, with plans to burn Bristol.'

'The deuce you have!'

The portly gentleman turned to the door of the sitting room.

'Blackwell, Hooperman, Cavendish! Get in here! On the double!' His voice rang round the corridors of the building and presently the sitting room was full of men.

'Now, this is Captain Weaver, one of my side men. Tell 'em what you've learned, Captain.'

'Sir, we have a satchel of messages that an invasion force has been repelled, but that we are to accept no payments from England except in silver or specie. We are told the French army, after capture, I presume, were carrying orders to march upon Bristol and fire the city.'

The diplomat looked from John to the other men in the room.

'Well? Well, you quill-pen soldiers. Where's our reports?'

One of them cleared his throat.

'We've been out of touch, with no despatches, most of the ferries have been tied up in harbour. Winter gales, sir, stop the packet boats sailing.'

'I know what winter gales are, you fool.'

'Well, sir, the last despatch we had was dated, er about twentieth of February, sir. That's three weeks, allow one week for the messenger, so a fortnight delay.'

'So, while we sit here our traders are told not to use English currency because it may be valueless. And we don't know anything about it. Right gentlemen. Action this day! And Captain Weaver, we will reach you at Mister Nyborgs office immediately we have further advice. I'll thank you for your prompt report, and wish you good-day, sir.'

When John returned to the harbour office a further surprise awaited him. Seated outside the door of the first floor office, a man in a strange grey uniform had removed his peaked hat and was mopping his brow. He stood to attention when John arrived.

'Captain John Weaver, monsieur?'

'Yes, I am he.'

'May I ask you for a document which shows your name, as to your identity, you understand, monsieur.'

John ushered the uniform man into the office and went through the papers on his desk. Eventually he found a bundle of business letters which had arrived by the earlier messenger, mostly from Lancaster. He allowed the man to note his name on each missive. The man nodded his head.

'I have a letter for you, concerning some dangerous cargo which is to be presented for loading on to your next ship to Petersberg. No one is to know we wish to ship this material, and you are not allowed to receive this letter until you agree to treat this in greatest secrecy.'

John was growing uneasy, and nodded to the messenger.

'I agree. Now please, give me your documents. I have much to attend to.'

He was handed a sealed envelope, and he waited until he could see the messenger making his way down the street before he opened it. Inside was a hand-written letter covering just one sheet of paper. It bore no sender's name or address. It read:

'General Napoleon Buonaparte has launched an invasion against England, to attack the port of Bristol, on the coast of England. The invading army is not a seriously trained detachment, it is called Le Legion Noire, and contains the following:

750 infantrymen with muskets

250 infantrymen with swords and lances

20 men to capture horses

100 men with oils and tars for fire-raising

The command will be an American Colonel Tate.

The landing will be by sea on the best tide after fifteenth of February and before the fifteenth March. After this time the detachment will be put ashore at any point on the English mainland between Portland and Lands End. It is not intended that any steps should be made to recover these men. Many of this detachment will be untrained volunteers and some conscripts.

Nota Bene. A Captain Richardson has sent a confidential memorandum to the British Admiralty warning of the risk of mutiny in British warships.'

The envelope contained one other piece of paper, which strangely, had no writing on either side. It was tightly folded, and enclosed in its own smaller envelope. Yet as soon as he opened it, he knew that it uniquely identified the sender of the message. In the centre of the blank paper, a tiny stain showed where the rich, heavy perfume had been applied.

Chapter 25

'We've completed the aqueduct, it's been filled with three feet of water for these four weeks, and apart from a few small fissures, the puddle is sound.'

Joshua Weaver was proudly showing Lars Nyborg the splendour of the great structure. The two men had met for the first time after the 'Diamant' had returned to London and Lars had taken the stagecoach to Lancaster, arriving late in the afternoon two days before, exhausted by the rigours of the uneven roads. He was staying as the guest of Joshua and Sarah Weaver, the house at Ryelands having been carefully prepared to receive their important visitor. Three additional girls from the village were cooking and serving at table, which Sarah was starting to enjoy. Already she was hoping that this way of life could continue even when Lars and John had departed. With the rising fortunes of the trade she felt Joshua could be persuaded to take additional servants and entertain a little more often. Since the death of Matthew Redfearn, John had many more merchants and bankers to meet. Four evenings a week the dining room and sitting room were in use, blazing log fires welcoming the diners and promoting easy conversation. Even John had noticed how much the house had changed, and complimented his mother on the glowing, polished rooms.

From the carriage on the river bank the five great arches certainly looked dramatic in the summer sunlight. The stone was the colour of honey, set off by shining white balustrades and coping stones. Even some of the rutted banks were beginning to take on an early mantle of fresh grass and wild flowers. The sparkling water of the River Lune made a welcoming sound as it rushed through the four main channels between the piers.

Lars nodded in admiration.

'A very fine structure, Mister Joshua. In Denmark, you understand, our whole life is conducted at sea level!'

The two men laughed, the shared joke a mark of amity. Lars continued.

'I have to admit I am surprised at the idea of one river crossing another on a bridge. Pray, tell me, who raises all the money for this remarkable structure?'

'Over fifty feet, Lars! Think of that, fifty feet above river water level. A man-made river, if you like, sixteen feet wide, and even a towpath on each side! Nothing like this in London, you know! 'His enthusiasm was more controlled when considering the financial question. 'The cost has been raised locally by subscription. Half a million English pounds raised by the sale of shares.'

'H'm. Joshua, I would very much like to own some of these shares. Are they freely traded?'

'They will be quite valuable, even though we don't start carrying traffic until later this year. The Birmingham canal shares are changing hands at ten times their face value. There is no reason why our own investment will not be similarly enhanced in due course.'

'And, Joshua, what is the name of the city at the north end. I do not know your geography very well. The end of this canal is in Scotland?'

'Bless my soul, Lars! Not Scotland! The market town of Kendal will be the most northerly point we can reach with our present skill. And even that will require a great tunnel. But we are learning so much about waterborne trade that in perhaps fifty years we will have the country linked with a lattice of similar canals.'

The provincial town of Lancaster, with its great castle over-seeing its every activity, was much smaller than Lars had expected, in contrast to his being overwhelmed by the size and activity of London. His enquiries had shown that London was ten times the size of Copenhagen, which itself was ten times the size of Lancaster. He was always conscious of the great span of wealth in England between the aristocrats and the labourers, the one insulated by their fine houses and carriages from the poverty and perils of the other. Overcrowding in Copenhagen was caused by the decision to constrain the growth of the city within the existing ramparts. In England, the crowded towns and cities seemed no more and no less than a traditional way of life.

On his recent arrival in London, however, everyone on the ship had been astonished to see moored in the fast-flowing estuary a dozen or more men-of-war, with no ensigns flying. Rowing boats and sailing cutters were plying between the ships and the shore, and one such pinnace passed close to the 'Diamant' and using a voice trumpet told the captain the Royal Navy had mutinied, and warned them to sail clear of the ships at anchor. Captain Junge turned to Lars Nyborg and John Weaver with a wry smile.

'Mister Weaver, sir, your navy has mutinied! Everybody knew this would happen one day, and yet your admirals do nothing. How can this be?'

'Captain, I wish I knew the answer to your question. I have good friends who sail in the Royal Navy and the conditions in which they work and sleep are impossible.'

'Well, just wait until the Frenchies hear about this! Then the French cats will chase the English chickens!'

The captain drew his finger across his throat in a dramatic gesture.

'I think not, Captain. The French crews need to nominate a committee before they can spread a top-gallant, and elect a new captain before he can alter course!'

'Mister Weaver, I just trust to God you are right.'

The sail-master hailed one of the passing cutters for one of them to take John ashore. Eventually, one of the small sailing craft came up on the lee side and waited for John to scramble down the rope ladder and jump into the narrow cutter. His sea-bag following on a heaving-line. John looked up and waved farewell to Lars and the captain. He turned to the coxwain of the cutter as the six oarsmen pulled hard against the swirling current of the estuary.

'Thank-you for the ferry. Where can you set me ashore?'

The coxwain seemed in singular ill-humour, presumably, thought John, because of the effect of the mutiny.

'Sheerness yards, that's all. Handy for the gallows!'

He laughed humorlessly.

'Well, cox'n, that will do fine for me. I have to be in London as soon as I can.'

'There's enough carriages and coaches full of admirals and commodores, running in circles, clutching their swords and praying Johnny Frenchman doesn't find out what game we're playing. They would like some company!'

John gave the coxwain a silver crown as he stepped ashore at the dockyard stairs.

On the dockside he was surprised to see ranks of marines drilling, the clatter of boots and muskets ringing across the cobbled yard.

'And what's your duty, landsman?'

John turned and saw a marine sergeant, with a pistol at half cock, pointing straight at John's chest.

'John Weaver, King's Courier. Urgent despatches from Denmark.'

He reached inside his coat and felt for the Letter of Free Passage. He handed it to the marine.

'What's this say?' he enquired.

'It says I am on the King's business, and must not be detained.'

'Right, sir, pass on.'

John tightened his grip on his bags and walked smartly across the side of the open dockyard, sensing the aim of the pistol still on his back. At the gateway, where marines mounted guard in large numbers, he was ushered into the guardhouse, and repeated the purpose of his mission. He enquired whether there was space in one of the returning carriages, and after some hesitation was offered a seat on a stage-coach which appeared to have been commandeered by the Royal Navy. Incongruously, four marines took the place of coachmen seated on the outside boxes, their muskets held between their knees.

Inside the coach, John found himself in the company of a naval lieutenant of about his own age. No other passengers were waiting, so the coach set off immediately. It soon became apparent to John that his companion had recently been drinking; his conversation was slightly slurred, and occasionally he stopped abruptly to belch or to mop his freely sweating brow.

'So you're from Denmark, eh? Good sailors, the Danes, good sailors but lousy fighters! Not like those scum at the Nore. Good fighters but hopeless sailors.'

'Well, that depends on what they have been instructed in...'

'Instructed? You don't instruct Suffolk pig-men. You hit them hard until they get it right. Instruction is for officers.'

He fell silent, wiped his soaking brow and put his head out of the window for a moment before slumping back in his hard seat.

'Teach 'em by fear, just ask Admiral Hood. That's how we get results.'

'Is that what you call your fleet at anchor at the Nore? Gotten results?'

'You speak very freely about His Majesty's ships. Perhaps you are competent in these matters.'

'Competent or not, I know how to run a sailing ship at a profit with less than forty men, and pay every man jack of them four times as much as you do, and feel able to enter any port without all my crew deserting and hiding in the brothels.'

The young naval officer looked at John with undisguised hatred.

'And how many enemy ships have you had in your sights? How many Spanish men-o-war with a hundred cannon bearing down on you? How many sailors do you see smashed to a bone-splintered pulp before you decide to call off the action? Methinks a shipful of Baltic timber must be about as hard to sink as anything on God's ocean. Or perhaps you are one of the gentlemen of the slave trade? That must be a most dignified pursuit for a man of taste. I'm told you can find a sweating blackie cabin mate to suit every whim...'

'Then, lieutenant, you've heard wrong,' snapped John with anger.

The journey continued without further discussion, which caused John to reflect upon the loss of the 'Laguna' and Jake's hellish tales of the 'Middle Passage' from West Africa. How little each man knows of his neighbour's business.

When, at last, the coach lumbered into the crowded traffic of the city the officer straightened his uniform and gave his brow a final wipe.

'I trust your mission proves more pleasant than mine,' he said to John.

'Oh! I just have to deliver despatches and reports. May I enquire what you have to do in this overpowering city?'

'I have to collect the executioner from Tyburn for our mutinous friends in the estuary. One Richard Parker and his zealots have need of his services. I wish you a good day, sir, and thank you for your company.'

The coach drew to a halt close to Hyde Park, on the western edge of the city. He enquired of the coachman the way to Whitehall and was directed across St James' towards the towers of Westminster Abbey. He had an address off Whitehall, and eventually found himself at the door of a house in King Charles Street. He struck the polished brass knocker, and presently the door was opened by a footman in a red and black tail coat, white linen and wearing a powdered wig. Recalling the instructions he had been given, he produced his Letter and asked to see 'The Honourable Simon'.

His hat was taken by the footman before he was ushered into a cold, bare waiting room, with a small window looking out on to an empty yard. After what seemed like an hour he was summoned by the footman and taken up the broad staircase. A pair of double doors led off the upper landing, and he was ushered through these into the presence of The Honourable Simon. Compared with the footman, the occupier of the office was completely colourless. A grey high-collared coat concealed everything except his close-cropped grey hair and a long, pale face. He barely moved as John sat on the offered chair.

'Captain Weaver? I hear from the embassy that you are to carry our despatches when needs arise. Please give me your Letter and the pouches.' He held his hand out abruptly, treating John as no more than another insignificant servant. John handed over the official pouch which he had guarded carefully on his journey. The Honourable Simon examined all seals before breaking them open and extracting the sheaf of papers and letters from within. There was silence in the room whilst the documents received a cursory examination.

'These all appear correct. I understand you have other associations in Denmark who may be helpful to us in our diplomatic discussions. Please describe the intelligence to which you are privy.'

'I have an informant who claims to have an ear in the court of Tsar Paul of Russia. As an earnest of his abilities, he has passed the following document to me.' He reached inside his coat to find the single page message giving precise details of the French attack on the South West of England, and the warning of mutiny in the navy.

Once again, the paper was subject to silent examination.

'This is a very strange document to have been secured by your man. I would have presumed this information originated in France, not Petersberg. Can you explain that?'

'Not fully, sir, except that I am told that the new Tzar has a close contact with Paris, and should not be judged as a necessarily strong ally in our affairs.'

'So we understand, er.. Captain Weaver. Our minister in Petersberg has made the same observation. But we are anxious to learn the nature of the Tzar's exchanges with Paris. We will pay for information in that regard, if accredited. Your man appears well-informed.'

'Not only in Petersberg, it would appear. I must admit, sir, a curious feeling to arrive at Sheerness and witness the mutiny about which I had been informed in Copenhagen two weeks earlier.'

For a moment the sleepy, grey eyes of The Honourable Simon fixed their stare upon John Weaver.

'I will thank you, sir, not to make wild interpretations concerning the intelligence you bring to my office. That is my task.'

He looked down and drew open the drawer of the desk. He lifted out a small velvet pouch and, without even looking at him, dropped it on the desk in front of John.

'Captain Weaver, I imagine you will have had some expenses in your work. This will cover them until we hear further from you. Good-day sir.'

John took the pouch, bowed briefly, muttered his thanks and left the room. The footman was standing at the top of the staircase, and escorted him to the front door. He handed him his travel-stained hat as if his white gloves might be contaminated by the contact.

*

The eventual reunion in the Weaver household, for all its excitement, only served to make John yearn for Eugenie, who was staying with Lady Elizabeth in Copenhagen whilst both her men were in England. Lars had been quite adamant that with the English fleet seeking out the French navy at every opportunity, the North Sea was not a safe place. As a result, the celebrations for John's engagement to Eugenie in her absence, were restrained, limited to a fine supper in the dining room at the Kings Arms. A wind band of five men from the militia band provided music for the evening and thirty-five guests, dressed in their finest clothes helped themselves from the heavily laden tables. Joshua Weaver had invited most of the ship-owners and merchants who had interests in the Trading Company. They were introduced to Lars, and congratulated him on the way trade had continued to develop, even in the face of the gathering strength of the French onslaught. Jake Tempest was late in arriving at the supper, having been in Preston for a few days. When he arrived, he was elegantly dressed in a crimson London-cut coat, with deep collars and cuffs and overflowing with white linen. His buckle shoes appeared slightly unsuitable for the streets of Lancaster. Even John barely recognised him, and his parents allowed themselves to be introduced to him as a stranger before they realised the joke. The lady on his right arm was, if anything, even more stylishly dressed, in white silk set off with crimson bows exactly matching Jake's coat. The significance of the colour scheme was not lost on Sarah Weaver. Her hair, the colour of polished bronze, tumbled in great curls almost to her waist, with several curls drawn forward to lie invitingly across the expanse of her bare neck. When Jake introduced his escort, Miss Jenny La Monde to Sarah, she drew her to one side, as if meeting a special friend.

'Jake has kept you very well hidden until tonight. I must scold him for being so thoughtless. Now, tell me all about yourself, Jenny. Do you live in the town?'

'No, Mistress Sarah, I live in Manchester at present. I'm acting in a play at the Comedy theatre.'

'Really. How exciting. I hope you don't have to return to Manchester tomorrow.'

'No, Mistress. The play is closed for some weeks, because the owner has run away with most of the money.'

'You mean you're on your own? How terrible!'

She caught hold of Jake's sleeve.

'Jake, is this true? Jenny tells me she has been left all on her own in Manchester. She must stay at Ryelands for a few days.'

A few feet away, Joshua stood next to his son, watching Sarah and Jenny.

'Looks as if Jake has been paid his bounty and spent it in one day,' said Joshua, with a laugh in his voice. 'That's a very striking lady on his arm.'

'I don't think you need worry about Jake's bounty, Father. He has a magic touch where money is concerned. Let's meet the lovely lady.'

With an unequal number of ladies to accompany the gentlemen, the evening's dancing was severely restricted, not improved by the modest repertoire of the five musicians. Nevertheless, with plenty to eat and drink the celebrations for John's betrothal became mixed up with the warm reception accorded to Lars Nyborg. His easy, but correct manner throughout the noisy evening attracted the interest of the local businessmen, and in the relaxed atmosphere appointments were made in diaries and meetings contemplated.

Jake seemed in deep discussion with Lars, which gave John an opportunity to make some pretence of dancing the two-step with Jenny La Monde against the piping sound of the band and the rising conversation and laughter in the rest of the room.

'Are you Jake's brother? I'm so confused about who Mistress Weaver really is.'

John held the slender waist of his dancing partner and shrugged his shoulders. He laughed.

'Who knows? Mistress Weaver has brought up Jake and me as brothers, equal shares of rabbit stew and love to each of us. So I say we're brothers.'

'Then why is his name Mighty Jake Tempest? Who would ever think of such a name? I must say, on the stage the name Tempest is quite common, but that's just to look good on the playbills.'

'How long have you been an actress? It must be exciting.'

'When a gent like Jake is there to take care of you it's alright. But when the theatre owner runs off with the money bags it's miserable. Chucked out your rooms, screaming landladies calling you a slut, everybody wanting something free...if you know what I mean.'

She blushed, realising she might have hinted at a certain weakness. John squeezed her waist to reassure her.

'Don't get me wrong, Mister John. Jake is so kind and treats me like a lady. I always feel safe when he's around, he can take care of a girl...in every way, you know what I mean. One night, in Manchester, he took on two men who considered they owned me. They tried to strangle him with a horse whip. He flattened them on the road and tied them through their legs, you know where I mean, and he said that's what they did to 'uppity slaves on the ships.' When he said it, he made my blood run cold. But he always treats me as gentle as can be. He's my prince.'

John swung her round as the music came to an uncertain halt. He caught her expertly, holding her close in both arms., so that for an instant the firm shape of her body was pressed hard against his.

'I congratulate you on your estimation of men. Jake is my best friend, so I better respect his lady.' He released his hold and with excessive formality, offered her his arm before leading her back to the group where Jake was now seated round a table with several of the shipowners. On the white tablecloth, between the tankards and wine-mugs Jake was laying out playing cards, face downwards. In some intricate game, five or six men places coins on each card. John couldn't understand the process, but after a few swift moves Jake drew all the cash towards him, adding to the pile at his elbow.

'Goddammit, Jake, I'll never see how you make that trick work every time!'

'Too strong for me,' muttered another as he got up from the table.

'That man could make a profit from a stone!' complained another.

'Like the man who built the aqueduct, eh? Ha!' One of the gamblers laughed at his own joke.

Jake look round and saw Jenny returning.

'Here we are, gentlemen, Lady Luck has returned to my side. Watch your language and get your purses out and see what fortune awaits us!'

John stepped back from the gamblers and noticed how Jenny kept her hips pressed against the shoulder of her seated lover.

The night wore on, and in ones and twos the guests ordered coaches from the great yard below. One or two walked home through the poorly-lit streets, always staying in a group as long as possible. With much laughter Joshua Weaver and his present family of John, Jake and the effervescent Jenny La Monde climbed aboard the coach to take them to Ryelands. Lars Nyborg joined them and produced a bottle of sauterne for the journey. He had very thoughtfully brought a small copper cup, which was passed round. Then, when there was just a little left in the bottle, Jake easily climbed out of the window of the jolting coach and, standing dangerously on the window sill, reached up to offer the bottle to the driver. No one made a sound inside the coach until Jake's body slid easily back into the safety of the compartment.

Great cheers announced their safe return to the welcoming house at Ryelands

Chapter 26

The new Century dawned in bitter January weather, and the European states continued their blood-soaked games of chess. With Bonaparte installed effectively as Dictator and its internal affairs less demanding, France's neighbours felt under even greater threat. During the previous year Egypt joined Prussia, Russia and Turkey as countries that had all felt the fury of Napoleon's armies. As Joshua Weaver found, like many others in Britain, the cost of the war had to be met by the introduction of taxes and duties which affected everyone, except those too poor, in which case they could suffer the food shortages which beset much of Europe.

The Trading Company had continued to thrive until an unfortunate incident occurred when sailing under convoy in the North Sea guarded by the Danish frigate 'Havfruen'. Armed convoys had become a common practice by Britain and the Baltic countries. The Royal Navy had demanded the right to examine any merchant ships for war material. The Danish Captain Dockum had protested that the British had no authority for such an act, and the convoy continued into the Kattegat, with two of the company's ships, including the 'Falkon', crowding on the canvas while the British considered their position. Thus the Century had closed with the bitter winter winds made more piercing by the hostility between friendly trading nations.

*

John's quiet marriage to Eugenie had enabled them to set up house at the far end of Frederiksberg Alle, far away from the overcrowded city centre, and close enough to the Royal Palace at Frederiksberg to give them a feeling of security. As the fortunes of the Company grew, John found his time divided between Copenhagen and the ships. With his wife at home, he inwardly resented the amount of time he had to spend travelling on the fast-growing fleet associated with the Company. He was acquiring a greater practical knowledge of the agents in many of the ports, from Petersberg in the east to Liverpool in the west.

His greatest desire was to bring Eugenie to meet his mother and father, but recent skirmishes in the North Sea and the British pursuit of the 'Falkon' hardened his resolve to keep his new bride safe in her lovely home overlooking the trees and lakes of the park. They now owned a carriage and employed three servants and a coachman. Each morning John would be driven to the city gate at Vesterbrogade, and then he would walk across the city, calling upon shippers and traders on his way to the harbour. Lars encouraged John in building up the personal contacts with his customers.

Jake Tempest, an occasional visitor to Denmark, had visited John and Eugenie and found their social life very much to his liking. His tall, slender form, and distinctive braided pigtail had become a familiar sight escorting many of the city's beauties. Lars had quickly recognised his talents, and paid him a commission on every overdue payment he collected in the country. Both John and Jake learned to ride horses elegantly, rather than the 'farmer's seat' they had found adequate for getting round Lancaster. Fast horse riding became an essential skill to get around the gently undulating country, whether taking ferries from island to island or crossing the mainland of Jutland. The fastest way of getting messages to London was by mail-coach or horseback to Hamburg, where a regular ferry crossed the North Sea to Yarmouth or Maldon. Even so, the rate at which the agents could get messages to the company was a hindrance. John raised the question with Lars and Jake.

'Why don't we build some small, very fast boats, rigged fore and aft, with a small crew designed just to carry messages and mail. In England we would have to apply for a licence to carry the King's mail, but we would be speedier than anything at present.'

'Except for one thing,' interrupted Jake. 'If everybody's navy assumes the right to stop us and open the mail-bags, we'd soon be accused of stealing it ourselves. Until all these emperors stop fighting I suggest we just carry our own documents. Just think of it, our bills, letters of credit, promissory notes and even cash will be carried quicker than anyone else's. That would really put us ahead.'

*

Eugenie was growing bored with the city whilst her husband never seemed to be at home. She would like to visit England, particularly London, if only to buy some dresses in the Pall Mall of her imagination. Still, John wouldn't hear of it.

'If you think it is dangerous crossing to England, why can't I go to Petersberg? Lots of my friends go there in the summer, where they say it's beautiful.'

'Eugenie, my dearest, Russia is in the hands of a madman. I would be very concerned if you were there.'

'Is that what the countess tells you?'

John looked at his wife, and sensed her doubts created by his enforced secrecy.

'Why the countess? She is no concern of mine.'

'Then why do you see her so secretly? Do you think I don't know?'

'Know what? I have no connection with her.'

John felt his world starting to spin, like a ship at the centre of a storm.

'John, my dear husband, say what you like, sometimes I can smell her perfume as clearly as if she was standing in our bed-chamber. I find her notepaper, perfumed like a common sailors' keepsake, hidden in your linen. Do you think I am an idiot?'

'Eugenie, you must believe me, the messages I receive from the countess are only concerned with threats to the safety of our own lives. You don't understand...'

'John, please don't tell me I don't understand. That's what every cheated wife is told. Now, I'm not interested in fighting you. We have a lovely home, and I love you very dearly. But you know that if Lars was ever told you are spreading your seed in more than one furrow you would be finished. So, my beloved, the choice is yours.'

John felt sick at the interpretation his wife had put upon what was not only innocent, but essential to protect the interests of hundreds, maybe thousands of people. As if to compound his difficulty, a message was waiting for him when he arrived, weary and unrested the following morning at the harbour office. The familiar plain envelope was waiting in the pile of the morning's documents. He tore it open and read the brief, unsigned message.

'You must be at the residence at 4 o'clock today, Tuesday.'

At noon he climbed aboard one of the wagons heading out of the city, laden with goods.

'Here's a crown, driver. Drop me at the Rundel as soon as your horses can manage.'

When he jumped down and hurried along the tree-lined road he knew what action he had to take, whether anyone else would agree. He unlocked his front door and called to Eugenie.

'We're going out at three o'clock, so get dressed as prettily as you like. We are taking tea with the countess.'

He stepped out of the room before she could protest. He found the coachman working in the kitchen, flirting with one of the maids while pretending to polish a black iron pot.

'Carriage at three o'clock, sharp, into the city. You'll wait for the mistress and me.'

'Yes, sir,' replied the surprised coachman, not used to such blunt orders in the middle of the day.

In the dining room John found some cold lamb and a bowl of fruit. He ate a couple of hurried mouthfuls when Eugenie entered the room. She kissed him lightly on the cheek, and pretended to act like an innocent young maiden.

'Why has the countess asked us to tea? Does she want to see what I look like, so suddenly?'

'No, my wife. I have some vital business to discuss, and it will do you no harm to be present. At least allow me that.'

'Yes dear, of course. I'm sure you haven't been all morning arranging this charade with her, have you?'

'Eugenie, all I can do is place the truth before you. If you care to disregard it, I will have to try again.'

With great sweetness in her voice, Eugenie looked straight at her husband and replied, 'Of course, my dear. I quite understand.'

In the lengthening shadows of the winter afternoon, the carriage pulled up in front of the Residence, a small, graceful house set amongst trees on the north side beyond the city. From the upper floors the waters of the Great Sound could be seen through the trees, and where the winter left bare branches, the distant shore of Sweden could be seen. John understood the house belonged to a relative of the countess, who lent it to her on her ever longer visits from Russia.

The coachman jumped down and rang the door-bell. When the door was opened by a butler a brief conversation followed and then the coachman signalled for his passengers to enter.

To John's embarrassment, the countess was dressed in a flowing dress of the finest white lace, completely plain, but more inviting to the eye than the most skilfully cut Parisian gown. Every shadowy contour of her body could be glimpsed through the delicate weave.

The presence of Eugenie, dressed in her favourite tea-gown with a light cape, was obviously something of a surprise, which the countess did not readily conceal. A great commotion was made of ordering additional cups and plates and more of the small Danish cakes which made ladies' afternoons bearable.

'Eugenie, my dear, I haven't seen you since your marriage, except at these fearful suppers everyone seems to take in town.'

The conversation was difficult, and John knew the countess was nervous about speaking in front of Eugenie. Then he could maintain the hollow conversation no longer.

'Countess, it is quite in order for you to talk of our business in front of my wife. We have no secrets except this one. So please speak freely, and be assured, your words will go no further.'

The elegant woman seemed to consider John's words carefully, before replying, having uneasily made the decision in his favour.

'Well, I have received some news by a courier this morning. I am told that Cousin Paul is laying immediate plans. Do you understand that? Immediate plans to shut the Baltic Sea to the British. There, now you know the full import of my concern.'

John looked in astonishment.

'How can he close the entire sea, just like a walled garden? It's not possible.'

'It is completely possible and I'll tell you how. He will invite Denmark and Sweden to form a more effective League of Armed Neutrality with Russia. You know the slogan 'neutral trade in neutral ships.' Britain will be driven to intercept cargoes for France and Spain. If necessary Cousin Paul will put a Russian Merchantman in the Great Sound as bait in the trap. The day that a neutral ship is stopped by the Royal Navy, Russia will demand the neutral states close their ports to British ships. By that means he can cripple supplies of timber to Britain and soften her for the French to attack. But Cousin Paul's interest is simply to get France looking west towards England instead of east towards Russia.'

John still had difficulty grasping the meaning of the evidence of crude treachery. He had no training in European politics.

'But we're trading every day with Russia and the other countries. It would put an end to...'

'You understand? Put an end to British trade, but everyone else will be twice as busy as a result. Now has the real meaning got home? It is a quite brilliant plan, too clever for Cousin Paul. I'm told the idea was invented in Paris, not Petersberg. Your problem is that every British ship is in danger. That's all I can say.'

'Then we should present our intelligence to the British Embassy without delay.'

The countess turned upon John with the venom in her speech which he recalled hearing once before on a distant balcony.

'The British Embassy is a club for old men to sip their French wines and Spanish port. To them, a state secret is the name of the ambassador's mistress, and a spy is the butler at her keyhole! I implore you, John, do not tell anyone at your embassy.'

John felt his mouth go dry when he realised he might be the only British citizen to have any knowledge of this fiendish scheme, and he had to get the information to London without any delay whatsoever. His mind was calculating means of carrying the message, and he paid scant attention to the trivial conversation between Eugenie and the

Countess. Under these unusual circumstances, it became obvious he must bring the tea-party to a close. Eugenie was obviously enjoying herself, perhaps reassured by the evidence of the countess' role as an informant rather than a rival. She nevertheless viewed the beauty of her hostess with some concern. John , ever the English sailor, had never been slow to react to her own body. He could hardly be insulated from the sensual heat of the countess, just because she was also a highly-placed informer. Then she was aware of Irena's hand on her own.

'You probably view me as bidding for John's favour, no? How can I tell you, dear Eugenie, much as I adore these quiet Englishmen, I have no possibility of drawing him from your side. Please, let us be good friends.'

Eugenie paused for a moment, weighing her thoughts, looking from John to Irena.

'I will view the future with your comments in my mind.'

She considered her words gave sufficient uncertainty to keep everyone on their toes.

As they climbed into their carriage Eugenie was talking freely about the mysterious countess. But John heard little and understood less.

'We must go to London immediately,' he announced at last.

'Really, dear. You'll enjoy that.'

'Not me, Eugenie. Both of us. I've decided how we will do it. You will dress as a man, my servant perhaps, travelling with one bag between us. If we have the 'Cavalier' sailing from Copenhagen as I hope, we can board that as passengers and arrange to be landed at one of the ports in Essex. Take the Stage to London and thence to Lancaster. How does that sound?'

She looked at her husband in wide-eyed amazement.

'My darling man, it sounds quite mad. Why can't I dress properly?'

'Let me explain. I'm sorry, I was so occupied with my own thoughts I gave little time to you. Look, my darling, what we have heard today could start by destroying our business and end by seeing England invaded by France. I know it sounds impossible, but that is not our job. We need to leave others to consider the import of our information.'

'Yes, yes,' she cried impatiently. 'But why dress up as a man?'

'Right. I consider it essential two people have this information firmly in their minds, not in writing, you understand. If anything happens to one, the other carries the same details. I will tell you exactly how to find my connection in London. But we can travel light and fast as working men, attract no attention, invite no molestation.'

'Yes, if those are the risks, I agree. Look! Why is the coachman taking us through the city?'

'So I can go to the British Embassy and see if I can carry anything for them. Tell the Lords and Ladies I've got a fast boat and they'll give me a pouchful of documents. More importantly, I'll have a Letter of Free Passage for the journey. Then we must see Lars and get his approval.'

'For his sister to be presented to London society dressed as a labouring man? He should be very surprised!'

Darkness was settling over the city by the time they returned home, with a thousand jobs to complete to enable them to board the 'Cavalier' the next day and wait for a fair wind and tide to bear them to England.

'Dear John. I do understand how unfair I was to doubt your love for me. But I knew nothing of Irena's special interests, you understand and if I had seen her in that sea-mist of a dress I would have assumed the very worst. But I do believe your word.'

'Thank you, my own countess.' He kissed her upon her parted lips as he held her close.

'There is just one problem, John. For the next few days I am to pose as a man, wearing man's breeches and that dreadful moleskin coat. I'm sure the last thing you would want would be to be seen on one of my brother's ships slipping your hand inside the shirt of a common working man...which means tonight is the last opportunity...'

*

The trap so cunningly set by the Tzar was unwittingly baited with a convoy of Danish ships escorted by a valiant Captain Krabbe in command of the frigate 'Freya'. He fearlessly positioned his small ship between the six Danish merchant ships and the British warships who were enforcing the blockade of French and Dutch ports. Eventually, the convoy anchored off the port of Dover whilst the English sent Lord Whitworth to negotiate with the Department of the Navy in Copenhagen.

Whilst Captain Krabbe was feted in Copenhagen as a returning hero, the Tzar reminded his neighbours in the Baltic that Britain could not possibly be permitted to act in such a tyrannical manner, and as the year drew to a close the Treaty signed in St Petersberg confirmed the Armed Neutrality of Sweden, Denmark and Norway, Prussia and Russia. Every port in the Baltic was closed to British ships, and ships in port were seized. However, the Tzar was unaware that British ships tried to avoid the Baltic and its ice-locked ports in winter.

Britain responded by seizing one hundred and forty-nine foreign ships in British ports.

But the threat to her navy was clear to see. Lord Whitworth returned from Copenhagen convinced that the Russians were the driving force. If France was able to make an alliance with the neutral states, she would have access to combined navies capable of protecting her fleet of invasion boat assembling in Boulogne.

Even the newly-married Sir Hyde Parker, lowering his sixty-year-old frame into bed beside his eighteen-year-old bride, realised the bitter winter outside the steamed windows of the well-named 'Wrestlers Arms' in Great Yarmouth, might conceal an enlarged French fleet.

Chapter 27

John Weaver and Eugenie were waiting to return home to Denmark. John read the news in the Gazette with growing apprehension as the European protagonists took up their positions like witless prize-fighters squaring up to each other unaware of the rich and unseen wagers on the outcome.

Eugenie had grown impatient with the limited vistas of Lancastrian life. The weather was bitter, the streets broken and uneven, and the life after sunset was concerned mainly with returning home in safety. The giant labourers who, she learned, had been building the strange canal by the sea, still roamed through the towns looking for work. Even the clothes she had bought from dress-makers in Preston and Manchester she would happily leave in the gardrobes at Ryelands. Large gracious houses enfolded in the hills outside the city were the preserve of the gentry and a few successful manufacturers, and entry through their portals was most carefully constrained. Eugenie was conscious of the social ladder in the English counties and recognised that her hosts had only ascended as far as the first polished rungs. The glittering steps of silver and gold were, as yet, beyond their reach.

The only lasting memory of her visit was the warmth and affection of Joshua and Sarah Weaver. In particular, Sarah treated her with a deep affection, which Eugenie suspected was for 'the daughter she never had.' As Eugenie had scarcely known her own parents, who had died when she was small, a very special bond grew quickly between the two women.

One of the company's small, fast ships would be due in Kings Lynn on the Norfolk coast, but with no proper passenger cabins, they would once again travel as Mr Weaver and his clerk. By this time, John was well known and respected by most of the fleet captains and mates, so he considered Eugenie's disguise could be relaxed a little when the ship was at sea.

The bitterly cold journey across England to the port was made slightly easier by the frozen ground, when the toll roads were well-built. Nevertheless, their final arrival at the 'George' Inn was a welcome relief from the cold and the nausea created by the rocking coaches by day and the noisy smoke-filled coach inns by night..

The following morning they left the blazing fires of the inn to check along the wind-swept jetties for the ship that was to carry them across the stormy waters to the calm of the Kattegat. At last, the schooner 'Unity', with the red ensign at her gaff and the new, red and white company flag at her mast-head was found, made fast alongside two spritsail coastal sailing barges. The crowded harbour appeared strangely quiet, possibly awaiting the late winter sunrise.

The two passengers crossed to the 'Unity' and hailed to anyone on board. Presently, a heavily bearded man appeared from below decks. His huge frame was made even bigger by a collection of heavy-weather clothing of many layers.

'Hello, Mister Weaver. I am Hanson, Mate of 'Unity'. Quick, get below.' He assisted them over the ship's rail. 'You weren't followed, were you?'

'I don't think so. Why do you ask?'

Hanson looked round nervously.

'Press gangs, Mister Weaver. The Press Gang gutted this town yesterday, like a fishwife with a net of herring.'

'Dear God, have we lost any men?'

'Two, I think. One other might have run away without his pay. I hear some Admiral Parker is putting a huge fleet to sea from Yarmouth. Every time they stop in port more than a week half the crew jump ship. So out go the press gangs again and try to round up a scratch crew of goat men and chimney sweeps.'

'How soon do you expect to get clear of this place?'

'The captain's at the customs house even now. When he returns we'll be ready to take the tide, even if we have to anchor in the roads for a wind.'

'Mr Hanson, I don't understand. Are you a British ship?'

The giant sailor smiled slowly through his beard.

'British, Danish, Chinese, we can be what you want, sir. I speak good English, like most of the crew. Captain Bliss is as English as navy grog, but between us we can manage most tongues!'

Hanson showed John and his 'clerk' a small cabin with a narrow cot against each side, otherwise completely empty. As the space between the cots was no more than two feet, their travelling bags made the space look overcrowded.

Captain Bliss announced his arrival by a shout to the mate.

'Hands to moorings, Hanson, stand-by fore and mains.'

He looked briefly into the cramped cabin.

'John Weaver? Captain Bliss. Welcome to the 'Unity'. I'm going to get down the river on the ebb and then we can talk.'

When he had gone, John turned to Eugenie.

'Right, you stay here, George, and don't forget you're a man until I decide it is prudent!'

248

John scrambled up on deck and watched as the sails were shaken out.

'Use me as crew, Captain. I'm not here for a holiday.'

'Thank God. I didn't care to make such a request, but that damned press gang has left us very light. If you will look after the foredeck, Hanson can help me aft. We've only got twelve seamen, including a promoted sailmaster. My cook has decided he can make money at the George Inn, so we will have biscuits most of the voyage.'

'My man George can do the cooking. He fancies himself as a gourmet!'

'Well, this is good news indeed. Hanson, let go aft! Let the tide catch her. Mr Weaver, let go forward as we swing! This could be a good voyage!' He rubbed his hands in anticipation.

In the bitter cold the schooner drifted silently down the harbour and into the open waters of The Wash. To John it was like the Bay he grew up with, but without the majesty of the Westmorland mountains. For a moment a pang of homesickness cast a shadow across his mind, hardly the emotions of a twenty-six year old European merchant trader. Yet as the off-shore wind gathered its strength and bore the 'Unity' away from the low-lying shore-line, John was oppressed by a strange air of finality, as if this strange port was closing a chapter in his life. Perhaps reading his thoughts, Eugenie joined him on deck, remembering to stand at a respectful distance from him.

'Do you think we'll ever be here again? I have a strange sense that something has changed.' Her whispered comment exactly reflected his own misgivings

'Well, George,' he said in a loud voice, 'We'll soon be working out how to enter Copenhagen without a sail-full of chain-shot!'

At the end of the afternoon watch, as the pale sun set over the distant land, Captain Bliss and Hanson, the Mate and John Weaver, discussed how they would approach the hostile territory of Denmark.

'The custom house has warned us anything might happen. With the winter weather, messages are so delayed that no-one knows whether we are at war with God knows who. So, for this day, at least, we'll keep the union flag at the gaff. If we make good headway, we'll go Danish tomorrow. By God, this North wind is as cold as the Pope's wife! Make sure all hands have sheepskins and fur caps, please, Hanson.'

The warm, smelly skins and hats were handed out, with great amusement, their sizes and smells varying greatly. Each skin was secured with a rope girdle or a leather thong, and some of the sailors improved the comfort with strange fur additions, to cover ears, hands or faces. When everyone had taken their selection from the sacks, each admired his shipmates, like children being kitted out at the orphan's home, laughter and back-slapping adding some welcome warmth to the fading dusk.

John looked at the chart lying on the table in the small deck-house. The five hundred miles to Skagen, the 'Skaw' to English sailors, at the north of Denmark could be crossed by sunset on the third day if the wind stayed fair. Then the ship could continue overnight before feeling her way to Kronborg castle, where she would be examined for paying the Sound Tax entering the Baltic, if everything was normal.

But the following day, as the sun appeared above the swirling sea-mist it cast its cold light on the sails of two great men-o-war sailing parallel to the course of the 'Unity' about a league to the north. They gradually drew closer, making about the same speed as the schooner. Presently, the huge sail spread of the nearest warship stole all the wind from the 'Unity' and she soon lost her surging progress. The great warship eased her own canvas, to sail ever closer, possibly not realising the small ship would be unable to steer when she lost headway.

When it seemed that the 'Unity' was effectively out of control, a cutter was lowered from the deck of the warship, and amid shouted orders, proceeded to row across the turbulent water between the two rolling hulls. John saw what was happening and told Eugenie to get below decks and try and find somewhere to hide. He certainly hadn't planned for this style of intervention.

Mate Hanson threw a rope ladder over the side, and had seamen waiting to take any thrown mooring lines. Sure enough, lines came aboard and were made secure.

Presently, a uniformed head appeared above the bulwark rail.

'Lieutenant Boston of His Majesty's ship 'Bellona'. Permission to come aboard.'

'Mister Boston, we welcome you aboard the schooner 'Unity' from the port of Kings Lynn.'

The officer was smartly dressed in uniform overlaid with a great fur-lined cape, already stained white where the salt water had dried out. His escort consisted of two young midshipmen, small, pale-faced boys, trying to appear threatening in their uniforms. Their pinched, sea-sick faces hardly struck terror in the crew of the 'Unity'.

'Where are you bound, Captain?'

'Kronborg for Duties and Taxes, then Copenhagen.'

'Don't you know we are at war, for God's sake?'

The captain looked at the lieutenant, taller than himself, surmounted by a tricorne which made him appear taller. The captain turned to his substantial first mate.

'Mister Hanson! Did anyone have the courtesy to tell us in Lynn that His Majesty had bravely declared war against the great marching hordes of Copenhagen?'

'No sir. The press gang said they wanted volunteers for a warm voyage to the Indies. I almost joined them myself!'

The lieutenant was getting angry.

'Be that as it may, we want some information from your navigator. We are concerned about the passage into the Baltic, keeping away from the Danish coast.'

'Well, lieutenant, you would be well advised to take the Swedish coast, pass the island of Hven and Saltholm on your starboard side.'

'Show me.'

The Captain took the lieutenant into the deck house. John Weaver followed them in, anxious to learn as much as he could about the plans of the Royal Navy.

As they pored over the chart the captain pointed out the islands which lay like two monstrous ships in the restricted waters of the Sound.

'Why don't you avoid Copenhagen altogether? If you took the Great Belt you would not attract any attention at all,' suggested John, anxious to get the warships away from his adopted city. 'You could be in the Baltic before anyone knew you were there.'

'Are you sure?'

John nodded.

'With this wind, I'd use that route every time.'

'Right. I have the King's authority to recruit a good navigator as pilot. I won't take the captain, I'll take this man.' He swung round and seized John by the thick material of his sheepskin.

'Then you'll be aground even in fifty fathoms. He's a sail-master, not a navigator.'

The lieutenant laughed and slapped his thigh.

'I'll still take this one! When I see a man on deck still clutching a pencil I know I've got a navigator. What's your name, man?'

'John Weaver, travelling under Letter of Free Passage to His Majesty's Ambassador Plenipotential...'

The lieutenant interrupted him.

'Well, then, we had best get you to your destination as soon as possible. Hanson, get this man's gear together and we'll leave you unhindered.'

The captain started to protest, but the lieutenant turned his back.

While the exchange had been taking place, the warship was now close alongside, her lower spars almost touching the swinging gaff of the 'Unity'. High up on deck a man in an elaborate uniform, covered with gold braid, with a high tricorne, leaned over the bulwark and shouted through a speaking trumpet to the party on the deck of the 'Unity'.

'Lieutenant! Get back on board immediately. Put him in irons if he gives trouble. Move!'

'Aye, aye sir.'

John was bundled over the side of the 'Unity', followed by the three men in the boarding party and his travel bag, lowered on a rope. He turned to see the face of the captain.

'Take care of my man George. Tell him to get to the Frederiksberg office and wait for me there.'

The captain waved, and shrugged his shoulders.

The cutter was now almost trapped between the massive, steady hull of the warship and the lighter, rolling hull of the 'Unity'. As the sailors lowered their oars to pull across the few yards that separated them the sea dashed the cutter hard against the wooden wall. With a short scream one of the oarsmen was smashed in the face by the loom of his trapped oar. Blood spurted from his face as he released his grip on the oar. It swung further and hit the next man low in the ribs.

Within seconds, the boat was being tossed between the two ships and John made sure he was the first to grab the wooden rungs which made a firm ladder up the sloping side of the warship. He was the first on deck, whilst the chaos in the boat below had sailors throwing down ropes and rope-ladders to their shipmates being battered in the icy waters.

The warship quickly pulled away, opening the waterway between the two ships. The last thing John saw was the 'Unity' drawing away, her sails once again filling with wind and actually making better speed than the heavy warship. On the stern of the 'Unity' a small figure waved a fur cap towards the clumsy hull.

He was quickly escorted below the main deck and was astonished at the massive structure of the huge ship. Every timber was twice the size of anything he had ever seen, despite all his experience of sailing and building merchant ships. Monstrous black cannon blocked every space, bundled sleeping hammocks were tied up against deck-heads, ropes and stores in boxes and barrels were fitted into every corner. He was taken into a cabin already occupied by three officers. They greeted him in silence and ignored his presence altogether. He threw his bag into a corner of the cabin and sat on it to consider the unenviable position he was in, caused by his own stupidity.

While he sat dejectedly he reflected on the savage twist of fate which had put him a prisoner on board this hideous man-o-war and unceremoniously separated him from the woman he loved. He was confident that Eugenie could continue her deception on the friendly ship 'Unity' but many trials could lie ahead for all ships heading for the freezing waters of the Baltic.

After more than an hour a quartermaster appeared at the low door of the cabin and saluted.

'Mister Weaver, sir. Captain would like to see you in the day cabin.'

Nervously, John got to his feet and followed the quartermaster, up two companionways and then aft into a cabin which had square-paned windows looking out over the stern. The cabin seemed to be full of officers in smart blue uniforms, decorated with gold braid and more elaborate frills than he had ever seen on a ship before. The man who presumably was the most senior came to meet John at the door, his hands firmly clasped behind his back. No effusive greeting here, thought John.

'Mister Weaver, I understand. My regrets if you have been incommoded by our request for your services.'

'Sir, I am travelling under a Letter of Free Passage as a courier. The Foreign Secretary will hear of this interruption.'

'No he won't Mister Weaver. We are taking every measure to bring you to your destination. So I will listen to no more complaints. I have a hundred and thirty men on this ship who, three days ago, were spreading pig dung on the meadows of Norfolk. You have little to complain about. Now, to ship's business.'

He turned to the table which was covered with charts and sketches of the seas round Denmark and the Baltic.

'Our fleet has sailed with a meagre compliment of pilots, Weaver. You can be our pilot into the Baltic. Understood?'

'Understood, Captain. What is your destination?'

'Why, Petersberg, of course. Put a sixty-four pound ball in the Tzar's trouser-tackle, eh?'

The officers duly laughed at the feeble joke.

'The trouble is, we have little experience of these waters. Jamaica, St Kitts, Guadeloupe, my men could find them with their eyes closed. Three years in the Indies, most of us. Now this.'

John advanced to the table.

'How much are you drawing?'

A voice round the table answered.

'Twenty-one feet, in fresh water.'

'How close to the wind can you point?'

'Not more than a point for'ard of the beam. Slightly closer in low seas.

'Then pray for a good northerly like today and take the Great Belt. Plenty of clear water, a sheltered anchorage all the way through. Just hope the wind doesn't veer to the south. Then we're in trouble on either passage.'

The conversation turned to questioning about the relative merits and hazards of the low shores of Denmark.

The following day, to John's startled gaze, the sea was transformed. Coming up on deck of the 'Bellona' he observed they were surrounded by dozens of equally huge men-o-war. He attempted to count the ships as they pitched and rolled in the rising wind. He estimated there were more than twenty large ships, and a similar number of smaller vessels, some of which were short, squat hulls with two masts. He had never seen such a varied fleet.

The north wind was bringing snow and ice down on the straining ships. Ropes and spars were encrusted with ice, the bulk of the black cannons on the top deck looked less threatening with a soft pillow of snow on the barrels. In the thrashing waves, gravestones of ice were tossed against the hull. Smaller pieces made a continuous rattle as the great ship surged through the deadly waters.

The fleet was spread across a wide expanse of the sea, and signal flags seemed to be hoisted and lowered with remarkable speed. Without even seeing the charts, John could sense that the fleet was following a leading ship far to the east of Zeeland, and eventually, through the snow-heavy wind, he recognised the steeper coast of Sweden revealed ahead. The fleet turned south and with a strong following wind headed for the narrow, treacherous Sound which led to the harbour of Copenhagen on the western side, and the Swedish port of Malmo on the East.

'Not exactly amongst friends, eh?' The speaker was one of the officers with whom John had been speaking in the Captain's day room.

'I doubt they would attack a fleet this size.'

The land on each side was closing the channel down to less than two leagues and he could see the sharp outline of the castle at Kronborg, the historic Helsingor Castle which had defended the approaches to the capital many times in the past. John noticed the officers watching the battlements through their telescopes, calling to each other as flags were raised on the distant battlement.

'Here they come!' exclaimed an officer near John.

Then the thunder of cannonfire rolled across from the fortifications. The fall of shot could just be seen in the rough water, a league or more from the 'Bellona', although other ships in the fleet were closer.

The great fleet swept past the distant fortifications without slackening or exchanging fire, and as the final glimpses of the sun set over the land, ships were swung into the wind and the thunder of anchors being dropped brought the fleet to an uneasy resting place for the winter night. Surveying the unusual scene, John could make out one or two spires of Copenhagen. The masts of ships, presumably in the harbour, appeared like a bare forest before the city. Closer at hand, the fleet seemed engaged in energetic visiting. Cutters were launched in the icy sea, gold braided officers came and went from ship to ship, bundles of charts were carried into the dayroom. The night seemed to be full of activity.

*

In pitch darkness, John was called from his cramped cot and told to make his way on deck. The morning watch was coming on deck at four o'clock, muffled up with every available garment.

'Mister Weaver? A change of plans. You realise where we are anchored?'

'Surely. I estimate we're almost aground on Saltholm. One fluke in the wind and we can walk ashore on the island.'

'There's plenty of water, I'm told.'

'Who told you?'

The officer pointed out of the stern window.

'See that? H M S Elephant, flagship of Admiral Nelson. If he tells his ships there's sufficient water, even God would not dare argue. Now, our orders are to watch for his signal and then round the southern end of the Middle Ground shoal and sail northwards up the Kings Sound, right on the Danes' doorstep. Your job is to pilot us round the shoal.'

'Wanting twenty-five feet or more of water? Have you got sounding lines ready. Tell your leadsmen we must not cross the five fathom line.'

As the light improved, the full magnitude of the task ahead could be measured by every admiral, captain, seaman and deck boy. Across the flank of the city had been created a wall of anchored warships, perhaps thirty in number, each under bare masts, with battle ensigns blowing stiffly in the south-easterly breeze. Beyond the Danish fleet, the fixed forts and batteries, the distant Trekroner forts and, John knew, the massive batteries of the Citadel would be levelling their cannon eastward. To every eye, the Danish fleet was prepared to repel any attacker.

The British fleet was similarly preparing, the strange routines of charging the cannons for attack were keeping every man working. Each great gun grumbled on its carriage, to be loaded and run out through the open ports.

'How many of these brutes on this ship?' John indicated the nearest cannon as he spoke.

'Seventy-four guns, mostly twenty-four pounders. We boast eight hundred pounds of iron in a single broadside. Crack a basket of Danish eggs with that lot.'

'Why? Why are we here?'

'I think The Frenchies want to capture the Baltic fleets. So we arrived unbidden to spoil the party.'

At the end of the morning watch, as if by magic, the British fleet appeared to bloom as dozens of sails were shaken out and trimmed to catch the southerly wind. Calls from the foredeck reported as the anchor cleared the sea-bed. The Captain stood beside the two coxwains at the ship's wheel. He was surrounded by his officers, in descending order of authority across the raised poop deck. He summoned John to his side.

'Can you bring us round, just tell me the heading you need?'

'We must get further south than this.'

'Look, man, d'you see that cutter over there. Spent all last night they did, marking the southern end of the sound. They're our mark.'

'They are not in the right position for five fathoms. They don't understand the strength of the wind over current, especially with all this ice coming down from the Baltic. We must stem the current and get further south before rounding the middle ground shoal.'

'You're a fool, Weaver. Look, there goes Agamemnon, well to the north of us. We all have a position to take up. When Admiral Nelson announces his plans I'm not going to be the last into position.'

As if to add veracity to his words, the morning air was suddenly shattered by a thunderous rippling explosion, which seemed to last for several seconds.

"Polyphemus' has opened fire! Now 'Isis'! Let's get into the line. Coxwain, steer west-by-north by compass.'

John looked across at the familiar coastal landmarks, fearing that this huge, deep-draft ship would be dragged by the current.

Suddenly the yeoman, telescope to his eye, yelled at the top of his voice.

'Agamemnon's flying yellow and red. Good God. She's aground! She's on the shoal, look at her, she's been driven down on the shoal!'

By this time the barrage of broadsides was becoming a continuous roar of brain-fogging sound. John could feel the actual pressure of the explosions on his chest, yet 'Bellona' had not fired a single round.

'Coxwain, head Nor-nor-west by compass. Port gunners, lieutenant, fire when first ship is in line! Note your targets as we take position.'

John turned to the magnificently-uniformed naval captain, feeling helpless before the majesty of the ranks of officers.

'No, not yet, Captain, keep heading west, we're too close to the shoal!'

The first broadside of the port-side cannon was terrifying. The deck seemed full of recoiling cannon, whipping tackles, and stinking smoke. The intensity of noise was quite beyond John's preparations. The sound so smashed into his ears they kept reverberating with the same intensity after the first terrible shock wave had passed. Yet still he heard the screams of those 'goat men and chimney sweeps' struggling with the cannons in the nighmare of the lower decks for the first time.

The broadside caused the ship to roll to starboard which may have contributed to the great hull sliding on to the mud and shingle of the feared Middle Ground. The proof, if any were needed that the ship was now stationary was the speed at which the floes of ice clattered down the side, from the stern towards the bows. Officers and men looked over the bulwark at the current flowing past the ship, the awful truth undeniable.

'Yeoman, signal to flagship, 'Bellona' aground. Will continue action from here.'

The ignominy of being impotently skewered on the shoal, watching the rest of the fleet sail past in line to battle stations was partly relieved by the helplessness of watching H M S Russell make exactly the same error, pressed by the current into the invisible sea bed.

Chapter 28

The hundreds of men on the 'Bellona' could only watch the progress of the battle in relative safety. From time to time, the wind caused the ship to swing, allowing her guns to bear on the most southerly ships in the Danish line, and a thundering broadside would bellow across the water. Otherwise, she contributed nothing to the battle which raged until the middle of the afternoon watch. Cutters with flags of truce could be seen plying between H M S 'Elephant' and the Copenhagen shore. Then, without warning, before they could approach the Danish line a huge explosion rent the trembling air of the battle. One of the largest Danish ships, about a league to the north of the 'Bellona', exploded with a great flash of flame. The impact of the huge explosion a few seconds later shook every timber of the 'Bellona' and made every rope and block shake. To John it was like a punch in the chest. His ears had not become accustomed to the day's cannon fire, and this new thunder simply added to the continuous roar in his head. From their safe stand the helpless crew of the 'Bellona' silently witnessed the unthinkable fragments of the crowded man-o-war hurtling high through the scorching air.

Flag hoists rippled up and down the fleet's halyards, conducting and controlling the onslaught, and then, in response to a distant signal, relayed swiftly from ship to ship, silence fell across the opposing fleets, crippled and burning in the fading sun of the second day of April. The word 'armistice' ran through the hushed gun-decks. But no rejoicing warmed the air while the fearsome hulk of the Danish man-o-war blazed and finally settled in the timber-strewn water.

*

When John eventually stepped ashore from one of the many small boats which were tending all the ships in the harbour, he found a city torn between grieving for the victims yet rejoicing that the skilled gunnery of the Danish ships had forced the legendary Admiral Nelson to negotiate with The Crown Prince and agree a peaceful solution. In a tragic irony, the news arrived in the confused capital that the mad champion of the League of Armed Neutrality, Tzar Paul, had been assassinated two weeks before Admiral Nelson had drawn up his fleet toe-to-toe with their former Danish allies. Thus it was that with the succession of Tzar Alexander, France lost her voice in the Baltic.

The lifting of winter was allowing more activity in the harbour, but the laborious task of hauling the battered warships back into the naval yard across the harbour was preventing the movement of merchant ships. John hurried to the office and found the building locked and barred. Groups of people in the street watched the returning ships with grim interest, and John asked one of them whether they had seen a ship called 'Unity' in the harbour. He described the shape of the schooner, but could learn nothing of the ship. He hurried through the streets towards the Nyborg house and anxiously rang the door-bell.

Lars called down when old Klaus opened the heavy door.

'John! At last! Am I happy to hear your voice! Is Eugenie not with you?'

Briefly, John outlined the events which had separated him from Eugenie and the 'Unity'. As he spoke, Lars was pulling on a heavy coat and offered John a better garment than he was already wearing.

'Klaus. Mister John and I are going to get horses from Peter's stable, and we'll ride over towards the Citadel, to get the best view of the Sound. But we will be back here in no more than six hours time. Is that clear?'

Tired and cold, John was hardly prepared for the gallop round the ramparts, but at least he felt he was doing something useful to find Eugenie. Lars had brought a small spyglass with him, and as the sea came into view he stopped from time to time to examine the ships tacking down from the north. When they reached the foreshore, Lars pointed up the coast and led the way as fast as the horses could carry them. He knew there were many inlets where ships might have taken shelter during the bombardment. But as darkness fell, the two men regretfully concluded there was nothing more they could do that night. They returned to the house at Frederiksberg, and stabled the horses for the night.

To John's surprise, the door was opened by Jake, who appeared to have taken up permanent residence. The house was exactly as he had left it more than six months earlier, polished and dusted, the servants silently curious at the absence of the Mistress. The travellers threw off their mud-caked coats and boots, and fell into the deep chairs while Jake organised the servants to get hot water ready and to find hot food.

'By God, John, it's good to see you again. When I heard the guns yesterday, after all the rumours in the city, I feared the worst. They say the British sent an ultimatum from Kronborg, to destroy the entire fleet or watch the city burn. I couldn't believe my ears. The rumours in the harbour as they hurried to drag the warships into the Sound started some panic. People thought the ships were being towed out for surrender, because most of them were without topmasts and spars. They sailed some of them with just two sails.'

The three men discussed the confusing events of the past days while the servants brought in trays of food. A large stone jar was carried in by one of the girls. It contained a strange, warm drink, presumably mulled red wine, with fruit and spices and a distilled spirit. The conversation flowed with the same ease as the warming elixir.

John casually enquired about friends in the city.

'How about Elizabeth Bowen? Has she been to see you?'

'Yes, she was very concerned about Eugenie not being home. I'll wager the embassy had news about the Admiralty's plans which would have made her nervous for your safety.'

John turned to Lars.

'Do you see your Russian Countess?' he asked as casually as he could, as if he had little real interest in the lady. Lars looked surprised.

'On occasions. She's always asking after 'The lovely English Captain.' But she left the city before the storm broke and I presume she will be in State Mourning for the murdered Tzar.'

John smiled.

'I don't think she was his greatest champion, do you?'

'True indeed. Perhaps even greater reason to be seen in black in the Winter Palace.'

The room fell silent for a while.

'She is a most unusually beautiful woman, Lars. I'm astonished she remains unwed.'

'Well, brother-in-law of mine, I don't think we should be sat here in the firelight discussing beautiful, unmarried aristocrats while your wife, my sister, is somewhere in the Kattegat with a boat-load of sailors...'

'Dressed as a man,' concluded John. 'You make me feel guilty.'

The following morning, a messenger arrived at the Frederiksberg house to report that the 'Unity' had been seen taking shelter in the Isefiord, less than thirty miles from Copenhagen overland, nearly three times as far to sail round the coast.

'Don't go, John. You could be two days looking for one ship the size of 'Unity' if there are many taking shelter. Even with those good horses we rode last night it would take three or four hours to get there. My advice is to stay in town and wait for the ship to make for home.'

'I feel helpless, almost uncaring, doing nothing. But I agree with you. Let's get to the harbour. We can call in to your house and make sure your old boy Klaus knows where we are.'

'He'll be witless by now. Remember, we told him we would be back in six hours. That loyal old man will have sat by the street door all night keeping a look-out for us.'

His assumption was correct. The old man's eyes were red with tiredness when he opened the door to the two men. Lars turned to make a brief apology. The old servant shook his head.

'It's not that, sir. I have been told by the Naval Division that my only son has been killed by the British gunfire. He was quartermaster on the 'Dannebrog' which exploded, I'm told.' The old man's weary, tear-stained eyes turned hesitantly towards John.

'They say the ship exploded while the flag of truce was flying from the British boats. I never knew the British could stoop to that.'

Lars made the smallest movement with his hand to prevent John making any reaction. A tilt of the head told John to get back to the waiting horse.

When Lars joined him they returned the horses to the stable and walked towards the harbour in silence. Eventually John spoke.

'I fear the English might not be well-received in the city at present. I watched that ship burst into a thousand pieces. I will never forget the sight or sound of it. We don't even know what Eugenie will be thinking when she hears what happened.'

'Then I tell you what we will do. When the smoke has blown away, when we have overcome our grief, we will have a great banquet to tie our country to yours. You can imagine Denmark and Norway, Sweden, Russia and Prussia, joining with Britain to ensure peace and profitable trade between us.'

'What about France? Do you think she will ever make peace with us?'

Lars shook his head.

'I don't think that is likely. Napoleon Bonaparte threatens us all. Perhaps we will be better placed when he has gone to his Maker. The Minister had a despatch at the turn of the year that an attempt had been made on Napoleon's life.'

*

Another day passed before news of the 'Unity' passing the harbour entrance arrived at the company office. Lars and John went to the quayside to watch the ship work her way into the harbour. John recognised the figures on deck, but could see no sign of Eugenie. As the ship drew nearer the fore-sail and main gaffs were lowered, headway just maintained with the two triangular headsails. Finally, as the first line was thrown ashore, the halliards were cast off and the sails were drawn down the fore stays and quickly secured by the two sailors on the bowsprit. At the extremity of the spar, twenty feet forward of the schooner's deck, the figure, standing precariously on the narrow footrope, waved to the two men on the quay.

'Good God! That's Eugenie! That's your sister balancing on the end of the bowsprit!' The two men waved frantically at the small, breech-clad figure.

'What do we call her? George? Eugenie? I suggest no embraces until we are in the privacy of the office.'

'I'm grateful for your advice, Lars. My first reaction would have been less restrained!'

Lines ashore and secure, gangway down, all sails lashed and covers ready for lacing, Captain Bliss reported the 'Unity' all secure, to Lars Nyborg. He turned to John.

'Mister Weaver, sir, I'm happy to return your wife to you, safe and sound. Without her, the 'Unity' would be ashore on Sjellands Reef.'

*

Returning to Frederiksberg in the crowded coach, the four passengers' excited laughter drew occasional disapproving looks from the crowded pavements. The seven hundred men who had been killed in the ferocious battle cast a deep shadow of sorrow over the city, made more painful by those rejoicing at the city's deliverance.

At home, the servants welcomed the return of the mistress of the house. Captain Bliss, with no family in the city, was invited to stay for a few days. Hot water, clean clothes and hot beef pie soon restored all the travellers to a good humour, and round the crackling fire the stories were exchanged. Captain Bliss gallantly explained how the sharp eyes of Eugenie had seen the first evil pinnacle of rock of the reef, the only stationary object in a sea of heaving ice and wind-driven spume.

'We were all so exhausted and cold ,I fear our attention was failing. There's men in this port tonight owe their life to you, Mistress Weaver. God bless you.'

Lars turned to his sister.

'When a sea captain says that to you, he means it.'

Suddenly Lars burst out laughing. Tears rolled down his cheeks. He was unable to speak, and began to gasp for breath. At last he exhausted himself, and was able to draw a breath.

'I have just appreciated the full, wondrous humour of the past few days. My beloved sister, pretending to be a Danish sailor, has saved a

British ship from running ashore, while my brother-in-law has been engaged as a British sailor to run a British ship ashore. In both cases, their actions, in different ways, have saved many lives. Is that not a demonstration that God has a sense of humour?'

By midnight, the strains and worries of the past days were taking their price. Beds beckoned, lamps were dimmed and fires banked up for the night. With their arms about each other, John took Eugenie to the elegant comfort of her chamber, stopping at each turn in the stairs to kiss her and run his finger-tips over her soft shoulders.

'Dearest Eugenie. I have had such fears. I was concerned that your disguise would create more difficulties than it was meant to solve. I worried that something unexpected would cause you to be in danger. Can you believe, I was uneasy that your monthly courses could give you away in such difficult circumstances. That's the depth of my concern.'

'Beautiful Captain, my monthly courses have most agreeably ceased for these past two months.'

She looked at her husband to see whether the significance had been recognised.

'You mean, my love, you are bearing our child? Can anything crown this day with more happiness?'

'You could try, my love.'

*

The cold, violent winter gave way to the easier days of spring. Just as the ice melted and dispersed, the countries round the Baltic warmed in their attitudes to each other. The demands and benefits of trade brought merchants together long before the Monarchs and Dictators had the courage to reach agreement. So it was, by the summer, the Treaty of Petersberg was agreed between Britain and Russia. On the twenty-third of October Denmark, with Norway and Sweden recognised the Treaty.

On the same day Eugenie was delivered of a son, called George, to be a constant reminder to his parents of the strange circumstances of his conception.

*

'What a wonderful justification for a celebration! We shall have a ball, even inviting the Crown Prince, to bring together Denmark and Britain in the person of this wonderful child.'

263

Lars was overwhelmed with the arrival of the small infant. He had long ago realised that no heir existed on his side of the family, and assumed that the Weaver family in Lancaster would be looking to the tiny creature to carry forward their name. Lars would make arrangements for them to visit Copenhagen as his guests, and meet the traders who formed the links in the chain which created wealth for each one.

As plans were laid, Lars allocated duties to each of his friends to take responsibility for different tasks. Jake Tempest made many of the arrangements, generally because his easy manner gave him access to the best advisers in society. One day he called on John, and for once he was obviously disturbed and worried.

'John, old friend, a most curious thing has happened. I have today received a document from a firm of solicitors in London.'

John looked at him with alarm.

'You haven't been sleeping with the dowager duchess again?'

'No fear. This is most strange. I think I have read it correctly.' He slowly read from a large piece of paper in his hand.

'To Mister Jake Tempest, sir. You are the sole beneficiary of our client, who refers to himself as DEAR FREND, who passed away some time ago. It was his wish that his estate should pass to you seven years after his death on the condition that you make no attempt to discover his identity in life. He states in his last will and testament that he bequeaths his worldly goods to you as truly as honest a man he has met. These are his precise words. The value of the estate, which has been converted to bonds and shares has a value on the first day of January in the Year of Our Lord Eighteen Hundred and One of..'

Jake's reading faltered. His brow was beaded with sweat. He wiped his lips with the back of his hand.

'.Fifteen thousand, seven hundred and eighty-four pounds precisely.'

A silence fell on the room. Jake held out the document for John to read for himself.

'That's what it says, Jake. I bet you it's one of your well-satisfied ladies. Dear Friend sounds good enough for me.'

'But you see how it is spelled? I know, even with my learning, that's wrong. So it must be someone who was as bad as me at spelling.'

'Maybe your father died a rich man. Putting everything to rights after all these years.'

Jake nodded.

'That's precisely how I account for it. Perhaps he has watched me all those years, even that your Mother treated me like her own son.'

'Well, me bucko friend, you're a rich man now.'

'Oh, fifteen thousand? I could find double that tomorrow if you wanted it.'

John could scarcely hide his surprise at the size of his friend's wealth.

'I congratulate you, Jake, on your good fortune. I've done well with the company, working here in Denmark. I must say that I find my loyalties to England hard to sustain. To watch that hideous battle last winter has left a dark cloud in my memory.'

'But John, that battle, surely, was to protect all of us trading freely in the Baltic? Blockades and closed ports are no good to us in the long run.'

'Not so. Our skill was applied to circumventing the blockades. That way we could demand more for our service.'

Jake's brow was creased in confusion.

'But just suppose Napoleon had seized the Danish battle fleet. They could have used them to destroy the English ships. Then where would any of us make our bed and earn a living?'

'Well, I find a hostility in the trade between England and Denmark which was never there before. With my new son, I think my heart is here in Copenhagen.'

'Then, John, let me be your shadow in England, for that is where I will earn my fortune.'

'And find your bride, I'll wager.'

When he was alone, John reflected upon the inheritance which Jake had received, equal to his own unexpected inheritance and made in precisely the same terms. Except that John had discerned the true name of their joint benefactor.

*

The third secretary to the Crown Prince carefully penned the first draft of the great speech. He amended the phraseology, adjusted the punctuation to make sure the words carried the import appropriate to the occasion.

'...our rejoicing at the peace between Denmark and her friends in England... the negotiations now taking place ...a solemn treaty between Britain and France, restoring the states of Europe to their historic peaceful custom, which We are confident will be agreed in the city of Amiens early next year...'

Chapter 29

The third summer of the new century brought peace among the European states, even France joining in the great treaties. In the Baltic, as in every other seaway, shipping was sailing with full holds and straining canvas. Sadly, the euphoria did not take such a firm hold in the city of Lancaster. Partly as a result of the development of Glasson Dock, but principally due to the rapid growth of the huge port of Liverpool, the River Lune carried a decreasing share of deep water trade. Coastal shipping was busy meeting the demands of local manufacturers, but the Northern Shipping Company found it was carrying little into Lancaster but more and varied cargoes into bigger ports closer to the new factories.

It was this change of trade which brought John Weaver back to his parent's home to forewarn the Lancaster shippers of the impending change in their fortunes. He had arrived in Liverpool on the 'Molly', an ungainly brig which had been a regular visitor to Lancaster in the past. Now, a full cargo of Baltic timber, flax and tar was consigned to the mills and yards of Liverpool.

On the Mersey dockside John was surprised to see Jake Tempest, standing apart from the waiting longshoremen as the ship drew alongside. His clothing and manner made it abundantly clear he expected someone else to handle the wet, clumsy mooring ropes. Even before they greeted each other John remembered the bare-foot orphan who had happily joined the Weaver household nearly seventeen years ago. As soon as the 'Molly' was secure alongside, Jake strode up the narrow gangway, looking aloft with the experienced eye of a mariner who has spent too long struggling with unyielding canvas. His first words of greeting to John were in keeping.

'Easy yards, easy canvas Mr Weaver?'

John shook his head in disbelief and started to laugh at his friend's manner.

'Jake, my friend, it looks as if a few tides have flushed the Mersey since you last struggled aloft! You'll be talking like Father's clients next. Never been aboard, yet every sentence had a larboard and starboard, topgallant and bottom-gallant!'

'Captain Johnny, you must understand, one's appearance carries more weight than one's knowledge these days.' He slapped John's shoulder in affection. ' Welcome home, John. We're all pleased to see you again. I have a couple of horses hired in the stables for a quick ride home.'

John nodded. 'That's welcome. I just have some documents to lodge at the custom-house and a brace of bags of mail, then home!'

As the two men walked round the busy deck of the ship they compared notes and experiences. Jake asked about Eugenie and her family as if she was his own sister. John told him about his terrifying experience in the naval battle, which had deeply affected him, every detail still burned into his memory.

John introduced Jake to the master of the 'Molly' before gathering up his sea-bag and the satchels of documents.

'Thank-you, Captain, for a quiet voyage, and never a shot fired!'

'Steady as you go, Mister Weaver and a safe journey north. There's more perils on the King's highway than there ever was afloat. Keep a pistol on your saddle and a blade in your boot-top.'

With such a grim warning the two men set off across the busy city to collect horses for the journey.

Part of their route took them across a new canal which John assumed extended from Liverpool across the Pennines to Leeds. It appeared narrower than the Lancaster cut, but already he could see boats and barges of different sizes making their way across what would once have been open fields.

'John, I want to stop in Preston, perhaps we should stay the night. I have some small business to attend to.'

'That has an air of mystery, Jake! Not one of your actresses, I trust!'

'No luck tonight. Just a visit to Preston Bank to collect some documents. I would be obliged if this visit remained confidential.'

John suddenly realised how much each of them had grown into their separate lives. But when they crossed the Penwortham Bridge Jake drew his horse close beside John's.

'When we are at the bank I don't use my name Tempest. I would be obliged if you would call me Mister John Sparrow. Some of these banks get so easily confused.' He winked at John.

'Not just the banks, either, Mister John Sparrow.'

*

The roadway from Preston northwards towards Lancaster was well-made with stone for several miles, but as the two men pressed north they came upon the recently completed tow-path running beside the Lancaster Canal. Overnight there had been a torrential rain storm which had thrashed on the slates of the coaching inn. When they awoke that morning and took breakfast the cellar of the inn was flooded. The two travellers could only hear the inn-keeper cursing as he struggled with the precious barrels. '....never seen rain like it! Midsummer and the Lord sends us winter weather...'

Now, the canal was well-filled and every few minutes they encountered horse-drawn barges, some travelling south clearly full of blocks of limestone. As they trotted north they took the turn-pike road which they followed as the more direct route. John could see the canal curving sharply to the west and then turning in a great loop, the embankment clearly visible above the level of the rain-drenched meadows.

Presently John noticed the name of the small hamlet which they were approaching. 'BROCK'.

'It takes its name from the river, I think,' said John. Indeed, in a few yards they came upon a stone bridge which crossed a turbulent river in full spate. They dismounted to look over the parapet of the bridge and John was astonished to see the surging flow of water fill the arch to its keystone, so that the water burst forth with a loud hissing roar. Down the course of the river they could see the tumbling water bending the trees and bushes along the steep banks, some uprooted and joining the surge.

'Presumably this river must pass under the canal further down. Look, you can see the embankment the far side of those meadows! There's going to be trouble here, I can see!'

As he spoke a horseman came galloping down the turn-pike and reined-up beside the two travellers.

'The canal's ready to burst! Can you ride? Aye, you ride as fast as your horse can carry you. Take the tow-path about half a mile and you'll see the stop-planks under the bridge. If there's no one tending them, do all you can to drop them in the channels. There's not a moment for delay. But haste! If the flow gets too fast you'll never get the planks in!'

John turned his horse and noticed Jake with a smile on his face, pulling his hat down and turning his collar up against the driving rain. The excitement of the headlong gallop along the narrow path was already spurring them on. The two horses pounded on the level path, their nostrils flared as the riders urged them ever faster.

Round a bend in the canal the next stone bridge loomed into view. As they approached they saw a man struggling with the long wooden planks which could be fitted into vertical grooves in the stone embankment each side of the waterway. Single-handed the task was impossible, but the three men lowered the planks in, struggling against the increasing speed of the flow of water.

When the flow had been dammed the bankman, who simply introduced himself as Ned ,said they should retrace their steps back towards the river, to see if the bank was sound. He climbed up behind John and the three of them trotted along the canalside, looking for signs of damage. Presently, as the natural level of the fields fell away John realised they were working back towards the point where the canal crossed the river. On the eastern side of the canal the water in the flooded fields was almost as high as the canal itself. Round the gentle curve the massive stone parapets of the aqueduct could clearly be seen above the level of the canal bank, but just before they reached them the three riders could see a gap in the canal bank, five or six feet wide, where the water poured out into the flooded field. John quickly realised the flood-water from the river had started to wash away the canal embankment, so that now the canal water was adding to the thrust of river water trying to pass under the single low arch of the aqueduct.

On horseback and on foot , the villagers had already started to collect, standing a safe distance from the swirling water as it escaped from the canal. A man started to give orders, which appeared to provoke the observers into action.

'We're going to need stone, and get it here fast. If any have got a wagon, take it down to the quarry at Bilsborrow or Inglewhite. The Canal Company will pay well, I promise you. It could be the best money you'll earn before harvest!'

'Some God-damned harvest that will be. Most of it will be in the Bay by now!'

The man looked round again. 'Then now's your chance, boys! But keep away from the arch, in case it goes. And one of you horsemen, ride downstream and clear the riverside at Saint Michaels and below.'

Some of the crowd hastened back towards the turnpike, shouting to each other, planning additional helpers, even laughing at the possibility of unexpected profit. Ned the bankman turned to John.

'If you're headed north, sir, can you get a message to the Company in Lancaster?'

'By the town hall, is that?'

Aye, sir, d'you know it? Get the bad news to Mister Cartwright as soon as you can, and best speed to you.'

They needed no more encouragement. For a fast gallop across the countryside leaving the turnpike whenever a better course offered itself the two horsemen raced each other, their serious purpose adding to the exhilaration of the chase.

'Fourteen miles by my reckoning,' shouted John above the clattering hooves and slashing rain.

'And a quart to the first man at White Cross!'

Even as they galloped they could see at each bridge over the waterway the bankmen struggling with the planks. The vigilance of the bankmen had already detected the surging flow of the canal water. Indeed, the rate of rainfall was already filling the cut above its normal level.

*

In contrast, the following day was fine and clear. The rain had washed many of the buildings and streets to a bright summer freshness. However, in the lower parts of the city, near the river and quaysides, the streets had been flooded. As the water drained into the Lune, the mud lay inches deep in the roadways. Passing carriages and wagons splashed the black slime over those people struggling about their business on foot.

Like days in his youth, John accompanied his father into the city, with Jake Tempest joining them. Their business, however, took on a more serious air, no longer the youngster anxious to learn from his father, but all three of them viewing the rapidly changing city with critical eyes. As they crossed the New Bridge Jake took his leave to attend to his own affairs in town. Yet on the city side the roadway was full, people running and walking, carriages and wagons alike caught in the crowd. John noticed a man pushing a cart with a chestnut oven smoking,, another cart with a brightly covered tilt over a display of shiny pots and pans.

'There's a great number of people wanting to be in town today, Father. I wonder what the attraction is. Look at them, struggling across Cable Street. Must be a circus in town.'

Joshua Weaver looked briefly at his son.

'Then you've been away a long time John. I'll tell you what these happy citizens are in town to see. They're bound for the Castle for some entertainment.'

John shrugged his shoulders, still without understanding. His father explained.

'While you have been learning to be a Danish gentleman and young Jake has been tutoring most of the actresses in Europe, we have had more serious affairs to attend to. Our noble gaoler and the county executioner have persuaded the Assizes that it would be an asset to hang our felons in the city rather than the inconvenience of the open moor. So now this cheerful crowd can witness their brothers being sent to the gallows and buy a new pair of breeches or a bolt of silk in the market within the hour. I believe they call it a hanging match day.'

John shook his head in disbelief.

'I trust we are not going to this dreadful theatre?'

'No, son, I'll spare you that.'

In the room which had been the spartan office of the late Councillor Redfearn the several representatives of the trading company were arriving, leaving their hats and coats outside. John estimated there were twenty or more men in the room. Several of them were smoking pipes and unbuttoning their waistcoats, as if preparing for a hand of cards. Joshua Weaver took John round and introduced him where newer members had not met before. The summer sun streamed through the dusty panes and cast a pleasant atmosphere on a room which John remembered with melancholy when occupied by the departed Councillor.

Joshua took the chair at the head of the table. Some of the others sat down but others leaned against the wall or stood by the window, apparently watching the activity in the Market Square below. To John the assembly seemed remarkably relaxed and at ease. Joshua welcomed everyone and assured them that he would endeavour to conduct the business with all due speed.

He continued. 'As you all know now, my son has just returned on the Brig 'Molly' from St Petersberg, Memel and Sweden, last port of call, Copenhagen. He represents our several interests in Denmark. I'll ask him to report.'

John looked at the audience, some of them chatting amiably amongst themselves, seemingly without a care and indifferent to the business under discussion. He felt they might not understand the problems ahead.

'Gentlemen, the Baltic traders have lost patience with Lancaster.'

For a moment the room fell silent and then voices were raised in protest. John raised his hands to silence the comments.

'The direction of trade is changing. Look to Liverpool and Manchester and Salford. Mills and factories demanding shipping space, wanting larger ships to trade with the World. Whatever we might like to think, the slave trade is not sufficient and without a doubt the abolitionists will be successful. The exports from this city can be shipped from harbours with much easier access, not waiting upon God for wind and tide.'

At the end of the room a large man in a brown coat and waistcoat, stretched tightly across an ample stomach sucked on a pipe and blew a great cloud of smoke into the air, He waved one plump hand in the air as if chasing away a troublesome insect.

'Weaver, or Captain Weaver as I hear you are called by some, but not me, you have been in foreign parts too long. Our city is changing swiftly and in a practical way, building new harbours down stream, our splendid canal delivering our manufactures to every English home, Mister Brockbank and his ilk building ever bigger ships. Some of us have invested in this city for two generations. We've built mills, docks, hard roadways and bridges. We've tilled our farms and sheared our sheep. Now you arrive home from the same countries who have engaged the last ten years in trying to destroy us and our ships, or countries who need us to keep the seas open. And still you bear their crude messages. Don't try my patience, sir, or I may propose we seek alternative partners. I say no more.'

The speaker had clearly gathered around him a number who shared his sentiments and took the opportunity to join in the criticism.

'Perhaps you haven't had time from your travels to see our splendid aqueduct, which I'm told is the finest in the country. Are we to leave that as a monument to the death of our city?'

John raised his voice above the rising hubbub of the meeting.

'Gentlemen, I don't come here as a prophet. I simply ask you to look at your own ledgers. Surely you will see the arrivals and sailings of our own ships is already halved. Don't be blinded by the trade round our own shores which keeps the quayside working. And I would add that you are still struggling to carry the canal across the Ribble, regardless of the excellence of the Lancaster crossing. At sea we have a saying, a cable is as strong as its weakest link.'

Joshua Weaver looked at the figure of his son, and was proud of his fearless remarks, although he found himself sorely divided between his son's view of the future and his own concern for the investment he had made in the city. In a similar manner the meeting was clearly divided and becoming increasingly noisy in expressing its division.

Presently, a man banged the table with his fist until the noise subsided. He stood up and introduced himself.

'My name, to those I haven't met before, is Simon Matthews.' He clumsily waved his right arm towards his audience. 'I had the misfortune to leave one of my limbs on the gun deck of his majesty's ship 'Requin' so I consider I have an interest in the manner in which we trade with our one-time enemies. And my feeling is that we can find a middle course between the shoals of the River Lune and the beckoning attractions of Liverpool. I propose to this meeting that instead of , on the one hand demanding that the trade comes to us in Lancaster, or, on the other hand, that we abandon all our hopes and move our tents to Liverpool or even Bristol, like the nomadic tribes of the desert, I would like to suggest we trade out of Liverpool when necessary, but directing our efforts to the benefit of trade to and from Lancaster and her neighbouring towns.'

Another speaker stood up, waiting for Mr Matthews to pause.

'I'll tell you why not, sir. Because the Liverpool ships and their agents and their longshoremen will charge us premium prices and keep all the profits in their city. If we dock our own ships with regularity we will find one day there isn't an empty berth. Our friend perhaps doesn't know the battles we have fought with the Merseymen on the Guinea Coast for the best of the negroes. Aye, bitter contests for the black ivory, not easily forgotten.'

Once again the noise in the room grew, as sides were clearly taken, the anger tangible in the room. Members of the company rose to speak, but were frequently shouted down by others. Joshua Weaver rose to his feet and managed to bring the meeting to order.

'Gentlemen, these are serious matters which must receive our calm consideration. I, as much as anyone in this room, represent those who have been trading partners from the beginning. Yet I recognise the changing nature of our trade..' He was interrupted by a number of members speaking at once. He continued. 'Yes, I know it is my own son who has so bluntly laid the risk before us, but I haven't heard any criticism of his statement of the facts.'

The company seemed once again to divide into two arguing groups, and Joshua considered adjourning the meeting. He nodded to his son, and inclined his head towards the door. Then, as if by a hidden hand, the room fell silent. Men nervously looked at each other, mystified by unexpected silence. One worked at a window catch and managed to open the small window, allowing the tobacco smoke to swirl out of the room. Below, even the Market Square was silent.

Then, the tolling of the Priory bell drifted across the rain-washed roofs and silent crowds that filled the rising ground from which the Castle dominated the city.

In the meeting room, a voice muttered 'God rest their souls.' Men crossed themselves and for a moment reflected on the two hooded felons hanging from the scaffold, one aged fourteen, guilty of stealing a lame horse from the stables of The Kings Arms Hotel .

Very slowly, with lowered voices and averted eyes, the members settled once again around the table. Joshua was about to take the opportunity to adjourn the meeting when he noticed Mr Matthews catching his attention. Joshua signalled for him to address the meeting. In a subdued voice he addressed the silent room.

'Gentlemen, I feel I can offer safe course to navigate our way out of our difficulties.' Again, he waved his empty sleeve towards his audience. 'When I suffered this adjustment to my rig, a grateful Admiralty decreed that I should receive an additional share of prize money, and we indeed had a very fruitful voyage, delivering to the Dockyard at Sheerness two valuable Frenchmen, loaded in the Indies. A number of us who were awarded prize money, fulfilled our ambitions and purchased shares in merchantships, even owning two outright. I can therefore offer to your company access to ships run by my Liverpool committee at no premium whatsoever.'

The meeting greeted this news in silence. Then Joshua spoke from the head of the table.

'I'm the first to recognise the benefits you propose. I would, however, with the greatest respect, suggest that our trading adversaries on the Mersey may quickly recognise you as a Lancaster trader in disguise.'

'I had considered that risk, so we have placed our business with the Preston Bank, in the name of one Squire John Sparrow, a land-owner with property in Westhoughton.'

'An admirable arrangement' agreed the meeting.

Chapter 30

Like planets in their varied orbits returning at intervals to the same alignment, so within six years the planets of Europe had once again aligned in opposition to Britain, passing through the bloodstained Zodiac of Ulm, Austerlitz, Trafalgar and Friedland. Napoleon Bonaparte, in the Decree of Berlin isolated the European countries from trading with Britain, who responded by closing her own ports to their ships.

In Denmark, dependant on her traders for her wealth, the greatest wish was to remain neutral. In common with his fellow traders, Lars Nyborg was limited to seeking business from Baltic ports already crowded with ships hungry for cargo. His agents in Petersberg, Riga, Memel and Dantzig were suffering in the same manner, bewildered by thriving trades sacrificed as a result of a distant treaty. At the same time, the Crown Prince of Denmark was in Kiel with his Foreign Minister, Christian Bernstorff, making preparations to defend the southern frontier between Holstein and the smouldering French territories.

John Weaver and Lars looked despairingly across the harbour, watching the movements of a few sailing ships. Several of their own vessels were alongside, with no cargo, and earning no money.

'We are in the trap now. France could invade us tomorrow if we trade with Britain. If we don't trade, Britain may take the matter into her own hands and attack us as the guardian of the Baltic Sea. An unhappy position for the company, even worse for you, John.'

'For what reason?'

'Because in this city you are considered an Englishman. You should take care, while trade is quiet, to avoid having to declare your interests. I would quite understand if you felt it prudent to attend to your family and keep out of the city as much as possible.'

For this reason, when a message was delivered from Countess Irena, John and Eugenie invited her to the Frederiksberg house. When her carriage arrived, John was shocked at her appearance. Having not seen her for a year or more, he was surprised to see that her black, elegant hair was now streaked with grey, surrounding a heavily-powdered face which, he could see, was lined and care-worn. Eugenie, like John, took care not to react to the tragic appearance of the enigmatic woman, who unsteadily stepped from the carriage. But once settled in the drawing room overlooking the park, she seemed to recover her poise.

'Your young son must be growing now. How old is he?'

'Nearly six, and growing tall. He's in the park with his nurse. They may be back before you leave.'

'Oh, Eugenie, I'm so happy for you to have a child, which has been denied to me. Now the family are waiting for a peaceful occasion to send me to the Mediterranean to die in the sunshine.'

'Irena! You mustn't talk like that. I'm sure the sunshine of Tuscany will soon set you to good health,' John exclaimed.

The countess raised her hand to stop her hosts.

'I've had too many Petersberg winters. When we there for cousin Paul's funeral it was as if the whole city was in mourning, freezing to death. It all seemed needless suffering for such a stupid fellow.'

'And now?' prompted John.

'Now? I will tell you. The Tzar and Bonaparte are preparing to divide Europe between them. You've heard of their meeting in the houseboat on the River Nieman? I hear they left that ridiculous Prussian delegation sat on the river bank and only invited them aboard when the treaty was signed. Do you want to know how they will exert pressure on Denmark? I shall tell you. The Russian Foreign Minister has told Sweden that if Britain is allowed any freedom to trade in Denmark, Russia will capture Finland from Swedish rule and declare it a Russian State. Rumours are flying, that after all the bloodshed we are going to be united in destroying your country, Captain John.'

Eugenie looked at her husband with ill-concealed alarm.

'Are you in danger, John? Are we all in danger, living here? Is our son safe, feeding the king's peacocks in the park?'

'Please, ladies. Please. We are as safe here as anywhere in Europe. I can't take you to England by sea on one of our ships, and I believe the Hamburg ferry is very unreliable. We're safer here than attempting to move.'

The countess nodded slowly.

'You are right, John. Your biggest danger is from the nonsense people talk in the street. The most important task must be to make sure the old men in your embassy know what is happening. Let me warn you, your ambassador is probably going to be removed from his post.'

'How on earth do you know that?'

'A good friend of mine was on the ship that brought a new face from London. A gentleman by the name of Sir Francis Jackson. Get to see him, John, tell him what your standing is in the city, and make him understand what is happening.'

'How can I possibly do that?'

'A friend of mine is at your embassy. She will get you an introduction. Go to the legation and ask for Margaret Hill, say you are from Irena. She will help.'

Later, when helping her into her small carriage, John noticed two men standing across the road. He pretended to give an address to the coachman.

'Are you armed, driver?' he whispered.

'Not loaded up, sir.'

'Then step into the house and get charged. There are two men across the street who I don't fancy.'

The driver looked across.

'Not our worry, sir. They're from the constabulary.'

As he finished, the two men stepped from the shadows and approached the carriage, one round the rear, the other round the horses heads.

'Captain John Weaver, sir?'

'Yes, that is me.'

'You are under arrest, sir, as a British citizen. We are instructed to take you to the city for examination. Countess Kaminskaya, you will please leave.'

The driver whipped up the horses and soon the carriage was out of sight in the evening light.

'You can get some clothes and explain to your family.'

John ran up the stairs and hastily explained to Eugenie. He picked up George, his childish fair hair brushed until it shone, ready for bed. John hugged the small boy and kissed him goodnight.

'Sleep soundly, little sailor. I'll be home in the morning.'

While the men waited, he gathered some warm woollen clothing into a bag and briefly kissed his wife.

'Lars and the countess can both help. Jake should be trying to get here from England. Don't worry, my love.'

The police cell in which he spent the night was, as ever, cold and noisy, new prisoners coming and going throughout the hours of darkness. Arguments and protestations echoed through the stone corridors and cells. Two British seamen shared his miserable cell, but as daylight dawned the other prisoners were taken away.

At about mid-morning, a police officer unlocked the cell door and invited John to the police desk by the street door.

'Captain Weaver, sir? You are to be released, but you will not leave the city except to travel to your home at Frederiksberg. You are forbidden to leave the country. A constable will verify your presence from time to time. Do not absent yourself from the city or your home. That is all.'

He gathered up his bag and stepped out onto the crowded street. A carriage was waiting, and the driver called down from his box.

'Mister Weaver? Right, sir, step inside.'

John looked into the coach, and was surprised to see the only occupant was a heavily cloaked woman. He took off his hat before climbing into the coach.

'John Weaver, ma'am. Who may I ask..?'

'Margaret Hill, Mister Weaver. Embassy first, then home.'

As the carriage rumbled through the streets, John spoke quietly to his companion. Under all her wraps it was difficult to determine her age, probably fifteen years older than John, well-dressed but not obviously fashionable. He mentioned the countess and her introduction. Margaret Hill nodded in approval.

To John's amazement, when they reached the pillared embassy building, it gave the appearance of impending disaster. Clerks were hurrying everywhere, bearing arm-loads of papers and books and putting them in wooden boxes.

'What in heaven's name is happening?' asked John.

'Oh, this is usual if there's a possibility of hostile action in the host country.'

John looked at Margaret Hill.

'Hostile action? War, is that what you mean?'

'Of course. Why do you think you were arrested? Our ambassador has been withdrawn, and now we have a special envoy from London, to talk to the Danish government.'

'Can I meet him? Tell him I have a Letter of Free Passage, and have often acted for the embassy in the past.'

She pushed him into a waiting room. 'Wait here.'

After a few minutes she returned and showed him to an office on the upper floor. She knocked gently and waited.

'Come!' shouted a voice.

John stepped inside. Standing in the middle of a large conference room was a tall man in a black frock coat, with deep collar and cuffs. He had a thin, pinched face, and seemed to be in a very bad humour. He was brusquely handing messages and papers to a number of clerks and officials who were nervously waiting beside him.

'Ah! You're Weaver are you? The fella we've had to rescue from the constabulary. Did they ill-treat you? I'll protest to the Foreign Minister tomorrow.'

'They treated me very well, sir. I have no complaint. I'm worried about the rumours in the city, which are very damaging to the reputation of the British.'

'Good, very good. We're not going to be threatened by these people. If the Danish government think they can calmly ally themselves with that little French toad we must teach them a lesson.'

John swallowed hard, feeling suddenly very nervous.

'These people are our friends, sir. We have no business to threaten them.'

'Ho! Ho! Mister Weaver the peace-maker! Let me just explain, the only remaining fleet left in Europe, apart from what Napoleon has already captured, is here in Copenhagen harbour. If those ships are seized by Napoleon the Baltic is closed to us forever, and Denmark will fall to the French.'

'That sounds like a nightmare...'

'It is, Mister Weaver. And we will make an unpleasant awakening for the French by taking the Danish fleet before anyone arises.'

'How can you consider you could ever take the fleet?'

'We are demanding surrender of all warships. I am seeing the Crown Prince and giving his country just seven days to deliver the ships to us.'

John lowered his voice.

'Sir, I don't think the Crown Prince is in the city. I think he is in Kiel. How will you negotiate with him?'

'Then we will go to Kiel to tell him our terms. These people must be made to understand.'

John stepped forward and almost laid a hand on the arm of the envoy. He resisted the temptation to physically hold the man back.

'Please, sir, don't you realise, the Danish fleet is lying in harbour out of commission? There are no masts stepped, no spars or sails rigged. It would take weeks to get that fleet ready for sea.'

'Ha! That's what Garlike was telling the Foreign Office! Rubbish! That fleet represents a threat to our country. The Danes will surrender it to us, or it will be destroyed, to the last piece of oak and the last pine spar. And you, as a local trader, may be recruited to carry out the task. I have the authority of His Majesty to recruit British persons in my undertaking. I shall call upon you when the need arises. You live on Falkoner Alle, near the Park, I believe. I bid you good-day sir.'

The meeting was over abruptly as Sir Francis turned to his staff. John left the chamber, shaking with anger. The lady he knew as Margaret Hill was waiting near the front doors.

'You look as if you've seen a ghost!'

'I have. I'm sure the Crown Prince will never surrender the navy to us.' He dismissed the offer of a carriage home, and wearily John returned home on foot, with a heavy heart. The door was opened by Lars Nyborg.

'John, my friend, I understand you were in prison. I'm told by one of the coasters that a fleet of British ships is approaching Skagen - fifty or more ships in a great fleet. If we can negotiate an alliance so that we hold the Baltic open, that would allow everyone to retain their honour.'

'Lars, that does not seem to be the idea. I've spoken to the British envoy. They are determined to destroy or capture the fleet.'

*

The rumours grew in the city, until the word circulated that the Crown Prince had returned victorious from Kiel with his ministers and was placing himself at the head of the defences of his homeland. Those who saw him returning to Frederiksberg Castle cheered the small procession of carriages. Eugenie and George and his nurse, standing by the pond, watched and waved their hands, although the important affairs of state prevented the occupants waving back. The little boy asked why they didn't wave.

'They will tomorrow, young man. The prince will wave when he sees you tomorrow. He will say 'There's young George Weaver Nyborg again.' Today they have many worries on their minds.'

But the following day, in the long summer evening, the Crown Prince left his castle in silence, taking with him his elderly and infirm father, to supervise the defence of the city from a safe distance in Kiel. He delegated the task of defence to a seventy-two year old General, Ernst Peymann, whose skill was principally in constructing water supplies. An unfortunate choice.

At Kronborg the Danish artillery along the ramparts of Helsinor Castle fired a twelve-gun salute to the majesty of the great British fleet sailing into Danish waters with flags flying. The promenading Danes covered their ears from the detonations and then waved to the brave sailors on the beautiful ships.

*

The ships lying against the dock walls and at anchor were idle, but on the quaysides, a nervous air drew people together, watching the movements of the British warships beyond the harbour entrance.

Lars and John were in the harbour offices, gathering up vital papers, bills of lading and manifests. Beneath the stone floor of the warehouse Lars had thoughtfully had shallow, concealed safes constructed, mainly because of the frequency of theft. But now, with the terrible uncertainty, he realised that everything he had created was at risk.

'When we're all secure here, John, you must go home and stay there. Let us agree that if things go amiss, we will use your house as the meeting place or to leave messages. I'm uneasy about my apartment in the city.'

As he spoke, a small boy appeared at the door.

'Mister Lars? Message from Captain Eriksson.' He held out a grimy envelope.

'Eriksson lives up near Vedbeck. He will see what's happening.'

He tore open the envelope and read the paper inside.

'Holy Mother of God! He says the British soldiers have landed and are occupying the town. Look at this, he says there are thousands of them! What on earth are we doing to protect ourselves? Good old Eriksson, he warns we should make all secure and keep out of the city. I hope he's safe.'

Lars turned to the small messenger.

'Where do you live, Big Boy?'

'Near the captain, sir. Vedbeck.'

'Right, lad. We'll find a wagon and all go home together.'

But that was not to be. As they drove towards the coast road, they found their way blocked by two tree trunks laid across the uneven roadway, guarded by a motley collection of defenders, dressed in a variety of makeshift uniforms. The civil guard wore yellow sashes over drab tunics, but volunteers had hastily stitched red collars to their shirts to mark their military intent. A strange custom had evolved in a few hours, so that men who were too vital to be on defensive duty, like bakers, millers and butchers, wore the white shirts of their trade as a mark of exemption.

Lars told the boy to find his own way along the road home. To the west, away from the coast road, some light gunfire could be heard. John found the local councillor, wearing a ceremonial hat, and asked him what the gunfire might be.

'Well, sir, it certainly isn't ours. I'm told the brave British have just attacked a fortress in the park gardens.'

'A fortress?'

'Yes, an old colonel built it as a decoration for the towns-people to enjoy. I think the British have mistaken it for the Trekroner Forts!'

With a feeling of unreality, the two men turned the wagon towards Frederiksberg. When they finally reached the house Eugenie greeted them at the door.

'Have you heard? The British have now landed in Koge Bay! Apparently, John, your friend Jackson is furious that he has missed the Crown Prince, and is continuing his negotiations with Joachim Bernsdorff.'

'How can he do that? That's the minister's brother! He isn't even in the government!'

'Well, one of the coaches passing told the maids there are fifty thousand soldiers marching on Copenhagen. Look, I wrote down the names the maids told me. Here. General Gambier is the top officer, then there is.. er. General Cathcart and General Wellesley.'

'God! They've got more generals than we have infantrymen,' said Lars. 'I understand our best soldiers are standing guard from Kiel to Hamburg. An invasion across the Elbe would be the final blow.'

The following morning, more rumours. The postman, with no letters arriving in the city, called at the house for his usual cup of chocolate in the kitchen and frightened the maids with fresh talk of the brutality of the British, including the wild men from the hills of Scotland, who reputedly fought without mercy, and wore short, coarse skirts! The young maids sat with wide, terrified eyes as he outlined the obvious dangers from a man '...who could lift his own skirt and yours with the same hand!' He also confirmed that the city was considered closed and under siege. The ramparts were guarded with cannon, manned by a few regulars, conscripted militia and volunteers.

By the evening, the first of the British soldiers could be seen setting up their guard posts on the high ground on which the palace stood. Suddenly, the tranquil tree-filled park became a sinister, unfriendly no-mans-land.

In September's early dawn, the bombardment of the city started, with British cannon firing from the high ground. The sound of the cannons, completely unexpected, shook the house and wakened everyone. Lars told them all to get warmly dressed, and he kept the maids busy telling them to make a collection of all the bread and pies, cold meat and smoked fish, things that could be easily carried if they had to leave the house. The street outside filled with horses and wagons as people decided to leave the city, and then they met the British soldiers bringing cannon and mortars closer towards the city walls. The sound of their bombardment was much louder, and almost continuous. Suddenly, there was a knock at the street door, a loud, imperious banging, demanding an entrance.

'Eugenie, take George into the back nursery, I'll tell all the maids to hide in the scullery. Lars, will you keep an eye on things here, there are pistols in my bedroom, powder, shot, everything.'

The banging on the door continued. John buttoned his coat and hurried to open the heavy street door. On the step, a young British officer, smartly dressed in a red tunic bearing elaborate decorations, white breeches and shiny black boots, saluted.

'Sir, we wish to use part of your house as an observation point. You will be well compensated, and I guarantee you will not be harmed by any of my men.'

John used his most superior London voice.

'Is that so, my man. Let me tell you, his Britannic Majesty's Embassy, of which this is a part, is not to be employed in warfare against...'

'You can forget your fancy ways, sir. If General Cathcart wants to watch his bombs falling on the city he will use the best building he can find.'

Without further ado, he beckoned to a handful of men waiting outside and they hurried through the door.

'Top floor, watch the carpets, don't touch the paintings!'

The stamp of the men scrambling up the graceful curved staircase rumbled through the house. They could be heard shouting from the maids bedrooms, where the highest windows in the house were dormers in the roof.

The officer turned to John.

'Thank-you, sir. Live in Denmark, do you?'

'Yes I do indeed. May I ask where you come from?'

'Norfolk, sir. Not unlike this dreadful country, flat and fertile. Just like their women, what?' He laughed at his own joke.

'And, my fine Norfolk fellow, do you think you can sink the navy from here?'

'Don't know about the navy, sir. Our orders are to bombard that city until the government surrenders.'

'Just bomb it with cannon? You must be out of your mind!'

'Bless you, sir, not just cannon. Oh no! Colonel Congreve, sir, a man of great invention, has provided us with his rockets. Wonderful things, fire and smoke, exploding and fizzing everywhere. Never seen them used before, but they should make short work of that place. I'm told we have twenty-five thousand rockets. You'll be proud to be British tomorrow, sir!'

John left the officer and found Lars busily loading the four pistols he had found in the bedroom. He had one small pistol of his own.

'Lars, that fool of an officer has told me the object. We've got to get into the city and speak to whoever is in charge.'

'John, you are going to stay here and look after your family. I've got no one to worry over me, except Eugenie, and she's as safe as anyone, guarded by you and the British army. Tell me everything you know, and perhaps you can have another talk to our loquacious lieutenant. I'll get into the city somehow.'

'But if the defending Danes don't shoot you, the British bombardiers will.'

'Then I shall ride in the darkness, and shout in Danish when I get to the ramparts!'

John checked on all the family and the maids, who emerged cautiously from the scullery when John told them to make some soup for the soldiers. When it was ready, two of the youngest maids carried the tureen and the dishes up to the top room where the soldiers were talking. With much joking and teasing, the five soldiers occupying the bedrooms asked the two girls to show them who's bed was which. The cupboards in which the maids kept their clothes were opened, and the girls were persuaded to hold up each dress against themselves, to show how they looked. The soldiers appeared to be quite correct in their manners, so John took the opportunity to ask one of them about the view of the city.

At one of the dormers a large brass telescope had been set up on a wooden tripod and the soldier showed him the spires and domes of the city. A map of the city was pinned to the back of the wooded door, and parts had been coloured to show the position of what John assumed were the British troops. The young soldier explained how the rockets would be launched from behind sloping earthworks.

'Frightening things when they go, sir. Even worse when they land. I've seen one rocket ruin a little house when we tried them at Foulness.'

'Are you happy to be here?'

'Happy, sad, I just do as I'm told, sir. These people don't fight very much. Not like in Holland, we were shot to pieces there. Bad place for soldiers, water everywhere. Couldn't move for water.'

The lieutenant came into the room to see what all the laughter was about as the soldiers teased the maids. He saw John at the window.

'There you are, sir. See? We can make sure our rockets only land on military targets.'

'But, in God's name, why don't you just attack the ships in the harbour?'

'I'm told that if we damaged the ships, or let the Danes sink them, we would lose them forever. This way, if we destroy the city and they surrender, we can reinforce the Royal Navy ships.'

'What a masterly strategy. Our generals are to be congratulated!'

Once downstairs, John looked through his bookshelf until he found a page in a book with a recent map of the city and Frederiksberg. He tore out the page and hastily sketched from memory the positions he had seen on the observers map.

'Lars, when you go, take this, in case it helps our cause. But you must explain to General Peymann that they will bombard the city until we surrender the fleet.'

That evening, under cover of darkness, Lars, wearing a dark cloak approached the city along the southern shore. In the bay he could see ships moored which he knew must be the British transports, bringing men and war material ashore. When he reached the city walls he edged nervously towards Vester port, but found the gates closed and obviously barricaded shut. He called out in Danish towards the top of the wall, and was greeted with abuse by an invisible guardian of the city's safety. However, a boatman punting a small barge along the moat called up from the blackness.

'Two kronor will get you into the city, sir.'

Through the cold darkness, he was punted, until the high wall terminated at the entrance to the harbour. Lars climbed up the sloping stonework on to a narrow ledge. He worked his way sideways, a foot at a time, until he reached the end of the towering wall. As he did so, he felt a pain low down in his abdomen.

'And where are you going to, my little beauty?'

The questioner was so close in the darkness, Lars could smell his breath and the sweat of a frightened man. He realised he was so close that the invisible guard had a bayonet pressed hard against Lars' stomach.

'I come as a friend. I must get into the city. I am a Danish citizen.'

'So am I, more's the pity. Where do you want to get to?'

'I must see the General.'

'Then you'll be a very lucky man. He's got a British musket-ball in his leg...'

Suddenly, the darkness was rent by a series of explosions, their blinding light illuminating the nearby streets. Lars took the opportunity to run into the city. The explosions continued, and he realised the sky was full of streaking fire and sparks, fireballs and the most terrible noise of the falling shells. He ran towards the centre of the city, and on one corner found two soldiers trying to smother flames in a small shop.

'Where's the General got his headquarters?'

'Try Rau's Hotel, in Kongens Nytorv. That's what I'm told.'

As he ran into the square, a fresh broadside of missiles crashed down upon the city roofs. The screams and shouts of terrified people filled the shivering air after the explosions had finished. One corner of the hotel had been damaged, but Lars was able to enter the front door before being stopped by four or five volunteers, armed with bayonet-carrying muskets.

'I must see General Peymann. I have news of the British intentions.'

Upstairs, he was taken into a large dining-room which was crowded with officers. Eventually, a Captain laid a hand on his arm.

'Lars? Lars Nyborg? I didn't recognise you. What's happened to you?'

Lars looked into one of the huge mirrors that decorated the walls. He saw his face was black with the filth of the explosions, and blood was smeared across his face and the shoulder of his cape.

'Don't worry about me. Should I know your name?'

'Captain Pedersen, I knew your sister Eugenie. Can I help?'

'Help? Help, my dear man? Do you know what is going on outside?'

The captain smiled.

'The British are just trying to prevent us making a treaty with Napoleon. The Crown Prince is in Kiel, already discussing a peaceful outcome...'

'Then will you tell the General the British, who have surrounded the city by land and by sea, are going to bomb us until we surrender the fleet. Tell him these rockets which are raining down so prettily will destroy us without the British having to move from the bedrooms of my sisters house in Frederiksberg. And if he is still too poorly to grasp the import of that, here is their map!'

The room had fallen silent as he spoke, the officers listening to his words. Even the bombardment had halted, as if to allow his message to be clearly understood. One of the officers studied the map with evident interest. From the open door to an ante-room, a voice called out. Lars turned and saw a portly, clean-shaven man propped up on a chaise-longue, his leg heavily bandaged and supported on cushions. He spoke with a hoarse voice.

'Take my word, sir, I know these British. They wouldn't dream of using their rockets to destroy any European city. Rockets are for fighting the Chinamen.'

Chapter 31

The British bombardment continued for four days and nights, the last day marked by the destruction of the Vor Frue church, its crashing, clanging, collapsing bell tower giving a visible and audible notice to the city. Not that any was needed where more than fifteen hundred citizens had been killed, many burned to death in the raging fires that left streets too hot to cross, horses killed in their blazing stables, food and water in desperately short supply.

The crushed body of Lars Nyborg was one of many killed by an onslaught of rockets which struck the dockside roadway, demolishing the front of one warehouse. The constable who searched his clothes for a mark of identity, found the carefully marked map and, wrote the word 'spion?' on the label tied to his burned clothing.

In Frederiksberg his family and friends awaited his return anxiously, whilst the soldiers watched the fall of the rockets on the city. In the midst of the battle, Jake Tempest arrived at the door of the house, tired and travel-stained. The noise of the bombardment surprised him, and he was alarmed to find the British soldiers walking freely round the park and the streets.

'Why aren't we keeping the soldiers out of the streets? They walk around the park as if they own the place.'

John smiled ruefully.

'At present they do own it. Some volunteers tried to fight with pitchforks and scythes, they say some of them didn't even have shoes, yet they gave a good account of themselves.'

'What about the people in the city?'

'I heard some have fled across the harbour to Amager, across the Knippels bridge, but then the British said they would destroy all the bridges and people were scared.'

Eugenie welcomed Jake and proudly showed him how tall George was growing. Jake clumsily sat the little boy on his knee, and sang a sea shanty about the ladies of Amsterdam. George laughed, sensing the disapproval of his mother. Jake had brought a large, wooden toy sailing boat, artfully carved from a large piece of driftwood with sails looking suspiciously like the material of a lady's nightshirt. When Jake had settled into the house, and Eugenie was putting the child to bed, he enquired about Lars. John spoke in a whisper.

'We haven't seen him for two days. He went into the city with some information I had got out of these soldiers. Vital information for those defending the walls, but since then, nothing.'

Jake looked out of the windows at the smoke rising from the distant buildings, and the soldiers leaning against the trees in the park. He lowered his voice.

'Listen to me. I've been sent here on a special mission. I've got a ship waiting off Kronborg, to sail back to England. You can bring Eugenie and George, no one will say anything, and you can get out of this dangerous place.'

'Special mission? What do you mean? Who sent you?'

'You know them, the people in London. I am commissioned to rescue some of our friends from danger.'

'Such people as who?' asked John, beginning to feel he knew the answer.

'Well, Countess Kaminskaya and some of her contacts.'

'You mean you are rounding up foreign agents?'

'Not so. The countess has been an agent of the British for years.'

'I know. I've been carrying messages for her many times.'

Jake started laughing.

'That's why I'm here. Your contact in London is the Honourable Simon?'

'How in God's name do you know that? I swear I've told no one, not even Eugenie when she travelled with me to London. How do you know all about it?'

'Because, my friend, I used your name. The Honourable gent sent a man to Lancaster to find you. Instead, he found me and said he wanted John Weaver. Well, I'm your best friend so I said I was you. He questioned me closely about the countess and whether I could rescue her. Of course, I knew Copenhagen and the countess, so he took me back to London and offered me a fast boat, lightly armed, hand-picked crew. I believe we also brought the army's pay with us!'

'Jake! You always astonish me. But why the rescue?'

'On the ship, one of the officers was talking freely to me. This war with Napoleon is not over by a long distance. The countess and some of her friends are under deep suspicion. When we leave this country, her life is in danger. She only has a few years to live and the English want to protect her, and the people who passed her the secrets. Now, I can say your family are under suspicion in the same way.'

John shook his head sadly.

'To return to England? I'm afraid that is something I would not consider. I feel I am amongst friends here. I am ashamed of what England has done to this city.'

Their quiet conversation was interrupted by insistent knocking at the door. Although it was open, two British soldiers were leaning against

288

the outside wall, watching the old man knocking on the door. John went to answer it and found Klaus, the old servant from Lars' house. He was dishevelled, covered in dust and shaking at the knees.

'Klaus, come in. What ever is the matter?'

'It's the house, sir. A bomb has fallen in the yard, one of the maids has been killed.'

'Is Mister Lars there?'

'No, I understood he was here, sir. He had shut the house, and told the maids to go away from the city, but this girl stayed. I should have made her go.'

'Klaus, don't blame yourself. Is the house secure?'

'Not really. The back wall has been blown open. Mister Lars had hidden many of the valuable things away somewhere.'

'Don't worry, Klaus. Get some supper, and then Jake and I will try and get into town.'

'You can't. The army are letting a few people leave, but allowing no one in.'

*

On Sunday the bombardment ceased. Quickly, the word spread around the city that the Crown Prince had agreed with the British an honourable end to the battle. Two days later, the bitter truth became clear to the embattled population. Detachments of soldiers and sailors marched into the naval yard. The ships of the Danish navy, consisting of fifty ships-of-the-line, thirty-five smaller ships and frigates and over twenty gunboats had been surrendered to the Royal Navy, including all stores and equipment. Dozens of ships, large and small, British and Danish would have to be pressed into service to carry the looted equipment back to Britain.

The soldiers in Frederiksberg left the house, first presenting George with an small wooden box full of shiny brass buttons, insignia and badges from uniforms. The officer-in-charge asked to be shown any damage or breakages and wrote a note promising to pay five English pounds for 'use and minor damages' to the house.

When he was satisfied no further threat existed, John left Jake in charge and rode into the city on one of the many carts carrying people back to their homes. He made his way straight to Lars' house, and found many of the windows broken. He walked round the yard to the back and, as he expected, found a hole in the rear wall of the house big enough for him to step into the kitchens without bending. Inside, he could see evidence of two or three small fires, and damage to the walls and decorations in the ground floor. The upper floor had escaped most of the effects except many of the windows were broken or cracked, with jagged shards of glass littered across the rooms. He could see no evidence that anyone had stolen anything from the unlocked rooms. He returned to the street door, considering how he and Lars could secure the gaping walls and windows. In the dust and broken plaster lying across everything in the hall, he found letters which had been posted through the front door. Two were addressed to Lars, the third was simply addressed 'To the Family of Lars Nyborg.' He carefully slit the paper and drew out the brief note.

'To the family of Lars Nyborg. We have to tell you with sadness that the dead body of Lars Nyborg has been found in the Hanvegade, his death caused by the collapse of buildings during the bombardment by detachments of British troops encircling the city. A member of his family is requested to present themselves at the Holmen's Church to view the departed and approve burial.'

John fell into the nearest chair, his mind in a whirl. Next to his wife and young son, Lars had represented the guiding light in his life. He found himself reflecting on his own father's encouraging words, always looking to the future, welcoming change, chiding those who would not accept the need. In Lars, this philosophy had found the means of expression. His boast that honest, skilful trade between countries could flourish in spite of the 'kings and princes' which drew his contempt, now left John crushed by the meaningless death of his mentor. With weary limbs and a heavy heart he turned towards the Nybrogade and the Holmen's Church.

*

The mourning at his home in Frederiksberg made a poignant contrast with the rejoicing voices in the street. Eugenie was heart-broken at the hideous, wasteful death of her brother, and for a while kept a distance between herself and John, as if he shared the responsibility of his countrymen for her grief.

In the autumn sunshine, the survivors of the outrage, with their friends who had come to look at the invading soldiers, walked through the meadows and parks, even attempting to talk to the British soldiers. Jake, taking advantage of his language and posing as an equerry at the embassy, managed to engage in conversation with one of the officers. He was taken to see the remaining unexpended ammunition hidden under the trees. The officer boasted of the brilliance of the attack.

'We had enough explosives here to sink the entire city, if we wished.' He showed Jake one of the strange rockets, part of a stack on a wooden board.

'Congreve rockets, hundreds, thousands of them, fired in the past five days. One day alone we fired six thousand! This is the war of the future, Mister Tempest. No more muskets and bayonets, no more brave men on horses, frightened men on foot...'

'And terrified boys on men-of-war,' interrupted Jake.

'Aye, sir, quite so. Bigger rockets could be the answer to all our tactics.'

As the officer spoke, a detachment of soldiers marched past, their tread almost silent on the parkland grass, the sound of their progress marked by the rattle of their muskets and equipment, a pretty tinkling sound in contrast to their grim appearance. The officer turned to Jake.

'Look at them, the kilted dwarfs! Steer clear of that band of killers. They've got knives in the stockings, in their boots, under their skirts. Should never let them loose with decent English soldiers!'

Jake studied the receding Scottish soldiers with interest.

'I expect they will be more agreeable when they've got their own rockets, captain.'

The officer turned suddenly, looking first at Jake and then at the soldiers.

'Don't even jest about it, Mister.'

*

In the silence of the house in mourning, essential plans still had to be discussed and agreed. Jake was arranging to collect his passengers. However, before he could plan for the departure of his ship, he needed to know John's own feelings.

'John, you could close down the house, taking a limited amount of valuables with you. Just think, Eugenie and George living in comfort in the English countryside. A good healthy life for you all.'

'Yes, Jake, and in another six years he will be old enough for the press gang. How old were you when you went to sea, twelve, thirteen?'

'Not if you've got a purseful of gold, John. You and I know the press gang is for those who can't afford to escape it.'

'I hear from Lancaster there are now crimp houses for recruiting for the military. What do they say? Saved from the palsy so he could die of the plague?'

'Oh, you know it's not like that. Anyhow, we will soon be at peace in Europe.'

'At peace, Jake, I would choose to live in Denmark. At war, with Lars one of the first victims, I must live in Denmark. In any case, my wage is dependent upon rebuilding the company in the Baltic, just as you may feel the English trade is your paymaster.'

Jake shook his head.

'Suppose the Danes don't want an Englishman at the helm? The trade could sink like a stone. Come home, John, and live in peace beside the bay.'

'Peace, war, it seems to me that Lars knew how to make a sound business out of either. I'll be happy to follow in his footsteps.'

'Then, Weaver, what shall I tell your father and mother?'

Jake was clearly losing patience with his boyhood friend. Just as a thirsty man values a single cup of water, so an orphan may show an undying love for those who show him affection at a critical time in his young life. John was alert to unspoken criticism in his friend's question.

'I would trust my parents to expect me to make my fortune in my own chosen domain.'

'Then let me tell you where our real fortune lies. I have seen in England the ship of the future. A ship driven by a steam engine. With masts and sails just as an additional horse in the shafts, not relying on wind or tide...'

'Yes, Jake, big enough just to carry the coal it needs, and a hatful of cargo. Boiling all that steam in a Baltic winter sounds a fool's errand.'

'Then we must each place our stake upon the unseen cards, and pray we have the ace.'

John nodded and smiled in agreement, thankful that he could part on friendly terms. In his grief at the death of Lars John could not bear the loss of his friend's esteem.

'You must also remember, Jake, there are four aces in the deck.'

Nevertheless, when the day dawned that Jake and his passengers were to depart, there was a real sadness in the house at Frederiksberg. Eugenie and John were not only saying farewell to Jake for an unknown time, but the countess, who, in her mysterious way, had played an important part in their lives, was leaving to die in a strange country. Two other ladies who Jake surmised had been engaged in passing secret information, accompanied her into exile. The door was closed on the carriage in silence, and in the late autumn gloom, with the smell of the drifts of fallen leaves in the park, the coachman started the long journey to Kronborg and the perils of the voyage to England. When the carriage turned the corner and disappeared from view, John put his arms round Eugenie and young George and gently guided them back into the sorrowing house.

*

Yet, in England, the London column in the Lancaster Gazette detailed the heroic victory of the combined activities of the army and the Royal Navy in depriving Napoleon of the great Danish Navy. Joshua Weaver was the first to announce to his friends in the Town Hall meeting that both his son, John, and his friend Jake would have been playing their part in protecting the interests of the King and the Country. A murmur of appreciation greeted his remarks. Then the clerk called the meeting to order.

'Gentlemen, we meet today to listen to representation of our neighbours in Kendal with regard to the Lancaster canal. I would like to ask...' he looked down at the papers on his desk '...ask Mister Malachi Brazenose to speak.'

The man who stood up had the florid complexion and well-fed outline of a successful farmer, to whom distant wars and closer famine held no dangers. He threw open his brown coat to reveal a brass-buttoned waistcoat enclosing his ample form. He stood with his hands on his hips, waiting for silence in the crowded chamber.

'Your committee, sitting in this chamber, many years ago, told the world at large that you could make a canal to extend from Kendal to Wigan. Even, gentlemen, I remind you that ten years ago you opened to public use, an isolated waterway, unconnected to any other stream or river, extending from Tewit's Fields in the north, forty miles to Preston in the south. Yet, as I speak today, fifteen miles of meadows have still to be engineered to bring this miracle to the people of Kendal. Yet what do we find? Not one man, nor even a boy, is engaged in this vital connection. I am reliably informed that the aqueduct you have built across the river here in Lancaster has drained your resources and your enthusiasm. Well, I'm here to tell you we do not consider the work of this committee is good enough.'

In his audience, faces were averted, blushes concealed, whispered comments passed behind hands. The speaker refreshed himself from a tumbler of wine, as the whispered complaints died down.

'I am also told that much of the land to be purchased to build this canal has been secured by a local owner who we have been unable to trace. I expect this committee to take every step to acquire this land before its price gives you further excuse for delay.'

293

Mr Brazenose shuffled through the papers on the table before him. He felt in his waistcoat pockets and finally withdrew a pair of spectacles which he adjusted on his nose before reading from one of the documents. He looked up for a moment.

'I am told it is the property of one Jake Tempest Esquire of the Duchy of Lancaster.'

His announcement produced a stunned silence.

Christopher Oxborrow

As a deep-sea mariner who has also worked in the heart of industrial England, the author has first-hand knowledge of the locations in this story. Nevertheless, to re-create the events and attitudes of Napoleonic times has demanded research into the history of the pioneers who drove the industrial revolution at the end of the 18th Century. Even to a qualified navigator the difficulties of communication and navigation at that time are hard to reconcile in today's electronic age. Yet the great feats of engineering remain, and the author's adopted city of Lancaster a worthy demonstration of this heritage.